PRAISE FOR

THE MISSING

"Suspense that can rip your heart open and leave you raw . . . The characters are absolutely fantastic, from the leads to the side characters. The setting is wonderful. If you enjoy suspense/thriller/romance novels, heavy on the suspense, then I highly recommend Shiloh Walker's *The Missing*."　　　　　　　　　　　　　—*Errant Dreams Reviews*

"Walker pulls it off brilliantly . . . [She] certainly has a future in paranormal and/or romantic suspense."　　　—*The Romance Reader*

"Great romantic suspense that grips the audience."
　　　　　　　　　　　　　　　　　　　—*Midwest Book Review*

CHAINS

"This book is a double page-turner. The story is thrilling, and the sex just makes it better—two great reasons not to put it down until the end!"　　　　　　　　　　　　　　　　—*Romantic Times*

"Breathtakingly wonderful . . . Smoothly erotic . . . Utterly amazing . . . Will definitely keep your pulse racing!"　　　—*Errant Dreams Reviews*

"Exciting erotic romantic suspense."　　　—*Midwest Book Review*

FRAGILE

"[A] flawlessly sexy suspense novel . . . Exhilarating."
　　　　　　　　　　　　　　　　　　　—*Romantic Times*

"An excellently crafted mystery and romance!"
　　　　　　　　　　　　　　　　　　　—*Errant Dreams Reviews*

continued . . .

"Suspense, romance, and an ending that I can't say anything about—because that would be a spoiler . . . I recommend reading this one."

—*The Best Reviews*

"Intense, sexy . . . Ms. Walker has created another unforgettable . . . fast-paced, edgy tale."

—*Fallen Angel Reviews*

HUNTER'S FALL

"Shiloh's books are sinfully good, wickedly sexy, and wildly imaginative!"

—Larissa Ione, *New York Times* bestselling author

HUNTER'S NEED

"A perfect ten! . . . [A] riveting tale that I couldn't put down and wanted to read again as soon as I finished."

—*Romance Reviews Today*

HUNTER'S SALVATION

"One of the best tales in a series that always achieves high marks . . . An excellent thriller."

—*Midwest Book Review*

HUNTERS: HEART AND SOUL

"Some of the best erotic romantic fantasies on the market. Walker's world is vibrantly alive with this pair."

—*The Best Reviews*

Hunting the Hunter

"Action, sex, savvy writing, and characters with larger-than-life personalities that you will not soon forget are where Ms. Walker's talents lie, and she delivered all that and more . . . This is a flawless five-rose paranormal novel, and one that every lover of things that go bump in the night will be howling about after they read it . . . Do not walk! Run to get your copy today!"   —*A Romance Review*

"An exhilarating romantic fantasy filled with suspense and . . . star-crossed love . . . Action-packed."   —*Midwest Book Review*

"Fast-paced and very readable . . . Titillating."

—*The Romance Reader*

"Action-packed, with intriguing characters and a very erotic punch, *Hunting the Hunter* had me from page one. Thoroughly enjoyable with a great hero and a story line you can sink your teeth into, this book is a winner. A very good read!"   —*Fresh Fiction*

"Another promising voice is joining the paranormal genre by bringing her own take on the ever-evolving vampire myth. Walker has set up the bones of an interesting world and populated it with some intriguing characters. Hopefully, there will be a sequel that ties together more threads and divulges more details."   —*Romantic Times*

THE
DEPARTED

SHILOH WALKER

B
BERKLEY SENSATION, NEW YORK

THE BERKLEY PUBLISHING GROUP
Published by the Penguin Group
Penguin Group (USA) Inc.
375 Hudson Street, New York, New York 10014, USA
Penguin Group (Canada), 90 Eglinton Avenue East, Suite 700, Toronto, Ontario M4P 2Y3, Canada
(a division of Pearson Penguin Canada Inc.)
Penguin Books Ltd., 80 Strand, London WC2R 0RL, England
Penguin Group Ireland, 25 St. Stephen's Green, Dublin 2, Ireland (a division of Penguin Books Ltd.)
Penguin Group (Australia), 250 Camberwell Road, Camberwell, Victoria 3124, Australia
(a division of Pearson Australia Group Pty. Ltd.)
Penguin Books India Pvt. Ltd., 11 Community Centre, Panchsheel Park, New Delhi—110 017, India
Penguin Group (NZ), 67 Apollo Drive, Rosedale, Auckland 0632, New Zealand
(a division of Pearson New Zealand Ltd.)
Penguin Books (South Africa) (Pty.) Ltd., 24 Sturdee Avenue, Rosebank, Johannesburg 2196,
South Africa

Penguin Books Ltd., Registered Offices: 80 Strand, London WC2R 0RL, England

This book is an original publication of The Berkley Publishing Group.

PRINTING HISTORY
Berkley Sensation trade paperback edition / January 2012

Library of Congress Cataloging-in-Publication Data

Walker, Shiloh.
   The departed / Shiloh Walker.—Berkley Sensation trade paperback ed.
   p. cm.
   ISBN 978-0-425-24521-7
   1. Psychic ability—Fiction. I. Title.
   PS3623.A35958D47 2012
   813'.6—dc23

                                                            2011036848

PRINTED IN THE UNITED STATES OF AMERICA

10 9 8 7 6 5 4 3 2 1

For my family . . . always. You're my everything. I thank God for you.

For Patti D. . . . you were the first one to ask when Taylor would get a story. The first. And I told you he wouldn't *get* one. I think I even called him a bad name. He's another one of those characters I never planned on giving a story to—I didn't think there was a story there. But I kept getting asked, first by Patti, then others: *But I want to know why he's the way he is.* *Why* is one of those questions that can be deadly for a writer—it starts all those strange little wheels spinning. I got asked *why* too many times about Taylor and those wheels started spinning. Turns out he had a story after all.

And because I'm *always* asking him for medical help, I think I should probably mention Klaus B. for that help. Thanks bunches!

AUTHOR'S NOTE

French Lick, Indiana, is a lovely old town . . . a lot of history runs through it and I wanted that for this story. But I took a little bit of liberty while writing it . . . putting in an extra resort, placing a jail where there isn't one, a florist shop. In reality, I wouldn't change a thing about the town, but for the book, I needed to change a few things.

I also made free with my fictional little special task force of the FBI— one headed by the hero, Taylor Jones. Taylor's in charge of some special people—psychics—and they work pretty hard to stay out of the public eye. I know his task force isn't portrayed very accurately, but, well, the FBI wouldn't let me come in to play with them . . .

ONE

"FUCKING crazy," one of the techs muttered, watching as Dez Lincoln stood in the middle of a desolate Iowa field with a smile on her face.

She was a beautiful woman—her black hair cut short, no more than an inch long, currently spiked up. Her skin was a light, smooth brown and her eyes were dark, so dark they almost appeared black, set under feathery, arched brows. Her body was all curves and long limbs, round hips, and a chest that was undeniably *female*. But there was no mistaking the strength—there was well-toned muscle to go along with those curves.

No doubt about it, she was gorgeous, and when she smiled, she could make the hearts of the men around her race.

But right now, her smile was fucking *freaky*.

Under her feet, they suspected, were dozens of bones. Unmarked graves.

The location of a serial killer's little playground. Or maybe his burial ground.

But she smiled. It was a peaceful, beautiful smile—a Mona Lisa smile, and it didn't belong in the place of death and decay, the tech thought.

Fucking *freaky*. He muttered it under his breath again and went to turn away, only to realize he was the subject of intense scrutiny.

Special Agent in Charge Taylor Jones was staring at him, and he did not look pleased. If Desiree Lincoln was fucking freaky, then Jones was fucking scary and that look never boded well.

Swallowing, he held that steely blue gaze and prepared himself for the fact that his head just might be rolling across the ground, figuratively speaking, in a second or two.

But all Jones did was stare at him—long enough to make sure the point was made.

Idiot.

Taylor Jones didn't much like having any of his people being called crazy—they were unique, all of them. If they weren't unique, they wouldn't work for him. But unique didn't make them crazy—and it didn't make them freaks.

The tech flushed and after another fifteen seconds, Taylor looked away.

Still, he knew the man's thoughts were echoed by a number of others. At least among the techs. Those on Taylor's team understood, on some level, how Dez's gift worked and they were no longer surprised by her reactions, even in a place as disturbing as this. Others, though . . . no, they didn't like to see a woman smiling when she stood in the middle of what was likely an unmarked, mass grave.

Perhaps, if he didn't know Desiree, he'd agree with them.

He knew her, though, and her gift had long since stopped

unsettling him. Other things about Dez might unsettle him, but not her gift. He knew she wasn't smiling because she stood atop the possible gravesites of murder victims.

She smiled because one of them, at least, would find peace tonight.

To Dez, that meant a lot.

Taylor wished he could find some solace in that, but all he felt was a fiery hot rage, carefully hidden under a cold, professional veneer. Somewhere, buried under all of it, was exhaustion.

He couldn't let that cold professionalism crack and he couldn't give in to the rage. Later, sometime much, much later, he could give in to the exhaustion, though.

They already had the killer in custody. *Correct that*, he thought to himself. The *alleged* killer.

Alleged, my ass. Keaton Weiss was a brutal, sadistic bastard who had spent the past fifteen years preying on the Miss Lonely Hearts type, stalking them, seducing them . . . then kidnapping them, raping them, and killing them. Their bodies had never been recovered, until one victim had managed to get away and that was how they had finally managed to catch Weiss.

And catching Weiss was what had led them here.

No . . . it was what had led Dez here.

All Taylor had to do was place her in the room where Weiss had committed untold atrocities on untold women and, one by one, the ghosts had started to whisper to her. Most of them, though, had been too weak, too faded, or still too traumatized to connect with Dez.

She would work with them and hopefully, over time, she could help them move on.

But one of them had been able to establish a tenuous link with Dez and that link had proven strong enough for her to lead them here. Here, they'd find the evidence they needed to put the bastard away.

Jones didn't have the gifts Dez had, but he knew his people, and judging by the looks on the faces of some of them, they had hit the crime jackpot here. Some of them were all but chomping at the bit to get out there and start their own hunt, but they knew they needed to give Dez her space.

If they screwed this up for her, the ghost may never find the peace she needed.

Some of the ungifted techs didn't quite understand that. While Taylor was impatient in the extreme and itching to get out there, he knew if that ghost didn't find any sort of peace, she'd linger with Dez.

And that would torment her.

He couldn't do that.

Not to her.

He tried to force up some semblance of the cold, hard shield he'd perfected so long ago—he didn't have any sort of special interest in Dez Lincoln. He wouldn't wish the unrest of an agitated ghost on any of his people; that was all. He needed them all at their best, all the time.

But even as he told himself that little line, he knew it for what it was.

Nothing but shit.

He most certainly had a special interest in Dez Lincoln. And he had from the very beginning.

Not that it mattered, though.

She was a member of his unit and that made her off-limits.

And even if that wasn't an issue, Taylor Jones didn't do relationships.

Period.

* * *

"WILL you find him? Stop him?"

It was the third time Tawny Lawrence had asked Dez that question. The departed so easily forgot things, especially when they were agitated, and Tawny was most definitely agitated. Agitated, angry . . . and as they'd drawn closer to her unmarked grave, she'd gotten sadder as well, as though she'd felt the gloom and the darkness looming over her.

But Dez didn't mention the repetitive questions—she simply answered as she had the first and the second time. "We have found him. He has been stopped. He won't do this to anybody else."

They were often confused—especially once they realized she could see them, hear them . . . talk to them. Some of them had spent years and years unable to speak to anybody, not even each other. A lot of the time, the souls of the departed were trapped in their own personal hells and until they could break free and move on, they weren't aware of anything or anybody.

Unless somebody like Dez could penetrate that shield.

Tawny's face, pretty and sweet, softened with a smile and, just like that, the darkness surrounding her began to lift. She didn't look like a ghost, didn't look like a murder victim.

In Dez's experience, the departed were a reflection of how they remembered themselves in life . . . a washed-out mirror reflection. Tawny's pale face faded even more and she closed her eyes.

"How long? Do you know?"

Dez said gently, "You disappeared seven years ago."

"Seven years . . . my God." She sighed and her image flickered. Then she focused on Dez's face. As her gaze focused, the air around Dez grew colder and the tension was thick enough to cut. *"My son. I have a son. Do you know what happened to him?"*

"Your ex-husband took him. Raised him—he misses you but it looks like his father did his best to make sure he had a good life. He's graduated from high school and he's in college. Going for a degree in criminal justice." A faint smile curled Dez's lips and she said, "I think because of what happened to you."

Something that might have been tears glimmered in Tawny's eyes. "*He's a good boy. I'm glad . . . thanks for telling me.*"

Dez wasn't surprised the woman had asked. She'd skimmed the file as they traveled up here, preparing for just this sort of thing. A lot of them had questions and nothing made it harder for them to pass over than *not knowing*.

Unwilling to be the one responsible for holding somebody back, Dez did her best to make sure she could answer whatever questions may come up. But she couldn't always answer every one, and often, those unanswered questions were the hardest.

"*What happens to me now?*" Tawny stared at her, her gaze sobering.

"That's not so easy to answer, Tawny. What do you think happens?"

Tawny just smiled.

And as easy as that, she faded away.

Once Tawny was gone, Dez turned and faced the rest of the team.

Her gaze locked on Taylor's.

He lifted a golden brow.

She nodded.

That was all he needed. Without a word from her, he turned away and the team sprang into action.

And just like that, Dez's job was done and she was relegated to the sidelines.

Good thing for her she'd brought a book.

She knew Taylor wouldn't be leaving here anytime soon.

TWO

"You're not supposed to be here," Taylor snapped, his voice flat and cold.

Dez ignored him, staring at the house with a rapt expression. The voices . . . they called to her. Their call was impossible to ignore. The whispers were like a siren's song in her head. Responding to Taylor's blunt statement was pointless, especially since she couldn't explain why she was here. She just knew she *had* to be here.

She hadn't been notified and that meant nobody thought her skills were required. If Taylor wanted her here, he would most definitely have called her.

After all, she lived just a little outside of Williamsburg. It wouldn't take her any time to get to the small, upscale subdivision where all hell was currently breaking loose. It made her gut hurt to think about the hell happening inside this posh, designer neighborhood. Some people thought bad shit didn't happen in places like this.

Dez knew better.

"There's a child in there," she said quietly.

"No, there's not." It was Colby Mathis, one of Jones's bloodhounds. Under most circumstances, she would have listened to him, agreed with him. She liked the guy, respected him, and she knew he knew how to do his job. He was the hard-core psychic and she was the one who talked to ghosts.

But he was wrong this time.

Because there was a ghost standing at the door of the house, staring at Dez with desperate eyes, her mouth open in a silent scream.

"He's got a child in there, Taylor, and if you all move on him like you're planning, he's going to kill her," Dez said, her voice strained.

Colby swore. "We don't have time for this, Jones. The fucker's slipped away from us before—he's *not* doing it again."

Taylor looked from Colby to Dez, and Dez stared into Taylor's eyes.

"Colby, give me one minute."

Taylor saw the frustration simmer in the other man's eyes, but the agent gave a terse nod and retreated, falling back a few steps as Taylor reached out and caught Dez's arm. He tried to ignore the soft, silken warm skin of said arm, just as he'd tried to ignore the way his heart had skipped a beat when she had moved to stand beside him earlier.

He hadn't even seen her, and he'd known it was her.

Felt it, somewhere deep inside.

Guiding her away from the crush of bodies, he said, "You can explain what you're doing here later. But for now, tell me why you think there's a kid in there when all my intel is saying otherwise."

Dez flicked a look past his shoulder. "Something woke me up

and I just knew I needed to be somewhere. *Here*. So I got up, got dressed, and headed out. Ended up here—I didn't even know you had a team here, by the way."

For a period of about five heartbeats, all thought stopped. Taylor could think of nothing else but those words—*got dressed*. Meaning . . . what? Had she been sleeping in pajamas? Something slinky and silky? Something sensible, practical? Or had she been naked, that sleek, warm brown body bare?

Blood drained out of his head and he clenched his jaw, jerked his attention away from her, and stared at the house until he could remember what he was doing, why he was here.

What he was about. He didn't have time to be thinking about Desiree Lincoln and her sleeping attire—or lack thereof. He had a job to do.

A mission. *The* mission. It was all that mattered. All that could matter.

But his body didn't want to listen to reason and he had to dredge up dark, ugly memories.

All of it necessary to ground himself, something he had to do around her, more and more.

He needed distance between them, a great deal of distance. But somehow, he didn't think she'd like it if he suggested she quit. And as his unit was rather unique, if she didn't, the only way he could get distance was if one of them requested a transfer.

Dez would never do it. She'd joined the FBI specifically to come work for him—she *needed* it.

Her dark brown eyes moved past him once again, lingering on the porch, and there was an expression in them that he had seen all too often. Haunted, angry, and determined. That haunted look appeared in her eyes for one reason and one reason only.

She had a ghost riding her.

Shit. He might have intel on the outside, but it looked like Dez had intel on the *inside*, and if she did, he couldn't risk a child . . .

"What do you see?" he asked, his voice flat and cold.

* * *

HER name was Richelle. In life, she had been a petite, pretty little angel, one who had probably driven her mom and dad insane, one they had probably loved dearly. Her death would have left a hole in their hearts and Dez wondered if they were the open sort . . . the kind of people she could sit down and talk to.

Could she tell them what she was? What she did? That she'd seen Richelle, spoken with her? Would it help them? Hurt them?

Could she tell them that Richelle had helped her save another child?

That's assuming you do *save her,* she thought grimly as she followed Richelle's wavering form down the hallway. Taylor was at her back, shadowing her every move.

It was just the two of them, and it had taken every persuasive argument she had in her arsenal to get him to do this. If there was a child in the house, they needed to get her out. Dez had eyes—the ghost would help her, she knew it, clear down to her bones, and she'd been right.

Richelle was doing just that. A petite, avenging angel. She was hauntingly lovely, and death had made her ethereal.

And angry.

Right now, her killer was ensconced in the front of the house, staring entranced out the front window and mumbling to himself.

Richelle insisted he had a girl with him, but Colby had spent the past twenty minutes saying otherwise. Hell, he was probably *still* out there trying to convince the rest of the team Dez was wrong.

Colby sensed people. *Living* people.

If there was somebody else in there besides their killer and Colby didn't feel her, then chances were, the child was dead, and by letting Dez go in *alone*, with nobody but a ghost for a guide, they would likely be giving the bastard a potential hostage.

Taylor, naturally, had agreed. So she wouldn't go alone. She could live with that—after all, she wasn't stupid.

Nor was she helpless. She held her gun in a loose, ready grip.

Hostage, my ass.

She might not be the typical agent and she might not be the badass some of them were, but she'd made it through the same training they had, and she still kept herself in pretty decent shape. The day she couldn't handle herself against a child-molesting, motherfucking pervert was the day she'd put down her gun and take up knitting—just let the ghosts drive her crazy, because she wouldn't be much use to anybody anyway.

"She's in the closet." Richelle's ghostly voice, audible only to her, drifted back to her. *"Gave her something to make her sleep."*

Dez hoped it was just drugs, but logically, she knew Colby was likely to sense a child, even one knocked out by drugs.

Not many things would keep him from sensing the presence of a human.

Dez wanted to ask Richelle if she knew what the guy had used but she knew it was a waste of time. Richelle was only ten—wicked smart and surprisingly clear minded, especially for one of the departed. But still, the child was only ten.

And now, she'd never get to see eleven, or twelve . . . never go to the prom, never get her first kiss.

Richelle stopped by the closet and Dez halted a few feet away. She looked by Richelle to the front room and then glanced over her shoulder to Taylor. He eased around her, the bulky bullet-proof vest he wore breaking the smooth, perfect line of his suit.

He stopped just a breath away from Richelle and his eyes, flat and hard, stared down the hallway, watching, waiting.

With him watching her back, Dez laid a hand on the doorknob. Slowly, oh, so slowly, she turned it.

* * *

OUT front, the rest of the team waited.

With Taylor in the house with Dez, Special Agent Joss Crawford was in charge and, unlike Jones, he didn't believe in keeping a polished veneer that never showed any sign of emotion.

So when the message came up on his phone, he didn't bother suppressing the urge to swear. No, it ripped out of him in a long, ugly torrent and then he looked over and pinned Colby with a stare. "You were wrong, Mathis. Lincoln found a child and she's alive."

* * *

TAYLOR suspected some manner of psychic ability was more common than people thought.

He didn't have any classifiable skill—wasn't telekinetic the way some of his people were and he couldn't talk to the departed, as Dez liked to call them. Nor could he home in on the trail of a kidnapped child the way one of his sometimes contract employees, Taige Morgan, did.

He recognized the gifted, though. It was how he'd lured so many of them to his unit. He recognized them—that was his gift, so to speak, that and knowing how to bring them inside, get them to work for him.

While he wasn't getting any of those vibes from this house, he wasn't the least bit surprised when the bastard they'd been sitting on came roaring around the corner, like he'd been somehow alerted to their presence.

Instinct. It wasn't that far removed from some level of psychic skill, and this pervert's sick needs were about to land him in the worst sort of hell.

His name was Edward Mitchell; he liked to pick up pretty little girls just shy of puberty, rape them, and dump their bodies in the James River; and he wasn't going to go down easy.

They'd almost made it to the back door and Taylor even had a believable story concocted to explain why they were in the house to begin with—they did have a warrant, but they hadn't bothered to explain that when he'd picked the lock on the back door. They'd had reason to believe there was a child in danger in this house and Dez was carrying that child in her arms now.

But as Taylor went to open the door for her, Edward came rushing down the hall, huffing and puffing, his pale, pasty skin gleaming with sweat and his eyes half wild.

"No!" he screeched.

And he raised a gun.

Taylor raised his own and fired, but the bastard managed to get a shot off. And as the sick fuck fell, lifeless, to the floor, Taylor turned. And the first thing he saw as he turned was the brilliant, dark wash of red staining the side of Dez's neck.

* * *

THE night passed in a haze of bloody memories, the wail of sirens and the bright, blinding lights of the emergency room.

They tried to keep him out in the waiting room.

But either the blood they saw in *his* eyes, the badge, or the gun he didn't bother to keep concealed convinced the medical staff that trying to keep him out was going to waste precious time.

Judging by the amount of blood Dez had lost, he didn't know how much time she had.

The child was already at the local children's hospital, alive . . . and that was all he knew. For the first time, he'd turned over the reins to another, allowing Crawford to take command while he stayed with Dez. God—Dez.

She couldn't die.

Not like this. Fuck, she couldn't die. Not Dez.

Although he knew her, too well.

She'd be okay with going down knowing she'd helped save a child, and that was what she'd done. The girl was alive . . . because Dez had shown up when she had. Alive because of Dez and the ghost of another victim.

Another victim . . . somebody else Taylor hadn't been able to save. Another scar on his soul. It didn't matter that he hadn't known. It never mattered. All that mattered was that he hadn't gotten there in time, hadn't pieced it together in time . . . and another child, another little girl had been lost.

Dez . . . would she become another scar on his soul?

Her face flashed in front of him, her warm brown skin a sickly, ashen gray, her eyes wide with shock. The blood had soaked her clothing. Mitchell, damn the bastard. Either he was a damn good shot or Dez just had lousy luck. Her vest would have protected her torso, but the bastard's bullet had hit her neck.

Stop it—he had to hold it together for now. At least long enough to make sure they took care of her. She was still alive. That meant she had a chance. But if he hadn't been right there . . .

"Don't think about that," he muttered, reaching up and pressing his fingers to his eyes. "Don't."

And he found he actually *could* push the image out of his mind, but only because it just wasn't acceptable. The thought of Desiree Lincoln's lifeless body was just more than he could handle. A hell of a lot more.

"Mr. Lincoln?"

Tired, so tired it never occurred to Taylor the nursing staff might be looking for him. It wasn't until the voice came again, and from a lot closer, that he opened his eyes and met the tired gaze of a man dressed in pale green scrubs. "Mr. Lincoln?"

"No. Special Agent Jones. But if you're here about Desiree Lincoln, then yes, I'm here with her."

"Ahhh . . . I see. My apologies." The nurse smiled. "It's been one of those nights. There's a small lounge just down the hall. I'm going to take you there, if that's okay. Dr. Frantz will be in to speak with you shortly." He paused and then asked, "Does Ms. Lincoln have any family we should notify? There wasn't much information in her personal effects."

Taylor shook his head. Dez's mother was still alive, living in the lap of luxury in West Palm Beach. He knew that because he'd researched everything about Dez when he'd discovered her. He knew all about how the girl had been abandoned—her mother had taken her to school one day and just never came back for her. Dez knew about her. But the woman was a stranger to her and it was in her file who to contact in the event of an emergency . . . or worse. Her mother wasn't on the list.

Taylor couldn't blame her. Why should she want to talk to the woman who'd walked out on her? Dez had gone through a series of foster homes after her mother disappeared. Nobody wanted the strange, pretty child who had talked to thin air.

Almost afraid to ask, he said, "She has some very close personal friends. Should . . ." He realized there was something hot and bright burning his eyes: tears. It was tears. Blinking them away, he cleared his throat and asked quietly, "Should I call them? One lives in Alabama. It would take her a while to get here . . . should she come?"

The nurse gave him one of those strained smiles. "You really should speak to the doctor."

"Just tell me if her friends should be here," Taylor said, putting a hard edge into his voice. "She risked her life to save a child tonight and if she's not going to make it, she's got a right to have friends at her side. Don't give me that official shit—just give me a simple yes or no."

The doctor appeared just then and though her smile was every bit as tired as the nurse's, her face wasn't quite so strained. "She came through the surgery and if you want to call her friends to donate blood, I'm all for that. She's going to need it. But she's a strong woman."

As his brain processed that information, he almost hit the floor. As it was, it took all he had just to stay standing.

Relief, Taylor realized, could be very, very painful.

THREE

THE last person Dez expected to see standing at the door to her hospital room was her boss. She didn't know exactly *why* she was so surprised to see him. He'd made damn sure she stayed in the hospital several days longer than she needed to, she was sure, and he had haunted the damn halls.

But why he was here *now*?

In his hot and sexy flesh . . . although his version of hot and sexy was actually the cool and polished version. His suit was a little too nice for the typical agent and his shoes were a little too pricey—custom-made, she'd bet. He could wear a suit like nobody's business, that was for damn sure.

Damn it, he was so put together. Looking at him just made her think about how much fun it might be to see what it would take to make him come apart. And those were thoughts she just didn't *need* in her head. *Down, girl,* she told herself as she eased up in the bed.

Frowning at him, she asked, "What are you doing here?"

"Taking you home." He flicked a glance at his watch and then looked at her. "Are you ready?"

"Why are *you* taking me home?"

"Because you need somebody to drive you," he said.

She resisted, just barely, the childish urge to stick her tongue out at him. Taylor Jones brought out all sorts of strange impulses. Childish ones. Wanton ones. Erotic ones. She'd long since adjusted to that very disturbing fact, but adjusting to it didn't make it any easier to fight.

Sighing, she asked, "Doesn't the boss have anything better to do than play chauffeur?"

"Don't worry. I didn't bring the limo." He came into the room and paused to study the neat stack of her belongings. "Has the nurse been in to take care of your discharge?"

"Hell, no." She scowled. "I think they suspect I'll sneak out the door and try to hitchhike. Then they'd have to deal with you." Absently, she reached up and touched the bandage on her neck, itching to take it off and look at the damage. But she wasn't doing it until she was in the privacy of her own home. The nurses around here made Nurse Ratched look like a pushover.

She shot Taylor a narrow glance. Probably had something to do with her boss. She'd heard rumors he'd terrorized the staff. He was good about that. He terrorized everybody.

"But now that you're here . . ." She leaned over and grabbed the call light.

She didn't bother to wipe her smirk off her face as the nurse appeared in under five minutes with all the paperwork, shooting Taylor's back a dark look before blanking her expression. Yeah, Taylor was definitely part of the reason the nurses were watching over her like she was in jail or something.

Bully, she thought, disturbed by the affection she felt for him.

She was just plain disturbed and she would be until she got the hell out of the hospital. Too much unrest in a place like this.

There weren't any active souls looking for her help that she could see, but she could feel the echo of their passing and it was like somebody was constantly stroking her spine with icy cold fingers. She was cold, damn it, very cold, and she wanted nothing more than to be out of here and snug in her own house, where she could be warm again. Nice, new house, no death there, never touched by anything but *her* presence and the presence of the builders, her friends. All hers. No lingering touches or echoes or shadows.

Damn it, she wanted to be home.

"Special Agent Lincoln, are you listening?"

Dez rolled her eyes and jerked her attention back to the paperwork the nurse had in front of her. She signed here, initialed there, and voiced her understanding over changing the dressing and when she was supposed to see her doctor for follow-up; her eyes started to glaze over with all the blathering all the medical types like to hand out.

Who in the hell needed sleeping pills? Just stick the insomniac in a room with a nurse doing discharge orders. That would knock out anybody.

"So, do you have any questions?" the nurse asked, giving Dez a bright, hard-edged smile.

It seemed to read: *Say no, please, so you can get the hell out of my hospital and take this prick with you.*

Dez narrowed her eyes. For some reason, she was oddly tempted to play dumb and act like she hadn't understood any of the words she'd just ignored. But she wanted out of here too much.

Giving the nurse a wide smile, she took a deliberate look at her name tag and said, "Ms. Lafferty, you've taken such excellent care of me, the next time someone from our unit is injured in the line of duty, I'm sure my boss is going to put in a special request just for *your* services."

She had the pleasure of watching the nurse's eyes tighten minutely around the corners.

Yeah, Taylor could be a prick.

But he got the job done.

Plus . . . he'd saved her life.

And she really needed to tell him thanks for that, too.

* * *

DEZ's full, firm mouth was set in a mutinous line as she was wheeled out of the hospital in a chair. The nurse had given her an innocent smile and insisted, "Hospital policy."

And it most likely was, Taylor figured. One person trips over his own feet and decides to sue and hospitals everywhere are going to be cautious. Still, he knew Dez hated it.

He had an urge to stroke his finger down the line between her brows and tell her to relax. It was all of five minutes, and after what she had gone through, what did it matter if she sat in a wheelchair for five minutes?

That's what he wanted to do.

Instead, he tucked a hand inside his pocket.

There was a thin, golden chain inside there, one he needed to return to her.

It had somehow fallen off her neck that night—he didn't know how. But after the paramedics had rushed her away, he'd seen it there, glinting in a puddle of her blood, and he had picked it up. The chain itself was damaged, but the slender cross wasn't. Although he didn't know the history of the bit of jewelry, he knew it was important to her. Dez didn't wear jewelry—just this piece, and she always wore it. To him, that meant it mattered.

He should have returned it before now, but he couldn't seem to. He needed it out of his sight because every time he looked at it, he saw Dez again, bleeding out under his hands.

Too close. It had come too close . . .

"Okay, Agent, if you'll bring your car . . ." The nurse stopped and stared at the black Mercedes parked in front of the double doors and then she looked back at him, disapproval in her eyes. "Is this *your* car?"

"It is." He smiled coolly, watched as the woman's shoulders went stiff and tight with indignation.

"You shouldn't park there."

Taylor lifted a brow. "I'll keep that in mind the next time I have an agent in need of your services, Ms. Lafferty." He hadn't missed the expression on her face when Dez had made that comment. Her lids flickered and she sniffed.

He might have said something else, but he knew he'd been a bastard to her and the rest of the medical staff in the days since Dez had been brought in. He wasn't inclined to apologize—he didn't care whether they cared for his attitude or not—but he knew he'd definitely done enough to incur their dislike.

A few minutes later, they were pulling away from the hospital and Dez sighed, the tension easing out of her body.

"How bad was it in there?" he asked quietly. Hospitals could be bad, bad places for some of his people, especially those who were more in tune with pain . . . and death.

"Bad enough," she admitted. "I need a few minutes of quiet. I feel like the death is sticking to me."

He could give her the quiet she needed, and in the forty minutes it took to drive to her little place outside of the city, he saw the difference some peace and quiet could make.

Her color returned and the soft, warm brown of her skin looked almost normal again. A night of sleep, a few days of decent food, and she'd be as good as new.

No thanks to you . . . you never should have let her go in there. Not her damn job, not what she trained for. You fucking moron.

He wished he could silence that voice.

Wished he could take more comfort in knowing a child lived because of Dez's actions.

Always before, it had been enough.

But for now, all he could see was her blood, so much of it, dark red, spilling out over his hands.

As he parked in front of her house, her eyes opened and she shot him a quick glance. "You never forget a thing, do you?"

"Rarely," he said.

And about her?

Never. He'd been to her house one other time, four years before. That time, her particular skills had been needed on a job and since he had been driving in her direction, he'd decided he would pick her up. It would save time.

Yes, all in the name of expediency.

With everybody else, yes.

Refusing to look at her, he climbed out of the car and grabbed her things from the trunk before she had the chance. Although she was supposed to be resting, taking it easy, he knew Desiree Lincoln. *Rest* wasn't in her vocabulary.

"Who is coming to stay with you?" he asked as he headed toward the front door.

"I don't need anybody staying with me."

"Who?"

She blew out a breath. "I asked a friend I know—outside the bureau. Julie's a nurse but she can't be here for a few hours. And you do realize, don't you, I'm not exactly on the clock and if I don't *want* a babysitter, you can't make me have one. You bullied me into staying in the hospital a few extra days, but you can't bully me into having a babysitter."

He reached the porch and turned to face her. Eyeing the bandage, so stark and white against her flesh, he let his gaze linger there for a pointed moment before looking back into her eyes. "If I do not have your word you'll have somebody with you for the next twenty-four hours, then *I* will be here watching you for the next twenty-four hours."

"That's gonna be boring. Did you bring any popcorn?"

Then she shouldered past him and dealt with the locks. He came inside and shut the door behind him while she reset the security system, trying not to think about her smart-ass reply. Why was it that when 99 percent of his people would tell him to kiss their ass, Dez issued a statement like *Did you bring any popcorn*?

If she would just work to keep him at arm's length, the way everybody else did, maybe it would be easier not to be so obsessed with her. So desperate for a touch, a taste . . . a night.

A lifetime, even.

Stop it.

She glanced over her shoulder at him and said, "Julie won't be here until after her shift at the clinic is over. So if you're really determined that I'm not to be alone, either you call me another babysitter or you make yourself at home."

Then she sauntered off into the depths of the house.

He found himself watching the way her ass swayed back and forth and wishing, really wishing, he had the strength to call her another "babysitter," as she called it. But he also knew there was no way in hell he was going to miss out on spending a little bit of time with her. Away from work. Out of that damned hospital.

Here. In her home. Where he could assure himself she was safe, alive.

Whole.

* * *

STARING into the refrigerator, Dez found herself contemplating the bottle of wine. It was too damn early, she knew. Plus, she was still a little off-kilter from the pain meds and she knew she'd be popping another shortly.

But still. Every once in a while, liquid courage did help things a bit and she needed something to help loosen her tongue because she couldn't seem to figure out the right way to go and talk to Taylor and tell him something very, very simple.

Thanks for saving my life.

"Are you hungry?"

She jumped, startled. Turning around, she stared at him and then she gaped, a little dismayed at the sight of him. He'd taken his jacket off. He'd loosened his tie.

Hell—it was almost like he was . . . *naked*. At least for Taylor Jones. Those suits of his were like armor, she'd always thought.

"Are you okay?"

Jerking her eyes away from his chest, she stared at him and stammered out . . . something. She didn't know what.

"Maybe you should sit down. You look flushed."

No, I look hot. As in turned on, she thought irritably. *All because my fricking boss undid the top two buttons on his pristine white dress shirt and loosened that damn tie.*

And the jacket. Mustn't forget the jacket he'd taken off.

Swallowing, she turned around and grabbed a can of Diet Coke from the fridge. Over her shoulder, she said, "I'm just thirsty. Tired. Nobody ever gets any rest in a hospital, you ever noticed that?"

"I've never had to stay in one," he said. "But plenty of my people have."

There was a weight in his voice.

Slowly, she turned and studied him.

That heavy, strange weight she'd heard in his voice was echoed in his eyes, she realized. It didn't show in his face—no, very little was ever revealed on that face of his, but those eyes . . . somewhere, just behind a rigid, steely curtain, she sensed a great deal of chaos. Pain. Guilt.

She remembered how many times she'd heard that he was at the hospital because one of them had gone down. This was the first time for her—she was rarely ever in a place where there was any action going on. But her best friend, Taige, had been hurt a few times and she knew, vividly, that Taylor liked to haunt hospital halls.

No, he didn't show much emotion to the world. But he felt it, she realized. He felt a great deal.

And suddenly, those words were a lot easier to find.

"You saved my life," she said softly, setting her drink down and crossing her arms over her chest. "I haven't said thank you for that."

"You don't need to. I never should have let you put yourself in that position."

Dez arched a brow. Oh, yeah, there was emotion. She was nowhere near the emotional bloodhound some of her colleagues were, but psychics, most of them, had similar natures and she could pick up the vibes well enough.

What she didn't understand was why she hadn't ever picked these up from him before.

Unless he was just having a harder time keeping it all hidden . . .

Pushing off the counter, she circled the island to stand in front of him. "There was a girl inside that house, Taylor. He would have killed her."

"We don't know that."

"Don't we?" Reaching down, she caught his hand and said, "Come on."

For just a second, he resisted.

She had no idea why she'd grabbed his hand. She was surprised as hell that she'd done it.

She was equally stunned when his fingers, long, cool, and elegant, closed around hers. She led him to the bathroom and left him standing by the counter as she faced the mirror. "This damn tape itches like crazy," she said. "I kept telling that nurse to find some paper tape. I think she liked ignoring me."

"You shouldn't be exposing that yet," he said, his voice gruff.

Dez rolled her eyes and made a face at him in the mirror. "Yes, Daddy."

Something flashed in the depths of his steely blue eyes—something hot—something that made her knees do the weirdest damn thing. Swallowing, she tore her eyes away from him and focused on her reflection, watching as she peeled the bandage away and revealed the neat surgical scar on her throat.

Dumping the bandages in the trash, she turned to face him. Bracing her hips against the marble countertop, Dez angled her chin up, let him stare.

He did. For long, long seconds. Then he turned on his heel and stalked out.

She caught up with him in the kitchen, grabbing his arm. "It's a scar, Taylor. A fucking scar. And I don't mind it. Hell, I'll wear it happily for the rest of my life. You know why? Because there's a little girl who is *alive*." She stared into his eyes and said, "Hell, even if I'd bled out, I'd consider it worth it, because that monster is dead—you made sure he'd never hurt another little girl."

A muscle jerked in his jaw. "Stop."

"Stop what? Pointing out the truth?"

He sighed and shoved a hand through his hair. "I *know* all of this," he said, his voice harsh, colder than normal. "I even knew you'd feel that way—willing to die if it meant the girl lived. But as I'm the one who had your blood all over my hands, and as I'm the one who allowed you to put yourself in that situation, I'd rather not relive it."

Her heart softened, something she really, really didn't need. Not when it came to him. That bit of flesh was already a little too compromised when it came to him. "Taylor . . . stop trying to be master of the world, okay? I made the decision and I knew, going in, it could be dangerous. I'd do it again, too." Rising on her toes, she brushed her lips against his cheek. Heat lanced through her but, as much as she wanted to, she didn't seek out his mouth. Instead, she started to lower back down. "You saved my life . . . thank you."

His hands closed around her arms. Oddly gentle, but firm. Unyieldingly so.

Dez's heart lodged in her throat as he reached up, his fingers hovering just above the wound at her throat. Hovering, not touching. A world of emotion crept into his voice as he whispered, his voice raw, "I can't stand seeing that mark on you."

Then he shifted his gaze and stared into her eyes.

She knew the man had feelings. She always suspected they ran deeper than most of her co-workers expected.

He never let it show, though.

Until now. That steel curtain, for just a moment, parted. Fluttered. Just beyond that curtain, she saw pain, misery, and guilt . . . and something else that stole the breath from her lungs.

Molten, burning, scalding heat . . .

The sight of that heat did something to her low, low inside her belly. Her heart skipped a few beats, then settled into a quick, rapid rhythm—a thousand butterflies trapped inside her chest. Butterflies with wings dipped in some seriously strong sort of aphrodisiac, too. Lust, hot and heavy, moved through her, and before Dez knew what she was doing, she had her hand on Taylor's cheek. "I'm okay, you know. I'm tougher than I look. Hell, I feel almost normal already. No surprise, considering you made them keep me several days longer than needed."

Then, tortured by the unexpected misery she saw in those steely blue eyes, taunted by unadulterated heat, she bussed his mouth lightly with hers. "I'm alive . . . and I'm alive because you were there, Taylor. So stop kicking yourself, okay?"

* * *

THE feel of her mouth against his was a delight he had never expected to feel, one he knew he didn't deserve . . . and one he knew he wasn't strong enough to turn away from.

When she would have pulled away, he reached up, cupped his hand over the back of her head.

He thought she'd pull away.

Was sure of it, even.

She was just trying to assuage his guilt, and it didn't surprise him. She was cocky, sarcastic, and very often full of attitude, but she had the gentlest, kindest heart . . . and he didn't deserve that kindness. She didn't pull away, though.

And when her mouth opened under his, it wasn't the sort of soft, pitying kiss he might have expected.

The heat, the hunger in that kiss might have laid him low . . . if he hadn't already been so starved for her. If he hadn't spent so many fucking nights dreaming of her. If he hadn't been half blind with need and guilt and desperation and too many other emotions he couldn't even begin to describe.

Slanting his mouth more firmly against hers, Taylor stared at her from under his lashes and was startled to realize she was looking back at him. Swearing, he jerked back and muttered, "Damn it. This is insane."

One slim, ringless hand came up, toyed with the placket of his shirt. "I always thought it was insane not to do something you really, really want . . ." Dez's gaze shifted up to meet his and his body tensed, whip tight, as she murmured, "And I've wanted this a very, very long time."

That elegant, long-fingered hand stroked down the front of his shirt. The smile that curled her lips was so smug, so sexy and female—if he hadn't already been rock hard and aching . . . fuck, he could have gone to his knees and begged just then.

And when her fingers closed around him, stroked him through his trousers, he almost did. The smile on her mouth widened. "Taylor, you want me, too. So, tell me . . . why is this insane?"

There was a reason. No. Not *reason. Reasons.* Lots of them. He knew it. But as those fingers stroked up, then down, he couldn't think of them, not a single one.

Staring into her sloe eyes, he dredged up a couple of those reasons. "You work for me. I'm your boss—this is a bad fucking idea."

"Then I guess maybe we shouldn't tell anybody."

Yes, that's a good idea . . . Shit. This wasn't happening. It couldn't.

* * *

DEZ could see the war being waged in his eyes and if she had any sense at all, she'd back off. She already knew she'd have a hard time facing him when she went back to work—hell, five minutes from now when the fog cleared from her brain—but she couldn't back off. She needed this, needed him. The ache was a constant, pulsing emptiness inside her and it grew worse and worse with every passing second.

Instead of backing away as common sense demanded, she teased the line of his mouth with her tongue and delighted as she felt him tremble against her. The subtle power in that lean body had always amazed her . . . and she could make him tremble.

It was a drug.

That would explain why her brain suddenly went beyond haywire, why every last nerve ending started to buzz and jitter and vibrate. Fisting her free hand in his shirtfront, she pulled him closer and sank her teeth into his lower lip. "Tell me something, Taylor . . . you ever turn that brain of yours off?"

He swore.

And she could almost hear it as the threads of his control snapped. His hands grabbed her, hauled her against him. Breathlessly, she laughed against his mouth and whispered, "My bedroom's down the hall."

But she didn't think he even heard her.

Five seconds later, Dez wasn't even sure *she* remembered where her bedroom was. She went from standing pressed against his body to sitting on the cool marble of the kitchen island, with him standing between her thighs.

Always, always, always Taylor Jones presented a remote, impassive mask to the world, but the man staring down at her now was anything but remote, anything but impassive. His steely blue eyes glittered with hunger, and harsh flags of color stained his high, elegant cheekbones.

As his mouth crushed down on hers, Dez barely had two seconds to think, to realize . . . all that hunger, it was for *her*.

But for all that burning hunger, his hands were gentle as he stripped away her shirt, infinitely gentle as he peeled it away. "Your skin is so soft, so fragile," he whispered, dipping his head to press a kiss to her shoulder.

"I'm not the least bit fragile," she said, her voice husky. She fisted a hand in the silky, short hair at his nape and guided his head to her breasts. "Touch me, Taylor. You have no idea how many times I've thought about this."

He buried his face between her breasts as he reached around and unfastened her bra, drawing it away and dropping it to the floor. When his mouth closed around one swollen nipple, Dez groaned. She started to arch her head back but the tender, healing flesh at her neck protested and she hissed out.

Taylor stiffened, pulling back.

But when he would have pulled away, she fisted a hand in the front of his shirt. "Don't you dare," she said. Catching his wrist, she guided his hands back to her, lowering her gaze. "I want to see you touching me."

His hands, tanned, lean, and elegant, looked so damned nice against her darker skin, she decided.

"You're not up to this," Taylor muttered.

But that didn't keep him from stroking his thumbs around her nipples and when she sneaked a look at him from under her lashes, she saw that he was also staring at the way his hands looked on her flesh.

Arching into his touch, she said softly, "Isn't that kind of up to me to decide?"

"You're supposed to take it easy."

She reached down and undid his belt, slowly released the button on his trousers, lowered the zipper. "Then we'll just have to drag out the whips and chains next time, huh?"

Slipping her hand inside, she closed her fingers around his cock and stroked. With a groan, he crushed his mouth to hers.

Those wicked, wicked fingers would drive him out of his mind if he wasn't careful, he realized.

Or maybe they already had, because there was no way in hell he could be sane and still be doing this. If he were sane, he wouldn't have stripped Dez out of her clothes, wouldn't be easing her body back so that she lay spread out over the cool white marble of the kitchen island. Her flesh glowed a soft, warm brown, her breasts round and full, her belly softly rounded. Her hips flared out, a sweet, sweet curve that had driven him insane pretty much from the beginning. Her legs, strong and sleek, parted for him as he moved up closer.

Dez stroked a hand down the front of his shirt and said, "You're still dressed."

He knew. He needed to do something about that, but first . . .

Between her thighs, the flesh of her sex was glistening and pink, already wet. Wet . . . for him. Fuck. Fuck. Fuck. Reaching down, he cupped her in his hand and as he pushed a finger inside her, he watched her face.

"I don't have anything with me," he said, his voice ragged.

This had been the last, the absolute last thing he had planned on doing—even though it was the one thing he wanted more than anything else on earth.

He was so unprepared, it was laughable. He had his hand between Desiree Lincoln's thighs, one finger inside her snug, wet pussy, and his cock ached like a bad tooth and the nearest fucking gas station was fifteen miles away.

Her lashes drooped low over her eyes. "I'm on birth control." Then she arched her hips against his hand, a shuddering sigh rolling out of her. "And that's not the only consideration . . . but I'm clean. Broke up with my last serious boyfriend a few years ago and haven't been intimate with anybody since him."

He knew she'd broken up with the guy—he even knew the date. He knew the guy's name, his address, his job. And he also knew that the last thing he needed to be saying was, "I have a physical yearly and I'm clean."

"We're responsible, reasonable adults," Dez said. She rocked against his hand once more and reached down, closed her fingers around his wrist, held him closer as she started to ride his hand slowly.

His heart slammed against his ribs at the sheer, sweet sensuality of it.

"Yes. And we should both know better."

Their gazes met. "Fuck it," she whispered.

He shoved his trousers down and tugged her to the edge of the island, steadied himself. Disentangling his hand, he lifted his fingers to his mouth and muttered, "Later, I'm going to taste you. All of you." Then he licked them clean before gripping her hips.

He had the pleasure of watching her eyes flutter as he pushed inside . . . slowly. Feeling that soft flesh yield and stretch around him as he took her. Slick, tight . . . so wet. Skin to skin. He hadn't gone skin to skin with a woman . . . ever. As he buried himself completely inside her, he pressed his brow to hers and stared into her dark, warm eyes, shaken to the very core.

"Dez," he whispered against her lips.

She brought her legs up, wrapped them around his hips.

"Make love to me, Taylor," she murmured.

How could he do anything but?

* * *

LATER, he kept his promise. *After* Dez called her friend Julie and told her she'd have somebody with her and would be okay through the night, of course.

And after Taylor did something she didn't think she'd ever seen him do.

He took the rest of the day off, calling in for personal time.

One very hot shower later, she was sprawled on the bed and he was sprawled between her thighs, her butt in his hands and his mouth against her pussy, his tongue stroking and teasing and making her so damn hot, she didn't know if her heart could handle it.

He tasted her, he tormented her, he teased her, and when she was sure she'd die if she didn't come, he rolled onto his back and pulled her on top of him. Sensitive and sore, her body unused to the demands after a few years of celibacy, she bit her lip as she slowly sank down and took him inside.

"I love looking at you," he whispered, his voice raw, rough. So unlike the cool, collected professional she was used to. The steely blue of his eyes was molten and hot, stroking all over her flesh like liquid, living flame. His hands cupped her breasts, plumping them together, teasing her nipples until each light touch was like an arrow of fire shooting straight down to her crotch.

Dazed, she rested her hands on his chest and rocked against him.

He lifted his head and caught one nipple in his mouth and Dez shuddered, shook, clenched down around him. It made him groan and the vibration of it against her flesh had her shaking all over.

Madness . . . she'd fallen into madness.

Actually, though, it was more than that.

She was insane and she was in . . . in something else that she wouldn't even think about. Not right now. Bending down, she crushed her mouth to his, linked their fingers, and started to pump against him, madly. Desperate. Driving. So full of need, so full of hunger.

She needed him—so much. The ache had lived inside her for so long and she'd ignored it for so long.

The thick ridge of his cock twitched, swelled inside her, and he shifted, adjusting her weight so that when she moved, she was pressing against him just . . . *there* . . .

She cried out against his mouth and went shuddering, shaking, and screaming into orgasm.

* * *

ALTHOUGH she wasn't surprised by the distance between them the next day, it did hurt.

She sat sipping her coffee and watching as he put his armor back on.

That suit, a little wrinkled and worse for the wear, hid a body she'd held pressed against hers through the night and she decided she really did hate those suits. He used them to hide.

And when his phone rang, she watched as he used that to put even more distance between them.

But she wasn't surprised.

As he finished taking the call, talking in terse sentences, she shored up her defenses. She had feelings for the cold bastard, but she knew a one-night stand with him wasn't going to change things . . . not for him. Maybe she'd hoped to get him out of her mind, and only time would tell if it worked.

When he disconnected, she lowered her coffee and glanced up at him. "Missing child?"

"Yes."

She nodded and asked, "Who do you think you'll call in?"

He tugged his tie on, tying it in smooth, efficient motions. "It was Taige Br—Morgan that called. She's already tracking."

"Taige?" For the past few years, Taige had been mostly incommunicado with the bureau. Ever since that last injury. Although the injury wasn't to blame. She'd gotten married, had a real life . . . finally. Dez was happy for her. Taige needed a real life, something outside the misery the other woman had known for most of her life. But if something was pulling at her, Taige wasn't going to ignore it, she supposed.

"Yes."

Recognizing the distance, and even more, recognizing the light burning in his eyes, she lifted her cup. "Then you'd better hit the road, boss. If Taige has a live one, it probably won't take that long for her to track the kid down."

He came closer and, for a brief second, her heart stopped. But all he did was angle her chin up so he could scrutinize her neck. Jerking her chin out of his grip, she said edgily, "I'm fine. They wanted me to have somebody with me for the day."

She pushed away from the chair and carried her coffee over to the sink. Suddenly it was turning her stomach. She dumped it down the drain and looked at him over her shoulder. "I had somebody with me all day . . . and all night. Now, if you don't mind . . . I need a shower."

* * *

THREE days later, she wasn't handling it quite so well.

Especially not after what he had just told her.

"I'm *what*?" she demanded.

"On leave. The next three months."

"Oh, hell, no, I am not."

Taylor barely glanced at her. "Yes, you are. You took a nearly fatal injury and—"

"Oh, kiss my ass, Jones. This is not about my injury," she snarled. She had the presence of mind, just, to slam the door shut behind her before storming over to his desk. Leaning over it, she glared at him. "This is because of what happened. Be enough of a man to admit that."

"All right." Taylor leaned back and folded his hands over his belly.

It was hard, she realized, harder to look at those hands without thinking about how they had felt on her body.

"I'll admit it. I will not deny a strong attraction on my part, and it was unwise for me to act on it."

"Unwise," she mimicked.

"Unwise, foolish, unethical. Take your pick."

It hurt. Unethical, yeah, she'd give him that. It had been unethical. But unwise? Foolish? No. Not for her. Hearing him describe it that way was like having him jab little needles into her heart. "And your solution is kicking me out."

"I'm not kicking you out. You *do* need time off to fully recuperate." Then the mask fell away and for a brief moment she caught a glimpse of the man who'd so desperately made love to her.

The man who had held her like she mattered. That was what hurt the most, she realized. He'd made her feel like she mattered . . . mattered to *him*, almost the way he mattered to her.

Dez had never mattered to anybody before. Not personally, at least, not really. And now she was being reminded, again, of just how little she did matter. That it was Taylor delivering her that message was a double blow and it was painful enough to leave her breathless.

"I can't do my job when I've got you on my mind, Desiree. I just can't." He said it in that flat, cool voice and every word was a slap.

"So this is *my* fault." She didn't blink, didn't let him see how much this hurt. It wouldn't do any good, and damn it, she had her pride. Some of it, anyway. What little she could scrape up off the floor.

"No. It's mine. But I can't head the unit if I'm on leave." He continued to stare at her, and once more, his blue eyes were blank and cool. Emotionless. "Can you think of a suitable replacement?"

She glared at him. No. She couldn't. Without Taylor there, walking the razor's edge that kept this unit going, they'd go under. They were too damned important and she knew it, but too many others outside the unit just didn't *get* it.

"So I get the short end," she murmured, her voice hoarse and ragged. She wasn't going to cry, damn it. She wasn't.

"Would you just *think* for a minute?" he snarled. "It's not like you don't need the time off."

"But three *months*?" Her voice broke. She couldn't . . . three months. The voices . . . no. The ghosts that haunted her all too often. They pulled her from her sleep if she didn't seek them out. She couldn't go three months—even thinking about it was enough to make her head threaten to split, that darkness edging up on her. It was hard enough to get through a week without following those whispers. As long as she answered them, she could stay sane. But if she didn't . . .

Now he wanted her to take three months away from it?

And three months without seeing him?

He doesn't want to see you anyway.

Yeah, she was getting that picture.

"You need to take the time off," he said flatly. "And you need to rest. And we . . . need time to get our heads on straight." Something she couldn't quite read moved through his eyes as he studied her face.

She couldn't read it, but it hurt—left her heart aching and empty.

Get our heads on straight.

In other words, he wouldn't change his mind, wouldn't try to find a way to make things work—even though she knew, without a doubt, he had feelings for her.

"What's the purpose of getting our heads on straight? Tell me that." Oh, hell. Even *she* could hear the catch in her voice now.

"We have to get back on even footing."

"Or . . . ?"

He didn't answer.

Dez swallowed. "Shove your three months, Taylor. I quit."

I quit—

Taylor jerked his head back as she said that. Then he shook his head. She couldn't. He knew Dez, knew how she needed . . . *fuck*. Yes, he knew how she needed what she did. It *wasn't* a job for her—it was a need.

"You can't quit," he said quietly. "You and I both know how much you need your work—we know what it does to you when you don't work."

Dez's mouth twisted in a bitter, ugly smile. "Obviously *we* don't or you wouldn't be pushing me out for three months because *you* can't deal."

Alarm screamed in his head as she reached down, pulled out her ID, her weapon. *Fuck—*

"Desiree, be reasonable."

Lashes swooped low over her eyes and she murmured, "That's exactly what I'm doing. I'm not taking three months—double the time the doctor said I needed—and hell, I can talk to ghosts just fine without hurting my neck. I don't even need *six* weeks. I'll go insane if I spend three months away from what I need to do. Since you won't let me do it here, I'll do it on my own."

She slammed her shield, her ID, her weapon on his desk.

He caught her wrist. "Don't do this, damn it." She couldn't leave . . . even as he thought maybe it was for the best—for him. Yeah, it might be better for him, but it would be hell for her. She needed this. Shit. What had he done? She couldn't leave.

"Give me a reason why I shouldn't." Her eyes, dark and soft, bore into his, challenging.

Something hovered on the tip of his tongue. But instead of exploring that, he gritted out, "Because you'll regret walking away from your job."

Dez shook her head. "I didn't *walk*. You shut me out." Her eyes lingered on his face, and then she reached up, touched his cheek.

His heart slammed against his ribs and he had to fight the urge not to nuzzle that hand, not to grab her, beg her not to leave. Fuck—not seeing her? Then, even that paled.

Away from here, how would she get what she needed? How would she get *enough*? The voices, her ghosts, they'd drive her mad.

As she turned away from him and started toward the door, he came out from behind the desk. "You can't walk away from this team, Dez. I won't allow it," he said, forcing his voice to be flat and cold—no emotion, damn it, because letting something *other* than his head speak was what had caused this. No emotion— nothing but logic. Nothing.

Dez paused at the door and looked back at him. She lifted a brow at him. "You won't allow it," she murmured, cocking her head. Then she sighed and opened the door. "Sugar, you just don't seem to get the picture here. You don't have a choice."

Their eyes met, held, steely blue on darkest brown. She was the one to look away first.

"Good-bye."

As she closed the door behind her, he could have sworn he heard something crack.

But it wasn't his heart—he wasn't so fucking stupid that he'd allow himself to fall for a woman he couldn't have. And even if he *was* that stupid, surely he wouldn't compound it by chasing her away.

Except Taylor knew that was exactly what he'd done.

Shaken, he slipped a hand into his pocket and pulled out that slender gold chain. The one he still hadn't returned to her. The delicate gold cross hung there, swinging back and forth.

FOUR

Fourteen months later

MY *angel. It's almost time. Fall.* The pen paused over the paper while the hand holding it trembled. *I think about you every day but this time of year is always so hard. My angel. My pretty, precious angel. My one and only.*

Tears came. Blurring the words on the paper. But still, the pen moved. Still the words flowed.

* * *

IT was late.

Few people remained in the office. But Taylor Jones wasn't surprised when his administrative assistant appeared in the doorway just as he clicked his briefcase closed.

"I assume you'll keep things under control while I'm gone?" he said, giving Gina Berkle a quick look.

She didn't smirk, but she might as well have. The look in her hazel eyes accomplished the same thing. "Yes. Don't worry. The place won't fall apart because you're taking a few weeks off. I held it together last year; I'll do the same this year."

He nodded, his mind already on his trip. It wasn't anticipation that flooded his mind, or excitement. It was, plain and simple, dread. This was a duty, something he had to do, something he needed to do, something he did every year.

And it hadn't gotten easier over the years, either.

Not that he expected it to.

"May I ask you a question?"

Taylor looked up, frowning. He'd forgotten about Gina. She was watching him, an odd look in her eyes. "You can ask. Whether I'll answer depends on the question."

But it wasn't the question he'd expected.

"You *are* coming back, right?"

Taylor stared at her, perplexed. "Why wouldn't I?"

Gina came farther into his office and sat down, smoothing her skirt down. "Hell, I've said this much," she muttered, absently rubbing her hands together, staring down at them. Then she looked back at him. "You don't see what we see every day."

"And that is . . . ?"

"Yourself. The look in your eyes." She chewed on her lower lip. "I imagine you've read my personnel file, right? I mean, this is the FBI. And you're a paranoid bastard anyway. You probably know my shoe size."

"Actually, no. Your shoe size has nothing to do with your job." But he knew where she was going with this. "And relax, Gina. I'm fine."

"Are you?"

"I said I was." He resisted the urge to snap at her—oddly touched that she cared enough to say anything. Just about everybody else would have ignored it, assuming they even noticed anything was wrong. Shit, most of them would probably lift a glass in celebration if he decided to put a bullet through his brain. "Stop worrying."

"I can't." She shrugged and gave him a weak smile. "You haven't been fine since Dez Lincoln was injured on the job."

You haven't been fine since Dez Lincoln was injured . . . No. He hadn't. Shit. Closing his eyes, he took a deep, slow breath and then looked up, stared at Gina. "That's enough," he said softly.

She fell silent and looked away as he filed a few more documents and shut down his computer.

He ignored the roaring in his ears, ignored the pounding of his heart. He just had to get out of here—and maybe buy a big-ass bottle of Jack Daniel's on the way home. Good ol' Jack. His dad had always liked his Jack from time to time. He could lift a glass in his dad's memory, even. At least one memory that wasn't too fucking painful.

His flight didn't leave until 10:20. He could get plastered, something he rarely did, and maybe he could have a peaceful night of unconsciousness.

"Sir?"

Slowly, he looked up and saw that Gina had risen from her chair and stood nervously in front of his desk, her hands twisting at her waist. She stared at him, her eyes miserable as she bit her lip.

"Yes?" he asked, forcing the word out through a tight throat.

"Is it?"

"Is it what, Gina?"

"Is it enough?" She shook her head. "You can be a cold guy to work for, but . . . well . . . you've always been fair. You've never *not* been fair. And . . . well, like I said, you don't see what I see every day. I saw my last boss in the days before she decided to kill herself. And too often the look in your eyes looks too much like hers. I didn't say anything then and now I have to live with wondering if maybe I could have made a difference—I won't do that again. Not ever. So if this is out of place, I'm sorry, but I'm not living with that on my soul again. I look at you and see something too close to what I saw then. I can't be quiet this time. I just can't."

Taylor closed his eyes. He heard the nervous tremble in her voice, knew why she was so upset. And he understood why she'd made herself say this—forced herself to do it.

Gina had been the one to find her boss dead. But he wasn't about to off himself. He didn't deserve that easy of an end.

He made himself look back at her. "I said I'm fine."

She continued to stare at him and her gaze told him she wasn't convinced.

"Gina, I'm fine." No, he wasn't. But he wasn't going to put a gun to his head, either. Forcing himself to smile, he added, "I've got too much to do to kill myself anyway."

There was still the mission, after all. If nothing else, he still had that.

Always that.

Gina weakly returned his smile. "Well, I guess that's one way to look at it."

"Yes."

He came out from behind the desk and hesitated. It was weird, he realized, to know that somebody was worried about him. Most people around here wouldn't give a damn if he died, other than how it might affect their jobs. "Was there anything else?"

"On that topic?" She gave him a wobbly smile. "No. Other stuff? I'm sure it will come up. I know what to call about, what not to call about . . . except . . . ." She grimaced.

"What is it?"

She glanced past his shoulder, like she didn't want to look at him as she asked, "What do I do if we get more of *those* calls?"

Now it was Taylor's turn to grimace. In a gesture that had become automatic, he slid a hand into his pocket, fingered the golden chain. For the first few months, he'd told himself he'd send it to her. Return it. It was hers, after all.

Then he told himself he could drive it out there . . . once he had time. He could at least look her in the face, perhaps apologize.

But he never did it. And he knew he wouldn't. He couldn't, for some reason. He needed that small connection, that small piece of her. Idly, he rubbed his finger across the chain and then looked at Gina.

"If she calls, call me." But he hoped it didn't happen. He was going to have enough to deal with, just getting through the next few weeks.

The last thing he needed was to think about dealing with *those* calls . . .

* * *

"PLEASE. Take it."

This was the part of her new life that wasn't so easy.

Staring at Myra Downey's wrinkled, tired face, Dez Lincoln gave her a weak smile. "You know, I don't much like doing this," she said, accepting the check with a strained smile.

"I'm seeing that . . . in your eyes. You got a lot of pride, I can see it. Just like I can see that if I hadn't offered this money, you wouldn't have asked." Myra curled Dez's fingers around the check and shook her head. "What you've given me is more valuable than what I'm giving you. And I think you know it. Peace is something I've not had in years, not since he disappeared."

A watery smile curled her lips and she reached down, touched the faded gold band on her left ring finger.

Dez suspected the ring hadn't ever left her hand for longer than it took to wash her dishes or take a bath. Myra closed her eyes and when she looked back at Dez, there was such peace, such tranquillity in her eyes. "You don't understand the gift you've given me, Ms. Lincoln. The peace I feel. Yes, now I have to grieve all over again, but now I *know*. Now I can have peace . . . and it's because of you. Now I know he didn't just walk away from us." Her voice broke and tears gleamed in her eyes. "He didn't just leave."

"No." Dez came off the couch and wrapped an arm around the old woman's shoulders. "Your Jimmy loved you and the kids. With everything he had."

"Yes." She closed her eyes, nodded. "Yes, he did. And because of a couple of fool kids, he's lost to us. But not forgotten. And now we can put him to rest."

Myra sighed and looked around her home. "Even without him, we had a good life—I was determined to see to that, determined to show our children a good life. But there wasn't a day that went by that I didn't think of him, not a day that went by that I didn't miss him, long for him . . . people told me to move on, you know. Move on, find somebody else—they said I deserved that. But he was all I wanted." She looked at Dez and whispered, "Does that make me a fool?"

"It makes you a woman who loved her man, I think." The knot in her throat wasn't going to fade anytime soon, not sitting here confronted with this woman's strength—her determination and her unfading, unfailing love. Forty years after her husband's disappearance and she still loved him.

Now, Myra could put him to rest. Now, she could finally let go and move on.

Looking down, Dez stared at the check she held and nausea churned her gut.

"Stop it, Ms. Lincoln."

She looked up and saw Myra watching her.

She had a silver brow cocked and was watching her with a knowing smile. "You didn't ask for it—I offered it, and I do it happily. Now go on. I imagine you've got more souls to help rest."

* * *

THERE was a grim-eyed detective leaning against her car.

"How much did you take her for?"

Dez didn't flicker a lash. She still hadn't looked at the check.

"There wasn't a business arrangement, Detective Morris."

The blond snorted and drew a cigarette from behind his ear, tucked it between his lips. He didn't light it. As a matter of fact, Dez was sure she'd seen that same cigarette between his lips the day before. It looked kind of worn and ragged.

"That wasn't precisely my question, Miz Lincoln," he drawled. "I asked how much you took her for."

He waited a beat and then said, "Maybe what I should ask is this: Did she pay you any money?"

"She did." Dez wasn't going to lie about it. Standing on the bottom step, hands hanging loose at her sides, she met his blue eyes levelly.

It wasn't easy to look at him. He bore a disconcerting resemblance to one rat bastard she'd hoped to forget about over the past year or so. Of course, it hadn't happened.

Tate Morris continued to watch her, his eyes narrowed and thoughtful. Finally, he sighed and shifted his attention to the scar on her neck. It wasn't an ugly scar, not as far as scars went, at least. The surgeon had done a damn neat job, she had to give him that. But it was still a scar, a pale slash against her darker skin, and it stood out.

"How'd you get that scar?"

"Cut myself shaving," she said without blinking an eye.

He grinned and shook his head. "You're a smart-ass. If it wasn't for the psychic bullshit, I'd find you ridiculously appealing, Miz Lincoln."

"My heart breaks over the fact that you don't, I assure you."

"Yeah, I can see that." He shoved away from the car. As he headed toward her, his gait loose and easy, he tugged the unlit cigarette out from between his lips and tucked it behind his ear again. "I've done some checking up on you ever since you called in and reported that body. Appears you've got a habit of being around bodies, Miz Lincoln. Especially dead ones."

"I wouldn't call it a habit. More like an occupational requirement."

"If you were a coroner or funeral director, even a cop, I could understand that." He stopped less than two feet away, much too close.

Dez didn't back away. He was doing it on purpose—trying to throw her off, trying to intimidate her. She'd dealt with far, far worse on a regular basis. She didn't give a damn. Smirking at him, she asked, "Are you going to ask me my whereabouts on the night he died? Because when it comes back that he *is* Myra's husband, you're going to look pretty silly, seeing as how he died before I was born—that's a pretty good alibi. You know, with me not being *alive* and all."

"Damn. I really could like you." He shook his head and sighed again, shooting a look over her shoulder at the house. "But tell me, how come you're so certain it's her husband? Hm? Why are you so certain?"

Dez smiled serenely. "Maybe a little birdie told me." Or a ghost. "Or maybe I'm psychic."

He snorted. "Don't start that bullshit with me, angel, okay? I'm not as easy to fool as a lonely old lady."

Dez was tempted to point out that he obviously didn't know Myra very well. Myra was nobody's fool. But before she could, she heard it. A voice on the wind . . . so faint.

. . . *Help me* . . .

A whisper of cold danced along her spine.

A voice, young and desperate and strong.

Dez swallowed. Not again. Not already. She was so damn tired, worn to the bone, and she was always cold now, so cold she ached with it. Closing her eyes, she shored up her shields, steadied herself. It took less than five seconds. She could do this—she might pay for doing another job right on the tail of this one, but she could handle it.

Looking at Detective Tate Morris, she gave him a brittle smile. "I'm sure you've checked me out, from birth on up to now. If there was any way you could think to discredit me, you would. And we both know you didn't have any luck . . . don't we?"

"I guess we do," he said slowly, nodding.

"Then there's really nothing left for us to say. You have a good day." She went to step around him. But then, because curiosity had a grip on her, she reached inside her pocket, tugged out a card. "If you're so moved, I wouldn't mind knowing how the investigation turns out."

He accepted the card but when she tried to go around him, he caught her arm. "What's wrong?"

"Nothing." The whisper was already back. *Help . . . damn it, can't anybody help . . .*

There was an edge of desperation there. What was this?

"Don't tell me that," Morris said, shaking his head. "Five seconds ago you were fine, and then your pupils go all pinpoint—now they are all dilated and your skin's cold. You don't look like the pill-popping type, either."

Dez pulled her arm away. "I have to go."

Help me . . .

* * *

THAT morning, she woke up in Springfield, Missouri.

By sunset, Dez Lincoln was pulling into French Lick, Indiana. It had been one hellaciously long day and she knew it wasn't about to end yet, either.

Her hands were icy, but despite that, sweat trickled along her spine.

The voice was driving Dez mad. The ghost was trying to drive her mad.

Pulling her too hard, too fast. And now that she was here, it was loud. So loud. It was almost a scream in her head.

Swallowing, she turned off the narrow, two-lane road onto a drive that led to a small cemetery.

Strange—

Most of her ghosts were people not at rest—unfound souls. Murder victims. And although *some* of them were found and laid to rest, many of her ghosts weren't.

There was something odd about this, though.

She could feel it, like a buzz in her brain.

She bypassed several dozen stones before she found the one she needed. She had no doubt it was the right one, either.

After all, he waited there for her.

Her ghost.

According to his grave marker, his name was Tristan Haler.

He had been a boy when he died, but just barely—hovering on the edge between boyhood and manhood. And when he turned to look at her, she saw something in his eyes that backed up her suspicion—too much knowledge.

"Why did you call me here?" she asked softly.

"I . . . I *didn't mean to,*" he said, his voice insubstantial and distant. "*You can see me, hear me, though, can't you?*"

"Yes. I see those who've left this world."

To her surprise, he laughed. It wasn't a happy sound, though, and the temperature around her dropped. She didn't shiver, but she couldn't stop the goose bumps from breaking out along her skin.

"*Those who have left this world,*" he echoed. "*You make it sound so easy. Like I checked out of a hotel. Like I picked this—wanted it.*"

He looked at her then, and his gaze was hot and angry, even as the air around her grew colder, tighter, all but freezing the oxygen until it felt like she was dragging in air straight from the Arctic. "*I didn't.*"

He went to his knees, staring at his grave. "*But everybody thinks I did. My mom and dad, my sister. They all think I killed myself. I didn't.*"

Dez closed her eyes. Then she looked at him. "You're certain. Do you remember?"

"*What happened . . . ?*" He looked away. "*No. But I know I didn't do it. I know what they think I did. I wouldn't have done it. I know who did, though. And I know why.*"

Dez shoved her hands into her pockets.

Just barely, she resisted the urge to swear.

Well. The good news was . . . he was from around here. If he was from around here and she could find out enough information on her own, or maybe even just freak out the killer enough—

once she found him—maybe he'd confess. She didn't have the resources she'd once had, and helping murder victims was a lot harder than it used to be. And somehow, she knew this boy wouldn't move on until he had justice.

It was written all over him—he had a mission.

Okay. She could handle this. Maybe she wouldn't have to make a phone call. That was all she wanted. To get through a few more jobs without making those damned phone calls.

Actually . . . *all* of her jobs without making those phone calls.

But even as she thought it, she found herself pulling out her phone. Found herself running her thumb along the keypad, the number burning bright in her mind, even though she insisted she didn't *want* to make that call.

She'd have to call him eventually. She knew it in her gut.

And it was enough to make her heart skip a beat, make her knees go weak, make her belly clench. *Will he come this time or send one of the others? . . . Will I see him?*

Taking a deep breath, she shoved all of that aside. It didn't matter, couldn't matter. This mattered—the boy, the job, the lost. They were what mattered now.

Focusing on the boy, she asked the question—whatever his answer was, it was one that mattered, because *this* was what held him back, what kept him from moving on. Something else she knew in her gut.

"You know who did. You know why. How about you tell me?"

She was expecting some story about teenage angst. Jealousy. Anger. Maybe even the loneliness or bullying that was so common these days.

What she didn't expect was the answer she got.

He stared at her with a grim, sad expression and replied, *"Because they were going to kill a girl . . . and I wouldn't go along with it."*

FIVE

I *wanted to see you today, my angel. But not yet. When it's time.*

Almost time.

I think I'll bring you pretty yellow flowers this year. I think you'd like yellow.

Pen continued to scratch over paper, pausing only from time to time.

Perhaps a new dress? Would you like a yellow dress? I saw one and I think you would like it. I don't know much about girls' dresses, but I think you would like this one. I also have a surprise for you, pretty angel. But I can't tell you yet. Soon, though. Very soon.

* * *

"WHAT was Tristan like?"

His sister shot her a look from under a fringe of heavy, dyed-black bangs. She stared at Dez for the longest time, not answering. Dez was already prepared for several long days of getting absolutely nowhere.

But to her surprise, Tiffany Haler sighed and actually answered her question. "What's it matter? He's dead, isn't he?"

"Yes." Dez kept her hands tucked in her pockets, stared straight ahead. Damn it, she was tired. It had been nearly one a.m. before she'd managed to find a bed to collapse into and what little sleep she'd gotten had been fitful. Tired or not, though, she had a promise to keep. Judging by the restless burn inside, she didn't think she'd have much time to do it, either. "Tristan's dead. But that doesn't mean he doesn't matter, does it?"

"No." Tiffany tucked her chin low and hitched her bag up on her shoulder, mumbling under her breath, "It's a bunch of bullshit, though. Bull*shit*."

"What is?"

Tiffany shot her a look. "Nothing. Look, lady, just leave it alone. It's not like there's some story of the week to go with this. Tristan wasn't some kid who got bullied to death, and he wasn't into drugs. He just . . ."

The girl's voice broke. And for a second, her natural shields, the reticence that kept Dez from reading many people, slipped and she felt something from the girl.

Doubt.

It was enough.

Seizing it, she said softly, "A bunch of bullshit . . . him killing himself?"

Tiffany stumbled. Under the heavy makeup she wore, it looked like she'd gone rather white, too. "What?"

Dez shrugged. "Well, from what I can tell, your brother had a lot of things going for him—a girlfriend who adored him, decent parents, a lot of friends, scholarships. We're not talking some poor little rich boy, we're not talking some scared, confused kid—he seemed like a genuinely nice kid. I think he even had a good relationship with you, didn't he?"

"He . . ." Tiffany looked away. She chewed on her lip, her eyes closed. Then, quietly, she whispered, "Everybody loved Tristan. He was a good guy, you know? People . . . they listened to him. Even me."

A harsh breath shuddered out of her and she looked back at Dez. "I used to get a lot of grief around here. Hell, I still do. You know what it's like being different?"

"Actually, I do."

Tiffany sneered. "You probably don't have a clue. I don't just mean being black. But I mean *different*. Half the school thinks I'm a lesbian. I'm not, but they used to tease me all the time . . . and then one day, Tristan heard. One of the guys—Beau Donnelly, some hotshot on the football team, he grabbed me. Said some things. It got back to my brother."

A smile, somehow both sad and proud, curled the girl's lips. "He waited until the guy was out of school. Then he beat the shit out of him." She slanted a look at Dez and added, "Then he told me I had to start standing up for myself, too. He might not always be around—said something like, 'The bullies stop when you make it clear you won't be a target, Tiff. So why are you being a target?'

"I stopped being a target." She pushed a hand through her hair, her hand shaking. "He was right. It's not always easy and I get into fights some, but most of them have figured out that I'll fight back now. I'm even *more* likely to, with him gone."

"Why is that?"

"Because I have to," Tiffany said simply. "He got in a lot of trouble for that—almost got kicked off the team—he could have lost his scholarships and he knew that, and even though my parents understood, they grounded him for three weeks. But he did it for me. And now he's gone—I owe it to him."

"Maybe you owe it to yourself," Dez said, her heart breaking. She understood, better than the girl knew. But she doubted the girl would get that—kids always thought they had a lock on unique problems. And it didn't matter, anyway. Not in the long run. She could understand without the girl realizing she *did* relate, all too well.

"You know, your brother doesn't sound like the type who'd take the easy way out. He just doesn't."

"No." Tiff reached up, wiping away a tear, leaving a black smear of eyeliner. "But he left that damn note . . . and it's his handwriting, you know?"

A shiver raced down her spine only seconds before she heard Tristan's voice.

"It's not my damn handwriting. I can tell you who wrote the note, although the fucker will lie about it."

Meeting Tiffany's eyes once more, she smiled. "Thanks for talking to me. I appreciate it."

She kept quiet until the girl disappeared from sight, saying nothing, not even looking at the ghost standing next to her.

Then, still keeping her gaze focused straight ahead, she murmured, "Well, then, you need to tell me who he is. Where I can find him—and Tristan, we need to move quickly if you're right about them killing some girl. I don't want another person to die if I can help it."

She felt his rage—felt it in the sharp cold that cut through to her bones—felt it in his misery.

"His name is Kyle Spalding. He used to be one of my best friends."

"And how do you know he wrote the note?"

From the corner of her eye, she could see the derisive smirk on his face.

"Because that's what he does. He forges handwriting—it's, like, his thing."

* * *

TAYLOR Jones knew he shouldn't be doing this.

Twenty-five years had passed since he'd lost this child. The first one he'd failed . . .

Logically, he couldn't carry this burden, but logic and the heart, logic and grief, they didn't mingle well.

He'd been fourteen, after all, and he hadn't even been watching her—he'd been at school. Football practice, something he hadn't wanted to do, but it was expected, after all.

He was a Jones and the men did sports.

Just like the women learned to cross-stitch and cook and marry the *right* sort of man.

Even though Anna had only been six, she'd already begun learning both skills, while their mother drilled into her head all the needed bullshit about what sort of clothing she should wear, how she should sit and speak and act . . . at age six.

Personally, Taylor had thought it was all a bunch of bullshit, Anna expecting to "marry well" as the main goal in her life—it was so fucking archaic, straight out of something from a book in a time long past, he'd always thought.

But their family had a lot of bygone traits and skills.

Like his father's habit of keeping a piece on the side.

His mother's habit of ignoring it.

A functioning alcoholic, that's what Elsa Jones had been, floating through their grand house, sipping her cocktails and pretending to be the happy wife at all the social functions, just as a good mayor's wife should.

It all fell apart after Anna disappeared. Sweet, pretty little Anna—his baby sister, somebody who had made him laugh. Made them all laugh, even Mother at times. But then Anna had disappeared and everything changed.

His father tried, Taylor knew. The old man did his damnedest and Taylor, at least, had that. But Elsa . . . a couple of years after it happened, Elsa took one of her cocktails and made it special.

She never woke up.

Taylor wasn't entirely sure he had even grieved over her death. Harsh, strident words still echoed in his ears all these years later and nothing he did could block them out.

Why weren't you watching her?

Elsa—he was at school.

Taylor closed his eyes, resting his hands on the cool wrought-iron balcony, staring out of the family estate. Fuck, he hated this place. He should just sell it. Not that it would sell easily.

Never mind the fact that it was one big-ass piece of land, with a big-ass house. Never mind the fact that the real estate market was still struggling out in these parts. Never mind that it was in the middle of nowhere.

But he couldn't sell the manor—couldn't walk away.

His dad hadn't been able to, either. He'd stayed here, searching for Anna, waiting and hoping, until he just withered away after Taylor went to college. It was like he'd held on just long enough to make sure his one remaining child would be taken care of and then he'd given up. The doctors said it was a heart attack, and yeah, Taylor could believe it.

A heart attack—a broken heart . . . weren't they sort of the same?

Both he and his father had adored Anna.

A pretty, wide-eyed little princess, too precocious, too smart for words.

The knot in his chest swelled, threatened to destroy him. Savagely, he swore, lifted his hands to press against his eyes. The breeze drifted by, blowing his hair back. It was cold, carrying that sharp scent unique to fall, and it was another blow. It had been a day just like this when she'd disappeared. Just like this—

"Shit." He passed a hand over his mouth. He had to stop this, had to. If he didn't, it was going to drive him insane. It was worse this year for some reason, even worse than last year.

And he wondered if maybe Gina hadn't been right, if maybe there wasn't something of his mother's weakness, or worse, inside of him. If maybe one of these days he wasn't going to look in the mirror and decide it would just be better if he gave up—on everything: on himself, on the mission, all of it.

A year ago, he wouldn't have even considered asking himself that question.

But lately . . .

No.

Shoving a hand into his pocket, he gripped the golden necklace that had become his talisman. His strength. No. He wasn't going to get that close to the edge. He wasn't there now and he wouldn't be. Carefully, he pulled the chain out, opened his palm so he could stare at it. Focus on it.

He was fine. Or as close to fine as he'd ever be.

He was just fucking fine. And maybe if he said it often enough, he'd even believe it.

* * *

SHE hadn't even been in the little town of French Lick a full day and she was being led around by the nose, it seemed. By a ghost. *So what else is new?* she thought glumly.

"Why are we *here*?" Dez demanded as she climbed out of her car and stared up at the hotel.

Actually, *hotel* didn't seem quite the right word to describe this place.

It was a huge, sprawling wooden affair, made to look more rustic than it was, designed for people with money, she imagined, people who wanted to pretend they were roughing it while they took a weekend away with their kids. They'd use the child care offered by the hotel while they went to the casino and gambled, let their kids swim while they sipped cocktails by the pool.

You're being cynical, she thought. A screeching child went running down the sidewalk, whooping with laughter and chased closely by a grinning, if exasperated, father.

Tearing her eyes away from the sight, she looked at the boy with her. The ghost. The only children she had in her life—the only children she'd likely *ever* have.

"Why are we here?" she asked again.

Tristan grimaced. *"They are doing it here."*

"Doing *what* here?" She crossed her arms over her chest and hoped, prayed this boy was wrong. So many of the dead were—it was easy. They confused things and it was understandable. Life, death, fiction, reality, it all became a blur for them.

But some of them had a better grip on reality than others—some had a core of pure steel and this boy, this boy who had been so close to being a man, who never would be . . .

A core of steel? Hell. Think titanium. Sighing, she looked at him. He wasn't wrong.

Tristan stared at her. *"I already told you. They are going to kill her. They might already be doing it . . . or have done it."* For once, the composure, the certainty on his face cracked and he looked scared, confused. He looked like a kid and he broke her heart. *"I don't even know how much time has passed, because I can't remember . . ."*

Dez knew. "It's been three months since you died." She watched as his eyes cleared. "I told you this . . . remember?"

They'd discussed this. Twice.

"Three months . . ." His eyes closed and he looked like he was trying to remember. Slowly, the strain on his face eased and he nodded. *"Yeah. We talked. Three months. That means it's October, right? That means it's October. Almost Halloween . . . ?"* He stared at her and for a moment, his image was clearer, sharper. And the air became colder.

"Yes. Halloween is in two more days."

Tristan's image flickered, wavered. *"Then it hasn't happened yet—they won't do it until Halloween. We can still save her . . ."*

* * *

HER first look at the hotel had already told Dez everything she needed to know—it would be way too pricey for her peace of mind if she just did the rack rates. No help for it, but she'd be damned if she paid rack rates.

So she called a friend. The travel agent had a line on all sorts of good deals. Even then, it wouldn't be cheap. Fortunately, Dez had money in her account and it was even more nicely padded now since she'd deposited the check from Myra. A check that had been far too generous.

Forty-five minutes later, she was checked in, following a uni-formed bellhop to her room—assuming you could call his pseudo-safari gear a uniform. She smirked a little, shaking her head. But hey, she wasn't carrying the suitcase or even her vanity case. If they wanted the bellhops wearing pseudo-safari gear or even real safari gear, so be it.

Once he'd tackled the dangerous task of stowing her suitcases in her room, she gave him a couple of wrinkled ones from her pocket and shut the door, studying the room. She'd spent the previous night sleeping at a roadside motel with a full-size bed. The mattress had sagged in the middle and it had creaked and squeaked every time she moved.

This room looked like paradise.

Good thing, considering how much she was paying.

Sighing, she made her way over to the bed and collapsed, facedown, without bothering to strip off her jacket. She barely had the energy to toe off her shoes. Five minutes horizontal—that was all she needed. Just five minutes.

It took only forty-five seconds for him to find her.

The temperature in the room dropped and she sighed, turning onto her back and watching as Tristan shimmered into view. *"You can't sleep!"*

"I'm not," she said simply. Sitting up, she braced her elbows on her knees and stared at him. "I'm tired, I'm stressed, and I just needed a few minutes."

"We don't have a few minutes." He started to pace, something that managed to stir up the air currents in the room, making it feel like the air conditioner was on. She was glad she'd left her jacket on. *"We have to start looking for her now before it's too late."*

"Okay." She rubbed her hands over her face and stood up. "But you've got to help me out. Where do I go? How do I start?"

She expected him just to give her a blank stare.

But to her surprise, he gave her another one of those grim smiles.

"We should see if any of my so-called friends are around."

"And where do we find them?"

"In the water park . . . most of us used to work here." His image wavered, shoulders going up and down almost as if he'd sighed, and a strange, whispery sound slithered through the room. *"It's how it all came up. We had this thing going—not quite a club, really. We thought we were too cool for that. We called it a fraternity. We didn't do mean shit—a few of them tried but I can't stand mean shit. We were talking about our senior year—making it memorable. I was all for that— something people would never forget. But then . . ."*

His eyes closed a moment, then he opened them and looked at her. A smile twisted his lips. *"I thought I was the one in charge, you know? I was such an arrogant idiot."*

Her heart broke for him.

"Have you remembered anything else about that night?"

"No." He shook his head. *"It doesn't matter, either. All that matters is this."*

It wasn't all—she could see that. He was still clinging to his rage, and that rage was going to chain him here if she didn't help him. But for now, she'd go along with it.

What they'd done to him, it did matter, it had to matter. But she wasn't going to harp on it now. Not when they might be running on so little time. Giving him a smile, she said, "If you say so, Tristan. If that's what you want. Well, then—let's go look for these so-called pals of yours."

SIX

"So everything's ready for tonight?"

Brendan Moore leaned against the wall, studying every-body. He saw excitement. He also saw fear and nerves. He didn't give a damn. It was going to be a party to remember—just the way they'd all planned. Nobody could get in the way now. They all knew what would happen if they tried, too.

Besides, it was too late to stop things.

Beau smirked and lifted his beer to his lips. "Oh, yeah. It's ready. Man, people are going to *freak*."

"I still say we should have stuck with Halloween."

"Shut up, Kyle," Brendan said, rolling his eyes. "The party tonight is the best way to do it. It's supposed to be about senior year, anyway, not Halloween. Everybody from school will see it, *and* we'll be in the middle, too—nice little alibi in case anything gets fucked up." He paused and looked at each of them. "Not that anything is going to get fucked up, right? Mark, you took care of all the security shit, right?"

Mark nodded, rocking a little, tugging on his lip. He wanted a drink. Needed it, but his stomach was fucking burning. If he had a drink, he'd puke. And he needed to quit drinking—that was part of why he was in this mess. Started drinking, hanging out with these assholes. He couldn't believe they were doing this. Shit, he should have listened to Tristan, back when they still had a chance to talk to somebody about Brendan . . .

"Mark, damn it, get your head out of your ass."

Jerking his head up, he stared at Brendan. His heart raced, his gut rolled. But he managed to smile. "Sorry, man—just running things through my mind, ya know. Don't want anything to get fucked up."

Brendan stared at him for a long, hard moment and Mark hoped none of the fear he felt showed in his eyes, on his face.

Finally Brendan looked away and Mark wanted to heave a sigh of relief, but he didn't dare. Couldn't let the guy know how scared he was, what he was thinking. Not Brendan. Not Beau, either.

* * *

THE noise was cacophonous—pushing past the level of deafening. Even before she drew near, Dez bolstered her shields. With that much noise, she'd need it. Even though she didn't have the same connection to the living that she had with the dead, she knew better than to go unshielded, especially around chaos.

It was going to be hard to pinpoint much of anything—damn it, she was the worst possible person to be doing this job. Worst possible person to help Tristan, it seemed, because he needed somebody who could connect with the living—all she could do was connect with him, and his memories were too fractured. He had *no* connection to what had happened after his death, just a desperate need for justice, to help this girl, wherever she was.

Sighing, she pushed through the door and immediately a blast of muggy air wrapped around her. For a moment, it chased away the cold and she paused, enjoying it even as her eyes went wide at the sheer chaos she saw before her.

No. It wasn't chaos. Chaos didn't quite touch this.

Happy chaos didn't even touch it. The shrieks of joy coming from the kids, the shouts and giggles. Without even realizing it, a smile curved her lips and she stood there, letting it settle over her.

There weren't many times in her life when she'd seen such . . . delight.

A pint-sized tornado came blasting her way. Dez froze, watching as an exasperated mother followed, grabbing the girl before she could get around Dez and make it to the doors.

So many sensations, so much emotion—all of them wrapping around her, flooding her. There was laughter, exhaustion, frustration, exhilaration—but overall, almost everything she allowed to filter through her shields felt . . . *right*.

Dez stood there, all but wallowing in it. It was so exhilarating it took a minute to realize that something felt off. Wrong. Completely off. Utterly wrong. And terribly *foul*.

A whisper of evil, underlain with terror. It skittered along her shields like a slimy little beast trying to push its way inside her soul. She swallowed, closed her eyes, and tried to focus on it, but it was faint. So faint.

Aware of the fact that she was catching attention standing there, she showed her wristband to the teenager sitting a few feet away from the door. Once she'd done that, she just wandered around the huge, open-air room, no destination in mind. Just wandering, trying to get a lock on that faint, insidious taint of *wrong.*

It lay in the back of her throat like poison and she was glad she hadn't eaten anything—she just might have started puking.

"Are you looking for something?"

Dez suppressed the urge to shiver as Tristan appeared at her side, too close. And cold—much colder than he'd been before. Being here was hard on him. She could see the icy glitter of rage in his eyes, see the emotional upheaval in his disturbingly solid form.

Uneasy, she glanced past him and saw one of the children staring toward them. No . . . at *Tristan.* The look in the little girl's eyes was a mix of fear and amazement. Damn it, Tristan was manifesting too fully. Looking around, she saw a rocky grotto with a sign—*Over 18 only.*

Excellent. Many younger kids were more sensitive to the paranormal—she had to get him away from them before they started pointing at him. If too many kids began pointing at a guy no parents could see . . . well, she didn't want to think about that. Draw no attention, a good motto.

"We'll talk in a minute," she said, heading for that grotto.

Once they were there, she sat on a lounge chair that let her see much of the water park and she started to study things. "Looking for something? Yeah, I guess. But I don't know what it is." She waited a beat, and then asked, "Do you have any idea?"

Tristan shook his head no. His eyes closed and for the briefest moment, his image faded. But then he looked back at her, and his form strengthened once more and that glitter of rage in his eyes was even stronger. Bad, bad sign . . . too angry, getting too angry. *"I don't know anything, damn it. Shit, this is a waste of time. We need to go find Kyle, Mark. See if they'll talk.* Something."

"No." Dez shook her head. "If I wasn't meant to help, I

wouldn't have heard you. I'm here for a reason—believe that. And there's something here, I can feel it."

The words had no sooner left her lips than she heard a bell. It was no delicate chime, either. It was loud, echoing through the cavernous room. And for some reason, the sound of it sent shivers racing down her spine.

Like a puppet on a string, she found herself rising and following that sound, listening to the shrieks of laughter as she left the secluded grotto. Moments later, she stood at the entrance of what looked to be a huge fort, and at the top, there was what looked like an oversized wooden bucket. A *very* oversized wooden bucket. The sight of it made her gut clench and she didn't even know why.

It started to tip.

The sound of laughter and shrieks grew louder and all the while, she grew colder and colder.

Swallowing, she closed her eyes. Something was wrong . . . so very wrong.

Tristan said her name, but she barely heard him. Barely even realized he was there. Dread crept through her. Although she knew it was the very last thing she should do, considering where she was and how many people were around her, considering what she suspected was going on, Dez lowered her shields.

Logically, she could have expected nothing to happen, really. After all, the living didn't call to her. But if that was the case, she wouldn't have felt so overwhelmed just by the sheer delight of the children in this place, she supposed. Logically, she shouldn't have felt much of anything.

Maybe that was why it was so overwhelming when the wave of terror, pain, and desperation almost sent her to her knees. It hit hard, so hard and fast, in a rush of words and sensation and emotion.

First, it was panic. Just sheer panic, followed by pain that wracked her body. Dez clutched her chest, felt like she was choking, gagging. But it wasn't *her*. Then it eased, faded away, replaced by a ragged burn and a dismal, heavy weight in her heart, in her mind.

The knowledge of death, coming soon.

I'm going to die . . . will anybody know? Does anybody care? Do they even know I'm gone—

The thought fizzed out, replaced by the sheer, utter terror, weariness, and pain, so much pain. And cold, mind-numbing cold. Something roared in Dez's ears and for a minute she didn't know if it was something she was hearing, if it was adrenaline or something else.

Finally, though, she realized it sounded like a *real* sound. But not one she was hearing. It was coming from somewhere else— some*one* else. Water. Rushing water. Lots of it.

Like a woman mesmerized, she continued to stare at that oversized bucket. There was the barest idea forming in her mind, but she couldn't be right. It just wasn't possible. It was unreal even to consider it. The sound of children's laughter echoed all around and she swallowed, bile churning in her gut.

Nobody would do that. What kind of sick fucks would do that—*how* could they do that? . . .

Another stream of thoughts blasted her, mostly incoherent, but so full of terror. *Oh, God . . . somebody, please . . .*

And in that moment, Dez managed to uproot her frozen feet and she was able to move.

* * *

"WHAT the . . . ?"

Mark blinked as he saw the chick eyeing the bucket. She was

rubbing a hand over her chest, like she was having trouble breathing, too. His mom did that. She had asthma and he'd see her doing that when she was having more trouble than normal.

But something about this woman had him thinking she wasn't needing an inhaler, though. She had a look in her eye, a weird one, one that froze him to the bone. His bowels were about to turn to water, but there was something besides terror.

Relief. Yeah. It was relief. If somebody knew *now*, if somebody did something *now* before Brendan's damn plan got put into motion . . . Except she was walking away. She turned on her heel and walked out.

No—

He blinked, his eyes blurring. Denial burned inside him and he wanted to scream, wanted to rage. *Fuck, fuck, fuck.* His hands shook and he needed a drink, needed it so bad. Tipping his head back, he stared at the ceiling. *God, I can't do this, I just can't . . . But how do I stop it? . . .*

Tristan had tried. He'd been so much tougher, so much stronger and braver. And look what they'd done to him. Mark was a fucking pussy. But if he didn't do something, say something— and *soon*—he'd have to live with this. If he tried and failed and they killed him, so the fuck what?

A breath shuddered out of him. He couldn't live with it. He knew it. So he either needed to *do* something or just fucking slit his wrists and be done with it now, because he couldn't be part of this. It was killing him already.

He took a deep breath and swiped at the tears that had leaked out of his eyes. He needed to do it now. Before he lost his nerve again. Hoping his voice wouldn't crack, he called out, "Hey, I need to go take a piss, man!"

Luther, the forty-two-year-old ex-cop who worked with him

in the afternoons, said, "You already did, and would you quit talking like that? Your mother would kill me if she heard you— she'll think *I* taught you to talk like that."

"I'll be back in a few." *Maybe. If I don't die of a heart attack* . . . He stood and automatically glanced at the security cameras. That was when he saw the woman again.

She hadn't left . . .

She was striding down the hallway. Heading back toward the water park area. And she had a heavy duffel bag slung over one shoulder. One that didn't look like any swim bag he'd ever seen. Her eyes glinted with determination and Mark swallowed.

What are you doing?

And for reasons he couldn't explain, instead of hiding some- where and making an anonymous call, he found himself heading to the water park. He got there just as she was pushing through the doors. Trailing after her, he watched as she breezed by the lifeguard checking the wristbands—they should have checked her bag, he thought as sweat collected and trickled down his neck. They should have checked—it was the rules.

But they didn't and he even knew why.

She walked around with that *I belong here* attitude. Luther had told him all about that attitude. If you act like you got a right to be someplace, a lot of people won't even question it. She acted like she belonged there, like there was nothing unusual about the bag she carried. Like there was nothing unusual about her walk- ing, fully clothed, toward the three-story water fort.

Mark's radio buzzed, but he ignored it. Water was all over him now, but he ignored that, too. Nothing mattered now except her. She was near the edge of the first floor of the fort now, let- ting that bag slide off her hand. Something about the way she caught it made him think it was heavy. Very heavy, despite how easily she carried it. She dumped it on the ground and then turned, looked up at the water bucket.

His heart leaped into his throat at the look in her eyes.

Oh, fuck. She knows.

Then she slanted a look his way.

* * *

SHE'D known he was following her almost from the second he came inside. She'd felt him, even through her shields. Felt his torment, his confusion—shit, he was almost as screwed up as some of her ghosts.

Dez stared at him, her heart so full of fury, it took a moment to realize what she was seeing in his eyes. There was terror, yes, but there was also something else. Relief. And hope.

One thought blasted at her shields, so strong and clear, she had to wonder if he had some sort of psychic skill— *Oh, fuck. She knows.* Shit, there was just too much stimulus coming at her here. It was driving her nuts.

"Yeah." She had to raise her voice to be heard over the water. "I know." Flicking her wet hair back from her face, she glanced at his radio, then back at him. "What do you plan on doing about it?"

He swallowed and glanced around, as though he expected the boogeyman to jump out at him. Then he just shook his head.

"What's that mean, kid? You plan on standing there? Doing nothing? Does it mean you're not going to tell me?"

"I'm not going to do anything," he said, his voice shaking . . . but certain enough. He was pale and she was pretty sure some of the moisture she saw on his face was sweat and tears, not just water.

She blew out a breath and studied his face. "Okay, then." She couldn't waste any more time. She'd already sent a message calling for the cavalry, although she had no idea when they'd get here. She'd dreaded sending that message, but if by chance somebody stopped her before she got up there . . . besides, as insane as *this* story was, she needed somebody to back her up.

Crouching down, she unzipped her bag. One thing the past year had taught her—be prepared. For everything. That might include needing things like ropes and such. Once she'd had to go down into a cave—an unmarked one, unmapped, to help one of her ghosts.

Yeah, the past year had been an eye-opening experience, all right. Standing, she met the boy's eyes once more.

He was staring at the rope, that odd look still on his face—dismay, confusion . . . and hope. Then he met her eyes. "Hurry. She's been in there a long time. I . . ." He closed his eyes and swallowed. "Just hurry. And be careful. They've got things set to get all fucked up later tonight, but if they see you . . ."

"I'll be careful."

* * *

"WHAT?"

Taylor clutched the phone, certain he'd misheard Gina, because this couldn't be happening. Not now. Not *here*. Not *now*. *Not here* . . . here, of all the fucking places. If Taylor had still believed in God, he just might have thought the big guy was pissed off at him, or trying to tell him something.

This couldn't be happening.

"You heard me," she said, sighing. Her voice was grouchy. "You have the information, as she sent it to me, word for word. A water park? French Lick, Indiana, of all places. I did a Google search on it. It's in the middle of nowhere."

Taylor closed his eyes. Oh, he knew the place. He knew it well. "How urgent is this?" he asked, his voice gruff.

"When I texted her back, she told me things were going to go FUBAR at any second, although she's not giving me details."

FUBAR. Fucked up beyond all recognition.

He blew out a breath. "Okay. Get a team together—Crawford, I guess. Keep them on standby. I'll let you know if I need them here."

"Right away, sir . . . ah . . . did you say *here*?"

Taylor grimaced. "I'm exactly six miles from the hotel, Gina. I'll be there in under fifteen minutes."

"Ah . . . excuse me?"

"You heard me." He disconnected and shoved the phone into his pocket. This wasn't happening, damn it. He had to see Dez. Normally he was able to get somebody else to run interference— namely, Joss Crawford—but he couldn't wait however long it would take to get Joss here.

Not when he was all of fifteen minutes away.

Damn it, what in the hell kind of trouble had led Dez to his town?

A shiver raced down his spine and he glanced around the cold and forbidding family manor. Dez chased ghosts for a living now . . . they called to her. One must have called her here.

Anna . . .

No.

He wouldn't think about that.

* * *

SHE wouldn't look down, damn it. Hell. If she *did* look down, if she fell, well . . . hopefully the rope and rig would hold and if it didn't, she was high enough, she'd break her neck. Nice. Clean.

Quick. Although she sure as hell hoped she didn't do that to these kids in here . . .

Dez flinched when she heard a shout.

She'd been noticed. Shit. She'd known it would happen, although she'd liked to think it wouldn't. Nothing wrong with a fantasy life, right?

There was another shout, a scream.

She tensed and tried not to think about all the eyes on her. Seconds ticked by, turned into minutes, and she kept focused on her goal, on the destination. Dez had no idea how much time had passed when she realized the deafening noise was gone.

The water was silent—somebody had turned it off and now there wasn't a soul in the place that wasn't watching her. She didn't dare look away to check out her audience. She couldn't think about them. It was time to tie off again.

Her hands were shaking and her heart was racing—she *hated* heights. Nobody knew that, but she hated them with a passion. "Don't think about how high you are," she muttered. "Just don't."

She dared one glance—almost there. Almost . . . *almost* . . .

"What in the hell am I doing?" she whispered. "What the hell . . . ?"

*   *   *

"WHAT the *hell*?" Brendan came to a stop outside the water park and stared through the glass doors. What he saw had him ready to drive his fist into a wall. What in the *fuck*?

Had somebody told?

Why else would there be cops here?

Six of them, all in uniform, and all of them were staring up at the top of the water fort. The big, pseudo-wood structure wasn't what held their attention, though, and for one brief second, terror and rage almost blinded him.

For that brief second, he realized he was *fucking terrified* and he knew it, admitted it.

But then he saw the woman.

Walking on one of the exposed metal beams, like it was a fucking balance beam. As he stared at her, she stopped and knelt down, tying off like she was on some sort of caving expedition. At least that was what he *thought* she was doing. He wasn't sure.

She was so high up, but that was what it looked like.

And that was how they—

No. He knew he didn't need to think about that now. They needed to get her down before she fucked up everything. Shoving his way inside, he went up to one of the police officers and said, "Hey."

It was Officer Lipscomb, one of his dad's ass-kissing buddies— awesome. Lipscomb gave him a tight smile. "Brendan. You working today?"

"Kinda sorta. We got the party tonight. What in the world is that girl doing and why are you all just staring at her?"

Lipscomb gave him a pained expression. "We're being careful. We go yelling at her and she falls . . . right now, all she's doing is climbing. Doesn't look like she has any weapons or anything."

"But you can't *tell*," Brendan said. His mind raced and he blurted out, "For all you know, she's got something stashed on her and she's going to plant it in the bucket or something."

"We're watching." Lipscomb shrugged and shook his head. "Sorry, kid. We can't just assume she's anything other than crazy without proof."

"And if she *is* crazy and you had a chance to stop her?" Brendan snapped. "Shit, I'm calling my dad."

Lipscomb sighed. "And what will that do, kid?"

"He'll get the crazy bitch the fuck down."

"She's not a crazy bitch," somebody said from behind him.

That voice, cool as ice and unfamiliar, sent a shiver down Brendan's spine before he could stop it. But if he thought the voice was unsettling, it was nothing compared to what he felt when he looked up and met the coldest blue eyes he'd ever seen.

"Who the fuck are you?" He tried to make it come out arrogant and cool, the way his father would have.

But his voice cracked and he didn't know why, but he had the weirdest damn feeling he was fucked. Completely and royally fucked. The desire to run hit him hard and fast—so fucking hard and fast.

The man's eyes flicked over him dismissively and then he looked at Lipscomb. "Special Agent in Charge Taylor Jones, with the FBI. You have one of my people on the grounds, a Desiree Lincoln."

* * *

TAYLOR didn't know what in the hell was going on, but he knew the sullen teenager in front of him had something to do with it. It was written all over him. Sullen, angry, with cold, dead eyes— those eyes bothered Taylor. A lot. He might have been even more disturbed, but he saw the fear lurking in that gaze as well. Cold and angry, this kid, but he could feel fear. That was a good thing. If he could be afraid, he wasn't too far gone.

Taylor hoped.

Regardless, he didn't have time for the boy's attitude, though.

Focusing on the cop, he pulled his credentials out. While he wasn't sure, he had a bad feeling that "crazy bitch" the kid was referring to was Dez.

The cop was politer than some, hiding his irritation behind a professional smile. "I don't suppose your people would be a lady, would it? Looks kinda tall, dark hair?"

"That's not overly descriptive." He glanced down, then met the man's gaze. "Officer Lipscomb."

"Well, I can't see her particularly well. As you can see." He gestured vaguely over his shoulder and Taylor followed his hand. And saw nothing. So he followed the gazes of the other officers . . . who were all looking *up*.

Oh, holy hell.

Other than that silent curse, he didn't allow himself any reaction, though. Couldn't afford that, because he didn't want anybody to know he had no fucking clue what Dez was up to—and yes, it sure as hell was Dez up there gliding along a beam like some sort of whacked-out gymnast. Okay, even for her, this was rather odd behavior, he had to admit.

She came to a stop near the crossing point of two of the beams, bracing a hand on one of the central supports that ran from the ceiling down.

At that point, some moron with a megaphone decided she was secure. "Ma'am, you need to come back down. You're not authorized to be up there."

Dez looked down.

Taylor couldn't make out the expression on her face, but he saw . . . something. He also knew the exact moment she saw him. If he wasn't mistaken, her body stiffened in shock. Although from down here it looked like, for all he knew, she was just taking a breather before she stood up to continue her little dance across the ceiling.

* * *

TAYLOR.

Dez closed her eyes. After a count of five, she took another look. Oh, yes. It was him. Like she could miss him. She could be in a dark, crowded room with a thousand other people and if he was there, she'd know it, sense it somehow.

Swallowing, she dragged her eyes away from him. She couldn't focus on him now, because that bucket was right beneath her and she had to look. Either she'd find what she suspected she'd find or she'd look like she'd lost her mind, and possibly get arrested. "Wonder if he'll get me out of it," she muttered.

Then she braced herself and looked down.

As the avalanche of rage and grief and disbelief rushed at her, she whispered, "I think I'd rather get arrested."

She wished she was wrong. She'd rather be arrested; she'd rather spend the night locked up, hell, a week . . . a month. *Anything* but this.

Staring down at the restrained form, at those slumped shoulders and downcast head, a crack spread through her heart and started to spill black, bitter blood.

"Tristan. I found her."

Then she looked up and focused her gaze on Taylor. She reached for her phone and entered a number she hadn't used in over a year. She didn't bother calling him—her voice wouldn't hold for now. She was too angry, too pissed, too broken.

She just sent a text and tried to figure out what they were supposed to do.

* * *

THERE'S a girl in this bucket thing. Don't know if she's alive.

Taylor had to read it twice before he managed to process it.

Blood roared in his ears and for a second that dragged out into eternity, he couldn't even get his mind to work. Then time resumed and he lifted his head and stared at Dez across the feet and open air that separated them.

Even from here, he imagined he could see the torment on her face.

Dez might not know now.

But he did.

This one was alive. Dez had a way of easing the pain of the deceased but she'd never been as good with helping the living and their pain haunted her.

Son of a bitch.

SEVEN

THIS isn't happening.

Gnawing on his thumbnail, Brendan told himself this wasn't happening. It was just some fucked-up dream and he'd wake up and it would all be okay. Maybe he'd just had a few too many drinks, had let some of that pussy Mark's death-and-doom premonitions get the better of him. This wasn't happening—he'd wake up and it would all be okay.

But he didn't believe it.

Not really. It all felt too real. He knew it. He really was sitting in one of the conference rooms at the hotel, waiting to talk to the damn cops. He had to wait for his dad, and he had to talk to the cops. They all had to give statements.

Fucking statements.

Somebody was going to talk. Mark. Kyle. Beau . . . no. Not Beau—Beau had his shit together. But somebody. Shit, how had that stupid bitch known?

A door opened and Brendan looked up as his dad came in, followed by one of the detectives from French Lick's microscopic police force. It had maybe *three* people who counted as detectives, Brendan figured. And this one wasn't the one he'd been expecting to see.

Brendan didn't even know this guy's name.

He'd figured Dad would bring in Ron Langdon, his golf buddy. Not this guy—Brendan didn't even know him.

Just keep it cool. That was all he had to do, really.

They didn't *know* anything. Couldn't prove anything. And the only people who did know shit were either dead or people who'd be in as much trouble as he was if they talked.

No reason to panic, right?

* * *

"You can go on now."

Tristan looked sad.

"Is she going to live?"

"I don't know," Dez said, shaking her head. "But that's not up to us. We found her, and they got her out, got her to the hospital. That's all we can do."

He nodded, his image insubstantial, fading. He sighed and this time, when he flickered, he didn't come back quite so strong. *"Do you think you can find out what they . . . what they did to me?"*

"Is that what you want?"

He shrugged. *"Not so much for me. It doesn't matter to me, really. But I think my parents, my sister . . . they deserve to know."* He hesitated and then added, *"And I don't want them thinking that I was some fucking coward who decided to off himself for whatever reason. That wasn't me. It . . . you were right. It matters. I want them to know."*

"You're right." She gave him a gentle smile. "It does matter. And I'll see what I can find out."

She swallowed, continued to stare even as he faded more.

This time, when he faded completely, she knew he wouldn't be back. She didn't have to ask, didn't need to linger. There was finality to his fading that just felt . . . *complete*. Tristan had done the one thing he'd waited around to do—he'd saved a girl's life. At least, she hoped he had. If nothing else, he'd kept her from dying like *that*.

Arms crossed over her chest, she continued to stare down at his stone, feeling the dance of wind over her chilled flesh.

Dez didn't know how much time had passed when she heard the engine. It didn't surprise her, though. After seeing him show up at the hotel, she'd figured nothing could surprise her. Just *why* he was here, she didn't understand, but she wasn't at all shocked that he'd tracked her down to the small, privately owned cemetery.

The sound of a car door shutting, the quiet crunch of gravel as he moved to join her, every sound drew her muscles tighter and tighter until she felt ready to snap.

Instead, she forced herself to take a deep, slow breath. He was here because of the job, only the job, and once he got what he needed from her, he'd be gone.

Because he wouldn't *let* her matter. He wouldn't let her matter to him, so she wouldn't let him matter to her. It was a little mantra she told herself, and as long as she kept all of that in mind, she'd be fine.

Hell, it had been a year.

More than, and she was a grown woman, right?

He was here about the job, about the girl, and once she told him she couldn't help him much, he'd be on his way.

He came to a stop next to her, and for the longest time, neither of them spoke.

The tension in the air ratcheted even higher and she swallowed the urge to whimper as his heat managed to reach across the scant inches separating them, warming her when nothing else had done the trick. She swallowed the spit that had pooled in her mouth. Damn it, if he wasn't going to say something, she'd do it—do it, get it over with, so she could get out of here. She'd hoped she could leave, but she now owed Tristan more than that. And if she was honest, she knew she wouldn't have left until she'd at least *tried* to look around.

A quiet sigh drifted through the graveyard and she slid a glance over at Taylor. A sigh. From him? Such a human sound—like he was tired. Like he had such human weaknesses.

She looked away almost as quickly as she'd looked at him, though. He looked . . . hell. Too good. She'd always thought he looked good in those damn suits, but what in the hell was he doing out on a job in jeans? She opened her mouth, some snide question lurking *right* there.

But he managed to get a question out first. It wasn't one she was expecting, either.

"Are you okay?"

Dez gaped at him. Then she immediately snapped her mouth shut and looked away. "What?"

"You heard me. Are you okay?"

On unsteady legs, she moved away. "What do you mean, *am I okay*? Hell, why wouldn't I be? I wasn't the one who just got pulled out of the waterboarding experiment from hell, was I?" Absently, she bent over and straightened a flower arrangement, brushed a few dead flower petals from a marker. "Speaking of which, how is the girl? Is she going to make it?"

Taylor stared past her, his gaze lingering on something in the distance. "More than likely. They . . . whoever put her in there didn't seem to want her dead right away. She wasn't in any danger of drowning for quite a while. They . . . well, I don't have any men here but I talked to the locals. They found some weird wiring, timers—looks like things were set to do something later, but I'm not sure what yet. Somebody will talk, though. Or they'll figure it out if they aren't completely incompetent."

Dez thought of the boy she'd seen in the water fort, but she kept quiet. She needed sleep before she got any more involved in this and she knew how Taylor was.

And she didn't *need* to talk to anybody to think about what those timers might have been set for—flooding that bucket, maybe. Drowning her completely? Or something more sensational?

Dez felt that rage burn hotter, brighter. "Bastards." Something cool tickled her neck and she shrugged, stretched her shoulders. Looking back at him, she met his eyes, all but colorless in the dim light. "I can't help you. There's nothing for me to tell you. I just knew something was wrong."

"She's alive. The living don't call to you." His voice was a quiet, steady murmur in the night.

Meeting his gaze, she cocked her head. "No. They don't."

"So who is he?" He looked down at the stone and she wasn't surprised he'd pieced it together. He wasn't the boss for nothing.

Dez looked at the marker by his feet. "Somebody who's not here anymore. He's already moved on . . . and he can't help you, either. He was only here long enough to help her."

* * *

TAYLOR wondered if she was trying to make this harder on him or if it was just natural for her.

Sighing, he crouched on the ground, mindless of his jeans as he studied the marker. It was new, pale gray marble from what he could tell in the dim light, shot through with something that made it shimmer.

He read the date and managed not to flinch when he saw how old the kid was. Just a kid . . . only seventeen. "What did he have to do with it, Dez?"

Silence was his only answer.

Looking up, he saw her standing on the other side of the small graveyard, her arms crossed over her chest, her face lost in the shadows. Sighing, he scrubbed a hand over his face. "Come on, Desiree, help me out."

"Why?"

He could just barely see the glitter of her eyes. "How about so I can keep your ass out of jail?"

She snorted. "Nice try. They might *try* to throw me in jail for a few days and, hey, maybe they'll succeed, but they can't keep me there. I've got too good an alibi . . . unless they can come up with a way of convincing people I teleported that poor girl in there."

"They can still make your life hell," he bit out. "I can make that go away. You going to help me or not?"

"If they try to make my life hell for a few days, so what? I get a lawyer and deal." She shoved her hands in her pockets and rocked back on her heels. "You can't ride into small-town America, flash those shiny credentials, and think that makes everything okay, Jones."

"Or you can help me out and nothing happens. You're not going to jail here, damn it." Shoving to his feet, he spun away and stared off into the night. No, not here. He had enough nightmares here to haunt him for the rest of his life. Letting them try to put Dez in a jail that was no doubt full of old ghosts and older memories . . . no.

She might be able to deal, but he sure as hell couldn't.

Behind him, Dez laughed. It wasn't a happy sound, though. "And what are you going to do if they decide they want to lock me up for a while, slick? You can't exactly *stop* them."

"I'll tell them to yank their heads out of their asses, damn it," he snarled, shooting her a dark look. And they'd listen. They wouldn't like it. But they'd listen—he'd damn well make sure of it.

Dez just shook her head. "You really still haven't figured it out, have you, Taylor? You can't control the universe." She rocked back on her heels and added, "And you aren't my boss these days—you sure as hell don't get to control *me*."

"I may not be your boss, but that sure as hell doesn't keep you from calling me when your ass is in trouble."

Although he couldn't make out her face, he didn't need to see her clearly to know she was smirking at him. "Hell, Taylor. You think it's *my* ass that had me worried? My ass ceased to be your concern some time ago. It's not *me* who needs you right now. You have another problem you need to worry about. That girl needs you right now—she needs you to help them find who did that to her. Why don't you get back to her?"

Her words managed to drill into his heart, an icy cold lance. Yeah, he knew she didn't need him. That was one thing he hadn't ever questioned. Swallowing past the ache in his throat, he said grimly, "I'm here trying to do my job—you came here for her, so I'm trying to follow up on anything that might help her."

"And I'm telling you there's nothing I know that *will* help. At least not right now."

"Nothing—you want me to believe you got nothing for me."

* * *

DEZ was having the hardest time focusing. There was a whisper, something so faint, even fainter than Tristan's call had been. But Taylor's presence, his voice—hell, his *everything* drowned that voice out.

But she needed to focus.

This was important.

It was *almost* like a voice. Almost.

But it was so . . . faint.

Was somebody speaking—

". . . answer me?"

She jerked her head up and realized that at some point, while she'd been distracted by that not-quite voice, Taylor had closed the distance between them. Now he stood just a foot away, close enough that she could see him all too clearly, close enough that she could feel his warmth once again and if she leaned forward enough, she could reach out and pull him against her. Feel that long, lean body once more.

Although the look in his eyes was anything but amorous. She smirked as she looked at him, amused despite herself. Even now, even after he'd been such a fucking *jerk*, even after she'd missed him for the past year, and even after the hell of today, she still wanted him.

Damn it, she wasn't ever going to *not* want him, she realized. It just wasn't going to happen.

She wanted this man . . . plain and simple.

Needed him. Craved him.

He was her drug.

His eyes narrowed on her face. "Are you listening to a damn thing I say?"

"No." Dez smiled. "I can't say I am. And you know what's really wonderful about it? You can't do much more than snarl and growl about it. After all, you're not my boss, right?"

Abruptly she laughed. "Damn, no wonder you were always so pissed off when you had to call Taige in on a job. It must really grate on you to have to call in somebody you can't control. And this is even worse . . . you didn't call me in. I'm not even a loose cannon. I'm worse than a loose cannon."

Taylor opened his mouth, said something.

She never heard it, though. She heard something—it was like the soft sigh of the wind dancing through the branches. Louder than a whisper, but no understandable words.

It was a cry, though. A cry for help—she understood *that* much this time. And once more, that shivery brush touched her spine and she shivered before she could stop it.

He saw, too. *Damn* it.

He glanced around. "I thought you said he was gone."

"He is." Dez shrugged. "I'm just cold."

"You're not cold. At least not because it's cold out." He looked past her, and once more she saw his gaze lock, linger. This time, she followed his eyes, tried to find whatever it was that held his attention.

But all she saw was the garden of stone—monuments to the dead, to the lost. Was it one of them calling her?

Was it a call at all or just her imagination? Cemeteries were full of so much unrest, it could be nothing. It could be just the remnants of their passing. And it could be just her subconscious trying to give her something else to think about *besides* Taylor.

Just then, Dez didn't know. She couldn't trust her instincts when it came to him, because when it came to him, her heart was involved and that made things too damn complicated. Sighing, she looked back at him.

That alone was enough to make her ache. Make her hunger. Make her long for things she couldn't have. It was enough to make her hate him at times. She'd been such a fool, letting herself touch him. That one day hadn't been enough. All it had done was make her long for more.

"Just leave me alone, Taylor," she said quietly. That was what she needed. She needed him to leave her alone—desperately. "Go do your job and leave me alone. I'm not your concern."

"Not my concern?" He caught her arm, his fingers burning hot, even through her jacket. "That's where you're wrong. You called for help. That makes you my concern."

She tried to pull away, but he wasn't letting go and unless she wanted to get into a wrestling match—and actually, that idea held too much appeal—she wasn't going to get away until he decided to let go. Because she didn't like the idea of just jerking against his hold, she settled for glaring at him.

"*Wrong*, Jones. I'm *not* your concern. Haven't been for over a year. I quit, remember?"

"As if I could forget," he muttered. "Come on. You don't need to be here right now. You're already on edge."

On edge. Talk about an understatement.

As he started to walk out of the cemetery, she reluctantly fell into step next to him, steaming mentally and debating on whether or not she wanted to go along with his imperiousness.

"Whether you're one of my people or not, you brought me here and you need to give me something to go on. You also could probably talk to that girl and help her a hell of a lot more than these people here can."

She could refuse. She knew that. She didn't *need* to go anywhere with him. But the cold shivers running down her spine, the
echoes of the departed, the strange, disturbing whispers . . . no,
she didn't need to be here.

And she wanted to be out of here.

Badly.

If there *was* something or somebody here for her, she'd figure
it out soon. Preferably after she'd had some rest, a few hot meals.
She was so damn tired—too many jobs, too close together. She
all but ached with exhaustion. Maybe fate and God would be
kind, though, and this would turn out to be nothing.

She could use a break. Really.

Following Taylor out of the cemetery, she resisted the urge to
look back. If she had, she might have seen it as the moon came
out from behind a heavy bank of clouds at just that moment.

The silvery stream of light fell across one of the monuments
along the far border of the cemetery. There was an angel there,
her face upturned to the sky, her wings spread.

A sigh drifted through the cemetery, followed by a sound that
was almost a sob.

* * *

HOSPITALS were all the same in some aspects. Too brightly lit,
smelling of antiseptic and faintly of illness and death. The stink
of illness and death weren't necessarily something the average
person might pick up, Dez knew, but she'd been in too many of
these places. She couldn't miss it.

Then again, maybe it was her imagination. Maybe she knew
the death and the illness lingered and that lingering stink was
some manifestation of her mind. And what did it matter . . . even
though, logically, she knew why she was thinking about it. It was

a way to distract herself, just another mind game, something to keep from thinking about the fact that she was walking down the long, overly bright hallway next to Taylor.

A way to think about something other than the low, cold whispers she felt in the hall.

They were there. Some of the departed . . . not all of them rested, not all of them called for help. Some of them just lingered, their cold, dry touch like a skeletal hand on the nape of her neck. She could feel their presence and now that she'd allowed herself to think about them, to focus, her mind reached out and tried to lock on one of those whispers. Tried to grasp something real . . . a voice, something, *somebody* she could help.

But their voices, they were so indistinct, like listening to dry leaves skittering down a street. There were no words, hardly any feeling left to connect to those disconnected souls.

She jumped as Taylor curled his hand over her nape, his fingers digging lightly into her skin. "Stop it," he murmured, leaning in and speaking almost directly into her skin.

"Stop what?" she asked sourly. She would have glared at him, but the firm hold he had on her skin kept her from doing that, and she was reluctant to break that contact. Just like always, his touch made everything else fade away.

"You know what. You're not shielding. I can see it. Shield up or you'll be a mess before I even get you to her room." His voice lowered when she tensed and tried to pull away.

"You don't get to boss me around anymore, Jones."

She tried once more to pull away, but this time he herded her into a narrow dip in the wall. A quick glance showed that it led to the chapel. She glared up at him. To her surprise, he was glaring back, his pale blue eyes glittering at her, and his normally emotionless face was anything but. "I'm not trying to boss you around, damn it. You're walking around looking like you've got death dancing on your shoulders and you're not doing shit to stop it. Should I just *ignore* it?"

"What does it matter to you?" She shouldn't be looking at him. She told herself that, told herself to look away, to look anywhere but at him. She couldn't, though. She couldn't look away from his eyes. Swallowing, she rested her head against the wall and repeated, "What does it matter to you?"

A heavy breath rushed out of him, his shoulders rising and falling. His blue eyes, so fiery hot and so unlike the cool, icy professionalism she was used to seeing, bored into hers. "Just shield up, damn it." Then he shoved off the wall and stalked away.

Immediately, Dez sagged a few inches and covered her face with her hands. Damn it. *What in the hell* . . . Damn it. Her knees were shaking. Her belly felt all tight and hot and jittery, and damned if she knew why.

You damn well do know—

No. She wasn't thinking about that—

She took a deep breath and lowered her hands. Then she looked up and gasped when she realized Taylor had returned, silently. One hand came, curled over the back of her neck. "This is why it matters, damn it." He hauled her against him and as his mouth crushed against hers, her brain clicked off, shut down . . .

And her body came to life. After more than a year of existence, Dez felt like she was living again. His free hand gripped her hip, keeping her body pressed close to his while his other hand tangled in the short strands of her hair to yank her head back.

This wasn't just a kiss, she thought. It was . . . more. It was everything. He breathed her in, just as she breathed him in. After so much time apart from him, she felt complete again. Whole.

His tongue stroked across her lower lip and she opened for him with a groan. He didn't waste a second, pushing deep inside. She bit him lightly and his long, lean body shuddered, crowded her back against the wall.

Dimly, she knew they couldn't do this. Dimly, she knew they needed to stop.

But she didn't *care*.

He was touching her. Finally, he was touching her again and it was so wonderful, so beautiful, she thought she might die. And then, just as quickly as it had started, it ended.

He tore his mouth from hers, panting. Pressing his brow to hers, he stared into her eyes. "Damn you. You know why it matters."

"If it matters that much, you shouldn't have let me walk," she challenged.

He sighed, one hand restlessly kneading her hip. "It's because you matter that we can't do this, Dez." He closed his eyes and then pulled away. Not just physically.

Mentally. She felt it, that slow mental withdrawal. Her heart ached inside, and those words made it all that much worse. She *mattered*? Hell, if she mattered . . . then she shook her head. She couldn't think about this right now. She had a job to do. And not just the one that Taylor had brought her here for—she'd made a promise to Tristan and even if he'd moved on, she would still keep that promise. She couldn't leave until it was done.

She wouldn't acknowledge the disturbing sense that she had something else here that awaited her.

That disturbing sensation in the cemetery.

Those vague, faint whispers.

She needed to cling to something—cling to the fact that she could just finish this job and get the hell away from Taylor Jones before he broke her heart all over again.

*   *   *

HE'D lost his mind.

Taylor knew he'd lost his mind. The last thing on earth he should have done was put his hands on her. The last thing he should have done was put his mouth on her. The last thing he should be thinking about was doing it again.

But he was.

Damn it, maybe he really was closer to losing his mind than he'd thought. Not that it would take much of a push, being here. He needed to focus, needed to get a grip. Needed to get whatever information he could out of Desiree, get her *out* of this place, and then see if the team was needed here. He wasn't so certain they were, and if nothing else, he could still trust his instincts on that.

In short, he had no time to think about her, but as she pushed around him and strode down the hall in front of him, all he could do was stare at the sweet, round curve of her ass. He had to stifle a groan as he remembered digging his fingers into those curves, how she'd shuddered and moaned under him, how she'd rocked up to meet him.

His heart raced and his hands weren't entirely steady; his mind was focused on nothing but sex, Dez, and getting her naked. And then he realized that she was standing at a dead stop in the middle of the hallway. Standing still in that odd, eerie fashion that he recognized all too well.

He didn't have to see the look on her face to know what was wrong. He already knew—he could tell by the strange, odd tension emanating from her. She felt something. He didn't know what, but she felt something. Whatever it was, it broke her heart, too.

He wanted to reach out, touch her, reassure her, but after what had just happened, he didn't dare.

But he couldn't stay silent, either.

With the rest of his people, he could. With the rest of them, he could wait in silence even if the worry was killing him. But not with her. Although she was no longer part of his team, although she was no longer remotely connected to him . . . no. He couldn't remain silent and wait and hope she'd share some small piece with him.

Down the hall to her right waited the cops and he suspected a few doctors and nurses were coming in and out of the room—this sort of shit just didn't happen in French Lick, the middle of nowhere. Everybody wanted to look at the girl Dez had saved. She was already a hot topic of discussion and the story hadn't even broken yet.

Shifting his body to conceal her as much as he could, he looked down at Dez's face. "What's wrong?"

"I can feel her." She blew out a troubled breath and shot him a quick glance before looking away. "I shouldn't be able to—I'm shielded—but I can feel her. It's the hell she's in."

Then she gave him a sour smile. "I guess that's good news. I don't think I'd feel her this strong if she wasn't going to make it. Her soul is fighting hard. The soul and the body are usually pretty tightly linked. If her soul is clinging to life, her body is going to follow, I think."

The look in her eyes was sad and lost. He couldn't not touch her then, not considering how broken she looked, how defeated. Brushing the back of his hand down her cheek, he said softly, "You saved her life, Desiree. You shouldn't look so sad about this."

"Saved her life . . . after some punk bastards decided to torture and kill her for kicks. Shit. What good did I do in the end? She'll have nightmares all her life over this."

He narrowed his eyes, his mind focusing on that bit of information she'd let slip—damn her, he'd known she had more knowledge than she'd given up. But now wasn't the time to interrogate her. When she would have turned away, he caught her shoulder. "What good did you do? How about the fact that she now *has* a life to have nightmares? The nightmares will be brutal, but she's alive. She'll have a chance to live, to heal. That's a gift and you need to get that through your head. She'll thank you for it; her family will. You saved her life. Be glad of that."

"It's not enough," Dez whispered, her voice broken. "Not if she's got that kind of pain in her. I should have gotten here sooner . . ."

"If that's how it was meant to happen, it would have." As a tear slipped free and rolled down her cheek, he brushed it away. That was one thing he did believe in. His people might be able to do what some called miracles. Some people called it other things—*hoaxes* and *bullshit* were the more polite terms. But for the most part, people saw things like what Dez did as a gift. She'd saved a life and she was beating herself up for not doing more. If she'd been meant to do more, she would have. "You did what you were meant to do, baby."

It slipped out of him.

Her breath caught and she shot him a look.

It hung there between them, but what could he do, take it back?

Sighing, he stroked her hair back from her brow and said, "You did what you were meant to do. She's alive . . . because of you. She can heal because of you. She can have a future . . . because of you. It's a gift. Don't belittle that."

She gave him a smile, but he knew her heart wasn't in it. Her shoulders slumped and she edged around him, likely following some unseen trail of misery, whatever it was that had put that heartbreak in her eyes.

She wouldn't ever get over not saving that girl from everything. That the girl lived wasn't enough—hell, it wasn't enough for Taylor, either, but he'd take what he could get. Dez, though, she'd torture herself over this.

She could send off one of the lost, those who had already left this world, and do it with a smile, but a girl she'd saved, one who was alive, she couldn't find something good in that.

As they approached the small knot of people gathered by the girl's door, voices hushed and then went abruptly silent. As gazes cut their way and then shifted to the side, Taylor moved closer to Dez and rested a hand on her shoulder.

One of the cops, his face vaguely familiar, came away from the door. "Hey, there, Taylor. Long time, no see."

Taylor tried to place the face—the guy was familiar, there was no denying that. The smile . . . yeah, Taylor had seen that smile before. But it was the eyes that gave him away. Hazel, flecked with gold. The last time Taylor had seen those eyes, they had been bright with amusement. Not so much now, but still, he recognized one of his old friends from high school. "Blake . . . Blake Hensley."

"Yeah." He gave him a tired smile. "Can't say it's a pleasure seeing you under such circumstances." He glanced at Dez, and Taylor saw understanding, recognition flare in those eyes.

Taylor tensed, prepared to step in. Whether she still worked for him or not, *he* still considered her as his . . . no, one of his people, and he wasn't going to let her get hassled for doing her job.

But apparently, small-town cop or not, Blake understood something about professionalism, because he didn't lay into her right there, didn't start with the questions or anything. Although that might have more to do with Taylor's presence than anything else. Or perhaps the hospital.

She would have to answer the questions, would have to give a statement, but not here. Not now. She'd have some rest first and if Taylor had anything to do with it, it would also be at some place *other* than the police department. And he'd be there, too, if he could manage that.

"Is she awake?" he asked as the silence threatened to grow heavy and strained once more. Silence never bothered him, but he wanted this over and done so he could get Dez out of here.

The doctor glanced from Blake to Taylor and then at Dez. "Well . . . yes. But she's restless, scared. I . . ."

Taylor reached into his pocket with one hand, nudging Dez into the room with the other. Flashing the FBI credentials always distracted people. Whether he was here officially or not, he could run interference for five minutes. His gut told him that Dez could help the girl. As one of the cops moved as if to stop Dez, Blake subtly stepped in next to him. Taylor caught his gaze and smiled.

* * *

EVEN before the girl turned her head, even before their gazes locked, the scream of pain hit Dez's shields. It was a discordant, cacophonous wave, one that made her gut ache, her head pound, and her heart bleed.

But she didn't let it show. She showed nothing but a reassuring smile, knowing anything else would only make it worse. Although, hell, how much *worse* could it get? The pain . . . it shrieked and screamed, worse than any demon from hell, it seemed.

As the girl sensed her presence, she jolted, a half sob catching in her throat. She cowered in the bed, as though she expected

Dez to jump her and drag her back to that watery hellhole and finish the job. She trembled so hard, the bed started to rattle.

Dez stopped in her tracks. "It's okay, sweetie. I'm not going to hurt you." She held out her hands, showed they were empty, even though that didn't mean much. The boys who'd hurt her, Dez didn't think they'd used weapons either—just their hands and their words and their minds. So evil. So vile. So wrong. "You're safe here, sweetheart. Nobody can get to you in here. Nobody will hurt you now."

Big, pale eyes locked on Dez's face and the crack in Dez's heart widened even more. Fuck. This . . . this was killing her.

And Taylor said she'd *saved* this kid. Had she saved her or just helped break her even more?

"You want me to leave?" she asked softly. She glanced over her shoulder at the door. She knew Taylor thought she could help, but she didn't think there was a damn thing she could do that would ease this girl's pain. How could she do anything that would help? How could anybody? "I can go. You don't need to talk to anybody if you don't want to, you know. You can wait until you're ready."

There wasn't an answer. The girl, maybe sixteen, just stared at her through her long hair. Her face, soft and a little too round for modern society's strict standards, was pale. She had a round body as well, with the generous curves a girl like her would probably hate. Staring into those pale eyes, seeing the scratches, the scrapes, and the bruises, knowing what those boys had been willing to do, what they'd *wanted* to do, Dez had to fight the urge to scream.

"I'll go," she said, her voice husky. She was going to cry if she didn't get out of there. Cry and beg the girl to forgive her. But how could she?

She was almost to the door when the girl spoke. "You . . . were there."

Dez paused and looked back. "Where?"

"At . . . there." She looked away, her gaze bouncing around the room like she couldn't stand to look at anybody or anything. "Where they found me. Where you found me." She swallowed and then looked at Dez again. "It was you. You found me. Didn't you?"

Dez nodded. "I'm sorry I didn't get there sooner."

The girl started to sob.

Unsure if it was welcome, uncertain if she should just leave and call for one of the nurses, Dez made her way to the bedside. She reached out and laid a hand on the girl's shoulder. But the moment she touched her, the girl reached for her and then, just like that, she was wrapped in a desperate, clinging embrace. "Oh, God . . . I was scared . . ."

"Shhh." Dez stroked a hand down pale, soft blonde hair, staring out the darkened windows into the night. "It's okay. You're safe now. You're safe, I swear."

EIGHT

THERE are strange things happening around here—a terrible thing happened yesterday. I can't even discuss it with you, it's so awful. Perhaps it's best that you aren't here, my angel.

The pen paused, trembling over the paper. A heavy sigh filled the air as the days were counted out. Not that it was necessary. Only a few remained. The flowers were on order, the dress had arrived. Everything was set. And the world was in chaos.

It's not good for a young lady to see this sort of thing. Not good at all. I hope it all settles down soon. I want peace for our day together.
My pretty, perfect angel.
My only.

* * *

"Do you know her?"

"I dunno." Brendan shrugged and gave the detective what he figured was a tired but polite smile. He wanted to look frustrated and aggravated, without looking too pissed off—he was his dad's son, after all, and they were politicians to the bone.

"You can't give me any more details than that?" Detective George Stahley stared at him, his brown eyes resting on Brendan's face in a way that left Brendan wanting to fidget. He had a serious face, serious eyes, and he didn't seem too inclined to hurry up, either. Brendan wanted *out* of there. "You work there—hang out there. You and your boys are all over that place. But you've never seen that girl?"

As he spoke, he nudged the picture forward.

Brendan glanced at it and then back at the detective. "No. At least I don't think so. But you have no idea how many people come in and out of that place, man . . . um . . . Officer, or do I call you Detective?" He wrinkled his brow and shot a look at his dad—*I'm nervous, I'm tired . . . Dad, help me out . . .*

His father laid a reassuring hand on his shoulder.

Brendan looked back at the detective as his dad said softly, "Detective Stahley, it's a hotel. A popular one, with a lot of people. Surely you can't expect Brendan to remember every girl that's passed through there."

Stahley gave his father a polite smile and then looked back at Brendan, tapping the picture with his finger. "Look again." Then he reached inside the folder before him and pulled out a different picture, laid it alongside the shitty one he'd been pushing at Brendan for the past twenty minutes. "Here's a different one. We've got her name now, have a better picture."

This one Brendan recognized.

It hit low in the gut, almost like he'd been punched. He bit the inside of his lip hard to keep from saying anything, to keep from showing any reaction.

Shit.

She was looking down, like she'd been too nervous to look at the camera. She'd been like that when he met her, too. The one and only time they'd met in person. He liked the picture of her. It was why he'd chosen her. Something about that picture made her tits look huge and he'd had a whole lot of fun squeezing those big tits when they'd been getting things arranged. She'd stared at him over the gag, her eyes big and terrified, her skin pale. They had worn masks, all of them, except for when he'd grabbed her. Then he'd worn a hat, glasses. Could she identify him? Fuck. What if she could . . . His heart started to slam against his ribs as he realized just how fucked up things were. If she could identify him, it wouldn't matter if the guys didn't decide to talk. Why wouldn't *she*? The fucking bitch.

"Well?"

Brendan glanced up and shook his head, swallowed around the knot in his throat and gave him a game smile. He needed to relax. He had barely recognized himself when he looked in the mirror right before he picked her up. She couldn't place him. There was no way. "No. I don't think I know her, Detective."

* * *

BEHIND the one-way glass, Taylor stood next to Blake Hensley and watched as the boy lied.

Oh, he wasn't bad at it. He might be fooling his dad.

But Taylor wasn't fooled.

"He's lying," Blake said, his voice grim and sad.

Arching a brow, Taylor glanced over at him. "What makes you think that?"

"Shit, FBI man. I got eyes, the same as you. I see the same

things you do." He reached into his pocket and tugged out a mangled pack of gum. "That boy is lying or I'm missing my left nut."

Then he flashed Taylor a wide grin. "And I'm pretty sure it's still there—was this morning. At least I think it was this morning." He sighed and checked his watch, then rubbed a hand back over his head. "Yeah. This morning. This has been one hell of a day. We don't get shit around here like this, you know."

"Well, it's good you don't see many things like this." He focused on the boy again, watching the way his eyes would occasionally dart to the one-way glass, the way he had his arms folded over his chest—it should have looked casual . . . probably even passed for casual to the untrained eye. But he kept digging his fingers into his arms, every now and then, like he was fighting the urge to fidget.

And his eyes were just a little too wide—the pupils dilated.

He was still scared.

But more than the fear, he was *pissed*. It was an ugly anger, too. The kind of anger that Taylor had seen turn deadly in the blink of an eye. He hoped that detective in there had good eyes, because this boy, he was a time bomb.

Oh, he hid it. Hid it very well under a smooth layer of manners—his father had raised him well, but Taylor wouldn't have expected any less of the Moore family. They'd been the sort of family his mother had loved—a nice, well-established family . . . they'd been in the area for years; they had money. They had history.

And about ten years back, Joshua Moore had run for mayor and won. Taylor remembered him—the guy had been a schmuck in school and was probably still a schmuck now, but he was a smart one. He was raising another smart schmuck, it seemed.

Studying Brendan, he asked softly, "You know who he hangs out with?"

"Yeah. There's about five other guys." He sighed. "There used to be six, but one of them . . . the best of the bunch, actually, died about two months ago."

The hair on the back of Taylor's neck stood up. "Really? What happened?"

"Killed himself." Blake shook his head. "Got to tell you, doesn't make sense—Tristan was a good kid. Level, you know? And I can't see him, of all kids, being involved in something like this."

Tristan.

A piece of the puzzle clicked into place.

The boy's ghost had found Dez somehow—led her here. Yeah, that was it. Taylor knew it as well as he knew his own name.

Something else he knew . . . Dez was holding back on him. In a major way.

"The other kids—you going to talk to all of them, too?"

Blake started to answer, but out in the hallway, there was a commotion. Loud. Very loud. "Damn it, I got a right to be in there with my grandson!"

Taylor's brows arched.

Blake swore and turned around, heading out of the room. Curious, Taylor fell into step behind him. The man out in the hallway looked vaguely familiar, although it took a few minutes to place him.

Beard, he thought. Leon Beard. The only reason he even re-membered was because he could vaguely recall the man's daughter had married Moore, the mayor. Grandson—

Shit. Taylor rubbed the back of his neck and watched as Blake went to deal with the older man. "Now, come on, Leon. You know that's not exactly true. You don't have a right to be in there with him and it's not like he's in trouble. We just need to piece things together so we can help that girl . . ."

He was good, Taylor decided, keeping his voice low and easy, not getting pushy or anything.

Leon still wasn't pleased. "You trying to say my grandson had something to do with it?" the old man blustered.

"Not at all. I'm just saying he works at the hotel where she was hurt. Maybe he saw something that could help her. He's a good kid, right? If he could help her, he'd want to." Blake rested a hand on Leon's shoulder and gently guided him away from the room. "Why don't we go get you some coffee?"

As they disappeared, Taylor slipped back into the observation room, this time closing the door tightly behind him. He took up his former position at the window, staring at Brendan Moore, brooding.

Brooding . . . and wondering.

* * *

GETTING Leon Beard out of the station was about as easy as pulling a tick off, Blake thought once he finally got the asshole out the door. He wasn't overly surprised to see the old man show up, although he knew for a fact the mayor wouldn't have been happy.

There was no love lost between the mayor and his father-in-law. It had gotten public a time or two—thanks to Leon. Moore had handled it well enough and he did what he could to keep things civil, even though his wife—the kid, too—didn't seem to want to have much to do with the old man.

Nobody knew why, and Blake didn't much care as long as Beard stayed out of his way and didn't cause any problems. Today he'd almost caused problems. And damn it, Blake had wanted to watch the interviews—all of them. Muttering under his breath, he headed back down the long hallway, figuring he'd ask Jones to catch him up. Maybe they could grab a bite to eat.

Blake wouldn't mind needling the man about the FBI and shit. Had to be more exciting than working here in French Lick. It might be home, but it got damn boring sometimes.

But he came back to a mostly empty room. Two other cops were in there.

Jones, though, was gone.

* * *

DREAMS, so dark and ugly, haunted her sleep. Twisting on the bed, still clothed, Dez groaned as the images assaulted her. The girl, her name was Ivy, and she was crying . . . crying, even though her lifeless body was stretched out on a slab, cold and naked and dead.

Her eyes, empty and accusatory, stared at Dez. "You were supposed to save me," she whispered. "Why didn't you?"

"I tried." Dez wrapped her arms around her middle and shook her head. "I tried." Then she stopped, closed her eyes. "I *did*. You're alive. This is just a dream . . ."

When she opened her eyes and looked back, Ivy was gone. But there was another girl. Younger, so much younger—six? Perhaps seven? She had soft, buttery yellow hair, straight and wispy thin, framing a cute, elfin face. Her skin was bluish white in death and she looked at Dez sadly.

"You can't save me, either. I've been dead too long."

"I don't save the dead," Dez said, shaking her head. "I just try to help you move on. I can't save *anybody* . . ."

And the few times I've tried, I've failed . . .

The little girl continued to stare at her solemnly. *"Can't you? What about him?"*

Dez blinked. "Who, Tristan? Sweetie, he's already gone. He's passed on. I can't do anything more for him but keep my promise."

The little girl stared at her. Then she sighed and faded away.

Dez reached out a hand. "Wait!"

She took a step forward and in that way of dreams, everything shifted, faded.

Changed.

And she was in the cemetery, the one where she'd found Tristan. Standing at his grave. But when she reached out to touch the stone, the dream shifted. Changed. And she was in a field. It was empty, or so it seemed. When she looked down, she saw . . . a hole? What was that?

She knelt to look, but found herself falling. Hurtling hard and fast. And then she hit. The breath was gone from her body and it was awful, because she wanted, so badly, to scream. *Needed* to scream, because what she was looking at . . .

A broken doll.

She resembled nothing so much as a broken doll.

Except this doll had once been a living, breathing child . . . and as Dez stared at her, the girl's eyes opened and life flooded them. She stared at Dez and whispered, *"Find me . . ."*

As the girl's presence wrapped around Dez, as Dez recognized the presence of one of the departed, some of the terror faded, replaced by rage and misery. Swallowing the scream, she opened her mouth, wondered if she could speak. But this was just a dream and she could do whatever she chose. Swallowing the tears, she said softly, "Tell me what you need me to do."

The girl's eyes closed and tears of blood rolled down her cheeks.

"Find me," she whispered plaintively. Then she reached out a hand, thin and frail and streaked with blood. *"Just find me . . . I don't want to stay lost."*

Dez reached out. As her fingers brushed the girl's, the girl's body began to crumble, first to skeleton, then to dust.

Then the dream shattered . . . fell away.

With a gasp lodged in her throat, Dez jerked awake in the bed. Staring straight ahead, she pressed her fisted hand to her racing heart. "Shit," she wheezed. "Shit, shit, *shit*."

She wanted to tell herself it was just a dream, one brought on by the day from hell. Who wouldn't have a nightmare? . . . Who wouldn't have a bad dream? And if it had only been about Ivy, she could have even accepted that.

There was more to it, though.

A lot more. It just had that feel to it. "Damn it," she whispered as she huddled under the blankets. "*Damn* it."

She wouldn't be leaving French Lick anytime soon, she didn't think.

* * *

"SOMEBODY fucking talked," Beau growled.

Brendan glanced at him from the corner of his eye and muttered, "Shut the fuck up. We don't talk about this here."

Not here.

Beau grumbled but went quiet as they jogged down the steps and headed toward Beau's '73 Mustang. Once they were inside, though, Beau's silence shattered and he snarled, "Who in the hell fucking talked?"

Sitting in the back, Mark and Kyle both said the same crap— it wasn't them. They didn't know. Fucking assholes. Somebody had talked, he knew it. He'd figure it out. Brendan leaned back against the leather, his eyes staring out the window. Inside the car, he felt a little less exposed, so he knew he could probably relax a little. But he wasn't going to—as of now, he trusted nobody but himself. Not Mark, not Kyle. Not even Beau, and normally he'd trust Beau with just about everything. "What did you tell the cops?" he asked.

"Jack shit. Told them I didn't know the girl, had no fucking clue what was going on." Beau started the Mustang and pulled away from Brendan's house. For a few minutes, silence fell. "What do we do, Brendan? We got to figure it out and figure out what we're going to do."

Brendan knew that, hadn't slept worth a shit the past night, trying to play things out in his head already. He even had a plan sketched out. But it would take a few days to get it in motion. A few days, some time.

"Right now, we just shut the fuck up and wait. Nobody talks, you got that?" He shot Kyle and Mark a quick look and then shifted his attention back to the front, staring out the windshield. "See if we can figure out how that bitch figured things out."

"Yeah." Beau frowned. "Where in the hell did she come from, anyway? She's not from around here."

Brendan shook his head. He didn't know. But she wasn't the one who had him all that concerned. He was more worried about the blond guy—the one with the cold blue eyes. He'd gotten a name on that one. His name was Jones. As in Taylor Jones—owned the big manor just outside town. Not to mention half the fucking property in the area.

Brendan knew enough about the Jones family to be worried once he'd heard that name. He wasn't worried because the family was loaded—his own family wasn't hurting for money. Wasn't worried because of the freaky shit that had happened to the family years back.

No, what had him worried was the rumors that had floated

around about the sole surviving Jones. Taylor Jones—he'd joined the FBI out of college, Brendan remembered hearing. The FBI . . . did a lot of shit with missing children. Runaways, kidnapped kids. That sort of shit.

And now he was here.

The bitch didn't worry him. But Taylor Jones . . . shit.

"Kyle. You light up in here and I'm kicking your ass." Beau glared at Kyle in the mirror as the other boy rolled a joint between his fingers. "I don't want that shit stinking up my Mustang. That smell won't ever come out and my folks will kill me if they smell it."

"Oh, kiss my ass," Kyle snapped. "Like they'd ever notice. They're too busy fucking everybody else in town to notice anything."

A dark, ugly look entered Beau's eyes and his hands tightened on the wheel. "If you don't want me to pound you into the fucking ground, you'll just shut up, Kyle."

Kyle opened his mouth, but apparently something he saw in Beau's face made him take those words seriously. Slumping in his seat, he mumbled, "Whatever."

"Fuck you." Then Beau shot Brendan another look, his anger at Kyle bleeding back into nerves. His pupils were so huge, they all but swallowed his irises. "Nothing to worry about. You're sure?"

"Shit, you need to relax," Kyle said from the backseat. He closed his eyes and tucked away his joint. "We've got to play it cool, remember? And would you quit being such a damn pussy? You got any idea what water will do to evidence? Any evidence there *might* have been? It's gone now."

Mark was quiet, staring out the window.

Casually, Brendan flipped the visor down, checked his hair, then shot Mark a look, noticed the sweat beading on the other guy's brow, the signs of a sleepless night. Yeah, it was entirely possible Mark was just stressed, the way all of them were. But he wasn't so sure.

Out of all of them, Mark was the one he could see breaking the easiest. "What do you think, Mark? Any way they can link this back to us? Video shit, evidence? Anything?"

Mark glanced at him in the visor's mirror and then looked away. "I dunno. There's no way I could recover anything and I got better equipment than anybody around here for miles, including the cops." He shrugged. "But I'm not the forensics freak—that's Kyle."

"Yeah." Narrowing his eyes, he said, "You say you can't recover anything. What about the feds? Like FBI or CIA shit?"

Kyle sniggered. "This isn't CIA territory, Brendan. FBI, maybe—kidnapping and shit. But CIA? Not unless you been spying and shit on top of kidnapping girls and groping their tits."

Brendan looked back over his shoulder. Softly, he said, "I wasn't the only one who took her, man. Remember that."

"You were the only one getting his rocks off groping her." Kyle stared at him, smirking. "Hey, she's got nice tits, what do I care?" He went back to staring out the window.

Brendan decided he'd ignore the fucker for now. Ignore him, because Mark was a bigger problem. Looking into the mirror, he studied the pale, sweating prick.

Mark stared right back.

* * *

NORMALLY, Mark would have felt like bolting. He saw something ugly and evil in Brendan's eyes and it was more than just anger—he knew. Somehow Brendan was piecing things together and he was piecing them together in a way that involved Mark, even though Mark hadn't really done much. Except stay out of the woman's way.

That was enough for Brendan, though—people who might fuck with his plans were to be stopped, period. Mark hadn't stopped the woman, and if Brendan discovered Mark's part in this? Then Mark was due to get royally fucked over.

He could see the suspicion there, the wondering, the doubt . . . all of that simmering along with the rage. But Mark also saw something else.

Brendan was afraid.

For some reason that Mark wasn't going to look at too closely, that gave him some strength—enough strength to meet Brendan's gaze and not look away as Brendan asked, "So the FBI, then? Could they find anything?"

His gut clenched even thinking about that. The fucking FBI? "FBI—shit." He passed a hand over his mouth and shook his head. "I don't know."

"What do you mean, you don't *know*?" Beau shouted, slamming his fist into the steering wheel. "You're the fucking hacker genius, aren't you? Can they find the shit or not? What do you mean by *I don't know*?"

"I mean I don't *know*," Mark bit off. "It's not like I've ever been into the fucking FBI headquarters. Contrary to what you might think, Sherlock, I really have no idea what they are capable of." He collapsed back against the seat, all too aware that they were staring at him. Watching. All too aware of the doubt, the growing distrust and anger in their eyes.

Fear was an ugly, rasping whisper in the back of his mind. Instinct screamed at him to run . . . run hard, run fast. But the last thing he needed to do was draw their attention like that.

Especially when he didn't have a place to run *to*. Especially when he had nobody to trust.

"Dude. There she is." Kyle punched him in the arm and leaned over, staring out through the window.

Mark turned his head and found himself staring at the woman, watching as she lugged a suitcase out of the resort. Leaving—she wasn't leaving, was she? No. Shit, no. She couldn't leave—

The air in his lungs felt like it was disappearing, being squeezed out of him by some giant fist. "You think she's leaving?" he asked, trying to keep his voice casual.

"Shit, she *can't*," Kyle said, shaking his head. "She's, like, got to be a material witness or something, I'd think."

Or something . . .

Something. Shit. She couldn't leave. If he wanted to talk to anybody, maybe the first person he should try talking to was her. Half the cops around here were too busy kissing Brendan's ass— or his father's ass. But that woman . . . somehow . . . she had connections or something.

Yeah.

She was the one he needed to talk to—he hadn't missed the look that had passed between her and that mean-looking dude yesterday. Either she'd brought him with her or she'd called him here or something. If she left . . .

Keeping his voice bored and easy, he looked away from her and stared at the back of the seat in front of him. "You know, for the hotshot forensics expert, you aren't showing a lot of smarts." He shoved Kyle back. "People can still *see* in here, you know. Don't go staring at her so fucking hard, dumb-ass."

Kyle shoved back but settled in the seat. "Why the hell not? Everybody around here stares at everybody else—and she's *new*."

"You still don't want anybody noticing you doing anything

different," Mark muttered. Then he leaned forward, watching as Beau kept shooting glances out the window toward the lady. "We picking up the others or what? I ain't got all day. Dad's riding my ass and he'll be calling me in an hour or so."

"Why?" Brendan twisted around and looked at him, his eyes cold and hard.

"Because of this shit." Mark jerked a shoulder in a shrug. "You know how he is. He's going to want to check up on me nonstop and he already told me he wants me home by three. If I'm not, he'll be hounding me until I get there."

It was a bald-faced lie but to his surprise, he managed to get it out without stuttering. His dad had been surprisingly calm about things when he came to the station the day before. When Mark had babbled an apology, he had just said, in that easy, quiet voice, "Now, Mark, it's okay. It's not like I think you'd ever have anything to do with this."

That solid, simple faith had all but gutted him.

"Shit, just blow him off," Kyle said.

Mark opened his mouth to answer but Brendan beat him to it. "Fuck, Kyle, get your head out of your ass. This isn't the time for any of us to change how we do things. Mark's the 'good' boy," Brendan said, his voice heavy with mockery. "If he doesn't show up, what do you think his dad is going to do? He's going to fucking call the cops. And what's *that* going to do?"

Mark slumped back in his seat, the adrenaline draining out of him, his heart banging erratically against his ribs.

"Mark, we all need to get together and talk, though." Brendan stared at him in the mirror and, try as he might, Mark couldn't look away. "Maybe you should see if you can come over tonight."

Mark gave him a strained smile. "I'll see what I can do. But

you know how my folks are about Saturdays and shit. I'm supposed to be at church bright and early. Maybe next week."

"It could be too late then. We all got to do some talking."

"Then we try to meet and do it tomorrow," Mark said, his
voice flat. There was no fucking way he was putting himself in
Brendan's hands for the night. No fucking way. "I'm not pissing
my dad off, upsetting my mom, all because you got your panties
in a twist, Brendan. Deal with it."

Brendan's eyes narrowed. Then, slowly, he turned around in
the seat, staring at Mark. "What the fuck did you say?"

"You heard me." This time, his voice shook a little, but he'd
damned if he backed down. Where in the hell this inner strength
had come from, he didn't know, but he knew one thing—Brendan
was scared. And if Brendan was scared, he was going to try *fixing*
things. But Brendan's fixes were bad for others. Brendan's fixes involved things like killing Tristan.

Shit. Shit. And fuck.

No way.

And for some inexplicable reason, a strange sense of peace
washed over him, flooding him with not just confidence but reso-
lution, as he met Brendan's gaze and held it.

He knew what he was going to do once he got home, too. He
was going to try to find that woman—see if she had left the hotel,
left town. If she hadn't left town, he'd be able to find her. If he
couldn't find her, he'd just go to the police. Or maybe Luther.
Luther would know what to do.

One thing was damn certain—Mark was *not* going to spend
the rest of his life like he'd spent the last few months.

No way.

NINE

TAYLOR had two stops that morning. The first was easy. It was the florist shop where Leon Beard worked. He was just curious about the man's rather violent reaction—though, granted, most people wouldn't be pleased to hear their grandkid had to talk to the cops.

But it wasn't like Brendan had been *arrested*, or even questioned. He had to give a statement, something that should have been expected, considering the circumstances.

He might have even just ignored the old man, but for some reason, Beard made his skin crawl and his instincts scream. He couldn't rightly say he'd ever spent five seconds near the guy before and it was possible he'd imagined it. Possible. Not likely. Taylor didn't imagine much.

So he'd swing by the florist shop while he waited for Dez to emerge from her cave. She was his second stop. And if he knew her at all, she'd zero in on the one place where she could find caffeine and calories.

The florist shop was a profusion of autumn colors, pumpkins, and, perhaps not surprisingly, early Christmas décor. It was quiet, as quiet as a tomb, he thought. No music played; nobody greeted him as he came in. Beard's Floral was the only florist in town so they could be lousy with the customer service, he supposed. And small towns were still small towns. They got used to things and didn't much care for change.

But the man could say *hello*.

Beard sat behind the desk and, as Taylor approached, he flicked him one glance and then went back to his book. If he'd been there to buy flowers, he would have left. Simple as that. As it was, he veered off, taking his time to pretend to shop around. Along one wall, there was a display of framed artwork of the hotel. Another wall featured crosses. There was a profusion of angels, little cherubs that gazed innocently at nothing. And flowers, mustn't forget the flowers.

As he circled through the store and finally came to a stop near the desk, he found Beard watching him now.

"Anything I can help you find?"

"No. I would like to send some flowers, though." Taylor didn't need to speak with the man about the boy to get a feel for him. He already knew what he needed to know—he didn't like Leon Beard. He didn't know why, but he didn't like him.

"Who will they be for?" Beard reached for a notepad by his cash register.

"A young woman at the hospital." Taylor paused, watched as the man's mouth tightened. "Poor kid."

Something ugly flashed through Beard's eyes. Oh, yeah. It was official. He didn't like this man.

It took fifteen minutes to finish up. And as he left, he decided the timing was about perfect. He watched as a familiar car pulled onto Main Street. He wasn't the least bit surprised to see her. She wouldn't be able to resist the call of caffeine—or junk food—for too long.

* * *

IT was midmorning when she hunkered down in a booth at Denny's, absolutely delighted to find the chain restaurant in the little town. Small towns like this, they could be hit or miss on restaurants; she knew that for a fact. Denny's, though, she could trust. She could trust them to give her pancakes and eggs and bacon. And coffee. Couldn't forget the coffee.

She had her hands curled around her first cup and it smelled so good, Dez almost whimpered just at the scent of it. Bringing it up to her nose, she breathed it in and sighed, letting the warmth of the mug warm her hands. She wished it would do the same for her entire body.

The waitress standing by the table laughed. "Honey, you look like you haven't seen a decent cup of coffee in a month."

"You're not far off," Dez muttered, taking a sip. It was strong—strong enough to make a dead man's heart beat, or close. She groaned in satisfaction. She took another sip and then put the cup down, rubbing her hands together. The waitress was still lingering there, watching her, her eyes bright with a look Dez recognized all too well.

Curiosity.

"You're the one who found that girl."

Dez didn't respond. She hadn't even spoken to the police yet and if she said a damn thing to anybody before she gave a statement . . . no. Sighing, she lowered her gaze to the coffee and reached for the creamer.

"You don't want to talk about it."

Brilliant observation. She smirked a little and glanced up, cocked a brow.

"How did you . . . well, I guess you're not going to say anything." Then the waitress sighed. "I just get sick thinking about it. It's all over town. Not that French Lick is a big town anyway, you know? But everybody is talking about it. Nobody can understand how she got in there, nobody is talking . . . did she fall?"

Dez looked away. Fall? No. Ivy hadn't *fallen* in there, but she couldn't exactly point that out. Rubbing her temple, she took a deep breath and then looked at the waitress. "I can't talk about this. I'm sorry, but . . ."

A gust of cool air whipped through the restaurant and, absently, she glanced up. She wasn't the only one. She also wasn't the only one staring as Taylor Jones strode inside.

Dropping her head into her hand, she muttered, "How in the hell?"

"Taylor . . . I don't believe it . . ."

The soft, disbelieving tone in the waitress's voice caught Dez's attention and she slanted a look at them as Taylor drew near, watched as the woman's eyes widened, watched as she flushed.

"Hi, Anita." He smiled. "How've you been?"

Dez narrowed her eyes, speculating. Okay, now, this wasn't just some mild familiarity—a guy who'd been in town a day or two. Mind whirling, she thought back to the night before. Her head had been a mess—still was, but not quite so bad. The cop—he'd seemed to know one of the cops.

Put two and two together . . . Taylor wasn't exactly a stranger here. Shit. What were the odds? As a headache settled behind her eyes, she looked up and met his gaze. "Howdy, boss," she drawled. If he *was* known around here, that would explain why he'd been completely convinced he could control the universe . . . or at least the people around here.

"Can you give us a few minutes, Anita? I need to talk to my agent." Without looking away from Dez, he slid into the seat across from her and as Anita walked away, he studied her face.

"I'm not your agent," she said, keeping her voice low.

"You didn't sleep."

Dez rolled her eyes. "Did you hear what I said?"

Taylor's mouth twisted. Then he reached inside the blazer he wore—over jeans, she'd noticed. Still seriously relaxed for him. What in the hell was up with him? She was about to ask him but then saw the folded-up paper he pushed her way. Scowling, she reached for it, only to drop it like it was made of something toxic the second she'd skimmed the first few lines.

"Oh, *hell*, no." She shoved it back at him.

"Sign it, damn it."

"Shove it up your ass, Jones."

He narrowed his eyes and leaned over the table. Somehow he managed to pitch his voice so that she had no problem hearing every last word, but she knew nobody standing three feet away would hear a damn thing. "Sign the fucking contract—I'll shred it the second this is over, but you're signing the damn contract. I'm not letting you get hauled in for questioning and this is the best damn way to do it."

"And what if I refuse?" Dez folded her arms over the table and smirked at him. She knew it would be easier to just sign the damn thing. If he said he'd shred it, she knew he would. Taylor wouldn't go back on his word. It wasn't his way.

But she also couldn't see why in the hell this mattered so much to him, either. She honestly couldn't. Seeing the fury light up his gaze once more, she groaned and covered her face with her hands, pressing her fingertips to her eyes. "Why, Taylor? You want me to sign that fucking thing, then you give me a straight answer. Straight, no bullshit."

She heard the harsh, heavy sound of his exhalation and then a faint rustling sound. "Come on. I want to show you something."

She glanced up, saw the money he'd thrown on the table. Frowning, she said, "I haven't had breakfast."

"I'll bring you back. It's Denny's, for crying out loud." He lifted the menu, studied it with a scowl, and tossed it back down. "They serve it all day. This won't take but twenty minutes and you'll understand, I promise."

Hell. Giving him a dark look, she slid out from the booth, watching as he tucked the contract back into his blazer. They were the focus of much attention as they left the restaurant, and she had the bizarre desire to make a face at everybody over her shoulder as the door swung closed behind them.

She resisted. Barely.

"This better be good," she said, not bothering to disguise the bitchy tone. She didn't *work* for him anymore . . . why should she disguise it? And unless he had a damn good reason, she wasn't signing that contract, either.

"Just walk with me." He slid a pair of sunglasses on, shielding his eyes. He looked polished, smooth . . . even wearing the jeans and blazer. But when did Taylor Jones ever *not* look polished and smooth, completely in control?

Well, that day . . . when he was inside me. He didn't look so in control then. A wave of heat washed over her and she rolled her eyes, looking away so he wouldn't see the flush of color that flooded her cheeks.

Shoving her hands into her pockets, she stared at her toes.

The worn tips of her boots weren't exactly fascinating, but a lot easier on her brain cells than Taylor Jones.

Moments of silence passed.

She was about to grit her teeth and snarl at him, or swear and demand he say something, when she felt it.

It was a whispering, quiet rush. It started as a whisper but it got louder, oh, so very loud, until it was a roaring scream in her head, one that had her fighting the urge to clap her hands over her ears just to get away from the noise.

She shivered and backed away a few feet, but it didn't do any good. They still lingered, their presence wrapping around her, calling out to her. Familiar. So very familiar. It left her shivering, and automatically she huddled into her coat, reaching up to tug the collar closed. As the ghostly whispers danced along her consciousness, she realized that Taylor had stopped.

Foreboding crept through her and she looked up, found herself staring at the graceful old building. In elegant scroll across the windows, she saw the words *French Lick City Courthouse*. Below that, in small print, she saw the words *French Lick City Jail*.

"They wouldn't keep anybody here for too long. Just a few nights. Anything big goes to the county jail. But if they just wanted to talk to you, detain you for a couple of hours? If they decided to keep you overnight? You'd come here."

He wasn't looking at her.

But she could already tell he'd seen her reaction.

A fist was lodged in her throat, choking the air out of her as the presence of the departed edged in ever closer. She could hear them, feel them—faint, weak . . . and so many of them. There was an aged feel to their presence and it ripped at her heart. Fuck, how long had they lingered?

"This courthouse has been here for two hundred years, in some form or another," Taylor continued, still not looking at her. "And it was used more actively as a jail for a good long while. Small-town place like this, they did their own executions here for years—that stopped a long time ago, but I imagine there are still echoes. And just because executions stop, that doesn't mean *death* stops. I guess you can probably tell a number of people have died here.

"They are old, you know. I can't feel them, but even I know that. They are old and fragmented and some of those who died here *did* die for crimes they committed—you can't give them peace. Maybe you could help some of them, but as old as they are, you may not be able to help *any* of them. There may be nothing left but echoes."

Now he looked at her, pushing his sunglasses back onto his head. His steel blue eyes locked with hers and he asked quietly, "Do you really want to go in there? For a night? A few hours? Even for five minutes?"

Dez swallowed and shook her head, backing away one slow step at a time.

After she'd put about fifteen feet between herself and the courthouse, the weight of the departed lessened and she could *almost* breathe. Almost. Rubbing a hand over her chest, she whispered, "Damn it."

"Are you going to sign the damn contract or not?"

Slowly, she looked at him. "Is this why? You just want to make sure you've got a legit reason for me being here?"

"I want to make sure I've got a legit way to help cover your ass and this is the best way I can think of," he bit. "It probably wouldn't work as well anywhere else, but it will here. Are you going to let me help you or not?"

Dez took a deep, slow breath. Just that simple action hurt her chest. She couldn't imagine the hell it would be to walk inside that place.

She fucking hated old places like that. For this very reason. He was right, damn him to hell. She *couldn't* help all of the ghosts, but whether she could help them or not, they still whispered to her. Still called to her. She could help some. But in a place like that, she might end up going insane.

Her hands were shaking, she realized. Shaking and sweating. Blowing out an unsteady breath, she looked at him.

"Yeah. I'll sign it." Then she added, "But it's for this, and this only."

He nodded. "Don't worry."

* * *

HE felt like the first-class bastard most of the world considered him to be, but as they walked back to the café, he couldn't make himself apologize. It had worked.

If he had just *told* her the place was old, it might not have worked.

Showing her, springing it on her like that, had done what he'd hoped, and now at least, he could honestly tell the men in charge of the investigation that Dez was one of his people and she was here under his authority . . . and he could also tell them all that they couldn't and wouldn't discuss confidential investigations.

They wouldn't like it, and he didn't give a flying fuck.

It would work and he knew it.

It was dancing perilously close to abusing his authority, and if it were anybody but Dez . . . he blew out a breath and looked away. If it were anybody but her, he knew he'd do what he could, but in the end, the person would have to deal with his or her own mess. This was Dez's mess, but he wouldn't risk her going into a place that would push her to the brink of madness. Not if he could at all stop it. If it took him close to a line, then so be it. If Dez wasn't worth losing everything for, nobody was.

The contract would cover her ass, it would keep her out of the damn jail even for a few hours, and that was what mattered—that . . . and he had a feeling there was more going on here than the small police department was prepared to handle.

Ivy, their victim, wasn't local.

It was all too likely this was veering rather close to something he might have to take an interest in anyway. Especially since it had led one of his people here. Not that Dez was really *his* anymore. From behind the protection of his sunglasses, he could watch her without her noticing and he kept an eye out, waiting until that pale, ashen look faded, until her eyes stopped looking so tight and pinched, until her breathing became a little less ragged and the tension left her shoulders.

They were almost to the restaurant when she finally took a deep breath and some of that tension finally eased. She stopped and leaned against the building at her back, staring at him. "That was a low blow, you know."

"Yes." He crossed his arms over his chest and stared at her. He wanted to brush his hand down her cheek, soothe that line that still lingered between her brows. Then he wanted to pull her against him, warm her—she was still cold. Even though she wasn't shivering, even though she hadn't said anything, he knew she was still cold. They always lingered with her like this, left her chilled, and it was worse when it was those she couldn't help. Those disembodied spirits that were more echoes than anything else.

But he didn't. He couldn't. Instead he stayed there, waited, and watched.

"You can be such a fucking bastard sometimes, Jones," she muttered, shaking her head and staring off past his shoulder. "You couldn't have just warned me it was an old place and probably not the ideal place for me to be?"

"And if I'd said that, just like that, would you have taken me at my word?"

She stared at him, her dark eyes boring into his like she was trying to see clear through him. Disgusted, she admitted, "The hell if I know."

"That's what I figured. This way, I knew you'd get the point."

"So what do we do now?" she asked, staring at him, her face grim. She was still pale, despite the color slowly returning to her cheeks.

"You have to go give a statement. But I imagine you know that." He slid his hands into his pockets, because he ached to touch her. So badly did he ache to touch her. "I'll make some calls, though. We'll have them come to your hotel."

"I'm not staying at the hotel anymore." She brushed her hair back, a habitual gesture. Then she absently toyed with the silver chain around her neck and he found himself staring at her fingers, then the scar tissue—remembering that night, how close she'd come to dying. The days that followed.

And the day he'd taken her home . . . the day he'd taken *her*.

He couldn't think about that now. Slipping a hand into his pocket, he rubbed his thumb over the smooth surface of the golden cross he carried. *Focus, damn it*. Had to focus. He tore his gaze from her neck.

"That hotel, I swear, it's highway robbery," Dez said with a wry laugh. "How can it stay in business in this little place? Anyway, I was going to see if I could find a room to rent or something for a week or two. Either that or just a cheap hotel."

Don't, he thought, staring at her. He could offer her a room out at the manor, but he wouldn't. He knew he wouldn't, knew he *shouldn't.* This was the worst time in the world for him to be around her. And that was the worst place in the world for her to be. There was a possibility she'd find ghosts there, as well.

Assuming there *weren't* any ghosts there, even if he made the offer, she wouldn't accept. But it was a bad idea anyway. Not that she wouldn't figure it out, but he didn't need her at the manor and he didn't *want* her at the manor. His head was fucked up enough there as it was.

Fortunately, he had the willpower to keep from blurting that much out. However . . . he could do something for her. "I'll see what I can do about getting you a place to stay. Since you've signed the contract, we will pick it up."

Finding a place wouldn't be an issue. His family had had its hands in everything—including real estate. He didn't give a damn what happened to the money, but he did pay attention, simply because it was his responsibility. One of the rental houses had gone vacant a few weeks earlier—he'd gotten the e-mail from the lawyer who handled everything. As far as he knew, it was still sitting empty. She could stay there, once he'd made sure it was in decent shape.

It was better than a hotel, at least.

But in the meantime, they needed to find a place where she could give her statement. Shit.

"Stop glaring at me," Dez muttered.

"I'm not glaring at you." Shit. He probably was. Then he sighed and looked away. "How did you end up out here, Dez?" *Here—now. Why the hell here and why the hell* now?

"You've already figured out the answer to that. Why do you need me to spell it out?"

"Maybe because it's not adding up." He looked back at her and lifted a brow. "And maybe because you're not telling me everything."

She wrinkled her nose at him. Then she jammed her hands in her pockets and started to walk, ignoring the restaurant and walking down the sidewalk like she didn't have a destination or a goal in mind. He fell in step beside her. "Aren't you hungry?"

"After your little display back there? Hell, no. I may not eat for a week." She hunched her shoulders up and shuddered. "His name was Tristan. A nice kid. Strong. You know that saying, 'Only the good die young'? I swear, it could have been written with him in mind. This kid . . . Taylor, he was good. I'm talking solid-gold good. He stayed for one reason: that girl. He needed to save her and he wasn't going anywhere until he did it. He couldn't move on."

"So he knew about her. All along."

"Yeah." She lifted her head, staring off into the distance. "If you go back through the obits, or talk to people around here, they'll tell you he killed himself. They'll tell you, 'What a shame, we don't get it. He was such a bright, nice young man.' And he was—he was a nice kid, would have been one hell of a man. And they are right . . . they don't get it. They are clueless. That boy didn't kill himself. *They* killed him. Those boys who put that girl in there. They killed him because he didn't want to go along with their little prank . . . and he wasn't going to allow it. They killed him to shut him up."

"Fuck." He closed his eyes as he realized what she was saying. He'd already assumed *one* kid had been involved, but as a prank? A fucking prank? And they'd killed another to silence him. Taylor closed his eyes. "You're certain."

"Yeah. Pretty damn certain." She licked her lips and shot him a narrow glance. "There was a boy yesterday, when I was getting ready to go up in that fort thing—he had on some sort of security uniform, and his name tag read *Danvers*. That ring any bells?"

"There is a Mark Danvers on staff. He's eighteen, works in the security department at the hotel." Taylor frowned absently, going through his mental files, ticking off the faces until he came to the right one. "Skinny kid. Dark hair, cut short."

"That sounds right. He saw me. Could have called for the rest of security, done something to stop me from climbing out there . . . slowed me down a lot. But he didn't." She stopped now and turned to him. A cold wind kicked up, blowing through her short, dark hair. "He knew. He's involved somehow and he was scared to death, but he knew. And when he figured out what I was up to, he was relieved. Somebody needs to talk to that boy, and they need to do it without his buddies around. Soon, too, because if the others would kill to go through with their plan . . . what are they willing to do to protect their secrets?"

Taylor didn't even want to think about that.

* * *

MARK waited thirty minutes before he slipped out of the house. He took his bike. He didn't ride much anymore. Not since he'd started hanging with Brendan and Beau—the Mustang was so much cooler than a fucking bike—but as he pulled on the cold-weather gear he used to use back when he biked all over these roads, he felt some of the stress easing away.

He never should have started hanging out with them.

Never should have gotten so caught up in the idea of that shit. He knew it now, wished he'd seen then. Out in the garage, it was chilly, but he ignored it. He lived five miles outside of town. It wouldn't take him long on the bike, but man, he was going to freeze his ass off. He grabbed an extra fleece from the wall and tugged it on as he laid out the plan.

He'd look for her, first. Look for the woman, and then if he didn't find her . . . shit. He didn't know. Maybe the guy he'd seen hanging around. The blond guy. He wasn't from town, but there'd been something about him. Or maybe Luther. Luther would know what to do. Luther always had the answers. Shit. He'd figure it out on the ride. Riding always cleared his head.

The air laid into him with a cold bite, one that he welcomed. For the first half of the ride, he didn't make himself think, not at all. He just rode and let his mind drift.

But as he got closer to town, he made himself start thinking, made himself start trying to plan. If he couldn't find the woman, and if he couldn't figure out who the guy was, the next person was . . . who? Half the police department had their lips firmly plastered to the ass of Brendan's father. He didn't know who there he could trust. Luther seemed to be the right call, but Luther wasn't a cop anymore. Still, he would know who to trust, Mark thought.

So caught up in his thoughts, he was only dimly aware of the engine. He heard it, but he wasn't paying attention the way he should. And it didn't dawn on him until it was almost too late . . . it was coming way too fucking fast.

At almost the last second, he jerked his head—saw the vehicle, that sunlight glinting off the Mustang's gleaming windshield. Swearing, he jerked the handlebars. The wheel hit something and he went flying.

*   *   *

BEAU swiped a hand over the back of his mouth and told himself he hadn't just done that. What the hell had he been thinking?

He'd just seen Mark and lost it—the fucking pussy had said something. He knew it. They *all* knew it. All of them. Shit, shit, shit. Mark was the weak one; he was the one who'd talked. They needed to just stop pussyfooting around and deal with it before he fucked them all.

He saw Mark lying crumpled on the ground and he gripped the gearshift—his hand sweating, his heart racing. He could do it now. Take care of it. It wasn't like he didn't have the vehicle for it.

Up ahead, he saw something, though. Through the trees—sunlight glinting off paint.

Shit. Heart racing, he pressed on the gas. Easy-like. Couldn't let anybody see him peeling out of there, right?

Shit. What the fuck did he do now? Wasn't like he'd *hit* Mark or anything, right? He'd go talk to Brendan. Brendan would know what to do.

TEN

So close to time.
    I wanted a more peaceful day for us, my pretty angel. My only.

But it was tomorrow, and it would seem there was no peace coming anytime soon. It was a concern, because unrest made people jumpy, made them look.

Not that there was much to see, after all. But still, it was a concern. But no one that would stop this special day. It only came once a year, after all.

* * *

You stupid motherfucker. Brendan stared at Beau, resisting the urge to get up and wrap his hands around the idiot's neck and just *squeeze.* "What in the hell were you thinking?"

"We know it's him," Beau said simply, staring at Brendan with a blank look. Like he wanted some sort of pat on the head.

"And your point is . . . ?"

"What are we supposed to do? Just be quiet and not say anything?" Beau shook his head. "We got to do something before he runs his mouth."

Across the room, Kyle laughed. "Shit, you've taken one hit too many in football, Beau. Anything happens *now*, it automatically looks worse for us, and since we're all friends, it looks worse on *all* of us. Can you at least tell us he hit his head hard enough that he won't remember what happened?"

Beau reached up and scratched at his scalp, looking confused.

"Guess we can take that as a no," Kyle muttered.

Brendan sighed. Kyle swore and then looked at Brendan. "What the fuck do we do now?"

Brendan shook his head and stared at Beau for a long minute. He had ideas. But he didn't want to do anything until he knew what was going on with Mark first. Shit. How in the world had everything gotten so screwed up?

He blew out a breath and shook his head. "Listen to me, damn it." He pointed at Beau and bit off, "Listen good. You don't do anything else. You got it? That was so fucking stupid."

"But . . ."

"No." Brendan shook his head. "Just shut up and listen. You could have fucked all of us. You don't tell the others; you don't mention this. It didn't *happen*, you hear me?"

"O-okay." Beau nodded, licking his lips. "It didn't happen."

Brendan turned away and shoved a hand through his hair, his mind racing furiously. "We need to just keep it cool, play it easy. We don't have school tomorrow, so that's good. And I heard my dad talking with somebody from the school board about either canceling school for Tuesday or setting up counseling and shit, because of what happened at the hotel and shit. They think we're 'traumatized.'"

He'd drop a few comments, see if he couldn't get his dad to throw his weight for an extra day off. They needed to make sure Beau wasn't going to lose his mind again—Beau of all people. Shit.

* * *

THE day that Taylor Jones dreaded was almost here. Tomorrow. Fuck. It was tomorrow. The flowers were already ordered—he'd taken care of that earlier in the week, thank God. Daisies. Anna had always loved daisies.

One more fucking day. Then it was behind him for another year. Another year for him to wonder and wait for there to be news. But there never was. Not that he hadn't looked, quietly. But the trail had long since gone cold. He wouldn't admit, though, not even to himself, that he'd never know what had happened to her.

One more day . . . and already, he couldn't think of anything but her, his sweet kid sister who made him laugh so easily. Part of him wished the damn phone would ring, that Dez would need him for something, just so he could escape these thoughts for a few hours longer. Until tomorrow, please God, just until tomorrow.

But Anna deserved better than that.

He'd been awake since before dawn and it had found him sitting in his bed, staring at nothing as he went back and thought of every last little detail about the girl.

Her smile. The way she laughed. The times she'd gotten him in trouble for pranks she'd come up with. And how he hadn't minded so much—because it had been Anna.

And he remembered the horror as they all realized she was missing. All these years . . . never knowing. The bitch of his job was that he knew he'd probably *never* know. That her killer would likely go unpunished.

"Anna . . . God, I'm sorry." A tear slid free and rolled down his cheek. Taylor didn't bother wiping it away.

He missed his baby sister.

* * *

DEZ climbed out of the car, ignoring the dry, skittering whispers that danced along her flesh as she placed one booted foot on cemetery ground. People who thought ghosts were stronger at night were clueless. Ghosts didn't care what time of day it was.

Right now the sun was a thin, watery light high in the sky and although she couldn't see a soul, Dez knew she wasn't alone as she made her way through the graveyard.

She didn't know why she was here.

Tristan was gone. She sighed and wondered if she could talk to his parents, if she *should*. She needed to find a way to give them the closure she'd promised their son, but right now, all she had was the knowledge that he hadn't killed himself. It was empty knowledge without proof.

But Tristan hadn't called her here.

Something . . . no, some*body* else had.

She couldn't see the soul. Couldn't even really *feel* whoever it was. The soul wasn't strong enough. Either too long dead or just too weak in general. But somebody was tugging her.

And there were others, too. Mostly echoes—not truly ghosts, just the remnants of their memories, the lingering of their emotions, echoes of their passings. She believed most of them had

truly passed on to what waited beyond . . . this was just like . . .
well, the afterdeath, perhaps.

Only a few of the souls felt *complete* enough to truly be called
ghosts and none of them were strong enough to manifest. The
rest, they were just the lonely echoes of their mortal lives. She
wondered if they'd ever find a way to let go, wondered what happened to their true souls if some remnant continued to cling. And
those were only some of the questions she had.

It was a terribly depressing thought, she decided.

Those whispery echoes, so forlorn and sad. Dez lowered her
shields as much as she could and reached out. "Hello?"

No answer.

"If you want to talk, I'm here."

There was *almost* a shivering sigh on the air—almost the
echo of a sound. So hesitant and faint.

"I'll hear you, you know. All you have to do is focus a little.
Reach out to me and just think about making me hear you. And I
will." She skirted around the base of a large marble angel, absently
stroking the petals of the flowers that had been placed there.

The silence lingered.

Sighs gathered and she felt the press of their presence, but
nobody answered.

Dez reached up, rubbing the back of her neck, frustration mount-
ing hard. She wanted so desperately to be able to help, but she didn't
know how. She couldn't reach out and focus until the soul actually
reached for her first. And there was nothing. Simply nothing.

The air was thick with sadness, heavy with it. It almost broke
Dez's heart. After another circle around the marble angel, she
ambled back over to Tristan's grave and crouched down, absently
picking up a few dead leaves and tossing them aside.

In the back of her mind, she heard more vague whispers. No words, nothing she could lock on. But there was somebody *there* . . . watching her. Somebody who *needed* her, or was at least aware of her.

It seemed the only time the departed were really aware of her was when they wanted her help. But this one wasn't reaching out. As the ghostly brushes against her subconscious grew stronger, colder, she shivered. Staring at Tristan's marker, she murmured, "At least I was able to help you, right?"

She jumped when there was a harsh, almost broken sound that echoed all around—it was so loud she *felt* it. It sounded like a sob. She could almost taste the tears.

Swallowing, Dez rose and looked around.

"Who are you?" she asked again.

But once more, there was nothing but the sound of the wind, and those ghostly, lingering sighs.

"I can't help you until you talk to me," Dez said quietly.

There wouldn't be a response, though. She could accept that. Okay. So she'd just come back. Give it time. Sooner or later, she'd get whatever connection she needed, because she couldn't rush this.

The ghost simply wasn't ready to speak to her yet.

Still, despite her unease, she was oddly hesitant to leave and she found herself doing another slow circuit around the cemetery. She might have done it endlessly.

But her phone rang, the jingling tune sounding strident and harsh in that place of silence and unrest. Jolting, she reached into her pocket and pulled it out in a rush, silencing the sound before it could shatter the quiet any more than it already had. Her heart was racing before she even lifted it to her ear. It was Taylor.

"Yes?" she asked, her voice creaking.

"I need you at the hospital. Immediately."

Swallowing, she closed her eyes. She didn't want to ask. She didn't want to—was it Ivy? What had happened to her? "Why?"

"That boy. The one you saw. He's been in an accident. Get here. Now." In typical Taylor Jones fashion, he delivered those words in a short, concise fashion and before she could ask a single thing, he hung up.

That boy. Mark. *Shit.*

Dez lowered the phone and cast one final look around the cemetery. "Whoever you are, I've got to go. But if you want my help, sooner or later, you'll have to speak to me."

The wind gusted through the cemetery as she headed back to the car, blowing the tail of her coat around her legs, sending leaves swirling around her in gusts.

And although she knew she wouldn't see anything, Dez knew she was being watched.

* * *

"I usually have to be in a town a few months before I have to visit the hospital twice," she muttered as she joined him in the hallway on the way to Mark Danvers's room.

Taylor just frowned. "If you really think he knows something, then we need to know now so we can have somebody placed here to watch him. This town is too small to be able to spare it unless it's absolutely necessary."

"Gee, I never would have thought of that," she drawled, giving him a look of wide-eyed innocence as she fell into step next to him. "The two or three stop signs in lieu of stoplights never would have clued me in to that. I'm surprised you even get cell phone reception here."

"Smart-ass," he whispered, nodding to the nurse as she came

out of the room. He caught Dez's arm and gestured to the doorway. "He's in there. You'll need to give the cops a minute to get the kid's parents out."

Dez shook her head. "I think you should leave them in there."

Taylor opened his mouth to argue, but she slanted a look his way. "He wants to talk. He's scared and he wants to talk . . . Give him a chance to do the right thing."

"And if he was involved in that boy's death?"

"I won't let him talk about that right now. I just want to know about the girl . . . and what happened today." She made a face at him. "I'm not new at this, you know. And it's not like I don't know what *not* to ask or anything. I can keep him from talking about shit he shouldn't talk about without a lawyer. But you need to at least give him a chance . . . and let him have his folks. I've got a bad feeling about this."

Hell. So did he.

Against his better judgment, Taylor nodded and stepped aside, following Dez into the hospital room.

* * *

IF the boy had looked pale and scared yesterday, it was nothing compared to how he looked now.

Pale and scared and bruised didn't even cover it.

He must have sensed the tension from his parents, because Dez and Taylor hadn't been in the room more than five seconds before the boy opened his eyes and turned his head to look at them.

Dez ignored the parents, focusing solely on Mark. She'd wondered if she would feel regret coming from him—regret for helping her yesterday—but so far . . . no. All she felt was exhaustion and pain. And fear. A lot of it.

"Hey." She studied the big-ass bandage on his head and wondered how many stitches were under it. "Don't take this wrong, man, but you look like hell."

He gave her a weak grin. "Well, maybe it's a good Halloween costume."

"You think they'll let you out to go trick-or-treat?" She moved around and eased a hip down on the edge of the bed, automatically sensing the best way to reach out to him, talk to him. He was tired of hiding, tired of being afraid, tired of lying.

He really did want to talk.

So she'd let him. And she'd hope his parents loved him as much as they seemed to.

"Nah. I scrambled my brains—they're keeping me for a day or so, they tell me." He closed his eyes and sighed. "Better off in here for a while, I guess."

"Yeah. I'm thinking so. Although I'm curious just how you ended up in here." She waited until he opened his eyes and looked back at her. Then she lifted a brow and asked, "You got any idea what happened?"

His mother reached over and laid a hand on his shoulder. "He already explained all of this. He lost control of his bike. It happens."

Dez ignored the mom. "You look awful scared, Mark. People who look that scared are usually scared for a reason."

A muscle jerked in his jaw. He blinked rapidly, like he was trying to get something out of his eye . . . or maybe like he was trying not to cry. A harsh sob escaped him.

"I wanted to tell somebody," he blurted out.

Mark's dad straightened. "What's going on here?"

"Dad, I wanted to tell you—"

The older man held up a hand. "I don't know what's going on, Mark, but you need to be quiet now. I want a lawyer in here."

"There's no need for one," Dez said quietly. "I'm not a cop."

Mark shifted his glance to Taylor and lifted a brow. "Don't tell me *he* isn't."

Dez turned her head and looked at Taylor. "Taylor. Can you go outside?"

Taylor narrowed his eyes.

"He wants to do the right thing." She held his gaze, silently begging him to listen. "Let him talk . . . and when he's done, we'll know if we need to have him protected—I'll tell you. You know I'll let you know. Later, the cops can talk to him. He's not going anywhere." She shifted her eyes to the boy and asked, "Are you?"

Mark swallowed and whispered, "No."

"Mark, be quiet. You don't need to say anything else," his mother said, glaring at Dez. "Whatever this is, we'll deal with it. I don't want you in trouble."

He laughed, but the sound was harsh and ugly. "I don't need to say anything? Damn it, Mom, I do, too. I *need* to, because *not* saying anything is killing me. I can't live with this inside me. And you don't *want* me in trouble? I *deserve* trouble."

"Mark . . ."

He looked up at his dad and said quietly, "You always taught me that when I screwed up, I had to accept responsibility. That's what I'm going to do." He looked back at Dez and said, "I want to tell you. He doesn't have to leave."

Taylor swore under his breath, then looked at Dez before looking back at Mark. "Actually, it's probably best if I do. Ms. Lincoln isn't . . . well, she's not bound by the same constraints that I am. Think of her the way you'd think of a doctor or a priest, for the time being. You can talk to her. But it's best that I'm not in here while you discuss this." Then he gave Mark a faint smile. "I've met grown men who lack your courage, you know that? As admirable as it is, it makes it harder for me to walk out . . . but I'm glad to see it."

Without another word, he turned around and left the room. As the door swung shut behind him, Dez looked back at Mark. "I don't want to know *anything* except what was going to happen yesterday and what happened today—I need to know about the girl and I need to know if you're in danger, Mark. Got that? I don't want to hear what happened months ago and I don't want you trying to tell me. You can tell the cops all that later . . . *with a lawyer*, damn it. Get a good one, one who can cut you a deal. But for now . . . Yesterday. Today. That's all . . . Am I clear?"

He stared at her and nodded slowly.

"Okay, then. Are you in danger? Did somebody try to hurt you?"

"Yeah." He licked his lips and then glanced at his mom when a harsh, startled cry escaped her. "I'm sorry, Mom. For everything."

He looked back at Dez and said, "It was Beau. I recognized his Mustang—he has a plate on the front of the car, it reads *BOKXASS*: 'Beau kicks ass.' I didn't see him, but I know that Mustang. I was riding, and he was almost on top of me, getting faster. I just jerked the handlebars, felt the wheel hit something. I . . . I don't know after that."

As his parents crowded around him, Dez remained silent. Finally, though, his father asked, "Mark, are you *sure* it was Beau? I mean, why would he do that?"

Mark started to cry then.

Deep, ugly sobs. There was poison in those tears, Dez suspected, poison that had been festering inside him for months and months. His parents stared at him, in complete and utter shock, for the longest time. Then, slowly, they looked at her. His dad was the first one to start to understand, and she saw that dawning horror, watched as he stumbled back a little from the boy who desperately needed him.

Rising, Dez moved and slid an arm around Mark's shoulders as she met the father's gaze. "You know what happened yesterday," she said quietly.

The older man nodded.

"Your son was there. He could have done two things: He could have screwed around and made it harder for me to help. Or he could have done what he did. He made it possible for me to help . . . whatever else happens, whatever you hear, remember that."

The mother continued to stare at them, mystified.

Dez ignored them and caught one of Mark's hands in hers. "You need to get this out, Mark. You said it yourself. It's killing you. Get it out . . . and let me help. However I can, I'll help."

* * *

IT was hours later before Taylor saw Dez again. The day had slipped away from him without giving him much time to think about Anna, and what tomorrow was. He'd get up early to visit her grave, to take her the flowers. God knew he spent a lot of time thinking about her anyway, no matter where he was.

He stood in the hallway outside the small hospital lounge, where Mark's mother was alone, weeping. The family's day hadn't gotten any easier. In fact, after Mark had made his confession to Dez, it had gotten worse—so much worse.

The boy had started having seizures. Apparently he'd had a lot of trouble with them when he was younger, although they'd leveled off as he'd gotten older. The stress, Taylor imagined. Especially once it was discovered the boy was showing signs of going into alcohol withdrawal.

Like that family didn't have enough on their hands, he thought, staring out the window as Mark's mother fought to control her sobs. Her husband was in the room with their son, and she'd been in there as well, up until twenty minutes earlier.

But now . . . now she was out here, crying as though her heart was breaking.

Taylor suspected she hadn't wanted to break down in front of Mark—so hard for parents to always stay strong around their children. He guessed she needed a few minutes to get the tears out without upsetting her son. He couldn't blame her.

One thing was certain, though. Mark wouldn't be talking to the cops for a few days yet. While part of Taylor was impatient, there was another part of him that thought this was better—the sooner the boy talked, the sooner the other boys would know. Then they'd have time to shore up their defenses even more.

For now, Mark was as safe as he could be, safe and being kept from all visitors . . . including cops and friends. Until they had the withdrawal symptoms and the seizures under control, Mark's visitations would be very, very limited. And very controlled.

When Dez showed up and came to stand beside him at the window, he spared her a quick glance.

"She looks like she's had her heart ripped out," Taylor said, his voice flat.

Dez sighed. "It's only going to get worse. Wait until he confesses that he knew three of his friends had killed Tristan and he hadn't done anything about it."

"Fuck." He shoved a hand through his hair and shook his head. "*Why*? Damn it, why didn't he say anything?"

"He was scared. Tristan, the kid who brought me here, he was the guy everybody liked; everybody respected him. Or almost everybody. Some of the kids were even scared shitless of him—on their own, they wouldn't have messed with him. You don't expect that kind of guy to become a target, but that's what they did—they targeted him, plotted his death, carried it out, made it look like he'd merrily had a poisoned cocktail. They got away with it, too. Mark was scared it would happen to him. In his shoes, how do we know we wouldn't have done the same?"

"You wouldn't." Taylor snorted and shook his head. Then he sighed. "But in the end, he did the right thing . . . and I think he knew they would try to do something. They still might. Telling you took guts." He paused, then added, "There's somebody watching over him. It's not a cop from the department, though."

Dez narrowed her eyes. "What do you mean, it's not a *cop*?"

"Calm down. It's actually better this way. Right now, everything is still quiet—nobody knows but his family, you . . . and this friend they got on the door. An ex-cop," he said, a faint smile tugging at his lips. "Retired from Louisville and moved back home a few years ago. And it's somebody who volunteered—a guy by the name of Luther—he works with him at the hotel. He's friends with the family and when he heard about what happened, he showed up here, offered to watch over him. Seems like he'd suspected something was bothering the kid."

"Ex-cop. Cop. Same thing." She reached up to toy with the chain at her neck, a worried look on her face. "We're sure we can trust him?"

Taylor gave a short nod. "I'm sure. You'll probably feel better if you talk to him, get a read on him yourself. But he's got a look in his eyes. He's pissed. Good and pissed. Anybody wants to hurt that kid, they'll have to go through him. He's already kicking himself for not realizing how bad the kid was messed up inside."

"Woulda been nice if he'd said something to somebody," Dez muttered, shaking her head.

"He probably didn't realize it was this bad," Taylor said. "And the boy hid everything very well. His dad is a counselor, you know that? A counselor—didn't realize his son was an alcoholic."

"He hid it well." She blew out a breath and glanced back at the mother. "I wonder if I should talk to her."

Taylor grunted and stepped aside. She lifted a brow at him and he said, "You already know you're going to talk to her."

"And you know this . . . how?"

"Because you came over here." He glanced toward the woman and then back at Dez. "You can't stand to see suffering. It's in your nature to try to ease it if you can. If you didn't think you could, you wouldn't have come over here."

"And it's not possible that I came over here to talk to you?"

His only response to that was a smirk.

Sighing, she looked back at the woman. Then she lifted a hand to the glass window, pressed her palm flat to it. "Her pain is enough to steal my breath away. I can't hear her thoughts well, but every now and then, even through my shields, I hear something—she keeps thinking how close she came to losing him. And then she keeps wondering what she did wrong, how he could have done something so awful."

"Do you blame her?"

"No." She looked at him. "I'm angry at that boy—so angry. But I've also felt his pain, his fear. And it would have been so easy for him to pretend ignorance, or try to stop me. To just keep hiding under the covers. He's trying . . . that's more than the other bastards will ever do, I guarantee you that."

She closed her eyes and squared her shoulders. Then, taking a deep breath, she opened the door and slipped inside.

ELEVEN

Talking to Mark's mom had been hard. By the time she was done, Dez's heart was battered and bruised. By comparison, going to Ivy's room felt a little easier. Like trying to juggle three chainsaws instead of four, perhaps.

Her parents were sitting at her bedside, there was hospital security at the door, and Dez was scrutinized within an inch of her life. Jeez, the rent-a-cop took his job seriously. But she was kind of happy to see it. At least she knew anybody else going inside that room would get the same hard once-over.

She hoped.

As the girl on the bed turned toward her, Dez summoned up a smile. It wasn't easy. Ivy still looked so battered and worn. But when she saw Dez, a tired smile lit her pretty face.

"Hi!"

Dez stopped at the foot of the bed. "Hey. You're looking better."

Ivy made a face. "No, I'm not. But I feel better. I get to go home tomorrow."

"That's good." She glanced at the woman on Ivy's left and gave her a polite smile. "Ma'am."

Dez looked back at Ivy. "Have you talked to the police?"

Terror turned the girl's eyes all but black. She cowered into the bed, clutching the blankets to her. "Nuh . . . no. I . . . I can't tell them anything. I don't remember . . ."

"Ma'am, we've already discussed this. Ivy doesn't *remember* enough to help. I don't know who you are, but I won't have you upsetting her—" This came from the big-ass guy sitting next to her. As he spoke, he came out of the chair, taking one step toward Dez.

Dez lifted a brow at him. *Sweetie, if you think that's going to do anything to intimidate me, you need to think it through a bit more.* "Upsetting her?" Dez said quietly.

"Yes, upsetting her. She didn't sleep—she *can't* sleep." The girl's mom glared at Dez, her eyes snapping.

"I can understand that." Dez looked away from the man, away from the woman, and focused on Ivy. "And if you can't remember, then there's not much you can do to help, I suppose."

Taking a chance, she lowered her shields. Things were so fucking weird here, anyway, she didn't know what she'd get from this girl. Not much . . . but enough. Ivy wasn't being completely honest. She didn't remember much of what happened *here*, but she knew something about who'd hurt her. Who had taken her. "Tell me something, Ivy. How well are you going to sleep knowing the boy who did this to you is still out there?"

Ivy whimpered, bringing her hands up to cover her face.

"Damn it, that's it, you get out of here." The man reached to grab Dez, and she stepped back.

"You don't want to do that," she warned.

"Joey . . ."

The soft, broken sob came from Ivy.

"Sweetie, it's okay, I'll get her out."

"No. You . . ." Ivy lifted her face to stare at Dez. "She's right. Oh, God, you're right . . ."

She started to sob. As her mother leaned over and wrapped her arms around her, she glared at Dez. "How can you upset her like this? You have no idea what happened to her!"

Ivy shoved her away. "Shut up, Mom! Yes, she does. Don't you know who she is? Oh, God. Lady, I'm so sorry."

"Ivy . . ." Dez sighed and rubbed her forehead. "Sweetheart, it's okay."

"No. No, it's not." She swallowed and eased away from her mom, batting away the hands that tried to hold her. She made her way to the edge of the bed and just sat there, her feet barely touching the floor. She looked so young, so scared.

Her eyes met Dez's, held them. "Mom. Joey . . . this is the woman who found me." She looked away from Dez to the man— Joey—and then back over her shoulder to her mom. "She saved my life. And I'm sorry if it upsets you, but you know what? She's right. I'm not going to sleep knowing that freak is out there."

"Oh, God." The woman stood up, lifting a hand to her mouth. "You . . ."

Dez hunched her shoulders up, tuning the mom out. She didn't want this, didn't need it. She moved forward and when Ivy lifted a hand, she caught it in hers. "Do you know who he is?"

"No." Ivy shook her head and tears glimmered in her eyes, so dark and soft.

Bambi eyes, Dez thought. Absently, she reached up and

brushed a strand of hair back from the girl's face. "Okay. Is it that you can't remember all of it?"

"I . . . I don't know." Ivy looked away and sighed. The tears slid free and she reached up, wiped them away. "I don't think I'm ready to talk about it yet, though. Can I . . . can I take some time? I'm supposed to come back down here. Talk to the cops in a few days. Can I talk then?"

"Nobody can make you talk at all," Dez said softly. "But if you really want peace, if you want to fight and take back what he took . . . your best bet will be to talk. But nobody can make you do it."

Ivy looked down, plucking at her gown. "I don't want to sleep because I hear his voice. I don't think it will stop, maybe not ever. But if I don't try . . ." She shook her head. "I think I want to talk." Then she nodded, slowly. "Yeah. I think I need to."

"Brave girl," Dez murmured. She pressed a gentle kiss to Ivy's forehead. "Brave girl."

"I'm not brave." Her breathing hitched in her chest. "I'm so scared. I think I'll always be scared."

"Baby, it's completely possible to be scared and brave at the same time. Being brave sometimes means doing what you're scared of." She chucked the girl under the chin. Then she reached into her pocket. With a mental wince, she realized she was running damn low on her cards. "Here. You ever want to talk, call me. Doesn't matter what it's about. But that's a personal number. Confidential and all. Just for you, not your folks, not the cops. Just you."

After one more smile for the girl, she turned and walked away. Out in the hallway, she heard the guy—a stepfather?—calling out to her. She ignored him. She had no desire to talk to him or to the girl's mom. Not anybody.

She just wanted her bed. Damn it, she was tired.

* * *

"You going to tell me what's going on?"

Taylor looked away from his study of the parking lot and found Blake studying him.

"Right now?" Taylor checked his watch and then looked back up at the cop. "Not much of anything, thank God."

Blake made a disgusted sound and flopped down into the chair across from Taylor, staring at him.

Taylor ignored him. He was waiting for Dez to leave. She'd disappeared some twenty minutes ago, to the fourth floor, where they'd moved Ivy. Taylor hadn't been at all surprised, and if he had her pegged right, she'd be down here in no time flat. She'd want to check on the girl, comfort her a bit, and then she'd beat a fast retreat.

The parents were already trying to get information on her, but Taylor had put out word to keep Dez's personal information just that—personal. It wouldn't have worked well elsewhere, but it was working here. So far.

Fortunately, Ivy's folks weren't from around here; otherwise they'd know all they had to do was loiter around town and make conversation with the locals. People there had already ferreted out her name. Not much else—yet. But soon they'd have more. He couldn't stop it.

"What's up with the Danvers kid?" Blake asked.

"Bike wreck." Taylor slanted a look at him. "Head injury and he's got a history of seizures. Ugly mix. What, you can't get that info yourself? And what's it to you, anyway?"

"Don't give me that shit." Blake slashed a hand through the air. "If it was just a damn wreck, that hot girlfriend of yours wouldn't be here."

The hair on the back of Taylor's neck rose.

Blake narrowed his eyes and leaned back, crossing his hands over his belly as he studied Taylor. "I did some nosing around last night—online, kept it nice and unofficial, although I wouldn't be surprised if the detectives have already run her background. The past year, her name's popped up in some very interesting ways."

"You can't believe everything you read online," Taylor drawled, shrugging. He knew, for a fact, that the stories online about Dez barely even touched the surface. Most of the things over the past year were minor. Of course, the *National Enquirer* could have a fucking field day with even the most minor stories, but they didn't even touch on what Dez was capable of, the miracles she'd accomplished.

Blake just grunted. "What's really weird is the fact that before this past year you can't find hardly even a mention of her anywhere. I know where she lives. Virginia." He paused and added, "Same as you."

"Several million people live in Virginia," Taylor pointed out.

"True." Blake leaned forward, elbows braced on his knees. "But several million people don't have a rep for being psychic, do they?"

Shit. Taylor met Blake's gaze. "You realize if you go around handing out stories like that, you'll get laughed off the police department, right? And, Blake? If you can't hold a job with the French Lick Police Department, you aren't going to find another police department willing to hire you, I don't think."

"Is that a threat?" Blake stared at him, his gaze flat. And rather unimpressed, Taylor thought.

"Just a comment—pointing out the obvious." He sighed and rubbed his hands over his face.

Blake snorted. "Do I look stupid to you? I don't plan on

spouting any sort of shit. Like you . . . I'm just pointing out what's obvious to me. Smoke follows fire and all that. Your girl? She's smoke. Which means, she's following fire."

"Fire?" Taylor stared at Blake.

"Yeah. Meaning Mark." He stood up and glanced down the hall. "He used to be a good kid. Maybe he still is, I don't know. But if she's hanging out here around him, well, my gut tells me there's trouble."

Taylor followed Blake's gaze and saw Dez as she cut down the hall—not toward him, but a different way.

"So. Is there trouble?"

Taylor sighed. "With Dez, there's almost always trouble. Doesn't mean it's the sort of trouble *you* are looking for."

* * *

IT was almost nightfall when Dez slipped out of the hospital. And she was walking to her car when she realized one small but crucial detail.

Stopping dead in the middle of the parking lot, she planted her hands on her hips and swore a blue streak. That didn't make her feel any better so she stormed over to her car and kicked the rear tire.

It was hard enough that she felt it even through the heavy black boots she wore, but it still didn't take the edge off her irritation. Sighing, she turned around and leaned against the car, staring off into the distance, watching as the sun continued to sink slowly below the tree line.

In another thirty minutes or so, it would be dark. In a few more hours, she'd be too tired to see straight.

And she didn't have a place to stay. Did she just go back to that dump on the side of the road where she'd stayed the other night?

Shit. Probably. Her back screamed even at the thought. But unless she wanted to sleep in her car . . .

Her skin prickled and although he didn't make a sound, she wasn't surprised when Taylor came to stand beside her. Clad in his sport coat and jeans, his face emotionless, his steel blue eyes unreadable, he leaned against the truck parked next to hers and studied her face.

"Where are you staying tonight?" he asked bluntly.

She resisted the urge to stick her tongue out at him.

"Why?" She sure as hell wasn't about to tell *him* that she didn't have a place to stay.

Taylor sighed and rubbed the back of his neck. "Damn it, Dez, can you ever just answer a damn question? You didn't have a lot of time to look around today. Did you book a hotel or what?"

Caught off guard by the sharp tone in his voice and the glint of temper she saw in his eyes, she actually let herself answer. "No."

A second later he tossed something at her. She barely caught it before it smacked her in the face. Scowling at the key she held, she shot him a dark look. "You know, my mother always taught me that throwing around objects with jagged edges could be dangerous."

"No, she didn't," Taylor replied. He reached into his pocket and pulled out a piece of paper. "That selfish bitch took off before she could teach you anything."

She sighed. "True."

He held out the piece of paper and, despite her aggravation, she took it. Opening it, she found a computer-generated map. According to the directions, the destination was about five minutes away.

"It's to a rental," he told her. "It's got the bare minimum in furnishings, but it will work for the short term."

Rubbing her thumb over the key's grooved edge, she frowned. "How much?" Like she was really going to be picky. But still. It was the principle, right? And she *did* need to be able to afford it.

"It's taken care of—all you need to do is get your ass over there and sleep, preferably before you collapse." Shoving off the truck, Taylor started to stalk away.

Oh, no.

She caught his arm. "Wait a second, slick. You're not my boss, remember?"

"According to that contract, I am. Short term. But the contract has nothing to do with the house—you need a place to stay while you're here. I'm familiar with the area and found you a place. It was more expedient." He glanced down at the key she held and then back up at her. "Would you rather sleep at some hole-in-the-wall hotel and spend the next three or four days trying to find appropriate accommodations and spend money you needn't spend? You can always go back to the dive where you slept the other night. Maybe you'll get lucky again and not get a room with bedbugs."

Gripping the key so tightly the edges bit into her hand, Dez glared at him. "Why do you have to be such a bastard?" she demanded.

"It comes naturally." He pulled his arm free and moved as if to walk away but, instead, he paused and reached up, touched her cheek.

Unless she was seriously mistaken, his face softened, and the steel of his eyes warmed. "Dez . . . go to the house. There's some food inside. Eat. Get some rest. You need it."

His gaze dropped to her mouth and her heart skittered in her chest, dancing around crazily. But he didn't kiss her. His hand fell away and he walked off, his sneakered feet silent on the paved parking lot.

Gripping the key and the map, she closed her eyes and counted to ten.

How come this bastard was still managing to drive her crazy? A year out of her life and he was *still* driving her crazy?

Except he wasn't exactly out of her life, now, was he?

And she hadn't been able to keep herself from dreaming about him, either. Thinking about him. Wanting him. Shit. No matter how hard she tried, he still dominated such a huge part of her life, even if it was just when she was trying *not* to let it be that way.

Sighing, she looked down at the key and the map, and then back up just in time to see him slip back into the hospital. Just in time to see him look back at her. Their gazes connected and time fell away. Her heart seemed to hitch inside her chest and she could hear the echo of it pounding in her ears, hear the roar of blood.

Swallowing, she found herself wanting to drop the key, the map . . . everything. And just go to him.

But she'd tried that before. And even though it had been amazing, he'd pushed her away, pushed her so far, in the end, he'd pushed her completely out. There was still a hole inside her over that.

Sighing, she tore her eyes from him and turned to her car.

Why in the hell had she gone and fallen for somebody like him anyway?

* * *

THE rental house was a far right turn from what she'd been expecting. Quaint and quiet, it looked like a little storybook house built of stone, complete with a sloping roof and a door made of gleaming oak, and when she let herself inside, the scent of herbs and potpourri danced lightly in the air.

Hell.

Why couldn't the place smell of mold and cat urine and dog shit?

It would have been a lot easier on her mental balance if she could have found a reason to be mad at him about finding her a place. A lousy place, a miserable place, a dirty place . . . any of those things would have given her a reason to be irritated.

But he'd found her a fairy-tale cottage.

Her heart melted a little and she pushed off the doorjamb, pausing long enough to lock it and check the security system. He'd made notes about the password and she set it before moving inside and studying the little place.

He'd been right about the furniture—there wasn't much. But what there was—if she wasn't mistaken, it was new. The couch and the chair in the living room were new. The two-seater table in the kitchen looked pretty damn new. Up the narrow, twisty little staircase, she inspected the bed and it looked new as well.

Sighing, she sat on the edge of the bed and rubbed her hands over her face. "You make it so damn hard to be irritated with you, Taylor," she groused.

At least he made it hard for *her* to be irritated with him.

Everybody else didn't seem to have a problem at all getting irritated, staying irritated. Everybody else could tell the bastard to take a flying leap. Dez, though, she wanted to be the one to take the flying leap—right square at him. Take a leap and never let him go. Unless it was to strangle him when he did stupid shit that involved pushing her away.

He cared about her. She knew he did. Hell, if he *didn't*, he wouldn't be so intent on pushing her away. He'd probably be just fine with fucking her until he was bored with her. "At least I'd have something then," she muttered. Brooding, she lay on the bed and snagged the edge of the quilt, pulling it up over her body.

She knew she should go downstairs and eat, knew she should get undressed and shower.

But she was so tired, she ached. And the exhaustion pulled at her, dragging her under. Even as she slipped closer to dreams, she was dimly aware of how cold the room had gotten.

By then, though, she was already too far gone.

And when she opened her eyes, she was no longer alone.

She'd connected with the departed in her dreams before. It wasn't often. But sometimes it seemed they could reach her better when she slept. Maybe her shields were just too solid when she was awake.

Maybe she was more receptive in her dreams.

She didn't know.

She just knew she was dreaming . . . and she knew the girl in front of her was no longer alive. Something about the style of her clothes, the cut of her hair made her think it had been a few years since this girl's death.

Forcing herself to smile, she sat up and met the girl's blue eyes.

She looked like she would have in life—not the pale, washed-out reflection of most ghosts, but normal. Blonde hair, so pale it was almost silvery. Big blue eyes. And when she smiled, Dez imagined she'd have dimples. She stared at Dez solemnly, her face sad.

"Hi, there," Dez said quietly.

The girl just stared.

Dez sighed and leaned forward, resting her elbows on her knees. Jeez, if she was going to show up in her dreams, couldn't the girl at least talk to her? If not, then she'd rather have hot and nasty dreams about Taylor. At least then she could get off. But she kept the frustration hidden and just gave the girl another reassuring smile. "You can talk to me, you know. I can hear you. And I'll try to help. But I can't until you start talking to me."

The girl looked down. "I . . . I'm not supposed to talk to people I don't know."

"Well, then. I guess we should fix that. I'm Dez. What's your name?"

"Dez . . ." The girl frowned. "I'm . . ." Her frown deepened and she shook her head. "I don't remember."

She started to cry. Dez came off the bed and, instinctively, she went to hug the girl, but even as she drew close, the girl's seemingly solid form wavered and fell apart. She wasn't solid enough to touch. "Sweetheart, it's okay. You'll remember sooner or later."

She hoped. How awful it was not to remember even *that*.

The girl just shook her head and continued to cry. And as Dez watched, she faded away completely.

In the very next breath, Dez woke up. But the lingering cold told her she wasn't entirely alone. Drawing her knees to her chest, she grabbed the blanket and wrapped it around herself, staring into the room. She hadn't turned off the lights, but she wished she had.

Ghosts might not care about light or the lack of it, but a dim room would have made it easier to tell if there was somebody trying to manifest. This one was weak. Very weak.

Closing her eyes, Dez lowered her shields. That faint echo—just a prickle along her senses—remained. The ghost was either *there* or trying to be.

Dez didn't know for sure which one it was.

She closed her eyes and eased her shields down, careful not to do anything else, not yet.

"Hello?" she called out, keeping her voice easy and soft.

There was no answer. Huffing out a breath, she slid out from under the blanket and stood up, glancing around. She looked down and realized she hadn't even taken her coat off. She slipped out of it and draped it over the foot of the bed.

"You know, I can tell you want to talk. You wouldn't be coming around me if you didn't," she said conversationally. She unzipped one boot, then the other, slipping out of them and leaving them on the floor. "So why don't we talk?"

There was a warbling little breath of a sound. Almost a sigh. Almost a whisper. But nothing else.

"What is it you want to tell me, sweetie? I can't do much for you until I know what you need." Staring into nothing, she waited. Still nothing.

And that lingering echo faded, leaving her alone.

"Damn it." Dez rubbed a hand over the back of her neck, staring at the floor. That hadn't exactly gone as planned.

But then again, *nothing* here had gone as planned. Tristan hadn't been what she'd expected, discovering Ivy hadn't been what she'd expected . . . and she didn't even want to *think* about the complications with Taylor. Now she was dealing with a shy little ghost who only seemed to creep out while she slept.

"Hell, this is going to be a pain in the ass."

TWELVE

IT was time . . .

The flowers were gathered. Yellow flowers for the lovely angel. Pretty and perfect.

The tears threatened. But there was time for tears later. Tears mustn't mar their day together, after all. Later. After their special day. They'd be together all day—a day of joy. After that, there would be time for tears.

* * *

"HI, sweetheart."

Taylor's phone had been silent that morning. So far. Still, he woke early and made his sojourn to the cemetery where Anna rested along with his parents. The daisies, bright and cheerful, wouldn't last long, but they were her favorite. She'd get nothing else from him.

Sitting by her monument, he stared down at the ground.

He'd spent too many days like this. Holding vigil at the foot of the marble angel and wondering. Wondering, yet dreading what would happen if he ever found out. Would it break him, knowing what happened?

She was gone, he knew. He knew it in his soul.

Maybe that was why he'd never brought anybody out here. Wasn't like he couldn't. Wasn't like he didn't have the resources. Hell, he had somebody here now . . .

His gut wrenched. No. Just—no.

Still, with a hand that shook, he reached into his pocket and pulled out that golden chain. Stared at it.

There was a reason Dez was here. Why she was *still* here—in this town. Deep inside, in a place he didn't want to look at, he was starting to suspect those connections were a lot more complicated than he wanted to think about.

But he wasn't going to look at any of that just yet. Not today. Definitely not today.

* * *

"WHERE in the hell are all the kids coming from?" Dez stared grouchily at the crowded Denny's and wished she'd thought to stock up on coffee for the house. Although she wasn't quite sure where to buy groceries. Would she be here long enough?

"No school today." The waitress smiled, but it looked strained. "Fall break. They were off Friday and today. Plus"—she grimaced— "they'll be off tomorrow, too, it looks like. The school board thought it would be good to have a day off, but offer counseling for those who needed it." She sighed and glanced around, her eyes lingering on one table where a couple of teenage girls leaned against each other. "They've had a rough few months, these kids. Rough few months."

Dez was silent as the lady wandered off. Bending over her coffee, she brooded. Canceling school—was that the smartest thing? Letting those responsible for this out for more trouble, it seemed like. At least in her opinion.

But maybe they'd be smart, maybe they'd realize how obvious they were getting. Maybe they'd stop and nobody else would get hurt. And maybe pigs would fly, she thought. Too much arrogance here. Arrogant people rarely thought they'd get caught.

Which meant she had more work to do—she had to do whatever she needed to do to make all of this stop. She had to do it for Tristan. For Ivy. And now for Mark, as well.

* * *

"HAVE another drink, man." It was finally getting late enough to make this work. All fucking *day*, Brendan had waited. At least out here they didn't have to worry about trick-or-treaters. *Nobody* lived on this stretch of road but Beau and his folks.

Careful to keep the other guy from touching him, he pushed the bottle into Beau's hand. The gloves were as thin and close to flesh-colored as he could find, but they didn't feel like skin.

"Shit, already gonna be sick," Beau grumbled. "What the fuck went wrong, man?" He grabbed the bottle and lifted it to his lips, missed, and spilled half of it down the front of his shirt, adding to the stink in the car.

They were in the garage with the door closed, the engine off, although it wouldn't stay that way, not if Brendan got Beau drunk enough. The bastard was just too fucking erratic. You couldn't trust somebody who went and did that kind of crazy shit. Hell, if Mark died, they were all screwed. *All* of them, because everybody who knew Mark would be looked at closely.

That was why Brendan was taking steps now. Kyle would back

him up, he knew. And Kyle could lie with the best of them, could do it under stress, too. He'd head over to Kyle's in a little while, crash there. He already had the groundwork laid. His eye throbbed like a bitch and Beau's right fist was swollen. It had taken some doing to get the drunken idiot pissed off enough to take a swing, but he'd managed. They'd had a good day, though, hanging out in town, messing with each other, flirting—Brendan knew how to make sure Beau stayed in a good mood, and that was what he'd done.

Right up until it was time to get Beau in a bad mood, in a scared one—a worried one. The kind of mood that would make the boy want to grab a bottle.

And that was just what he was doing now.

When he was asked, Brendan would say Beau had been in one of his moods—they'd both been worried about Mark and, besides, they'd gotten into fights before. He'd say he'd gotten out halfway between their houses and hoofed it over to Kyle's. Nobody would ever know.

Everything would be cool. Whether Mark died or not. Because Beau wasn't going to be around to screw things up. And even if Mark lived—once he realized the shit he could be in, he'd straighten the hell up. Otherwise, Brendan would find a way to finish the job Beau had fucking failed to.

"Who the fuck is that crazy bitch, anyway?" Beau asked, his voice slurred and heavy. He looked at Brendan, his eyes glazed. "How'd she fucking know? She did *know*, right? How did she know?"

"Beats me." Brendan studied the bottle of Jack Daniel's he held—it was only about a little over a third empty and he hadn't had much more than a mouthful. Beau was a big guy, though, and he liked to party. He could drink. All Brendan needed was for him to drink himself unconscious, though. That was all he needed. "Hey. Quit bitching and just have a drink. We're supposed to be forgetting about all this shit, right?" He pretended to take a swig and passed the bottle back to Beau yet again, watched as Beau eyed the bottle and sighed morosely.

"Maybe somebody told her . . ."

Narrowing his eyes, Brendan shrugged mentally. "Maybe so. Shit, then we're *fucked*. What in the hell is going to happen? Man, you . . . your scholarship. Could you lose it?"

Beau's face paled and he upended the bottle, drinking long and hard. "Fuck that pansy Mark—had to be him. Should have just ran his ass clear over."

"Yeah. You know it was him."

Another drink. And this time, if Brendan hadn't caught the bottle, Beau would have dropped it.

"Fuck. What do we do, man? Don't wanna go t'jail," Beau mumbled. Then he closed his eyes and leaned his head back against the headrest. "Shoulda listened to Tristan, y'know. Shoulda. He said this was fuckin' nuts. Was right . . ."

As Beau slipped into unconsciousness, Brendan narrowed his eyes, resisted the urge to brain the bastard with the bottle. Fucking Tristan—all these assholes, still talking about him.

But he didn't do what he wanted—he just watched. He just waited.

And once he was certain Beau wasn't going to wake up, he lodged the bottle between Beau's legs then turned the keys in the ignition, left the window cracked. He hadn't been the one to swipe the bottle earlier—that had been Beau's handiwork. It had come from Beau's daddy's liquor cabinet and he'd even probably admit that . . . later.

He didn't wipe the car down, either. Didn't want it *too* clean. The rest of them thought he didn't pay attention, but he did. He was in and out of Beau's Mustang too often and knew if it was *too* clean, well, that would look weird, right?

So he left it. And he took his clothes. He'd slip out the back. Shutting the door tight, with the Mustang running, he left the house. Beau's folks were out—they'd be out at the casino partying for hours. Or out with their "friends." Shit. Friends. Beau's parents were into swinging—everybody knew it, they just pretended not to.

By the time they got home, Beau would be dead. Carbon monoxide poisoning—it was a bitch, and classic cars still weren't quite as good at eliminating that carbon monoxide—a handy little fact Brendan had researched a while back. It would all look like an accident. Wasn't like Beau hadn't gotten in trouble for drinking before. He'd even passed out in his car before. A fact that was known by more than a few people, since he'd done it in the school parking lot—fucking moron.

He could already hear all the crap. Everybody would talk about what a shame it was, such a terrible waste, a horrible accident. And if only his folks had been home. Brendan smirked, pleased with himself. He'd wait about fifteen minutes, make sure.

Out on the side, in the shadows, of course. Beau, like Brendan, lived outside of town on one of the bigger pieces of land. There was some privacy out here, so he could hide himself just fine. Well enough to make sure nobody showed up in time to save Beau.

* * *

TIFFANY Haler didn't know why in the hell she was there. Wasn't like she *gave* a fucking crap about Beau Donnelly.

Fucking asshole. Maybe *that* was why she was here. She'd heard about what happened to Mark Danvers and it made her belly hurt. She liked Mark, even if he did hang around with these losers. She'd always liked him. She wouldn't be surprised at all if

Beau had something to do with what happened to Mark. He was mean enough. Mean as a snake. Mean as a dog who'd been trained to do nothing but rip out another dog's throat.

Nibbling on her nail, leaning against her moped, she tried to decide if she wanted to go to the door of the house. Big, brightly lit, so pretty in the night. Not like her house . . . not anymore. Her mom stayed in her room and either cried or read. Her dad locked himself in his garage. And they both forgot about her. It was always dark, always cold.

At *her* house, the lights were rarely on.

Her mom rarely spoke. Her dad looked like he'd aged twenty years. Everybody was sad. Everybody was broken. All because of . . .

Unable to look at that brightly lit house, a place that looked like it *screamed* welcome, she looked away, staring into the darkness.

Something shifted in the dark. If she hadn't been staring *just there*, she never would have seen it. Never. But she was looking, and she saw the boy walking away—saw him stop and wait in the darkness. Like her. Staring at the house.

Just like her.

She reached for her phone, not daring to do anything until she saw the shadowy figure turn away and disappear into the night. Each minute seemed to be a lifetime, but she figured it was probably only five or ten minutes. She should wait longer, make sure he didn't come back.

But somehow, she didn't think she could. Somehow, she suspected there wasn't any more time to wait.

Swallowing, she fished out the card Desiree Lincoln had given her and punched in the number as she started across the street. As she drew closer, she thought she heard a faint roar. Faint . . . but pretty damn familiar, and as she got closer, she knew exactly what that sound was.

"Oh, shit . . ." Her gut clenched. Curled.

As a sleepy voice came on the line, she started to run.

* * *

PLEASED with himself, Brendan cut across Meyer's Field.

There wasn't a Meyer around, hadn't been for years. But the field was still called Meyer's Field. He kept to the fence, along the line of the side where the trees ran thick, not wanting to risk being seen, although shit, who the fuck was out—

He saw the outline of somebody out there, then. If the moon hadn't been full, shining down in just the right way, he might not have seen it. It *was* a person, right? He didn't think there was a scarecrow or anything out there. What the hell? Standing so still, staring down. Staring at what?

No. It was a person.

In the middle of the field, so fucking late—

What the hell?

Hissing out a breath, Brendan went still and continued to stare, creeping along, barely daring to move, barely daring to breathe. He was quiet—couldn't be seen now.

Damn it, what the hell was it with people fucking up his plans?

* * *

"IF the boy interrupts us, I'll be so unhappy."

There was just the faintest crunch of twigs breaking. Fainter, getting fainter. Leaving them, the boy was leaving. Good.

Their time together shouldn't be interrupted.

"We don't have much time together, do we? My pretty little angel." The flowers were already spread out, an offering. "I hope you like them. It wasn't as easy to get them as I'd hoped. Not the perfect ones I wanted for you, at least."

Perfect, everything for the angel must be perfect. Perfect for their day together. The only time they had together, every year. The day was almost done and then it would be a year—*no*.

It shouldn't have happened this way. "My angel . . . my one and only. Damn it."

There was a sob, harsh and ugly. She'd threatened to tell. *Why* had she done that? Didn't she know? Hadn't she understood?

It shouldn't have happened this way. It hadn't been meant to happen this way. Anger, guilt, grief, and longing—they were a poisonous mix. "You were so sweet and lovely. I want you back."

Tears fell and were ignored.

"I miss my angel."

* * *

DEZ jerked on her wrinkled clothes, the phone wedged against her shoulder. It rang and rang—four rings for Taylor Jones was a hell of a lot of rings. When he finally answered, he sounded a lot more awake than she felt.

"We need to get out to Beau Donnelly's house. And I've no clue where it is. Can you come get me?" she said.

"Yes. Why?"

"Weird phone call. Hell, *everything* about this town is weird. Is there something in the water, or what? I don't know if it's anything, but my gut says something's wrong."

"I'll be there in ten minutes."

Dez was dressed in another minute and spent the next five minutes curled over a cup of nuked instant coffee, shuddering at the taste of it. Spying the cabinet, she opened it and saw granola bars and cereal. Yeah, Taylor had stocked it with basics. Healthy basics. Typical. But she wasn't going to be picky. She grabbed a granola bar and tore it open, eating half of it in one huge bite.

She shoved another one in her pocket. She couldn't keep going on steam and nothing else. Well, steam and caffeine.

She saw the flare of headlights and headed toward the front door, coffee in hand. Whatever they had to deal with, she'd need more caffeine to do it. She was outside, shivering in the cold night air, by the time he'd stopped in her driveway. Climbing into Taylor's car, she shot him a narrow look. "You look ridiculously awake for one in the morning," she muttered.

"You rely on caffeine too much," he replied. "What's with this phone call?"

"I don't know." She glanced down at her phone as if it would tell her more than it already had. "We're going to Asher Road. I did a Google search."

"I know where it is. Tell me about the call."

"You know where it is," she echoed, rubbing her brow. "Of course you know where it is. It was Tristan's sister. I met her the other day. Talked to her briefly. Gave her my card. I didn't really expect her to call me and then she does, roughly fifteen minutes ago, and she's babbling about some shadow she saw and how this boy Beau is in trouble."

"Did she call the cops?"

"I told her to." Dez rubbed her temple. "But she hung up on me."

"Did *you* call them?"

Dez shot him a sour look. "I did better. I called the FBI."

Taylor sighed and grabbed his phone from the console. Closing her eyes, she leaned her head against the back of the seat and hoped she hadn't made a mistake in not calling the police right away.

It took only five minutes to get to the house, but those five minutes were an eternity.

* * *

THE second Dez promised she was on her way, Tiffany disconnected, ignoring anything else the woman had to say. All she
could think about, all she could hear was the rumble of Beau's
Mustang. That gleaming, vintage Mustang. Inside the garage. The
closed garage.

A moan lodged in her throat as she peered through the filmy
curtain and stared inside. She was pretty sure she could see Beau
in there, inside the car. Unmoving.

Tiffany's dad tinkered with cars. He liked them. A lot. Once
upon a time, Tiffany had even worked with him on some of the
cars he'd bought to restore and sell. Older cars, they didn't have
that nifty exhaust system that eliminated most of the carbon monoxide. Plus, she knew that even *newer* cars could eventually put
off enough of the noxious gas to kill a person—it had happened in
California back around Christmastime a year or two earlier.

He was sitting in there, in that silent, deadly poison. Swallowing, she slipped her bag off her shoulder and then checked the
ground. There were flowerbeds and she'd have to trample the flowers. But if she could bust through wood at karate class, she could
break glass, right?

She did a practice kick first, felt the glass give a little under
the heavy, weighted toe of her boot. Damn, she was glad those
things went almost all the way to her knees. Then she whispered,
"This is something you'd do, Tristan. Asshole or not." Gritting
her teeth, she set her stance and then struck, driving into the
window with all the force she had.

Glass shattered.

She used her bag to knock as much of it out of the way as she
could before she climbed in. Pulling the neck of her shirt up over

her mouth, refusing to breathe, she ran to the door and hit the button to lift the garage door. As it started to lift, she saw the lights
pull into the drive.

She wanted to cry in relief. But she could see Beau. And he
wasn't moving.

*   *   *

"Is he going to make it?" Dez asked quietly, gripping Tiffany's
hand. Her mother sat next to her, her face pale, dazed. But there
was a glint of pride in her eyes as she stroked a hand down her
daughter's hair. Pride. Love.

Taylor stood in the door, his face troubled. He glanced back-
ward and then at her. "I don't know. The carbon monoxide levels
must have been pretty high. Any chance he has, it's because he
was rescued when he was." He looked at Tiffany and gave her a
rare smile. "Any chance he has is because of you, Miss Haler."

Tiffany fidgeted. "I shouldn't have waited. I knew something
was wrong," she whispered. "But I was scared."

"You were scared, but you still did something," Dez said.
"That's more than a lot of people would have done."

Her mother leaned over and hugged her. "You gave him a
chance, at least, sweetheart. I'm so proud of you." She sighed and
added, "Proud enough that I'm not even going to ask you about
sneaking out right now."

"But we're going to ask," her father said flatly. "Later."

The girl shot him a quick glance and then looked down. "Yes, sir."

"I need to speak with my boss, sweetheart." Dez squeezed
Tiffany's hand again. "But I'll come back by, make sure you're
okay. If I hear anything, I'll let you know."

Tiffany nodded. "Thank you for coming when I called," she
whispered.

"Thank you for calling me." Dez gave her a crooked grin and then stood up, her tired, aching body screaming in protest. She rubbed her gritty eyes and headed toward Taylor. She knew him too well not to hear everything he hadn't said.

"So. Two teenage boys in this hospital. Both of them worked at the hotel where Ivy was found. Coincidence?" She didn't bother mentioning Tristan just yet. Falling into step next to him, she shoved her hands into her pockets.

"I'm not much for coincidences. You?"

"Nope. What in the hell is going on?"

"That's what we're going to find out, I suppose." He sighed and rubbed his neck. "Whether we're here officially or not. Have you been to see Mark?"

She shrugged. "I peeked in. The cop on his door is taking the job seriously. His mom said the seizures aren't easing up."

"They probably won't until the withdrawal wears off. Stressing his body too much."

Dez sighed. "That poor kid."

Taylor just grunted.

"We going anywhere in particular?" She glanced at him, walking along at his side and wondering why.

"Yeah." He slid her a narrow look. "To figure out what in the hell is going on, since *you* keep getting dragged into this."

"Well. You could just leave me to swing. But you insisted I sign that damn contract. So . . . what's up?"

"That damn contract is keeping your head in one piece," he reminded her. "As to what's up . . . Hard to say but it looks like somebody else besides Tiffany was out there tonight—last night. Area where somebody might have been watching the house for a few minutes. So far the car is showing a number of fingerprints, but nothing on the bottle but the boy's, the dad's, and a partial from a third person—my gut says that's probably from the store, though. If he had anybody in the car with him, they either didn't touch the bottle or they gloved up."

"Smart," Dez murmured.

"Yes." Taylor glanced at her. "He has a history of getting in trouble. Drinking. Fighting. This isn't a surprise to anybody around here. There are some abrasions, swelling on his right hand, looks like he popped somebody tonight."

"How many buddies did he have in that little group of his?"

"Six, originally. But with Tristan gone, it's down to five. Now it's down to three with Mark and Donnelly here. The other two, a Keith Sutter and Lee Grogan, aren't as intrinsic to the group, from what I've heard, but we need to speak with them."

"We?" she echoed.

He stopped now and turned, facing her.

Sighing, she turned and met his eyes.

"You're involved in this whether you want to admit it or not. The girl called you. Without the two of you, that boy would be dead. Hell, we're *still* trying to locate his parents . . ." His voice trailed off and he shook his head. "They looked closer around the grounds because Tiffany said she saw somebody. That's why they looked. If they'd just come over to answer a 911 call, they might have taken things as they appeared. A stupid boy doing a stupid thing. Assuming there's more to this, if any justice is found, it will be because of you—because you established a connection with that girl and gave her somebody she could trust. Like it or not, you're in this up to your butt, Lincoln."

"Why don't you kiss my butt?" she muttered, turning on her heel and storming down the hall.

Yeah, she was involved. But she damn well didn't *like* it.

Taylor caught up with her at the coffee machine. As she

plugged quarters in, he said, "That stuff is going to eat away at your stomach lining and you know it."

"You say the sweetest things, Jones." She sighed and rested a hand over her heart. "Is it any wonder I went to my back for you the minute I had you alone in my house?"

Hearing an odd, strangled sound from him, she shot him a look from the corner of her eye. His tanned cheekbones had harsh red flags of color to them—but he wasn't blushing. No, it was more than that. He looked . . . ravenous. Yeah. That was it. The steely blue of his eyes had a hard, hungry glint to it. It was enough to make her heart race, but she'd be damned if she showed it. Still, it made her feel a little better. He wasn't immune to her, even now. No more than she was immune to him.

Good.

"What's the matter, Jones?" she asked, forgetting about the coffee and taking a step closer to him. "Cat got your tongue?"

"Damn it, Dez," he growled.

Blinking at him, she whispered, "Is that all you got, Jones?"

"Why are you doing this?" He tore his eyes away from her, staring past her shoulder as though the secrets of the universe and the mess they had on their hands were written on the wall in disappearing ink and he had only moments to memorize it all. "Don't we have enough to deal with without this crap?"

"This . . . crap?" she mocked. "Is this crap?"

Sidling closer, she breathed in his scent, wished she could just lean in against him and let him take away every problem in the world. Wished he would *want* to.

"This crap," she repeated. "You want me. You care for me. I want you. I care for you. And once this job is done, we don't work together anymore. So why is it crap? Why is this such a problem for you?"

Tilting her head back, she stared at him, into those steely blue eyes that held so many secrets.

But he had no answer for her. Sighing, she turned away, staring at the coffee machine again. But she didn't need the caffeine now. She was wide awake. Wide awake and miserable.

He had a point, she supposed. They had enough on their hands and she didn't need to be stirring up her old heartbreaks on top of it. She just couldn't help herself. Not where he was concerned.

Tired of it, tired of the pain that came along with him, she walked away from the coffee machine. She needed to be away from him for a while. From all of this.

When this is over, I want to go to Tahiti. For a month. Someplace warm and sunny. And if she was lucky, she could find a deserted strip of beach where no ghosts would linger, where she could be alone inside her head.

Not that she would.

She'd find another lost soul, another one of the departed, another ghost. Somebody who'd pull her into a mess and have her give everything she had. And then another and another.

Until eventually, there was nothing left of her to give. Until she wasn't much more than a shell . . . just like them. She might still be alive, but she was turning into a ghost herself, she suspected.

* * *

WATCHING her walk down the hall, her head down, shoulders slumped, Taylor stared at her. She looked so tired. He reached into his pocket, touched the necklace as he stared at her retreating back. Then he groaned and looked back at the machine and considered the poison it spitted out as a poor excuse for coffee.

She never used to drink that much coffee. She'd lost weight, too.

Just leave her alone, he told himself.

But he didn't. He got the coffee, but laced it liberally with cream and sugar, hoping maybe they would provide a buffer to keep the coffee from eating at her stomach lining. Then he fed a couple of dollars into the various vending machines. He knew Dez. She liked her sweets. She could get a Hershey bar. If she ate a damn apple first.

She needed several hours horizontal, not that he expected she'd take them here. Probably better off if she didn't. But she could damn well get some food in her belly and she could sit down, stop pacing, and try to relax. He'd see to it. Assuming he could find wherever she'd disappeared to.

It wasn't that hard to find her, in the end. It seemed he could always find her. She was tucked away inside the small chapel, her knees drawn to her chest, her eyes locked on the cross hanging above the dais. "Leave me alone, Jones," she said quietly. "I don't want to talk to you."

"Then don't talk." He held out the candy bar.

Her gaze locked on it the way a shark might stare at a seal, he supposed. With hungry, intent focus. But when she reached for it, he pulled it back. "Eat this first," he said shortly, pushing the apple at her.

She glared at him. "I don't want a damn apple."

"You're swearing in church," he said mildly.

"And you're teasing a woman over chocolate. Both are probably akin to tempting fate." Then she made a face and glanced toward the front of the church. "Sorry," she mumbled.

He smiled as he realized she was blushing. "Eat the apple, Dez. Then you can have the chocolate."

She groaned and then reached out, snatching the apple from him. She crunched down. After she'd swallowed the first bite, she said, "You know, we're not supposed to eat in here."

"What are they going to do, arrest us? And somehow, I don't

think Jesus cares if you eat in here. Isn't there a passage in the Bible that says 'Feed my sheep'?"

"I'm not a sheep." Sighing, she just took another bite. "Besides, I don't see why you care if I eat or not. Haven't we already established we're not . . . whatever?"

"Do we need to be . . . whatever for me to care whether or not you're eating? Whether you're sleeping?" He curled a hand over the back of her neck, stroking his thumb over the sensitive skin under her ear. "You don't sleep much, or you haven't lately, at least. I can tell. And you're losing weight. When's the last time you took a break, Desiree?"

With a brittle smile, she said, "Three weeks ago. Before I took a case in Arkansas. I was going to take one after that case but this one came too hard." She took another bite and then, in a singsong voice, added, "Too bad, so sad."

"And how long was that break?" Three weeks wouldn't have her looking this drawn. While he didn't do it if he could avoid it, he'd had her work cases close together before. They'd never worn on her this hard.

She swallowed and lowered the apple. Her head dipped and she sighed. "Just a weekend." Abruptly, she slammed the apple into his lap and stood up. "If you want me to eat, you'd be better off saving the interrogation until I'm done, you know."

"Okay. A weekend. And before that?"

She paced in front of him, her hands tucked in the back pockets of her jeans. But she didn't answer him. Putting the half-eaten apple aside, he stood up and went to her, catching her arm. "How *long*, Dez?" he demanded.

She glared at him. "Four months. The last few cases ran together on me and it took four months to get everything wrapped up and done. Okay? It's been almost five months since I've gone more than a couple of days without having ghosts whisper to me. I had a week. Before that? The jobs would last a few weeks, maybe a month. I'd have three or four days of peace before they started again. But it's nonstop. Ever since I walked. I get no peace; I get no rest. It's worse than it was before I came to you. Are you happy?"

Fury punched through him but he shoved it down, lashed it under control. Fury wouldn't help her—it would just feed the wild desperation he could see in her eyes.

Staring into her tormented, tired gaze, he reached up and cupped her cheek. "Happy?" He stroked his thumb over her lip.

"Yeah." She jerked back from him and stalked away, like she couldn't bear to have him touching her. "Are you happy? I couldn't take going those three months of leave without helping— I *know* I couldn't. It would have driven me crazy."

She glared at him, rage all but vibrating off of her. "*You* know it, too, and don't deny it."

"Okay." He closed his hands into fists, resisted the urge to reach for her. It was something he'd forced himself to admit over the past year. Too long—it had been too long, and he never should have touched her and forced himself into that position.

She sneered at him. "Okay? *Okay?* You stand there and say *okay?* You push me out and now you say *okay?*"

"I didn't *push* you out," he snapped. "You *walked*." And he'd wanted to come after her, every damn day. If he'd known she was suffering like that, he would have, too. But he'd thought she'd be better off . . . happier.

"I walked because you didn't give me a *choice*." She glared at him. "And now you get to stand there and smile in that lofty, superior way of yours, because—guess what? I might not have gone crazy this way, but I sure as hell am working myself into an early grave."

She pressed a hand to her belly and smiled at him, a brittle, empty smile. "So either way, I was screwed. I was destined either to lose my mind or to work myself into the ground. You're right—I'm no better off leaving than I was staying. Either I'm sick in the head or sick physically. Neither one is much fun."

She shoved past him, leaving him alone in the small, quiet chapel.

He lingered, waiting. Watching. Wanting so desperately to go after her. And once more, he found himself pulling that necklace out of his pocket. Closing his eyes, he thought back, remembering all those months ago when he'd wanted to go after her.

He hadn't. And she'd suffered. All this time, she'd suffered and it was his fault.

He'd thought he was doing the right thing—for both of them. Even if it wasn't what he *wanted*, it seemed like the right thing. Letting her go, when all he'd wanted was for her to stay.

Closing his eyes, he whispered, "Damn it, I don't know what to do . . ."

Then he opened his eyes and found his gaze locked on the warm, gentle glow of the cross on the wall. He knew what he *wanted* to do—it was what he'd wanted then. But it wasn't that simple. It was never that simple . . .

Why not?

It sounded like something Dez would say. Why wasn't it that simple? She didn't work for him now. That issue was solved. Sucking in a deep, desperate breath, he lifted his hands to his face, wondered what he should do.

For once, damn it, for once, I want to do what I want—what I need . . .

He looked down at the necklace he held. Then, before he could talk himself out of it, he turned and took off after her.

Hell, could he possibly make things any worse than they already were? For either of them?

* * *

THE parking lot was empty. But it didn't take long to spot her. She was storming down the sidewalk leading away from the hospital. It was roughly five miles to the house and it looked like she was going to walk it.

In the dead of night.

Shit.

Say something, he thought. *Stop her, damn it.* His mind was a raw, ragged wound and today, of all days—shit, today, yesterday, it was the worst possible time for him to be trying to think of something *coherent* to say to anybody. Especially the person who mattered to him the most. Dez.

But he had to say something. He just didn't know what. Didn't know what to think. His mind went blank. Words, the easy glib lines he could always hand out whenever he needed to do whatever he needed to do—they failed him. He needed to talk, needed to say *something*, but he couldn't.

He had to do something, though, and he had to do it fast, because if he let her leave this time, he wasn't going to have a chance in hell of getting her. Keeping her. And he was finally starting to realize that was exactly what he needed to do—what he wanted, what he absolutely must have.

Otherwise, he was going to turn into one of those shadows that haunted her. Maybe a living, breathing one, but everything that made him live would be gone. *Dez* made him live, damn it. He'd been dead the past year.

Fuck.

Jogging to catch up with her, he caught her arm. "Dez . . ."

He swallowed as she stopped in her tracks. "Get away from me," she whispered, her voice low and raw.

"You can't leave," he said. He jerked his hand back and shoved it in his pocket.

"Why the hell not?"

Without anything else to say, he latched onto the one constant he'd always had in his life. "We have to go back out to the kid's house. You're the only one who has any possible chance of maybe connecting to the one who did this, and if we wait much longer, even that chance is gone."

"Oh, for fuck's sake." She turned around and stared at him, her eyes wide with disbelief. "You want *me* to play bloodhound? Hello, have you forgotten? I'm the one who talks to ghosts, remember? I'm not the bloodhound. I talk to dead people."

"You're still psychic. You pick up on lingering emotions and in case you haven't noticed, you're picking up a hell of a lot since you've been here. If you expect me to think that somebody can try to kill and not leave a trace for you to pick up on, then you must think I'm past stupid," he said. He didn't entirely believe that line, but he didn't disbelieve it, either. Dez underestimated her abilities. She always had. And whether anything came of it or not, he'd have another hour or two to figure out what to say to her, how to fix the damage he'd done to them.

All before he'd even realized he wanted to take a chance at *being* a "them."

Fuck. Maybe he *was* past stupid.

Dez continued to stare at him, her eyes suspicious. He held her gaze, refusing to look away. She finally swore and broke the stare. He held out a hand and said, "Truce?"

She shot him a dirty look.

"Like hell. Let's get this over with so I can get the hell away from you."

THIRTEEN

Dez ignored the man next to her.

She wasn't up to anything else just then. Bad enough that she was in the car with him, bad enough that she knew she couldn't get away from him yet, get away from this town . . . she wasn't ready to look at him or think about anything remotely personal. So she ignored him. She'd stripped herself bare—*again*—and it had gotten her nothing.

Not that she'd expected anything different.

Not from Taylor Jones. Yeah, he had a heart under that ice-cold exterior of his, but damned if he knew how to *show* it. He wasn't going to change.

So she'd do her job. Then she'd get out of town. Get away from him. Let another ghost pull her in, suck her dry. Sighing, she rested her head against the window and closed her eyes, the bone-tired exhaustion sucking at her, trying to pull her into sleep, even though the car ride lasted only minutes.

The car came to a stop and she straightened in the seat, pressing her fingers to her eyes and rubbing at them. It didn't do anything to get rid of the gritty ache there, or the throbbing that had taken up residence behind.

"When was the last time you had a decent night's sleep?" Taylor asked, his voice low and soft in the silence of the car.

"What do you care?" she asked wearily.

"Can you answer the question?"

In response, she unbuckled the seat belt, but before she could climb out, he hit the locks for the door. Clenching her jaw, she stared mutinously ahead at the brightly lit house. The cops were still there, in a careful, controlled mess around the Donnelly household. But she didn't see any sign of a new car. Had his parents ever shown up? Did they even *know* yet?

"We've got a job to do, Jones," she said, forcing herself to keep her voice flat and cold. Wouldn't do any good to yell. Wouldn't do any good to get angry. She'd done that before and it changed nothing. "Let me out so I can do it. Then maybe I can try to get some sleep."

"Answer my question and I'll let you out."

Groaning, she slumped forward and covered her face with her hands. "Months, okay? I haven't slept well in months. It's like I *can't*. Are you happy? Now let me out." She slammed her fist against the door, half expecting another question, but to her surprise, all she heard was the quiet *snick* of the locks.

She slid out of the car and headed off into the darkness to the far right. That was where Tiffany had said she'd seen a shadow. Taylor wanted her to try to pick up something—if it was going to happen, it would be here, she figured.

He caught up with her before she'd taken even a few steps. He paced along at her back and she shot him a narrow look. "This is probably a waste of time," she said. "I'm not one of your blood-hounds."

"So you've said. But you do well enough. You catch emotion better than you think." His face was mostly lost to the shadows, but the moonlight caught his hair, gilding it with silver.

She looked away, tried not to think about how much she wanted to fist her hands in that hair again. It hurt to think about things like that—she knew she wouldn't have it again. Need was a vicious ache, in her heart, in her belly. Throughout her entire body, it seemed. Why did she have to want things she couldn't have? she wondered. Why?

Doesn't matter. In the end, it didn't matter *why*. It just mattered that she *couldn't* and she needed to get the hell over it. Muttering under her breath, she shoved a hand through her hair and stopped just outside the square of light cast on the ground by the busted garage window. Crossing her arms over her chest, she closed her eyes and lowered her shields.

Anger—

Determination—

Fucking have to do it myself—

Idiots—

She swallowed and jerked her shields back up, thrown off a little by the strength and clarity of those lingering emotions.

"Whoa." She pressed a hand to her brow and glanced over at Taylor. "Yeah, somebody was here, all right. It's a fucking mess of rage here. I'm not what you need, slick—you need one of your bloodhounds. But it's going to fade before you get somebody in. Emotions this strong don't last."

He stared at her, his gaze heavy and focused on her face. "Can you follow it?"

"I can try," she said. She sighed and pushed her fingers through her hair. "The question is, *should* I? We don't know what we're getting into out there, do we?"

"Everything points to it being one kid. We even know who." Then he looked away, his shoulders slumping. "But you're right. We shouldn't. Not just the two of us."

"The trail will be gone before we got anybody else out here." Her gut clenched. Everything in her resisted the idea of letting that trail go cold. But she knew better than to wander blindly into the unknown.

She looked toward the garage, then started toward the house, but as soon as she took a few steps, the trail already began falling apart. Not there, then. He didn't head toward the house. She circled around, shields down. She shivered a little as she brushed too close to Taylor, automatically jerking shields up between them—hard to work that way with a shield between her and *him* but nowhere else, an added strain she didn't need. But she had to do it.

The trail was strong in one area only. A straight line toward the back of the house, off into a darkness so complete, she wouldn't be able to see much of anything once they moved away from the house.

"Back there," she said quietly, looking at Taylor. Closing her eyes, she pressed her fingertips to them. Exhaustion battered her body and she wanted to sink to the cold ground and just curl up into a ball. Sleep for a week. Longer.

Instead, she lowered her hands and continued to stare off into the darkness. "But there's no way we can go back there. We're not here. *Officially.* How do I explain I need to go nosing around back there in the dark?" She sighed and rubbed her neck. She wasn't an idiot—she already knew the answer. "We come back. In the morning."

"The trail will be gone," he said, his voice soft, close . . . only a whisper from her ear.

She shivered and eased away. "Most likely. It won't be strong enough for me to track, I know. But maybe I'll pick up on something. It's the best we have."

"Then that's what we'll do." He reached up, curled his hand over her shoulder. "Come on. I'll take you home."

She just stared at him in the darkness, wishing she had the energy to argue. She didn't, though. Wearily, she muttered, "Whatever, Jones. What the fuck ever."

As his hand closed around her arm, she jerked away. "I can walk just fine on my own," she said, her voice cold.

And she did. One foot after the other, away from the maw of darkness at her back, away from the garage that stank of violence and pain. And away from Taylor—and oddly, even though she kept her shields up, she thought she could almost feel *his* pain.

But that couldn't be right. If he was hurting, it would be like . . . well, maybe he was letting himself care. Any other time, he'd shoved all that emotion so far down deep, he couldn't even feel it.

So, no. He couldn't be hurting. Not enough for *her* to feel it. Wrapping her arms around her middle, she stumbled on leaden legs toward his car. She just had to keep it together long enough to get away from him. That was all.

Then she could fall apart. That was all she had to do.

She slid into his car, still silently chanting that mantra. *Keep it together, keep it together, keep it together . . .*

She managed to do it until they turned off the street.

But the warmth of the car, combined with the strange way Taylor had of blocking out everything else, it numbed her. She never should have felt comfortable enough to sleep in his presence—

never. But she did. She was asleep within fifteen minutes. So deeply asleep, she didn't even wake when he stopped the car. So deeply asleep, she didn't wake at the sound of her name, or when he came around and lifted her in his arms.

* * *

PAYBACKS are a bitch . . .

Taylor had no idea who'd coined that phrase, but whoever it had been, he or she had known exactly what they were talking about. Crouching next to Dez in the cold, dark night, he stroked his fingers down her cheek and waited for her to wake up.

But all she did was turn toward him as much as the seat belt would allow, her lips parting on a sigh, her breasts rising and falling under the battered leather jacket she wore. He closed his eyes and focused on the ground, told himself to get a grip.

Then he set his jaw and looked back up. "Come on, Dez. You need to wake up now," he said, louder this time, keeping his voice flat and cold despite the fact that he was more than a little worried. Should she be this hard to wake up? Trying not to panic when she didn't stir, he reached out and closed his fingers around her wrist, holding it lightly.

Her pulse beat against his fingers, strong and steady. Her skin was warm against his. Under most circumstances, Taylor knew he wouldn't want to have some of the so-called gifts his psychics had—he doubted he was strong enough to carry the burdens they did. But in that moment, he wished he had *something* that would let him connect with Dez, just long enough to make sure she was okay. He knew he could take her to the hospital, but wouldn't he look like a fucking fool when it turned out she was just sleeping the sleep of the exhausted? Not that he really gave a damn if he looked like a fool, not for her. He *was* a fool when it came to her.

But he couldn't logically take her to the hospital when he suspected she was just exhausted. She'd just told him it had been months since she'd slept well. Months . . .

Sighing, he eased closer and slid a hand into her pockets, checking for her keys. She couldn't be a woman who carried a purse, couldn't make it easy on him that way. And she couldn't be easy enough to even have the keys in her coat pocket, either.

Gritting his teeth, he freed her from the seat belt and rested a hand on her thigh, gingerly checking her right hip pocket. No. Not there. He felt the bulge of them in her left hip pocket and he mentally started to count as he eased in, twisting his body a bit so he could get to them without touching her any more than he had to.

But then she turned in to him, tumbling against him, her face pressed to his neck, her body a warm, soft weight against his own.

Aw, hell.

He eased her back, keeping his hands on her arms even as she made a protest and tried to burrow back against him. "Shhh. It's okay, baby. Just go back to sleep." Because she was asleep, because he could, he pressed his lips to her brow before he pulled away, keys in hand. He shut the door and closed his fist around the keys, the jagged edges biting into his flesh. He welcomed the small bite of pain, hoped it might clear his head. It didn't do much.

Jogging up the walkway, he unlocked the door and used his master code on the alarm before he headed back out for Dez. He'd put her in bed, then he'd leave. Go home, pretend to sleep, then come back and they'd pretend like this night hadn't happened.

Everything still unresolved.

He opened the door slowly but Dez was curled over the console now and her entire body was tense, trembling. Lines of strain bracketed her mouth and as he crouched by the door, she groaned, harsh and low in her throat.

Scowling, he reached for her, working one arm under her legs, the other under her upper body. As he started to tug her closer, once more she turned toward him. Was it wishful thinking or did the tension in her body seem to fade? Was she suddenly more relaxed, curling against him, pliant and soft?

Wishful thinking, he told himself. *Just wishful thinking.*

She'd walked away, because he kept pushing her away, and damn it, he needed to figure out the right way to say what he felt when he looked at her or he was going to lose any chance he might have left with her. If he hadn't already.

You need to just forget about her, the ugly, cold voice of his conscience whispered. *You don't deserve a chance with her. Even if it were anything you* should *do, and you know it's not . . .*

But the barriers between them, as far as what he *should* do and what he *shouldn't* do, they were gone. Or mostly gone.

* * *

FIVE minutes later, he was settled on the edge of her bed, working her free of her coat, trying not to think about anything but that task. Once he was done with that, he dealt with the boots, focusing *just* on the boots. Not on the long legs clad in denim, not on the round curve of her hips, her ass, the breasts that had filled his hands so perfectly.

He wasn't going to think about the scar that marred her neck, or the way she'd stared at him all those months ago, that glint of challenge in her eyes as she said, *It's a scar, Taylor. A fucking scar. And I don't mind it. Hell, I'll wear it happily for the rest of my life. You know why? Because there's a little girl who is alive.*

That scar, the sight of it was like claws in his gut, and she was happy to wear it, and he wasn't going to look at it, or think about what happened that day when he brought her home from the hospital. Or what he did three days later. No, he was just going to put her boots down and cover her up, then get out of there.

He managed to put the boots down, side by side, taking the time to make sure they were meticulously straight, the toes lined up perfectly. Then, still not looking at her, he grabbed the blanket from the foot of the bed. Sheets rustled and from the corner of his eye, he saw her drawing up into a tight little ball, heard the ragged gasp of breath. It was dim in the bedroom, but he could see her face easily, thanks to the moonlight shining in. It fell in a silvery swath over her face and he could see the strain in the lines fanning out from her eyes, on her face. Saw her flinch, watched her mouth form the word *No*—

One of her hands balled into a fist and she jerked, her back arching.

The resolve to just get the hell out of there shattered and he crawled onto the bed, stroked a hand down her back. "Shhh. It's just a dream, Dez. Just a dream," he said softly.

Blindly, she reached out and he caught her hand. "Sleep, baby."

". . . can't . . ."

He stiffened, his eyes narrowing as he stared at her face. But her eyes were still closed. "Desiree?"

She twisted on the bed, squirmed. "Everywhere—damn it." Her voice was husky, heavy.

"What's everywhere?" he asked. He laid a hand on her cheek. "Open your eyes and talk to me."

She didn't, though, and he realized she wasn't really awake.

"They are." She sighed and curled closer to him. "All the

time. They never stop talking to me anymore, Taylor. I can't get away from them anymore . . ."

He didn't have to ask who she was talking about. Guilt weighed down on him. This was his fault. She'd managed to balance things just fine for years, but then he forced her to walk away, and it had upset the balance she'd found. "Are they here now? Are they talking to you?"

She was quiet. She was quiet for so long, he wondered if she'd slipped back into that dreamless sleep, but then she sighed. "No. I only hear you . . ."

With a satisfied smile, the tension faded from her body and she sank back into a deep sleep.

Taylor, unable to move, sat there.

FOURTEEN

For so many years, *cold* had been a part of Dez's life. The departed felt cold. The long empty nights she spent following leads were often cold. She went home to a cold, empty bed and she awoke to a cold, empty house.

She was more used to cold than warmth.

So it was something of a shock when she drifted awake and found herself surrounded by warmth. She stiffened, the breath locking in her throat as she stared at the wall straight in front of her, unable to move, hardly able to think.

A hand rested on her hip and in that moment, as her mind tried to figure out just what in the *hell* was going on, it started to move, stroking upward. She shivered, feeling an odd tickling sensation in the wake of his hand.

"It was a mistake insisting on the three months," Taylor said quietly, his voice muffled against her neck.

She lay still, not moving, hardly daring to breathe. Even when his hand rested on the curve of her nape, she didn't move. "I knew it then, even if I couldn't have made myself say it. I can say it now. It was a mistake . . . and I'm sorry."

Dez closed her eyes. Swallowing, she asked, "Why are you in my bed, Jones?"

For the longest time, he was quiet. Then, finally, he pressed a kiss to her nape and replied, "Because I seemed to have a lot of trouble walking away from you last night. I needed to tell you that, needed to tell you I was sorry."

"Okay. You told me. You're still in my bed."

He let go and she felt something fall across her neck. Reflexively, she caught it, but she didn't look down because he'd caught her hip and started to tug, slowly. A gentle, unyielding pressure.

She could have resisted it, but that would have felt more than a little childish. She settled for keeping her eyes closed—that was only a *little* childish, right? Even as she lay there clutching whatever it was in her hand, she kept her eyes closed. Even as Taylor guided her to her back and pressed a hand to her belly and even as her heart skittered and danced in her chest.

She couldn't look at him. She didn't dare.

"I have the hardest damn time putting you out of my head." Taylor brushed his lips over her cheek.

She had to bite her tongue to keep from hissing out a surprised gasp. *Don't listen to him. Whatever new game this is—*

Then his lips covered hers. Thought stopped. As his tongue stroked along the seam of her lips, Dez opened for him with a startled moan. *What in the . . .*

He rolled on top of her, his weight pinning her against the bed. His hands cupped her face, tilting her head back. "I missed you—fuck, why can't I stop thinking about you?" he muttered, his voice low and harsh, demanding.

Dez's head was spinning. This—shit. This wasn't happening. Her heart raced, pounding against her ribs so hard she could barely breathe. Tearing her mouth from his, she opened her eyes and glared at him as she shoved him back.

"What the hell, Taylor?" she demanded, disgusted to realize she wanted to cry. Damn it all. She blinked back tears and glared at him. "What in the hell is this? First you push me away, then you refuse to even discuss anything remotely personal, and then you spend the night *uninvited* and now you're pawing me. What the fuck is this?"

A dull red flush spread across his cheekbones and if she hadn't been so upset, so fucking aroused and confused, she just might have thought it was adorable—he was blushing.

But she was aroused, she was confused, and she didn't know what in the hell was going on. The tears clogged her throat and, staring up at him, she whispered, "What is this, Taylor?"

He sighed, stroking one thumb over her cheek. "Would you believe it's a wake-up call?" His gaze dropped to her lips again and then he groaned, pulling away from her and sitting on the bed with his back braced against the post. "You walked away last night, and I had the strangest damn feeling it was the last time—that if I didn't do something, figure out some way to talk to you . . . I wouldn't get any other chance. And I finally figured out that I needed it—needed . . ."

He closed his eyes and averted his face.

Dez felt her heart leap up into her throat. Easing upright in the bed, she stared at him, not daring to breathe, not daring to speak, to think. The tears were back, this time threatening to blind her and rob her of speech, but damn it, she wouldn't let them. She started to wipe them away and that was when she looked down . . . and saw what she held in her hand. What he'd been holding when she woke up.

Her necklace.

This time, she couldn't stop the sob, couldn't stop the tears. She had nothing of her past, save for this necklace. It had come from her grandmother—a woman who'd died when Dez had been almost too young to remember her. But she knew the woman had loved her. The *one* person who *had* loved her.

All this time, she'd thought it was lost—destroyed or tossed aside in the rush to save her life, maybe, the night she'd been hurt.

Through her tears, she looked up and stared at Taylor. "Where . . . where did you find this?"

"I've had it since that night." He stared at the bit of gold swinging from her fist, his gaze rapt, like he couldn't look away. "I . . . I kept telling myself I'd mail it to you. Then maybe I'd convince myself I'd bring it to you, and apologize. Make sure you were doing okay. But I couldn't let it go."

"Couldn't let it go?" She shook her head. "What is this? Damn it, what is going on?"

"I finally let myself admit something," he said, his voice raw and harsh. "I figured something out. Figured out what I need, Dez."

"Yeah?" She swallowed the tears clogging her throat. Hope tried to dance in her chest, but she didn't want to believe in it. Didn't dare. "What do you need, Jones? Do you even know how to let yourself need something?"

"Not a what, not a thing," Taylor said quietly. He looked back at her. "Who. *You*, damn it. And you've known it all along. Better than I did. I need you and I knew if I just let you walk last night, that was it. It was done."

"I *did* walk," she pointed out, lowering her gaze to the necklace for a moment before looking back up at him.

He gave her a faint grin. "But you didn't get away. You've been stuck with me all night, even now."

She snorted. She managed a casual shrug as she inspected the chain of her necklace. It was damaged, but that was okay. The chain wasn't the important part. She'd replaced it four or five times over the years. The cross was what mattered to her. "Circumstances, Jones. You can't claim credit for circumstances."

Taylor reached up, scratching at the light golden stubble on his chin. "Actually . . . there were no circumstances. I had no reason to take you back to the kid's house—I was just trying to stall and figure out how to make my brain and mouth cooperate."

Dez stared at him. "No circumstances. That's bullshit. We found a trail."

"Dumb luck." Taylor shrugged. "I wasn't entirely surprised when you picked something up, but I wasn't exactly expecting it to happen, either—like you said, you're not one of my bloodhounds. It was just a last-ditch effort to keep you from holing up in here away from me."

"Ahhh. Hmmm." She licked her lips and then, before she did anything else, she set the necklace down. Carefully. She couldn't lose it again. That he'd cared for it all these months made it that much more precious, she realized. Even if she wouldn't let herself acknowledge it. That done, she drew her knees to her chest and made herself think about what he'd just said.

He'd lied to her. Hell, he'd also kept something she treasured for over a year. Yeah. She should be pissed off. He'd lied, after all, right? But somewhere inside, instead of fury, she felt something that just might have been hope. Or even glee.

Pressing her face to her knees, she took a deep breath. She

needed to think and focus. Think. Focus. And get the hell away from him. Yeah. That was a good plan. She should get out of the bed and walk away. Without looking at him. Because if she looked at him, she was lost. So lost, so screwed. She swallowed and tried to send the command to her body.

Said body wasn't in the mood to cooperate.

Okay. So she'd tell him to leave. That would work, too, right?

Sucking in a deep breath, she opened her mouth.

But what came out *wasn't* an order to leave. Instead, she blurted out, "What the hell does it matter if I hole up away from you *now*? When did things change all of a sudden?"

And she made the mistake of looking at him. Her gaze locked with his and she fell into that steely blue—usually so cold, so flat and emotionless. But now . . . not cold. And while she couldn't entirely understand the emotions she saw there, there *was* emotion—a whole hell of a lot of it.

"Change?" He laughed, but there was no humor in the sound. "Oh, nothing *changed* exactly. Except for that wake-up call I mentioned."

Her breath caught in her throat as he rolled onto his knees and crawled across the bed. It should have looked awkward. Seriously, who could *crawl* and *not* look awkward? Obviously Taylor Jones. Caught in the blue of his eyes, she felt like she was being stalked and she couldn't have moved for the life of her.

He stopped only scant inches away and lifted a hand, stroking it down her cheek. "The past year has seriously sucked, Dez. I don't know if I can do any sort of relationship and chances are I'm going to fuck it up something awful. I'm probably going to end up hurting you. But if there's any chance at all that you and I *might* have something between us, I want it."

Shit. Her heart slammed against her ribs; her breath was trapped inside her lungs. This was happening—this was real. Staring at him, she swallowed back the dazed, delighted giggle that wanted to break free. No. She wasn't going to fall for this so easily. Hell, no.

"For how long?" she asked, clenching her hands into fists to keep from reaching for him. "While we're both here? Until you go back to D.C.? How long, Jones? If it's just until you're bored with it, then just get the fuck away from me."

With a featherlight touch, he stroked a finger over the scar on her neck. His eyes held hers. "Dez . . . I could live a thousand years and never be bored with you. And I don't know how long. Probably until you're fed up with me and boot me out on my ass." He slid his hand back to curve around her nape, his thumb rubbing back and forth over her skin. "But I don't have hard-and-fast answers. If you're looking for them . . . well, I'm no genius at relationships, but I don't think they *come* with hard-and-fast answers. We just do our best and see what happens."

Relationship. As his fingers slid up to tangle in her hair, Dez closed her eyes. She was sitting here, in bed, talking about a *relationship* with Taylor Jones.

Hell had frozen over. That was the only logical explanation for this weirdness.

His lips brushed over her forehead and she tipped her head back, looking at him. "You know how insane this is?" she asked, her voice soft. "I shouldn't even want to see you, talk to you. I've spent the past year trying not to think about you at all."

"Same here." A faint smile curled his lips. "Did you have better luck than I did?"

Dez made a face. "Every time I slowed down more than five minutes, I'd find myself thinking about you. Thinking about you, cursing the ground you walked on in one breath, and missing you in the next."

"I just missed you." His mouth brushed across her cheeks, first one, then the other. "Missed you, then I'd curse the ground I walked on. I've spent a lot of time wishing I could kick my own ass. Dez?"

"Yeah?"

"If you're going to kick me out, do it now, because if you don't, I plan on having you naked in the next two minutes."

Her heart skipped a beat and her breathing hitched. Pulling back, she stared at him, while inside her head a war raged. Kicking him out was exactly what she *should* do. She knew that.

But she wasn't going to.

"Two minutes, huh? Do I have time to brush my teeth?"

"It's closer to ninety seconds now."

She grinned at him. "You're counting—"

Before she could finish, he had her mouth under his. She shuddered and opened for him, wrapping her arms around his neck. He hauled her against him and twisted, rolling across the bed until he had her flat on her back and under him.

His hands flew over her clothes and although she wasn't counting, he had her clothes off pretty damn fast—it just might have been two minutes. As the last of her clothes went flying, she worked her hands between them and pushed him back when he would have covered her body with his.

"Now you," she demanded, grabbing the hem of his shirt in her hand and tugging on it. "I want you naked, too."

He scowled but pushed away, dealing with his clothes with the same speed and efficiency he'd used on hers. He came back to her, his body hard, strong, and warm, chasing away the cold that always seemed to linger. She groaned, all but wrapping herself around him.

His mouth caught hers and she bit his lip, then sucked it into her mouth. When he shuddered against her, she smiled. Against her belly, she could feel him, hard and thick. She worked a hand between them and closed her fingers around his cock, stroking him.

Taylor tore his mouth away. "Fuck, don't do that. I'll lose it right here."

"That's fine with me." She smiled up at him and continued to pump. The thought of making him shatter like that had her belly going hot and tight. He wanted her that much—this controlled, contained man wanted *her* that much.

He reached down and caught her wrist, stilling her actions. "It's not fine with me."

"Spoilsport." She squeezed him and then let go, still grinning. A thought occurred to her. "I don't have anything with me, Jones."

His lashes flickered. "Me, neither."

"I'm still on the pill." A blush crept up her cheeks but she didn't look away as she added, "I haven't been with anybody since you."

"Me, neither." He closed his eyes, pressed his brow to hers. "I can stop. Go to the store."

"Or . . ." She wiggled under him, stroking a hand down his back. "We can do something really stupid again."

"We could." He nipped her lower lip and then lifted his head, staring down at her. "Something really fucking stupid. We both know better."

"Yeah." She cupped his hips in her hands and met his gaze. Her heart, always so damned weak when it came to him, trembled and stuttered inside her chest. "Make love to me, Jones."

He braced one elbow on the bed by her head. "Say my name, Desiree. *My* name . . ." he muttered.

"Taylor. Make love to me, Taylor."

His mouth captured hers as he shifted and positioned himself between her thighs. "Wrap your legs around me," he rasped against her mouth.

As she did, he pressed against her, the broad head of his cock nudging against her exposed, slick folds. She whimpered and arched, rubbing against him. "Damn it, Dez, be still . . ."

She couldn't, though. Aching, all but dying for him, she tightened her legs around him and arched up.

Taylor swore and pushed, driving deep, burying himself inside with one hard, heavy thrust that tore a scream from her throat. Again, again . . . he shifted his body so that each thrust had his body stroking against her clit, a burning, taunting little tease—driving her insane.

* * *

HER eyes, so dark and deep, stared up at him, her gaze glassy. Drunk with need, drunk on her, Taylor cupped the back of her head and kissed her, dying for more. Bored with her? With this? Not in this lifetime. The little muscles in her sex clenched around him, milking him, clutching at him as he withdrew.

So fucking sweet, so hot and so wet . . . He groaned out her name against her lips as she shuddered under him. Her body went rigid against his, tight with the need to come.

He'd wanted this to last . . . but there was no way it could. No way *he* could, not with her. Not with how much he wanted her, how much he needed her. Nobody else had ever done this to him, shattered his control like it was nothing.

Taylor worked a hand between them and stroked his thumb over the erect little nub of her clit. Lifting his head, he stared at her, watched as a harsh, broken sob fell from her lips.

Her nails bit into his skin as she started to come and he gritted his teeth, holding back until he saw her going over. Then, and only then, did he bury his face in her neck and start to move again, hard, fast.

He muttered her name, blind to everything but her . . . completely and utterly lost in her.

* * *

"THAT was definitely something stupid," Dez murmured once she could breathe again.

"Yes." Taylor had her tucked up against him, her back against his front, one arm wrapped around her waist. "I plan on doing it again later."

"I like that plan. But why later?"

He nuzzled her neck before responding. "We have to go back out to Beau Donnelly's place."

And with those words, reality came crashing back in. Sighing, she eased away from him and sat up, dangling her legs over the edge of the bed. "Yeah. There is that. Shit."

Behind her, she felt the bed shifting. Despite his apparent change of heart, she was still caught off guard when he came up to sit behind her, wrapping her in his arms. "We may not find anything. Probably won't. But we owe it to that boy, to his family, to at least try."

"I know." Brooding, she stared off into nothing, wishing she could use her gift in a little more active fashion. "Don't suppose you've called any of the others out here, have you?"

Several moments of silence passed before he answered. "No. I've considered it a few times, but my gut is telling me that isn't the answer. You are."

Dez made a face. "Some answer I am."

"You're more of an answer than you realize. For this . . . for me."

Her heart did a slow, lazy flip in her chest. Trying not to let it show, she chuckled and said, "Wow, Jones. You've gone and turned all poetical on me."

"And you're still a smart-ass. Doesn't change the fact that you're the answer here. Everything's tying into you and you know it." He rubbed his lips over her shoulder. "We'll go out to the Donnelly place after you eat some breakfast."

"I'm not hungry," she said, sighing and easing away from him. But before she could take a step, he caught her wrist.

Looking back at him, she arched a brow.

"You'll eat," he said, his voice flat.

Dez narrowed her eyes. "Excuse me?"

"You need to eat. Has it occurred to you that part of the reason your ghosts are affecting you so much is because you're rundown and worn out, and stressed on top of that? Not eating isn't going to help."

"Oh, please." She rolled her eyes.

"Dez. It makes sense—none of my team has ever been able to work as well after they've been sick or injured. Extreme physical exhaustion is pretty close to sick. If you can't shield as well when you're tired, then it makes sense that they are able to talk to you all the time now."

For the longest time, she just stared at him. Then, setting her jaw, she tugged away. "Fine. I'll eat. But don't be surprised if it doesn't make a difference."

"It's not going to be an overnight thing," he pointed out. "You need regular, decent meals and regular, decent sleep."

"Fat chance," she muttered with a snort. "Last night was the first decent night's sleep I've had . . ." Her voice trailed off and she looked away. She'd slept well. And Taylor had been there.

Coincidence, she told herself. That was all it was.

FIFTEEN

THE Donnelly house was silent. Nobody responded to Taylor's knock and Dez was just fine with that. She'd rather not have to face the emotion of his distraught parents before she had to try to focus on some practically nonexistent trail. Finding that trail, assuming she *could*, was going to be hard enough.

First, she went back to where she had been the previous night and just stood there. Back when she'd first started training for this job, she'd had an instructor who had taught her how to meditate. Dez had hated it. It was tedious, boring as hell . . . and useful.

It was a way of blocking out everything but the *one* thing she needed to focus on. Right now, she needed to block out everything, and everybody. Including Taylor, including the fact that they were going to try out a *relationship*. Including the fact that they'd had mind-blowing sex not that long ago, including even the fact that she was almost positive she had bruises in the shape of his fingers on her ass.

Blocking all of that out, she leveled out her breathing and just . . . drifted.

Drifted until she came in touch with something that didn't quite fit.

There.

Faint . . . it was so faint.

A thin, insidious thread of rage. So tenuous and weak, even one false step would break it.

I'll just have to be careful not to break it, then . . .

She started to follow, one slow step at a time.

* * *

We had a lovely day together, my angel.
Although we did have an unpleasant interruption—I'm sorry
for that. You shouldn't have to tolerate such behavior.

The pen paused, tapping against the paper.
That punk. So rude.

I'm sorry he had to interrupt our time together, angel. It
won't happen again. I'll see to it. Not that it will be necessary.
He doesn't even see how easily everything is tied to him . . .

Again.

* * *

BRENDAN stared at his father, a distraught, terrified look plastered on his face, and all the while, he was thinking, *Fucking again . . . somebody fucked things up again . . .*

"Beau. You said Beau's in the hospital," he whispered. "In a coma. But I just saw him. Last night. And he was fine."

Not supposed to be in the fucking hospital. Should be in the damn morgue. What the hell happened?

"I know." With understanding, compassionate eyes, Joshua Moore reached out and rested his hand on Brendan's.

His wife sat at his side, sniffling delicately—all without ruining her makeup, Brendan noticed. Classy bitch—that was Jacqueline. She wasn't his mom—his mom was dead. Jacqueline was nothing more than a brainless bimbo who'd fuck his father's friends in exchange for favors. Brendan wasn't supposed to know, of course, but he did. He knew all sorts of shit about his dad.

And he bet his dad knew exactly what had happened last night with Beau, too. Looking down at the table, he waited until he had a few tears in his eyes and then he looked up. With his voice shaking, he said, "What happened, Dad? Was . . . is this my fault? We . . . we had an argument, you know. Nothing's been right ever since Tristan died. Beau was in one of his moods and wanted to get drunk and I didn't . . ." He closed his eyes and shook his head. "Man, I shouldn't say this."

"Come on, buddy. You can tell me anything."

He gave his dad a tremulous smile. "Yeah. I know. Beau was talking about taking some of his dad's liquor again. I didn't want to. We yelled at each other." He reached up and probed his eye, gave his dad a sheepish smile. "This . . . well, it wasn't from me and Kyle wrestling around like I said. It was Beau. I told him I wasn't going to let him get my ass in any more trouble and he called . . ." He shot Jacqueline a nervous look. "He called me a pussy. I shoved him and he hit me. I told him—sorry, Dad—I told him to fuck off and then I got out of the car and headed over to Kyle's. I . . . he didn't have a wreck or anything, did he? Was it my fault? I know he's screwed up in the head. Maybe I should have . . ."

"It wasn't a wreck." Joshua patted his hand. "It was an accident—a terrible one, but I think he got drunk and just fell asleep."

"Thank God for that girl Tiffany," Jacqueline said, her voice soft. She shot her husband a quick look and then lowered her gaze, sighing. "She's like his angel or something."

Brendan felt the hair on the back of his neck go up. "Tiffany?"

Both of them gave him an odd look and it wasn't until then that he realized he'd said it all wrong. Giving them a weak smile, he said, "I'm just all messed up. I want to go see him. Can I?"

"I don't know yet," his dad said, sighing. "I'll have to make some calls and see."

"Okay." He licked his lips and then, careful not to let anything show in his voice, he said, "What did Tiffany do? And what happened to Beau, anyway?"

"He fell asleep in the garage with his car running. Or maybe he passed out." The man sighed, looking exhausted. "I don't know. But for some reason, Tiffany was in the area and she heard his car."

"That engine," Jacqueline murmured. "It's hard *not* to hear it."

"Yes. She ended up breaking the side window and going into the garage, opening up the door. If he lives, it's going to be because of her."

That little bitch.

* * *

SURREAL wasn't a word that normally belonged in Taylor Jones's vocabulary, but today it did. The logical, normal part of his brain kept trying to intrude, but for once, the rest of him was louder, able to silence that logical, normal part of him.

Even now, as he trailed along behind Dez through the frost-covered grass, his brain was only half focused on the job. The rest of him was thinking about everything *but* the job.

Was he really going to do this? Try for some sort of relationship with her? Was she really going to give him that chance? Had he lost his *fucking mind*? Those were the thoughts eating up the other half of his brain as they walked through the meadow.

Still, half a brain was enough to notice when she tensed up and stopped. Under the beat-up leather coat, her shoulders were tense. Her head slumped. Her hands, hanging at her sides, curled into fists so tight, her knuckles were bloodless.

A soft, nearly soundless moan escaped her and everything in him demanded that he go to her.

But he didn't—couldn't—because that could too easily break the connection. So as much as he wanted to grab her against him and keep her away from whatever was hurting her, he shoved his hands into his pockets and held still, watching.

Watching her so closely, he knew the exact moment she started to tremble, the exact moment she started to sway.

Oh, fuck—

He lunged forward just before she would have hit the ground. Catching her shoulders, he pulled her back, bracing her against him and staring down at her face. Her eyes were wide and fixed, staring upward at something he'd never be able to see.

"Dez," he snapped out, keeping his voice hard and flat. "Come on, Dez, snap out of it."

She only whimpered, huddling back against him, shaking, shuddering. This was bad. Dez wasn't generally one of his people to get hit like this. It had happened before, but not often. Usually her connections were a lot more peaceful, a fact that he'd always been thankful for. He knew how to bring her out of this, but damn it, he didn't want to have to do that with her . . .

Unaware of the plea in his voice, he whispered, "Come back to me, Dez. Come on, don't make me do this . . ."

She tensed, almost like she was seizing. Squeezing his eyes closed, he gathered her against him and sank to the ground. *Fuck—*

Setting his jaw, he pressed his fingers to her neck, tried to pretend he wasn't stalling. Her pulse was strong and steady against his fingers, her skin warm. And her eyes, those dark brown eyes, were still locked, still fixed on whatever hell she'd lost herself in. Whatever hell she'd *stay* lost in until he pulled her out, or forced her out.

Lowering his head, he pressed his brow to hers.

"Dez . . ."

She jerked again, the motions of her body unnatural, harsh and erratic. Her hand came up, almost nailing him in the side of the head. One of his psychics sometimes had what looked like a grand mal seizure with her visions and this was too fucking close. And it was *Dez*, damn it.

A strangled, choking sound left her and he swore. Shit, he had to get her out of whatever she was lost in—*now.*

As a fist closed around his heart, he lifted his head and stared down at her head. He closed his eyes and took a deep breath. Then, before he could talk himself out of it, he lifted his hand.

Before he could strike, though, abruptly, she screamed. And then, just like that, her eyes cleared and she sagged against him, gasping for air. Small, broken sounds, almost like sobs, escaped her lips.

"Oh, God, oh, God, oh, God . . ."

* * *

I⊤ was almost an hour before she could focus enough to think.

How did some of the others *do* this? she wondered. Nausea, pain, and grief swirled inside her and she wanted to gouge her eyes out, scrub her brain with bleach—*anything* that might undo what she'd gone through.

What that girl had gone through . . . *Oh, God, that poor baby . . .*

Wrapped up in a blanket, curled in the corner of a couch, she stared down at the glass of whiskey Taylor had pushed into her hand and tried to get her throat to work so she could speak.

"You ready to talk?"

She looked up at him and noticed lines of strain fanning out from his eyes. Odd. She'd never seen that on him before. She sipped from the whiskey and distracted herself by looking around. She didn't recognize where she was—didn't even remember how they'd gotten there.

"Where are we?" she asked softly.

Taylor sighed and came farther into the room. He sat on the ornate coffee table, just inches away from her, elbows braced on his knees. A bitter smile twisted his lips as he looked around the room. "My . . . home, I guess you'd call it," he said.

She blinked. "You . . . you *guess?*" she said.

"Doesn't feel like home." He shrugged. "The manor hasn't been home to me in a very long time. But it is mine. I don't live here. I only come here once a year. It was closer than the house where you're staying, though, and I wanted to get you someplace warm."

Then he glanced at the whiskey and added, "And someplace that had something for you to drink. You looked like you needed it."

"Yeah," she murmured faintly. She stared at him for a moment and then shifted her gaze to the room. It was . . . enormous. She thought of the little, squalid apartment she'd grown up in with her mother, back before the woman had abandoned her. Most of the apartment could have fit in this room. Swallowing, she looked back at Taylor. "Man. I had a feeling you came from money, but this . . . well. This is a little more opulent than I'd bargained for."

"Money doesn't mean a whole hell of a lot, sometimes," he said brusquely. A bitter smile came and went. "People think it can solve all ills, fix all problems. It doesn't."

He shoved up off the table and moved away, stalking over to the window and staring outside. The stiff set of his shoulders, the rigid line of his back, they spoke of pain. And more, she could *feel* the pain in him. She wasn't always able to pick up much from him and she was glad of that. But right then, she could feel so much misery inside him, it almost swamped her. She suspected it was because her shields were just about decimated, thanks to whatever had hit her earlier, leaving her more vulnerable.

She wanted to go to him, but she wasn't sure she could handle the pain in him just yet.

"I take it whatever made this place stop being your home—that was something money couldn't fix."

Taylor closed his eyes. "Yeah." Then he blew out a harsh breath and shot her a narrow glance. "But I don't want to get into this. We've got other problems on our hands. The boy. And whatever it was you felt out in the meadow."

* * *

As Dez lowered her gaze to stare at the glass of whiskey, Taylor stared at her. She was still off—her color ashen, her hands shaking. Every once in a while, a shudder would wrack her body and he'd glimpse something in her eyes that just about tore his heart out.

Whatever it was, he couldn't protect her from it, either.

"What happened out there, Dez?" he asked softly.

She shot him a look through her lashes. "I . . ." Her voice trailed off and she sighed, leaning back into the cushions of the couch. "I've been aware of something ever since Tristan moved on. A ghost. Old. Faint. Her presence . . . she feels young."

Taylor tensed. His heart slammed against his ribs. Casually, he leaned back against the windowsill. "She?"

"I think." She gave him a strained smile. "And I can't even be sure that's who I touched today. I do know today was a girl." She lifted the glass to her lips but her hands were shaking so hard, the whiskey was splashing out.

Taylor went to her. Dread curled through him, flooding every last inch of him. *Not Anna, not Anna, not Anna . . .* Automatically he started to slip a hand into his pocket, only to realize the necklace wasn't there. Fuck.

Dez's hands were shaking. Focusing on that, he covered her hands with his, steadied them as she sipped, and then he pulled the glass away. "What happened?"

She looked at him, her eyes all but black with horror. "He called her his angel."

Tears burned in her eyes and her voice broke. "His pretty and perfect angel . . . his one and only." A harsh sob left her, and for a moment she was quiet as she struggled to get herself under control. She took a deep breath, then a second. When she looked back at him, her eyes glittered with rage, with hurt, with horror. "I can't see either of them, not yet. She's too fractured and I was lost inside her. I'll try again—I have to. She's a very big part of why I can't leave yet. I just feel like I'm still supposed to be here.

Although why she's pulling at me like this, I don't know. I've never connected with any of my ghosts like this."

She took a deep, shaky breath and rested her head back against the couch. "I hope I never do again."

Taylor felt like he was going to snap. He wanted to rage—wanted to scream. Instead, he took a sip of the whiskey he'd poured for himself. Cool. Be cool. He didn't know if this was anything connected to him at all.

Like hell—

No. He might not have any documented gifts, but his gut rarely steered him wrong. And everything inside him screamed a warning. This was Anna. After all these years . . . *Anna.*

And, coward that he was, he wanted to force Dez to leave. Not just the house, but the entire fucking town. Keep her the hell away from here, so maybe she couldn't ever establish the deeper connection she needed to solve this one. Then he looked at her, her dark, soft eyes locked on his eyes, and he felt his heart all but shatter.

What if that deeper connection came from *him*? Things had gotten weird for Dez from the get-go here. She'd had an odder, deeper connection almost from the time she'd stepped foot inside the town. No, he didn't have any connection to Ivy, to the boys who'd hurt her. But he had one to this town that went deep—very deep. And Dez had a connection to him. Psychics worked on a different wavelength than others. Sometimes those connections defied logic. He'd seen it happen more than once.

Was *he* the reason all of this was happening now?

Swearing, he turned away, slamming his glass down on the mantel. Whiskey splashed out but he barely noticed. He gripped the icy marble in his hands. Blood roared in his ears, and grief, pain, tore through him. *Anna—*

The misery he'd seen in Dez's eyes, the horror.

No. Not Anna . . .

Lifting his head, he stared at the back of a silver frame. He kept it turned away because he couldn't stand to constantly see her face when he was here.

* * *

DEZ stared at Taylor's back, her belly in knots. What . . . ?

A wave of agony all but swamped her. She gasped, pressing one hand against her belly as she stared at him. Oh, shit—what in the hell?

A voice, familiar, whispered, *Not Anna, not Anna . . .*

Taylor . . . ? Oh, shit.

And yet again, that true psychic skill that had been so erratic became clear. The words were distinct and solid and real. She *knew*, as well as she knew her own name, that voice had come from him.

No.

Oh, *no.*

Rising, although she wasn't sure she could trust her legs to support her, she made her way over to him. The second she touched his back, the wave of grief intensified and she had to bite her lip to keep from crying out. She did, biting down until she tasted blood.

She stroked the rigid muscles of his back, studying his face. He wouldn't look at her, and that was strange. Taylor *always* seemed to be looking at her, she realized. Always.

But right now, he was staring very intently at a photo frame. Or rather, the back of it.

Dez closed her eyes.

"Dear God." She reached out and turned it around. But even

before she looked, she already knew who she'd see. The child was beautiful. And she had Taylor's eyes—that steely blue, although they didn't have that cool, untouchable look on the girl. The same gilt-edged hair, though. Even the same smile. The resemblance was eerie.

Taylor stared at the picture, a muscle jerking in his jaw.

And tears on his face.

Dez felt her heart shatter into a million pieces.

Reaching up, she wiped the tears away. He caught her wrist and shifted his gaze from the picture to her face. His eyes, not so cold now, but burning hot and intense, bored into hers. "Is it her?" he rasped.

Dez said softly, "I haven't seen her outside of a dream."

"Is it *her*?" The demand was unmistakable.

"Yes. I think it is."

The grip on her wrist tightened—bordering on pain—but she just stood there. Then, abruptly, he jerked her close. He went to his knees, then, and pressed his face to her belly.

Broad shoulders shook as he cried.

* * *

"WAS she your daughter?"

They were the first words spoken between them in hours. Dez felt him jerk in surprise. Then he lifted his head and stared at her. "No . . . Anna . . . she was my little sister."

Dez winced and touched a finger to his mouth. "I'm sorry." Pushing a hand through his hair, she asked, "How old was she? And you?"

"I was fourteen." He shifted on the couch, rolling onto his back and pulling her on top of him. "She was six."

"So young. Both of you." Pressing her lips to his chin, she

hugged him, wishing she could do something, say something. But she'd already shattered him. He knew something bad had happened now. Anna hadn't just wandered off and gotten lost, although God knows that would have been heartbreaking enough.

"Yes." He stroked a hand up and down her back, restless, like he couldn't stop touching her. He'd been like that for the past few hours, even as he cried, even as she held him. Like the simple act of touching her was comfort to him. Perhaps it was.

She could feel the tension in him and even before he spoke, she suspected she knew what he was going to say. Already dread was a heavy weight in her belly.

"You need to know what happened that day."

Lifting her head, Dez stared down at him. "I need to help her," she said quietly. "She's weak—not much she can give me. So the more I can get on my own, the better my chance of helping her."

His gaze was turbulent, but his voice was level as he said, "Don't forget who I am, what I do." His mouth twisted in a humorless smile. "I know the drill. Hell, I fucking *wrote* the drill."

"That you did." Reaching up, she cupped his cheek, stroking a thumb over his lip. "For Anna. All these years, I've wondered what drives you. A lot of people think it's political aspirations, or just some insane workaholic taking it to the limit. But you've got demons like I never imagined, Taylor. All of this was for Anna, wasn't it?"

He closed his eyes. "I don't want armchair psychology, Dez. Especially not right now. What I do, I do because I want to." Gently, he nudged her off and sat up, scrubbing his hands over his face.

She sat as well, resting a hand on his shoulder. "Want? Sugar, *want* would sort of imply this makes you happy. You've never been happy a day in your life."

"Why the fuck *should* I be happy?" he bit off. He shot to his feet and started to pace. "She was just a baby."

"And you were just a kid. Whatever happened, it wasn't your fault."

"I know that!" He spun around, his eyes hot, burning. And broken. So broken. "I fucking know that. But she was still a baby . . . and then she was gone. Just like that—gone. And I wasn't even there to protect her. I should have been."

He sank to his knees, staring at the floor. "I should have been. I was at the school—fucking football practice. I hated it. But I did it because I was a Jones and we Joneses did what we Joneses always did. She was here playing . . . and then she was just gone. And nobody knows why or what . . . or who."

He looked at her with haunted eyes. "Who was it, Dez? Who took my sister?"

"I don't know." She went to him and knelt down in front of him. Catching his face in her hands, she pressed her mouth to his. Against his lips, she whispered, "But I'll do my damnedest to find out, Taylor. I promise you that."

His arms came around her and he hauled her close. Raggedly, he asked, "He hurt her, didn't he?"

"Yes. God, I'm sorry. Yes." *Don't ask me any more right now, please . . .*

She felt him nod, almost like he'd heard that silent plea. "If I find out who he is, I don't know if I can stop myself from killing him." She felt the erratic rise and fall of his chest. "I don't know if I want myself to stop."

Easing back, she cupped his face. "You'll do the right thing, Taylor. I've got faith in that."

"Don't have faith in me, beautiful," he muttered. "You'll just end up getting disappointed."

He pressed his brow to hers.

Dez slid her arms back around him. The silence between them stretched out and she closed her eyes, wondering just where she went from here. She'd be working blind, even with him here. Whether he liked it or not, she wasn't blithely sharing every last detail, every last bit. She'd share facts when she had them and when Anna gave them to her.

It might be a mistake, she realized.

But then again, there was an ugly, brutal knowledge already in her head that she didn't plan on sharing with him, either. At least not right now. He hurt enough as it was.

Over his shoulder, she stared at the picture of a sweet, smiling young girl. Although Taylor held her tightly, almost desperately, she could almost feel that cold, eerie touch.

She kept hearing that voice . . . *My pretty and perfect angel* . . .

And it was stronger now. As though Anna had realized Dez knew. And the girl wasn't going to wait any longer.

SIXTEEN

Things aren't getting better.
I keep hoping they will, that things will become calm.
Peaceful, although you had no peace for our day. But it's
worse now, worse than ever.

The writing was frantic. Erratic breathing filled the air.

I don't understand this. I don't.

The hand on the pen tightened.

* * *

THE sight of Brendan's car was enough to make Tiffany's belly
turn upside down. She hadn't been able to stay away from the
hospital for much longer than it took to grab a few hours' sleep

the night before. And her mother hadn't been able to tell her no, either.

But just then, as she huddled in the front of her mother's car, staring at Brendan, she wished Mom had argued, wished her mother had insisted she stay home.

Coward—stupid little coward.

Something touched her head and she jumped, only to feel like even more of a coward when she realized it was just her mom, stroking her head and watching her with worried eyes. "Are you okay, baby? Maybe I should have made you stay home, get some sleep." Her mouth tightened and she sighed. "It's not that I don't appreciate what you did for Beau, but it's not like you two were friends—he was so awful to you." She shook her head. "That's it. You're going home."

"No!" Tiffany grabbed her mom's arm before she could start the car. "It's not him." Turning her head, she watched as Brendan disappeared into the hospital. "It's not him . . ." Swallowing, she gave her mom a weak smile. "I'm just still kind of freaked out. Come on. I bet I'll feel better once I see him."

As they climbed out of the car, she pulled her phone out. She had to let that lady know—let her know that Brendan was up here. That wasn't good.

"Tiffany, why are you in such a hurry? Slow down a little . . ."

"I can't . . . I . . . ah, I have to use the bathroom." She winced as she lied, but she couldn't slow down. Why was Brendan here?

* * *

BRENDAN knew he couldn't do anything.

Not now.

He'd have to find another way to handle Beau, damn it. But he'd look in, see him. Couldn't fucking believe this. What the hell? He'd thought he was done having Halers screw up his plans with Tristan being out of the way. And now Tiffany?

Standing over Beau's bed, staring at his slack face, he tried to figure out just what in the *fuck* had gone wrong. Why had Tiffany been there?

"The doctors think he could wake up."

He looked at Kadie, Beau's mom. She was still wearing her slut clothes from the night before, her makeup smeared from crying, her hair disheveled. Brendan made himself smile. "I bet he will. You just wait." He wasn't lying or trying to comfort her, either. The way his luck ran, of course Beau would wake up. "Why don't you get yourself some coffee or something? I'll stay with him."

"I don't want anything. Although I wouldn't mind using the bathroom." She grimaced and glanced down at her clothes. "Beau's dad brought me some clothes. He ran down to get some food—with his diabetes, he has to eat. But I do want to wash up and change. I just didn't want to leave him."

She came around the bed and gave Brendan a kiss on the cheek. When she did, he could smell the smoke, the beer, and the sex on her. Keeping his eyes downcast, he stared at the still boy in the bed.

"You're a good friend," she said softly. "Such a good friend."

He waited until the sound of her heels faded before he lifted his head.

"A good friend," he muttered. "Surrounded by fucking *idiots*." Shooting a look over his shoulder, he headed around the bed and took the seat Kadie had just vacated. Leaning forward, he stared at Beau. "So, what's up?"

There was no answer, just the monotonous, steady beeping from machines. He was hooked up to several and although Brendan wasn't going to dare, he imagined what it would be like to lean over and pinch off the tube that was connected to the oxygen tank. What would happen . . . ? He could see himself doing it . . .

"Hi."

Jerking his head up, he found himself staring into a pair of wide blue eyes. Those wide blue eyes, lined with heavy black eyeliner, were watching him with a disturbing amount of knowledge. And as he leaned back in his chair to meet Tiffany Haler's gaze, Brendan had the weirdest damn sensation run through him.

She knows . . . , he thought.

But as quickly as he thought it, he made himself push it aside. How could she know?

"Hey there, Tiffany." He smiled at her. "I hear you're a hero. Thanks . . . thanks a lot."

She cocked a brow at him. "Thanks?" For some reason, that seemed to amuse her and she started to chuckle. "Yeah. Whatever." She slunk into the room and settled against the wall, her gaze moving from him to the bed, studying Beau before shifting to the machines.

As her mother came into the room, he continued to watch Tiffany. If he wasn't mistaken, there was a hell of a lot of suspicion in that gaze. What the fuck?

"Brendan!" Tiffany's mother moved forward and he stood up, bracing himself for the hug. She'd always been a hugger, stupid old bitch.

"Hi, Mrs. Haler. Good to see you."

"Terrible circumstances, though." She squeezed him and eased back before turning to rest her hands on the railing of the hospital bed. "Well, he's looking better."

Tiffany snorted. "No, he's not." Then she lifted her eyes to Brendan and smiled. "But he's alive. That's a good thing, right?"

Once more, that odd, disturbing sensation returned. *She knows . . .*

* * *

WHEN Beau's mom returned, Tiffany slipped out. It was too much, having them all in there, especially with Brendan staring at her with his dark, flat eyes. Shark eyes, she thought. He had shark eyes. Lifeless and dead.

She headed to the nurses' station, unwilling to put herself anyplace where he might try to follow—and get her alone. She was too damn smart for that. One thing she'd learned after so much time being a target: don't make it easy for them.

She hadn't been out of the room more than sixty seconds when she heard him come out, too.

Slipping her hand into her pocket, she pulled her phone out, staring at the message that had come through on her way up to the floor. It was from Desiree Lincoln. *I'll be there in fifteen or twenty minutes.*

She'd be there.

But what could she do? Tiffany wondered. What was Tiffany supposed to say . . . *I saw a shadow, and the more I think about it, the more I think it was probably Brendan . . .* She couldn't *swear* to anything. There was just something about the way she'd seen the other boy looking at Beau, something about the way he stood there.

Something about the way he had watched her only minutes ago with those cold, flat shark eyes.

Fear was slippery and cold, turning her flesh to ice as she leaned against the nurses' station counter and smiled at Laney Boldary, one of her mom's Bunco buddies. "Hi, Laney."

"Hey . . . if it isn't the local hero!" Laney said, smiling broadly.

Tiffany flushed. Shit, she was tired of hearing that.

Her throat went tight as Brendan came to a stop next to her. She couldn't keep from tensing as he reached up and tugged on her hair. "That's what I was calling her," he said. "Saved my best friend's life. Maybe the local hero would let me buy her dinner some night."

Laney lifted her eyebrows.

Tiffany scooted away from Brendan before she even bothered to look at him. Once she had a few feet between them, she angled her head toward him and studied him.

He had half the girls in school all but drooling over him—she knew that. Yeah, he was cute, but he was an asshole. And that overlong haircut was way overdone, she thought. Hell, everything about him was overdone, including the way he stood there watching her with his hands in his pockets and that waiting, expectant smile on his face.

Like he just knew what her answer was going to be. People didn't tell *him* no, right? His fucking looks didn't even *matter*. The longer she stood there looking at him, the more certain she became. He'd been at Beau's last night. That look on his face . . . yeah. He had been there. Even the way he moved, the way he was standing right now was eerily familiar. The same way she'd seen that shadowy figure moving.

People didn't tell him *no*?

Wanna bet? Tiffany stared at him silently for a few seconds and then looked away. "No."

She watched as Laney lowered her head to hide her smirk. From the corner of her eye, she saw Brendan—saw the way he stared at her, like he couldn't believe what she had just said.

She was standing close enough that she saw a flash of something in his eyes, saw the way his shoulders stiffened. But it was gone, fast; that angry, ugly look was gone and once more he was relaxed and easy, smiling at her.

"Not even dinner? Lunch?" he teased.

"Not even a piece of bread from the cafeteria downstairs," she snapped, glaring at him, suddenly enraged. That bastard. It had been *him* last night—she *knew* it.

His eyes narrowed on her face, glacier cold.

Oh, God . . . She thought he'd been angry a second ago. She'd been wrong. So damn wrong. Fear could chase away anger in a heartbeat, Tiffany realized. Oh, hell. He knew. He knew that she knew—

She backed away a step, and then another—

Crashing into Dez Lincoln.

"Whoa, Tiff." One hand, soft and gentle, but strong, closed around her shoulder, squeezing lightly. "You need to kind of watch which way you walk, you know. Pay attention to what's around you."

Tiffany darted a look up over her shoulder at Dez before looking back at Brendan. He was still staring at her and those lifeless shark's eyes were looking at her like she was a bleeding seal.

"Do you pay attention to things, Tiffany?" Dez continued, still holding her shoulder lightly. Protectively, it seemed. "I do. I see things. People. I watch them. Notice them . . . I bet you do, too."

Abruptly, Brendan jerked his gaze up, staring at Dez. Those shark eyes had found a new target, Tiffany thought, dazed.

"Hello," he said quietly.

Dez smiled. "Hi, there." She moved around Tiffany and stuck out her hand.

* * *

COME on, you little prick.

She didn't want to be here—she had other things she needed to be doing. Taylor weighed heavy on her mind, and her heart broke for him, for Anna, for their parents.

But she hadn't been able to ignore that text from Tiffany, either. A cold shiver had danced along her spine—whether a reminder of the promise she'd made to Tristan or just a warning, she didn't know. But there were problems, many, many problems, and she couldn't ignore anything connected to this kid, she knew.

She also knew she needed to be here and Dez didn't ignore her instincts. Now that she was here, she was damn glad she was, even if she was pissed off, even more so, at this boy for pulling her away. She stared at him, all but daring him not to accept her handshake.

Not that he would—he wasn't the type. The cocky smile on her face was all that was needed to goad him into it. She'd pegged him with just a look, no psychic insight needed. Pampered little brat, had everything in his life handed to him, except for the things he'd needed, things like discipline, things like guidance, maybe even love. But she couldn't find much pity for him, not when his evil was already a stain on her soul—and she hadn't even touched him . . . *yet.*

Then he reached out and put his hand in hers. She could have crowed in victory, except she wanted to puke. She'd been prepared—hell, even if something about him hadn't already put her back up, she would have been prepared just by the way he'd been watching Tiffany.

Like a snake ready to strike. Only colder. A snake killed in self-defense or out of a need to survive.

This boy wasn't reptile cold. He was . . . evil. She could feel it now, with her hand in his. Evil, and angry. Images assaulted her. No true thoughts, thank God, but the images were almost as bad. She saw Ivy. She saw Tristan—oh, shit, this boy had watched him die.

She saw Beau. She saw nameless faces rolling through her mind, accompanied by the imprint of his anger, the echo of his rage, and it left her foundering. The icy, poisoned rush of his anger flooded her mind and his evil was choking her. Bile rose in her throat, burning to be free. Her ears buzzed and her eyes blurred.

There was one more image . . . she saw him writing . . . Her knees buckled and she swayed. Black dots crowded in on her vision as some of his thoughts started to filter through—*No, no, I can't handle that,* she thought, all but ready to scream it.

She thought she might *have* screamed it, thought she might fall into a whimpering, wailing puddle on the floor.

Then a hand touched her. A warm whisper chased along her skin. She steadied. Not completely. Just enough. Taylor was there. She hadn't screamed, she realized. And she hadn't fallen.

How long—?

Not long. Brendan was still standing there, staring at her, but he had a weird, dazed look on his face and his eyes were a bit glazed. Like he'd picked up something from her, the same way she'd picked up that vile, insidious evil from him. His hand tightened on hers and then, abruptly, he yanked it away.

Dez resisted the urge to wipe her own hand on her jeans. It wouldn't do any good. She'd still feel unclean, still feel so very dirty and fouled and destroyed. Instead, she just stared at him, trying to make sense of the images, particularly the last one. It was important. What had he been thinking . . . ?

He backed away, his face pale. He looked shaken, she thought.

Journal—it was a journal—

He crashed into one of the aides coming out of the room at his back. As both of them hit the floor, Dez lunged forward. Instinct drove her. The journal. "Are you okay?" she asked, not worrying if she didn't sound convincing, not worrying if she didn't *look* convincing. She knelt by his side with one thought in mind—for the first time *ever*, she wanted to connect with a living, breathing person.

She closed her hand around his arm and stared at him. He jerked back, his breathing erratic. "Hey, let go."

Dez just tightened her grip, staring at him. Her heart raced and her vision constricted, narrowing down until all she could see was him, all she could think was *him*, and that cloying, nasty evil. *The journal,* she thought, reaching out and trying to establish a link. *You've got one, right?*

She smacked into his shields—the living had stronger, more resistant shields than the departed and since she'd always been more drawn to the dead, they'd never worked on refining her abilities with the living. But she didn't let that deter her. Even when she saw him flinching, even when she knew she was hurting him, she pressed on.

A hand caught her arm. Taylor—

She shrugged him off. *Not now . . .*

More images, a rush of them, like a movie reel in fast-forward. She felt his panic, felt his confusion. The boy knew something was wrong, knew something was off. Too bad—

Yes—an intact memory. Last night. He'd written in it last night. She heard that rapid-fire succession of his thoughts. Beau, Jack Daniel's, the rage . . .

Gasping, she pulled away, and at the same time, she stood up, jerking him to his feet. "Okay, pal, you gotta watch where you're going." She gave him a brittle, hard smile. "Like I was saying to Tiffany, be aware of what's around you."

The journal. He kept track of *everything* in it, she suspected. She hadn't seen anything beyond last night's events, but her gut insisted there was more. Uncurling her hand from his arm, she backed away from him, bumping into Taylor's body.

Brendan stared at her, anger flicking in those cold, dead eyes. Anger . . . and fear.

"I'll keep a better eye out . . . Ms. Lincoln, right?" He smiled at her.

Dez just stared at him. If that little punk thought he could scare her the way he'd scared Tiffany, he needed to think again. She'd be careful around him, no doubt about that—but fear? No chance in hell.

Deliberately she held his gaze, and then she grinned at him and said, "You do that, kid."

Then she turned her back on him.

* * *

PULLING his mind out of the past, focusing on the here and now, was harder than it had ever been, but as the smug bastard stared at Dez, Taylor was able to focus just fine. Taking a single step, he put himself between the boy and the woman. As Brendan blinked and looked up at him, Taylor crossed his arms over his chest.

Behind them, the hospital worker finished gathering things off the floor. "Housekeeping will be over in a few minutes to mop up the spills," the man said. "Be careful of the wet areas."

Taylor nodded and waited until the man was out of earshot. "I guess you were distracted, worried about your friend."

The hesitation was so small, somebody who hadn't been looking for it never would have seen it. Brendan sighed, his face set-
tling into a sad, grieving expression, and damn if it wasn't
believable. "Yeah." He reached up and touched the bruise around
his left eye. "Distracted is one way to put it. We had a fight last
night . . . I don't want that to be the last time I talked to my best
friend."

"Hmm." Taylor reached up and stroked his chin.

Brendan gave him a sheepish smile. "Guess maybe I shouldn't
be saying that to you, huh? I heard how you're some hotshot FBI
type, right, Mr. Jones? Or is it Special Agent Jones or what?"

"Doesn't matter." What had Dez seen? he wondered. There
was something—he knew it. And whatever it was, it had her
either damned excited or damned spooked. What was it? He continued to study the boy, watching as Brendan grew more uncomfortable, watching as he squirmed and shifted his feet and fidgeted.

"Well . . ." Brendan shot a look around Taylor to peer at Dez
again. "I want to get back in there with Beau. It's a damn good
thing Tiffany found him, you know."

"Yes. It is. We're going to make sure she's well aware of how
much it's appreciated," Taylor said, emphasizing the *we*, watching as Brendan's lashes flickered, suppressing a smirk as that
flash of anger heated his eyes for the briefest moment.

The boy wasn't as good as he thought he was, Taylor mused.
"You go on in and be with your friend." He paused, then added,
"I want to speak with his mom while I'm here, but I won't take
up too much of her time."

"Why—" Brendan clamped his mouth shut.

"Yes?"

"Well, um, why do you need to talk with her?"

Taylor shook his head and gave Brendan his best deadpan

stare. "I'm afraid I can't discuss that with you. I'll leave you alone now. I need to talk to Tiffany, see where her folks are—I have to speak with them as well." He waited long enough to see if Brendan would have much of a reaction, but there wasn't one. Technically, he had no grounds to speak with anybody on this case. Of course, if he *was* going to be speaking to anybody, he wouldn't necessarily be informing Brendan of his plans . . . unless, of course, he wanted to see the kid's reaction. Or he wanted the kid to think people were on to him.

Possibly both . . .

For now, this just looked like a sad accident, but it couldn't hurt for Brendan to think he was being watched. Hell, he *was* being watched and it was probably a good thing for him to know it.

Brendan stood there for a few more seconds, shuffling his feet and trying his best to look unhappy, but all Taylor could see in his eyes was anger. The boy was pissed and trying not to show it.

Then he followed in Dez's footsteps and gave the boy his back, trailing along after her.

"You try not to worry too much about your friend. Considering how he managed to pull through the night, I wouldn't be surprised if he made it through the day," Taylor said. He'd hang around a few more minutes, though. He wasn't leaving that kid alone with Beau. He smiled at Brendan and added in parting, "I think I'll have a word with the nurse before I leave."

There . . . give the little asshole something to think about, and hopefully make Beau a little safer as well. Tiffany, too. As of yet, Taylor still wasn't here in any official capacity. He might have had a contract for Dez that he could whip out if he had needed to keep her out of trouble, but there wasn't anything yet to justify calling in his unit. Still, he didn't need to be here *officially* to make people uncomfortable.

Make them worry.

He made his way over to the nurse's station, staying in full view of the open door . . . in full view of Brendan as he slid back into the room.

The boy's eyes slid his way and then darted back to the still form on the bed. He was involved in this shit—it was all but written on his forehead.

Taylor would focus on that matter for now, and only that matter, because if he tried to split his attention between this and the bombshell Dez had dropped on him earlier, he would lose his fucking mind.

Even though, he realized, in some part of his soul, he'd already known this was going to happen. From the time he'd heard Dez was in his town, he'd known. *Should have tried harder to get her out,* he thought. But even thinking that filled him with shame. She could lay Anna to rest. Even if he had to live with the horror of knowing, Dez's continued presence here had something to do with Anna . . . and that meant Anna couldn't rest. And Ivy O'Malley lived because of Dez's arrival in town.

He was such a fucking coward.

SEVENTEEN

"Beau's mom doesn't seem at all surprised by what happened," Taylor said as he and Dez sat in the hospital cafeteria over bottled juice and coffee.

"He's gotten in trouble before," she said.

Lifting a brow, Taylor waited.

"I talked to Tiffany. Beau's not exactly known for being an exemplary kid. Drinking, fighting. He was well on his road to screwing up his scholarships for a while, and then things got better for a while. After her brother kicked his ass. Sounds like Tristan offered an olive branch and the two of them became friends of a sort. He straightened up for a while. But then Tristan died and things got worse. He's drinking again, wilder." She lowered her gaze to the apple juice he'd pushed on her—his bribe of coffee was still out of her reach, but she was drinking it because she knew under that hard-nosed line he'd drawn, he was only doing it because he was worried. And he *was* worried. She could feel it. It was kind of . . . well, *weird* having somebody worry about her like that. Worry enough to do something that would piss her off.

Nobody else had ever really cared enough.

"I need to get inside Brendan's house," she said softly, shifting her focus away from Beau and back to what had happened outside his room earlier. She lifted the juice to her mouth and polished it off. Then she slammed it down and demanded, "Give me my coffee."

"Why do you need to get inside his house?" He continued to hold her coffee hostage, tapping a finger on the side of the cup, staring at her with grim eyes.

"I just do. Give me my coffee."

"Dez . . . you're a pain in the ass." He pushed it over to her and leaned back in the chair, his arms folded across his chest.

The first sip of caffeine was both wretched and wonderful—hospital coffee was usually lousy, and this was. But it was strong, and hot, and Taylor had added enough cream and sugar to make it tolerable. As it burned its way down her throat, she studied him from under her lashes—the way the cotton shirt clung to the leanly sculpted muscles of his arms and shoulders, the way he stared down at the table, gold-tipped eyelashes shielding his gaze from her view.

And the strain on his face. He was tired. He never really looked tired, but he did now. Tired, and sad. Grieving, she knew. Why wouldn't he be?

Abruptly, she set her coffee down and leaned forward, straining to place one hand on his. "Are you okay?"

"I'm fine—shit." He turned his hand over and caught hers, squeezing her fingers in a grasp so tight it hurt. His head lifted and he stared at her, his steel blue eyes burning and intense. "Fuck, Dez. I'm *not* fine, but I can't discuss this now. Anna . . ."

His eyes closed. When he looked back at her, those raging emotions were banked and his voice was level. "What happened then is done, and regardless of whether we can figure it out, a few days here or there won't make a difference, I don't think. But what's going on *now*—a few days, a few minutes—that makes all the difference. We've already seen that. We handle this, then we focus on . . ."

His voice trailed off.

"Okay." She smiled at him. "It's not like I've got anyplace to go. No mean-ass boss riding my tail or anything."

A faint grin tugged at his lips. "I can ride your tail if you want."

Heat burst through her belly and a startled laugh escaped her. "Oh. Um. Sure. Please do. But . . . this first. That assaholic boy first. Brendan. Again, I need inside his house."

"Again, Dez, you're a pain in the ass." He leaned forward, his hand still holding hers, although his grip loosened. "Fine. Just *why* do you need inside his house? What did you see earlier?"

Just like that, she wished she hadn't had the coffee. It pitched in her belly and she had to swallow against the bile rising in her throat. That nasty little shit—he had gotten under her skin but good. Taking a deep breath, she told him, getting it out as quick as she could, trying not to dwell on everything she'd picked up from him.

There was a reason she preferred to deal with the dead . . . the people she helped were generally *decent* people who just needed to move on. She saw ugliness through their eyes, and she had to live with their pain. But she'd never felt that much vile, foul *evil* inside her before—pure, straight from the source, so to speak.

"So this journal. You want to find it." Taylor watched her from under his lashes, his thumb still stroking over the back of her hand. "Shit, Dez. We can't just sail inside. Officially, *we* aren't here, you know that, right?"

"So that should make it easier." Dez shrugged.

"And if you find whatever it is you're looking for?" He cocked a brow at her. "What happens when you find the journal? It's not like we can just take it. It's not like any of my people have legit reasons for being here. I can keep your ass out of trouble—I can't make things like illegal searches legal."

She made a face at him. "I'm not going to do an illegal search—although technically, anything *I* do . . . would it be legal or illegal?" She smiled at him serenely. "How does the freelance gig work, anyway?"

"Again, you're a pain in the ass." He rubbed his forehead. "Exactly what do you plan on *doing* once you're in there if you don't plan on searching for the damn thing?"

She shrugged. "I don't know. I'm kind of making this up as I go." Sipping from her coffee, she stared at the table, trying to figure out just what to do, which way to go from here. "He thinks he's in control, you know—thinks he's as cool as a damn cucumber."

"He's a spoiled, uncontrolled little asshole," Taylor said, shaking his head. "A sociopath in the making."

"He's already made." He might *think* he was in control, but he wasn't. Now, as far as cool went—he might be *cool* as in cold, but that was an empathy thing there. The boy had none. Looking at Taylor, she said quietly, "I don't even know if Tristan was his first victim. Touching him, it was like touching hell. There's so much wrong inside him, I wouldn't know where to begin if you asked me."

He lifted her hand and kissed the inside of her wrist. "I'm not asking." Blowing out a breath, he said, "The kid's dad is the mayor. That's one way in. We won't go in as anything official."

"What does his father being the mayor have to do with it? Especially if we're not *official*?" Dez scowled even as she fought the urge to melt as heat raced up her arm just from the light brush of his lips on her skin. He'd kissed her. In public. It hadn't even been anything remotely sexual, but it had been intimate—extremely. Anybody could kiss you on the cheek—friends, even distant friends sometimes did it. But for a guy to kiss a woman on the wrist . . . shit, that was intimate.

Swallowing, she reminded herself she needed to focus. In a very bad way. *The job. Think about the job.* She stared at Taylor, tried to do it in a dispassionate manner, and saw that he had a humorless smile on his face.

"That's easy," he said, shrugging. "He's the mayor. I go up, knock on his door. He'll let me in."

Dez lifted a brow, confused. She was missing something but . . . Shaking her head, she sighed. "Okay, you've got to spell this out for me, slick, because I'm clueless. Is this a small-town Indiana thing? You go knock on a mayor's door in small-town Indiana and they just let any old FBI agent in?"

"No." Taylor laughed a little. "It's got nothing to do with small-town Indiana, with me being an FBI agent, or any of that."

"O-o-okay . . ."

Taylor stood up, grabbing her coffee.

"Hey! I'm still drinking that!"

"Then get up and get it before I toss it out." He also grabbed the empty juice bottle.

She managed to save the coffee, glaring at him. "You're so fricking evil sometimes," she muttered. "What's the deal with the mayor, Jones?"

"That's easy." He shot her a sidelong glance before he turned and headed for the door.

She had to trot to catch up with him. Once she did, he reached down and caught her hand, absently stroking his thumb along her wrist. Her irritation abruptly fizzled and even managed to stay that way, although she was able to pretend it hadn't as she sarcastically said, "If it's so easy, why can't I figure it out?"

"Because you look at me and see me. You don't look at me and see a rich son of a bitch." He glanced down at her, then paused, reaching up to stroke her cheek. "I don't know why you don't see the son of a bitch. I am one. I know that. It never bothered me up until you came along. But that's all anybody else sees—the s.o.b. Here, though, they see the s.o.b. and dollar signs."

"Taylor." Reaching up, she closed her hand around his wrist. Then she leaned against him and pressed her lips to his mouth. "Don't delude yourself. I see the son of a bitch—he's part of you. But I also see the guy who paces the floor when one of his people gets hurt. I see the guy who went into a career that guts him and now I even know why. I see a man who looks at me in a way nobody else ever has, who makes me feel like nobody else ever has."

She settled back on her feet, turning her face into his hand and kissing his palm. She squeezed his wrist gently and then looked back at him. "I see the s.o.b., all right, because he's part of you. And I've always seen you."

"If you see me, then why are you still around me?" He pushed his hand into her hair.

She glanced around. Did they really need to discuss this here? Hell. They *were* here . . . She reached up and fisted a hand in the front of his shirt, tugged him close. "Because I see *you*. All of you. The s.o.b., the guy who cares too much and doesn't let it show, the man who turns my bones to mush with just a look. That's who you are and if you don't see it, then maybe I just see you better." She pressed a quick, hard kiss to his lips and then let him go, pushing him away. "Now, come on. We can't do this here."

She started down the hall at a quick pace. No, they couldn't do this here, and they couldn't do it *now*, period.

"Turns your bones to mush?" he murmured, falling into place at her side.

"Yes. I'll demonstrate later. Now enough . . ."

* * *

IT was a nice house. *Nice* with a capital *N*, Dez mused as Taylor parked in front of it. Although not completely *NICE* the way Taylor's was. Man, she didn't think she'd ever *seen* a house quite as *NICE* as Taylor's was. It wasn't even a house. He'd called it *the manor* and that seemed to describe it better than *house*. *Manor. Mansion.* Did they mean the same thing?

"He's not as loaded as you are, I take it," she said, squeezing Taylor's thigh and shooting him a quick look.

Taylor gave her a narrow look.

"What?" She smiled at him innocently.

"Are you going to make comments like that in there?" He put the car into park, but didn't immediately climb out.

"Nah. That would be kind of tacky, wouldn't it?" She turned toward him and continued to stroke his thigh, edging her hand higher, watching as the ice in his eyes melted, turned to blue fire.

"Tacky?" He snorted. Then he reached down and covered her hand with his. "If it's tacky to do it in there, why is it okay to do it in here?"

"Oh, that's easy. I'm not sleeping with the mayor. I *am* sleeping with you. Once I've had sex with you, that pretty much makes you fair game." She wiggled around and came to her knees, pressing her lips to his mouth. "You're fair game now, Jones."

She went to pull away, satisfied that she'd done enough to ease the tension in him for now. And hers as well. Her own was a monster in her gut, clawing and tearing to get free, brutal.

But she'd barely made it a few inches before Taylor snaked an arm around her waist. "Fair game?" His gaze bored into hers. "I'm fair game? Does that mean you are, too?"

She didn't even have time to get the words out before his mouth was on hers. Hard and hungry. So damn hungry. She was breathless by the time he pulled away, breathless and about ready to tear his clothes off and throw him in the backseat.

But when she slid a hand down the front of his shirt, he pulled away. Two seconds later, he was out of the car and she groaned, slamming her head back against the padded headrest. "Jerk."

Sighing, she climbed out of the car and joined him where he waited near the hood. "You ever have sex in the back of that thing?"

"No." His gaze dropped to her mouth and then he looked at the car, a thoughtful look on his face. "I'm not entirely sure I want to, either."

"I'll change your mind." She started toward the house. "Now, come on. I want this over with."

"Why? So you can try to talk me into having sex in my car?"

She shot him a look over her shoulder. "If I decide we're going to have sex in your car, Jones, I promise you . . . you'll thank me afterward."

* * *

OH, he was absolutely certain of that. A few quick strides had him by her side and he caught her hand, tugging her to a slower pace. "Don't be in such a hurry." Stroking his thumb along her wrist, he kept his expression relaxed even as he felt her tension skyrocketing. "If you look anxious or like you have a mission, that's going to tip Moore off."

"Moore . . . the kid or the mayor?"

"Both. But I'm more concerned about the mayor. I can probably talk him into showing us around the house, or *you* can—if

I remember him right, he was an arrogant prick in school and he'll be happy to show off whatever he has." He paused and glanced down at her. "But don't look like you're on a mission, or it's not going to happen. He wasn't an idiot when I knew him— he's not likely to be one now."

"Too bad." Dez blew out a breath. "Idiots are annoying but they are easier to manage. You can manipulate the hell out of them."

True. There wouldn't be any manipulating with Joshua. He mounted the broad brick steps, taking note of the small details— the security system, the solid oak door, and a series of complicated, although ornate, locks. The mayor took his family's security seriously.

He pushed the doorbell, still stroking his thumb back and forth over Dez's wrist, trying not to think. He'd devoted too much time to doing that. Couldn't think. Not now. Not until this was done—

Anna . . . an image of her flashed through his mind and the rage hit him, surging through him like a tidal wave. Rage and pain and grief—all this time. *Fuck*—

Cool hands touched his face. Soft lips pressed to his. "Taylor."

Distantly, he heard the door open, but he couldn't think. Couldn't do anything but try not to break under the fury and the pain. Forcing himself to stare at Dez, and only her, he wondered if he could do this. Could he? Could he manage it? Could he make it?

"You can," she whispered against his lips, and he wondered if he'd said the words out loud. "Just breathe. Just focus. Think about me right now. Think about this. We'll help her, I swear."

Pressing his brow to hers, Taylor gripped her waist and waited for the grief to level off, waited until he could breathe through the rage.

He heard somebody clearing his throat and slowly he lifted his head, found himself staring into an amused pair of dark blue eyes. They were familiar, he realized—Brendan's eyes. But not so cold and lifeless. Arrogant as hell, but not cold, not evil.

Easing away from Dez, he reached for the control that had gotten him through the worst shit imaginable. It let him push aside everything else and meet Joshua Moore's eyes with a smile. "Hello, Mr. Mayor."

Joshua responded with a hearty laugh. To Taylor's ears, it sounded just a little too hearty, a little too practiced, but then again, he'd always been the sort to look for things like that.

"Now, you can't call me Mr. Mayor, Taylor. We go too far back. There's a rule for that sort of thing, I'm sure." He grinned at Taylor and then shifted his attention to Dez, giving her a wide, easygoing smile. "Hello, Ms. Lincoln. It's a pleasure to meet you."

Dez lifted a brow. "It sounds like my reputation has preceded me."

"It's a small town." Joshua shrugged. He stepped aside and gestured for them to come in. "After everything you've done, how could anybody here *not* know your name? Come in, come in . . ."

Keeping an eye on Dez, Taylor followed her into the house, watching her. If there was anything here, she'd probably feel it fast, considering how everything here seemed to be affecting her so acutely.

And it was easier—the coward's way, he knew, to focus on her, to think about her. Because she could keep his mind occupied. As long as he thought about her, he didn't have to think about anything else. Right now, he *couldn't* think about anything else.

* * *

IT was all but black.

Dez had to slam her shields up the second she stepped foot over the threshold; otherwise, she just might have collapsed. Even through her shields, she could feel the ominous, heavy weight of it pressing down on her. Okay . . . maybe it was a good thing she wasn't generally a bloodhound, wasn't one of the empaths. Yeah, they'd be more equipped to handle this, but what if she'd walked into this blind and wide open?

She didn't know, but it might have sent her to her knees.

There was something so fucking wrong in this place.

Jackpot. She followed along behind the mayor as he led them into a spacious living room and gestured toward a nice little recessed area with chairs gathered around a fireplace. It was flickering brightly, although there wasn't a sound coming from it and she couldn't smell any smoke. Electric, she decided, studying the flames. They looked almost real, but not quite. Yep, she was going to analyze the décor while her brain processed everything around her. One small chunk at a time—much less likely to go insane that way.

As Taylor came to a stop beside her, he rested a hand— possessive, protective, and reassuring all at once—at the small of her back. "I wouldn't mind some coffee," he said. "And Dez is a caffeine junkie."

She glanced up at him and then at Joshua, realized he was watching them expectantly. He'd said something—shit. And she'd been completely out of it. So completely out of it.

Dredging up a smile, she met Joshua's gaze. "Guilty. If you make it as strong as they do at the hospital, I'll need cream and sugar, though."

"Oh, I think I can do a sight better." He smiled and gestured to the couch. "Sit, please. I wasn't expecting to have any company. My wife is out with a few of her girlfriends, and my son . . ." He sighed and the practiced, professional smile faded, replaced by something real, something worried. He rubbed a hand over the back of his neck. "Well, Brendan's out with his friends. Kid's having a rough time of it lately. Very rough."

Once they were alone, Dez moved farther into the room and gingerly settled on the edge of the couch, braced and ready to leap off in case anything bombarded her. She felt silly, but man, this place felt like a psychic bomb, ready to drop squarely on her head.

What she wouldn't give to have better control over this sort of thing. She wasn't used to this—she talked to ghosts, damn it. She wasn't supposed to have all these outside stimuli coming at her. It was driving her nuts.

"You okay?" Taylor asked, his voice low and soft.

"Yeah." She glanced up at him. "It's just . . . off. Everything in here is off." She glanced in the direction Joshua Moore had taken and murmured, "The man doesn't have a lick of psychic talent, though. Or it would drive him nuts just being in here. He'd be a mental case."

"That bad?"

"Worse." She shivered, wondering just how many years of hatred, of *wrong* were stored up in here. It wasn't a recent thing, though. Something recent—a few months, probably even a year or two— wouldn't hit her like this. She could connect to emotions, but for it to hit her in such a way, the problems here must have pretty much infiltrated the very foundation of this house. All but given it a spirit, she realized. A soul, even though there was no life attached to it.

An angry, restless, cold one.

Hearing footsteps, she looked up. By the time Joshua came back in, carrying a tray loaded with mugs, she had managed to hide any signs of unease, but damn it—she wanted out of here.

"Good thing Jacqueline likes to entertain," Joshua said, smiling as he set the tray down. "Otherwise, I'd be juggling three mugs of coffee and probably burning myself. Typical guy."

"Are you?" She made herself smile. "What's a typical guy, anyway? I mean, you're a mayor, right? Most guys aren't mayors."

"It's just a job." He gave her a charming smile and shrugged. "And I assure you, I'm very typical. Unlike Taylor here. A small-town boy makes good and all. Look at you, Taylor. FBI. Although I guess I can see why."

He looked down, focusing on the coffee. "Is it . . . well, does it help?"

Dez reached over and covered Taylor's hand with hers. She opened her mouth to answer for him, but Taylor turned his hand around, squeezed her fingers lightly.

"Help?" he echoed. "No. Nothing helps. But if it stops other kids from losing their sisters . . ." His voice trailed off and he shrugged.

"I'd think that would help, though." Joshua looked up, his darker gaze locking with Taylor's lighter one. "Knowing you do something to keep some other kid from going through what you went through."

"That's making me a more altruistic person than I ever have been." Taylor shook his head. "Nothing makes the pain stop. It fades; you learn to live with it. And yes, sometimes I can sleep easier knowing something I did will keep one more predator off the streets. But nothing really *helps*."

"Maybe nothing is supposed to." Dez squeezed his hand. "It's still unfinished. For you. Not knowing anything—that leaves the wound raw and unhealed. You'll start to heal once you know."

I'll give you that, I swear. She lifted his hand to her lips and pressed a kiss to it, then looked over at the other man. "So . . . you two were friends in school?"

Joshua shrugged. "Not really." He shot Taylor a quick glance. "The guy sort of got lost in his own world after . . ."

"I know about Anna," Dez said softly.

He nodded. "Not surprising, considering everything I've heard about you two. Although . . ." Abruptly, he closed his mouth and shook his head.

"Although what?" Taylor's voice was cool, his eyes narrowed slightly.

Joshua looked like he was going to brush the question aside.

Taylor didn't get brushed aside; Dez could have told the man that. But apparently Joshua Moore had already figured that out.

"Well, it's just that I'm sort of puzzled at the talk . . . and now I know for a fact it's not talk." He gave them a halfhearted smile. "I wouldn't think such relationships would be allowed, with your jobs and all."

Dez could feel the slow crawl of heat up her cheeks. Ducking her head, she reached out and grabbed a cup of coffee. Let him field this one, she figured. He was the one who insisted she sign the damn contract. He was also the one who'd kissed her. And the one who'd slept in her bed. And—

Chicken.

She mentally groaned and tried to figure out just what she should say, although she couldn't, for the life of her, find the words to even begin.

Taylor's hand curved around her neck, his thumb stroking her skin lightly. Just that light touch relaxed her. Eased her.

"Joshua, it's not really any of your damn business," Taylor said, his voice easy and mild, although she could hear the edge of warning there. "But Dez works with me on a contract basis. She's not a full-time employee with the bureau. Different rules apply."

"The FBI takes freelance work?" Joshua lifted his eyebrows, glancing at Dez. "Just what sort of freelance stuff can one do for the FBI?"

She smiled at him and sipped her coffee. Over the rim of the mug, she studied him. "I could tell you, but then I'd have to kill you."

He blinked and then did one of those laughs where he threw his head back, the sound of it ringing through the house. Considering how depressed, how *angry* the house itself seemed to be, the laugh felt like a mockery more than anything else, but Dez simply continued to smile at him.

"I guess I asked for that." He sighed and shook his head. "And you're right, it's none of my business. So . . . why don't I ask something that is. To what do I owe this pleasure, Taylor? Not that I mind the company or anything. But you've never been overly social."

Taylor glanced at her. Dez smiled at Joshua, still not sure where to go with this. "I thought you said you weren't friends in school."

"We weren't." Taylor shrugged, laying a hand on her thigh and stroking absently. "Joshua is a couple years older. But we still knew each other."

"Town this small, almost everybody knows each other." The mayor grimaced. "At least it used to be that way. We're growing, bit by bit. And you two haven't answered me." His eyes narrowed on her face, scrutinizing.

Sharp, this one. Yeah, she could see the arrogance, but he wasn't stupid with it. Okay, so how to proceed? He wasn't going to buy some ditzy *Oh, I just love your house . . .*

Staring into those dark blue eyes, she leaned forward, her hands laced together. Dez opened her mouth—closed it. *Shit, Jones, help me out here . . .*

Still staring at Moore, she opened her mouth again.

He lifted a brow at her. "Yes?"

And then, without even realizing what she was going to say, she heard the words coming out of her mouth. "It's your son."

"My . . . my son. Brendan?" He frowned and rubbed a hand over the back of his neck. Shoving up out of his chair, he moved over to the fireplace. "What about him?"

"Brendan. I . . . well. I don't know what all he's been through, but I did hear that he's close to Beau. I saw him earlier, and I was just worried about him."

Joshua braced an arm on the mantel, staring down at the brick flooring in front of the fireplace. "You and me both." He shot her a look over his shoulder, his eyes dark and stark in his face. For that moment, he didn't look like anything other than a worried father. Tired, stressed, and angry. "He didn't—shit, he didn't do anything I need to apologize for, did he? He's had some trouble before, but I thought we were past all of that."

"He hasn't done anything to me." She shook her head. "He . . . he just seems so angry."

Caution flickered in his eyes and a guarded expression fell across his face. "Like I've said, he's had a rough time lately. He's going to be angry. Besides, he's a seventeen-year-old boy. How many of them *aren't* angry at some point or another?"

"Of course." She settled back on the couch and hoped she hadn't just blown this, hoped she hadn't just screwed this entire thing up. "It's just he's had a really rough time of it. Beau. Mark. And I heard he lost another friend not that long ago."

His shoulders rose and fell as a harsh sigh escaped. "Tristan. Yeah. That was . . . rough. On the whole damn town, but especially on his folks, and those boys. They were tight, you know? Close. Especially him and Mark. Brendan was pretty beat up over it—I wanted him to talk to somebody but he kept telling me he'd be okay. He didn't want to talk. Maybe I should have made him, but . . . well. Anyway." He raked a hand through his hair and moved back to drop down on the couch, sighing. "Look, Ms. Lincoln—is it Ms.? Do I call you Special Agent?"

"How about Dez?" She shrugged. She wasn't about to lie to him—she wasn't an agent anymore.

"Dez." He had that politician mask firmly in place once more. "I appreciate the concern about my son, and I can assure you I'll talk with him. But you really didn't need to come out here for this. I can't imagine how much work you two have to do."

Taylor smiled. "Not so much work. We're not yet here in an official capacity."

Biting back a smile, Dez looked over at him. *Not yet official*— damn, he was good. He'd managed to make it sound like they could get official at the drop of a hat.

Something flickered in the depths of the mayor's eyes and Dez once more felt something brush against her shields—damn it, she was tired of this. She wanted her gift to go back to behaving the way it was *supposed* to behave—she liked speaking with just ghosts, thanks. She didn't like feeling all the extra, all the time. It was exhausting. Too much emotion coming and it strained her to the very edge of her resources just to keep up with it.

"Not here officially, huh?" Joshua leaned back, those shrewd eyes of his locked on Taylor's face, measuring, calculating. "I'm curious, then, why you two seem to be everywhere there's trouble. Why you were there the night my son gave his statement— why you were reading all of the statements. If the FBI isn't involved, why are you poking your nose in?"

"I was there because one of my people was involved in rescuing the victim," Taylor replied, his voice cool. "I have an interest in it. This shouldn't surprise you. And, for the record, I never claimed to be here representing anybody. If your police force makes that assumption—that's on them."

Joshua scowled. "Shit."

Once more, he came out of his seat. Had a hard time being still when he was nervous, Dez decided. He shot her a look and even before he said anything, she *knew* what he was going to say—no psychic skills required.

"I know about you, you know," he said softly. He stopped in the middle of the floor, legs spread apart, shoulders set. He had his hands in his pockets, head tipped slightly back. A guy braced for a fight, she decided.

"Do you?" She studied him, eased her shields open a bit, trying to pick something up from him. It was vague—just another one of those insubstantial little brushes against her shields, too vague for her to even define. "I'm curious about whatever it is you think you know."

He snorted. "Why don't you read my mind? Then we can discuss it."

"Buddy, if you think that's even close to original, you need to think again." She sighed and leaned back, stretching her legs out in front of her. She crossed her ankles and rested her head against the plushly cushioned couch. "I can't even recall how old I was the first time I heard something along those lines. Maybe seven or eight."

His bark of disbelieving laughter didn't grate on her nerves. Dez was used to skeptics—honestly, they were easier to deal with. They didn't expect anything from her.

"Look—I don't care if you think it's true, if maybe it is true—"

"Maybe?" She smirked. Rising from the couch, she hooked her thumbs in her front pockets and shook her head. "There's either a *yes* or a *no* to it. There's not a maybe. Either I had some sort of psychic talent that let me keep a girl from dying a grisly death in your charming little town or I didn't."

"Or, the third option, you're involved," Joshua said, his eyes cold now.

Behind her, she heard Taylor moving but when he would have gone past her, she caught his arm. "Don't," she said quietly. "Not worth it."

"Oh, you're so very wrong." He brushed her hand aside. "Watch where you go with this, Moore. Watch very carefully."

"Now, don't get your boxers in a twist," Joshua said, a bright, sharp smile on his face. "I never *said* she was involved. I said it was another option."

"And I said watch where you go with this." Taylor glanced at Dez, his eyes unreadable.

Damn it, she'd gone and turned this into a clusterfuck. Brooding, Dez stared at Joshua. What in the hell was she supposed to do now? Why had she blurted that out? Was she hoping he'd feel some pressing need to open up to her and then show her the kid's room and . . . and . . . what?

Blood roared in her ears. She needed to get up to that kid's room, damn it. Her heart pounded. Cold crept in, snaking around her.

Shit—

Abruptly, she realized just *why* she was cold. The front door of the house was open. Wide open. Turning her head, she found herself staring into Brendan Moore's wide, angry eyes. He looked at her, looked at his dad, then looked at Taylor. Then, just like that, he took off running, his feet pounding on the steps.

"What the hell . . ." Joshua muttered.

EIGHTEEN

"WHAT the fuck is this shit?" Brendan jerked his mattress up and tore down the zipper. It had been a bitch to put that thing on but he'd wanted a secure place to put his shit, and this was secure. Wasn't like Jacqueline was ever going to come in and flip his mattress or anything, right? The maid, all she did was change his sheets and text her boyfriend.

He shoved his hand in and jerked out the journal, ignoring the other stuff. The condoms, the weed, all of that, that was small shit. The journal, though, it could cause problems.

Hearing the footsteps, he felt something cold twist in his gut—*fear*—

No. He wasn't fucking scared. He was just tired of people fucking with him, tired of people fucking things up *for* him, and he was tired of that crazy bitch . . .

"Brendan." His dad knocked on the door.

"What?" He looked down at the journal, glanced at his bathroom. Needed to get in there, burn the thing. Best chance. Yeah. Starting toward his desk, he jerked open a drawer and grabbed the lighter in there.

"Open the door, son. Need to talk to you."

"Don't want to. Need to be alone."

"Brendan . . ." The doorknob rattled.

Brendan smirked. Like he wouldn't have fucking locked it.

Outside he heard voices—raised, irritated. *Fine, yeah, argue with my dad while I—*

Turning, he froze.

Dez Lincoln stood in the door of the bathroom. She rocked back on her heels as he gaped at her, a faint smile on her lips. "Hey, Brendan." She glanced back at the bathroom shared by his bedroom and the guest bedroom, then back at him. "Nice house. I would have killed to have my own bathroom as a kid."

"What are you doing in here?" Sweat slicked his palms. Clutching his journal, he stared at her. Outside in the hallway, he could hear his dad, still arguing with Jones.

He'd thought Jones was the problem. In the beginning, he'd thought that cool-eyed bastard would be the problem. But it had been this bitch screwing things up, bit by bit. Being at the resort. Showing up at the hospital with Tiffany. Being here *now*.

She sauntered farther into his room. With that smug smile still on her face, she glanced down. "Oh, hey, you keep a journal? I always thought about doing it. But I'm lazy. What kind of stuff you write about?"

"What are you doing in my room?" he snarled.

"Easy, kid." She laughed softly, shaking her head. "You should chill out a little." And she came closer . . . closer.

* * *

So damn angry. Unlike his father, she got a better read on him. It wasn't so much psychic skill that was needed, though. It was his face—he showed too much. Every thought, every action, they all showed on his features. An open book, she mused. And the closer she got, the more tense he got.

One hand closed into a fist.

Out in the hall, the men had gotten silent. She took another step, closer . . . closer . . .

He was fast, she had to give him that. Damn fast, especially for a wiry, mouthy little punk. He moved like a snake, striking out and attempting to deck her. She managed to squawk out a surprised scream as she dodged it—she'd seen it coming a mile away. He choreographed his moves as clear as day and she wasn't about to get hit, not until she had to, anyway.

He snarled and tried again. From the corner of her eye, she saw Taylor and the kid's dad bursting into the room and this time, she didn't move out of the way. His fist caught her in the gut and the air exploded out of her, even though she bent some, right before the impact, lessening the blow to some extent.

Joshua bellowed out the boy's name in shock. "Damn it, Brendan, have you lost your mind?"

Taylor didn't bother with words. He just caught the boy's fist before he could try another—not that Dez planned on letting him *land* another one. Brendan snarled and growled, sounding more like a rabid animal than a person. Taylor ignored that. In a matter of seconds, he had the kid's hands pinned behind him, while Brendan's face was pressed against the wall.

He wasn't hurt and Taylor wouldn't hurt him, but the kid sure as hell was pissed.

And scared now, because in the scuffle, he'd dropped the very thing he'd tried to protect—just as Dez had hoped. The journal lay open on the floor. And that wasn't the only thing. Apparently he'd done more than write in the journal. It held drawings on loose paper, now spilled out. No wonder he'd been so determined to keep it from her. Swallowing, she knelt down, one hand reaching out to touch the image of a familiar downcast face.

But she stopped, her fingers hovering just an inch away. Slowly, she curled her hand into a fist and pulled back. With her heart slamming away inside her chest, she looked up and stared at Brendan. Still struggling to catch her breath, she said hoarsely, "That's Ivy."

With his face pressed up against the wall, he panted out, "Fuck you, bitch."

Dez just stared at him. Fuck. This . . . this wasn't how she'd wanted this to happen. She'd just needed to know if the damn journal was *here*, not have the fucking evidence spread out in front of her. *Damn it—*

She'd screwed around the wrong way and now they were fucked. Royally. Even if they weren't officially connected, any evidence here would be tainted. She went to rise and saw Joshua. He was crouched on the floor, staring at the spread of pictures there. Staring at them in unconcealed horror.

As though he'd sensed her gaze, he looked up.

His voice was agonized as he rasped, "Is this why you were here? Did you know?"

Shit. What did it matter now?

"Yeah. I knew." She stared at him, hating herself for screwing this up, for ripping his heart out.

An anguished scream left him and he slammed his fist into the ground. Then he surged to his feet, his face pale, his eyes dark with fury. "Damn you," he snarled.

For a moment, she thought he was speaking to her.

But then she saw that he was talking to the kid.

Taylor let him go.

Brendan turned to face his dad, all big eyes and sadness. "Dad, what . . . what are you talking about?"

Joshua swooped down, grabbing one of the pictures. "This, damn it. I'm talking about this—what the fuck is this?"

"It's that girl." Brendan shrugged. "I thought she was pretty and I wanted a picture of her."

"Don't fucking *lie* to me," he snarled. "What the fuck is this?"

He grabbed the journal and that was when Brendan snapped— all but transformed, his handsome face going ugly with hate. "Give me that," he growled, lunging forward. Taylor stopped him.

Dez almost wished he hadn't as Joshua flipped through it. "Oh, God . . . oh, God . . ."

He looked at his son, shaking his head. "How . . . Tristan . . . you . . ."

Then he closed his eyes, going to his knees.

"Hey . . ." Dez, her heart a cold, miserable knot in her chest, moved toward him.

In the edge of her vision, she saw Brendan. Saw him spin, grab something—a guitar, it looked like an electric guitar. Taylor intercepted, coming between the father and the son before Brendan could bring the guitar down over his father's head. Dez heard Taylor grunt, watched as the instrument connected solidly with his forearm. The sickening, wet crack was terribly familiar— the sound of a bone breaking was a sound she'd heard before, a sound she never wanted to hear again.

She bit back her cry and circled around as Brendan eased back, watching Taylor with a taunting smile. "Stupid fuck," he jeered. "How you going to handle me with a broken arm?"

Dez got in front of him, keeping one hand behind her, hoping Taylor's instincts were as good as they'd always been. They were. A second later, she felt the familiar weight of his gun. She slid the safety off before she brought it out from behind her—never show your weapon unless you're prepared to use it. She didn't want to shoot this boy, but she would.

"He doesn't have to worry about handling you, kid," Dez said quietly.

His eyes went wide at the sight of the gun.

She smiled at him sadly. "I can handle you just fine. Put the guitar down, Brendan. Put it down. Nobody else has to get hurt."

He swung it back and forth, shaking his head. "You think I'm fucking *stupid*? You want to arrest my ass, take me to juvie or something."

Oh, Brendan—you wouldn't end up there after what you've done, she thought sadly. Assuming the locals could make the charges stick, and that would be dicey. She just didn't know. But she didn't say any of that. Instead, she nudged the journal with her foot. "Arrest you? Man, I'm not an official agent. I can't arrest you. And this? Hell, this shit is compromised now." She shrugged and grimaced—looking pissed off and worried wasn't at all hard. She wanted him to feel comfortable enough to put that guitar down, but she didn't see it happening.

She had a bad, bad feeling in her gut. Very bad. Damn it, she'd screwed this up. All to hell and back.

"Come on. Put it down."

He just laughed, backing his way out of the room, keeping his back close to the wall and his eyes on them.

They couldn't let him leave—not like this. No, the locals might not be able to arrest him for *this*, but Taylor could damn well have him arrested for assault, and that would buy them time for something—*anything*.

If he left, though, he was going to hurt somebody else. She could see it in his eyes, could all but feel it.

Apparently Brendan's dad had the same feeling. Or at least the same desire not to see the kid leave. Joshua, finally able to pick himself up, got to his feet. With fury and heartbreak glinting in his eyes, he glared at his son. "You're not leaving this house, Brendan. Don't even try."

Brendan sneered at him. "And how the hell you going to stop me? Fucking pussy."

"Enough," Joshua snapped. He took one step toward the boy and then blanched as Brendan grabbed something from the top of the desk near him. It glinted silver.

Dez braced herself when she saw the knife. It wasn't the kind that would be balanced for throwing, she knew. But luck wasn't running on their side today. "Put it down or I'm shooting," she warned.

"No!" Joshua reached out a hand.

"Pussy." Brendan gave the man a look of complete disgust, complete loathing. He threw the guitar down, shifted the knife to his right hand as he moved toward the door. "If I stab you with this, you still going to stand there and whimper and cry about her shooting me?"

"You're my son, damn it," Joshua said, his voice hoarse. Broken.

"So the fuck what?" He'd cleared the door and shot a quick glance toward the stairs.

"You're my son. I love you." Joshua shook his head. "And I should have seen how messed up you are. But if you leave this house, don't think that's the end of it. I'll have every cop I can find looking for you. You'll be arrested. I'll have you in the nearest—"

"Fuck you!" Brendan screamed. He threw the knife, but either luck smiled on them or Brendan's rage had cost him. The knife went wide, landing by the window. The boy didn't wait to see. He took off running.

Dez took off after him—

There are times when every second takes a lifetime. Even as she burst through the door, she knew, deep in her gut, it was too late. Too late for what, she didn't know.

Those seconds slowed to a crawl—Dez heard a scream. A woman's? Then there was a crash. Then another scream—Brendan's— and it carried through the house, ending all too abruptly.

With her heart in her throat, she ran for the stairs. There was a gaping hole in the middle of the railing along the landing, the wood ragged and broken. She didn't even remember getting down the steps, just that she'd been up on the second floor, then she was kneeling by Brendan's side.

He was breathing—barely.

"Oh, God . . ."

NINETEEN

"HIS spinal cord is damaged," Taylor said quietly as he settled into the seat next to Dez.

She closed her eyes. "Is he going to live?"

"Spinal cord injury." Taylor sighed and scrubbed a hand over his face. "Hard to say. It's a lower break—in the thoracic area. Had it been higher . . . well, who knows? His dad and stepmother are with him now. The doctors have him mostly stabilized."

"Stabilized." The sound of his scream kept echoing through her mind. "What in the hell does that mean, anyway? They . . ." She swallowed. "They're sure it's a break, right? Not just damaged or whatever?"

"It's broken. He landed on a table, hit it in just the worst possible way. Although if he'd hit a little bit higher, it would have been his neck that snapped." Taylor stared straight ahead, his face blank, voice flat. "He's got movement in his hands and arms, can feel about through his midchest. That's it." He shifted his gaze and stared at her. "They're still with him, and I guess anything's possible, but I'm not looking for any medical miracles here."

Dez shifted her gaze away.

"He can't stay here, though. They'll have to move him to a better facility, Bloomington or maybe New Albany or Louisville. He'll need further treatment and rehab."

Dez opened her eyes and looked at him. "This is my fault," she said quietly. "I *had* to know if that journal was there, but . . ."

"We both carry some blame here. We need to remember one thing, though. Nobody made him do what he did and nobody made him run. You gave him every reason *not* to run." He reached over and covered her hand with his. "He didn't need to run. He didn't need to try and attack his father."

He grimaced and looked down at his casted forearm. "And he didn't need to break my damn arm, either. Went my entire life without getting a broken bone."

"Well, no." She rested her head on his shoulder. "You have a broken bone now—two actually."

"Smart-ass." He closed his eyes. "Dez, this entire thing is a mess. All of it."

"Yeah." She didn't mention that it wasn't even done. There was no need. He knew. Her gut was still in knots over the task before them, the heartbreak they still needed to face. And the guilt—

Fuck, the guilt.

"God, what have I done?" She dropped her head into her hands and blew out a breath. "What in the hell have I done?"

Taylor rested his hand on the back of her neck. "Dez, you need to stop."

"I *can't*," she snapped, surging out of the chair and pacing the small confines of the waiting room. "I haven't been gone so long that I've forgotten to be aware of all possible outcomes. I knew what kind of kid he was—knew he wasn't stable—should have realized he'd react badly if he saw me there. *Damn* it—"

"And what if we'd waited?" Taylor stood up. His voice was cool and, once more, his emotions were hidden behind that steely blue curtain. "What if we'd waited? Dez, did you *look* at that journal at all? He was at Beau's house. You know why? Because Beau saw Mark and ran him off the road. He wrote it all down. He was afraid Beau's fuckup would lead back to him. And he also was worried about the other boys. What if he'd gone after them?"

Dez shook her head. "And what if he hadn't?"

"He was going to go back for Ivy."

She stilled. Her heart slammed against her rib cage and her mouth went dry. Wiping her sweating palms over her jeans, she stared at him. "What?"

"You heard me. He considered her an unfinished job. He'd set himself a goal of 'killing a bitch'—his words—before he turned eighteen and he was going to do it. She was his goal and he was going to kill her."

"No." Dez turned away, covering her face with her hands. Screams of fury rose inside her, but she kept them trapped. "You . . . hell. You read it in the journal?"

"Yeah. He had it all documented, neat as can be. His dad had me read it earlier—I finished it while you were in the chapel. It goes back eight months. There are others, though. His stepmom says he's kept journals for almost as long as he's been able to write."

The guilt was still there. She couldn't wipe it away as easily as that. And maybe she shouldn't be able to—oh, screw the maybe. She *knew* she shouldn't be able to wipe it away. She'd fucked up and she needed to take responsibility for it.

But she could bear that guilt, she reckoned. Especially if it meant Ivy would be safe. "He'll have a harder time hurting her now," she said quietly.

"Yes."

"Does that make it okay?" She turned and looked at him, her hands opening, closing into fists. She remembered the look of sheer hate, the rage—the *ugliness* she'd seen in Brendan's eyes. The pure filth she'd felt inside his soul. "He's so young. Could he be helped? Knowing she's safe now, that makes me breathe easier, but this doesn't make it okay for me. It *can't.*"

"It shouldn't." Taylor came to her and slid his arm around her waist. She sighed and rested her head on his chest, wishing she could get closer. Wishing she could find a way to fix all the mistakes she'd made over the past day. "If this made it okay for you, you wouldn't be who you are."

"Are *you* okay with this?" She curled a hand into his shirt, determined she wasn't going to cry over this. She wouldn't let herself have those tears. She wasn't sure she deserved them.

"No. But I saw a kid who was willing to kill you, me, his father. All because we were in his way. That's all it was, Dez. We were in his way. It doesn't make any of this right, but I'm not going to kill myself with guilt over it, either. We screwed up. We have to live with it. But he made the choices that put him here." He pressed his lips to her brow.

"He's just a kid."

"He's seventeen. Old enough to know he shouldn't kidnap a girl, that he shouldn't kill his friends. Don't use that 'just a kid' line, Dez. We both know better. Neither of us had the easiest childhood and we didn't decide to go and kidnap a girl, didn't decide to kill our friends, none of that." He eased back, studying her face. "You have to figure out how to deal with it on your own; I know that. But he made his own choices. And he knew they were wrong. He just didn't care."

She swallowed. Sighing, she eased back away from him. The memory of seeing those pictures spill out of the journal haunted her—seeing Ivy's face—*that* haunted her. Ivy . . . God, she wanted that image gone. So badly.

But she couldn't pluck it from her mind, just like she couldn't erase any other moment of this day. She had to live with it. "You're right. He didn't care. I have to live with knowing I did something that pushed him into running—and he had an accident that landed him in here."

"*We* pushed him into running," Taylor interjected. "We have to live with it—it was both of us."

"We," she echoed. "But he was old enough to do this. It's not like he was ten years old, twelve years old. We have to deal with it. So does he."

* * *

IT was night. Dark and cold—too cold, but Dez thought maybe it was just her. As Taylor pulled up in front of the cottage, she looked over at him. "Will you stay with me?"

"Is it a good idea?"

Her heart stuttered. He . . . hell. He hadn't changed his mind already, had he?

In the faint light coming off the dashboard, she saw the tired smile on his face. "Dez, that look hurts even worse than my arm," he said. He put the car into park, awkwardly, shifting around to use his left hand since the right was casted to just under his elbow. Then he turned and reached out, brushing his thumb over her lip.

"I'm not walking away. I meant what I told you—hell, was it only this morning?"

She swallowed. "Then why don't you want to come in?"

"You need to sleep."

"All the more reason you *should* come in." She covered his hand with hers, staring at him. "I sleep better with you around, Jones. At least I did last night. And . . . hell, I don't know what it is, but when you're around, I don't have this rush of *everything* coming in. It's like I'm more grounded or something. And around here, I desperately need it. It's peaceful."

A blond brow crooked up. "So basically you're just attracted to me because I'm boring?"

"Boring?" She laughed weakly. "No. Boring and peaceful are two different things. Come on inside, Jones. I'll even let you use the washer and dryer if you're worried about wearing dirty clothes tomorrow. The washer and dryer look like they are brand new—you can break them in."

"They are new." He leaned over and nipped at her lower lip. "I'll come in. If you call me by my damn name."

"Taylor." She touched his cheek. "Stay the night with me. Please."

"Okay."

Then she pushed him back, scowling. "How do you know if the appliances are new?"

"I own the house."

She was still gaping when he opened her door a minute later. He owned the house?

* * *

"You *own* this place?"

Taylor glanced at her as he rooted through the cabinets, try-ing to find something fast and easy that he could make her eat before they went to bed. "Yeah. Do you like chicken noodle soup or tomato better?"

"Chicken noodle. Unless we can do grilled cheese."

She wandered farther into the kitchen and peered over his shoulder as he glanced into the refrigerator. Yeah, the lawyer's wife had done a decent job stocking up on basics. "We can do grilled cheese."

"Good . . . are you cooking?" She headed over to the island and settled on one of the scoop-backed stools, gazing at him.

"Yes. Because I know you won't. You'll just go collapse in bed."

"Why do you own two houses?"

He frowned at her. "I don't."

"But . . . you just said you owned this one."

Taylor sighed. Tugging open one of the drawers, he rum-maged around for a can opener. "My family owned five houses here, including the manor. Now they're mine. So those, and my house in Virginia. That's six houses, not two."

"Six." She rubbed her eyes. Absently, she frowned at him as he studied the can opener and the can in front of him. "You need help?"

He grimaced at his casted arm. "I'm afraid I do."

She opened the can and nudged it over to him and returned to her perch, content to let him finish since he seemed so intent on doing it. "I can't believe some of this is happening, you know. Actually . . . *all* of it. But some parts seem very surreal. Like now. I'm sleeping with my boss. He owns six fucking houses."

"Technically, I'm not your boss."

She smirked at him. "Technically, you are, according to that contract. Although I guess we can tear that up."

"I already did." Using his casted right arm to steady the tub of butter, he scooped some of it into a spoon and dumped it into the skillet. "Well, figuratively speaking. The job that was never really a job is done and it's official. You're completely free of me again."

"Am I really?" Her voice was low and soft, husky . . . and it hit him like a sucker punch, straight in the gut. In the heart. Glancing up at her, he found her staring at him with heat in her eyes, a smile dancing on her lips. "What if I don't want to be free?"

"You might want to be careful there." He looked away—had to, before he decided to say the hell with cooking. She needed some food in her belly. He could strip her clothes away and have his way with her after she ate, damn it. And he insisted he could wait, even though his hands were shaking somewhat.

* * *

DEZ smiled at his back as he focused on the food. Either it required a great deal of his attention to grill those sandwiches or he was ignoring her.

She figured he was ignoring her.

That was fine. She'd been flirting with him more to keep her mind off everything else, anyway. Everything else—so much of everything else. Damn it all to hell.

Stop it. You can think about it more in the morning. You need to sleep, she told herself.

Needed to sleep. Needed him. Needed to set all of this aside. Tomorrow she'd go back to the hospital, face what she'd done. Again. But for now, she needed to set it aside.

It didn't take long for him to slip a plate and a bowl of soup in front of her and she stared at it for a good thirty seconds, trying to convince herself she could eat, that she *should* eat. Making a face, she looked up at him and said, "You know, I'm not hungry."

"Eat." He settled across from her with his own food.

"You're so damn bossy." She sighed and dipped a spoon into the bowl, stirring it around. "I'm not hungry."

"If I waited for you to be hungry, you might eat at the dawn of the next ice age. Eat . . . please."

"Damn. Jones, you just said *please*. I'm so impressed." She put the spoon down and picked up her sandwich, then dipped it into her soup, a faint smile curling her lips. Vaguely, she could remember eating like this with her grandmother. Those memories were so faint, they couldn't really even be called memories. But they made her smile. She reached up to touch her necklace, only to remember she didn't have it—the chain still needed to be fixed.

After she took a bite of her sandwich, she looked at Taylor. "Where was my necklace?" she asked him.

A shutter fell across his face, his eyes carefully blank. With controlled, precise movements, he laid his spoon down. His gaze shifted to some point past her shoulder, although she suspected he wasn't seeing any part of the house, or even her. "It was on the floor after the medics transferred you to the stretcher. I saw it and grabbed it." He slanted a look in her direction and then shifted his gaze off to the side again. "I'm sorry I didn't return it sooner."

"'S okay," she murmured, shrugging. "I was just wondering. I'd pretty much given it up for lost."

"I'll get the chain fixed for you." He picked up his spoon again.

She opened her mouth to tell him it wasn't necessary, but then she frowned, noticed how tightly he gripped that spoon. Hell, she couldn't have pried it out of his grip.

"I never should have let you go in there."

Dez tore off a piece of her sandwich and popped it in her mouth. Oddly, her appetite wasn't quite as dead as it had been. "You would have had a hard time stopping me, you know."

"I could have cuffed you and thrown you in my car," he growled. "Shit."

He shoved back from the island, hurling the spoon down.

"And I would have decked you. A girl would have died. We need to get past this, sugar. God knows the two of us are going to have enough to come to grips with, just dealing with everything going on here and now. I'm *fine*, so why worry about it?"

"Because I'm not fine!"

She jumped, caught off guard by the fury, the heat in his usually cool voice. He came off the stool, prowling the kitchen like a caged lion, his eyes half wild, his uninjured hand opening and closing into a fist. "I've got enough nightmares haunting me already, but none of them haunt me like that. I can't . . . I can't . . ."

His voice broke and he turned away.

Dez stared as he braced his uninjured hand on the counter, his broken one hanging at his side. Then he just stood there, head slumped. "You're all torn up inside over what happened to Brendan Moore and I won't deny feeling some guilt. But it's not going to shatter me, not going to keep me awake at night. None of it would have happened if he hadn't taken the road he'd taken. If he was four, five years younger? I might feel different. But you saw the same person I saw—that wasn't a child making those decisions. He knew what he was doing—*and he didn't care.*"

As he turned around and stared at her, eyes burning with

emotion, Dez's heart leaped into her throat. "You're going to feel bad about it, and I can't stop you," he said, his voice gruff, raw. Naked emotion shone in his gaze. "It may well keep you up at night. But you know what keeps me up at night? The sight of you lying on the ground, your blood all over my hands, and I can't fucking stop it."

"Taylor . . ." Slipping off the stool, she moved around the island, coming up to stand in front of him. She cupped her face in his hands, stroked a thumb over his mouth.

What did she say to him? Her heart ached inside her chest and she wanted, so badly, to take that pain from him. Rising on her toes, she pressed her lips to his. She couldn't just keep saying, *I'm fine.* He could see that. And saying it wasn't going to do anything to undo the nightmares, she realized, not if they ran that deep.

Maybe . . . she closed her eyes and pulled away, resting her head on his shoulder as the words she'd held inside burned in her throat. Maybe she could give him that. Would it help? Would it hurt?

Swallowing, she lifted her head once more and studied him. She stroked her hands down his chest, down to his sides. "Have you ever had something burning inside you, something you wanted to tell somebody for a long, long while, but you just couldn't?"

His lids flickered, but he said nothing. His uninjured hand came up, his thumb lightly brushing the scar on her neck.

"I could have said it a year ago. I meant it then. Hell, I could have said it two years ago, five . . ." Nervous, she realized. Oh, fuck, she was nervous. Was she supposed to be nervous? She'd never told anybody. Not like this. She thought she might have told her friend Taige, but that was different. Had she ever told anybody as a child? Her mother? Her grandmother . . .

Focus, damn it.

Biting the inside of her cheek, hard, she waited until that small, sharp pain cleared her head enough for her to think again. Then she focused on that steely blue gaze. Yes. She could have told him five years ago, easily. She suspected she probably could have told him within a few months of meeting him, not that he'd made it easy for her to love him—Taylor Jones wouldn't want anybody loving him. But she loved him anyway.

And it was time she let him know that.

Cupping his face in her hands once more, she focused on him—just him. He was her anchor, she realized. When he was there, he made everything so much easier, so much more real. She needed him.

"I love you."

* * *

FOR a few seconds, those words didn't want to connect in his head. No, that wasn't right—they *wanted* to connect, but some protective instinct just wouldn't let them, not immediately, at least.

He could feel the ridge of her scar under his thumb, the warmth of her skin. He could see the darkness of her gaze, the intensity of it. There was a small, solemn smile on her lips, so gentle and easy.

Closing his eyes, he let himself think about what she'd said— let himself think about the *words*.

Fuck. *Fuck*—

Abruptly, he caught the front of her shirt in his hand, fisted it, dragging her closer. He pressed his brow to hers. In a ragged, harsh voice, he demanded, "Do you mean it?"

"Now come on, Jones." She chuckled. "Since when have I ever said anything I don't mean?"

She might have said something else, but he didn't know

what—he couldn't say he even cared. He was too busy kissing her, his mouth all but devouring hers. And she didn't seem to mind at all.

Handicapped by his broken arm, he struggled one-handed with her clothing, determined to have her naked—*now*. She apparently had the same focus in mind, her fingers fighting with the buttons on his shirt, shoving it open, but she didn't mess with trying to get it off. Fine by him.

He wasn't too worried about his clothes, but hers were a different story. The shirt, it had to go. Same with her bra, her jeans, her panties, although his fingers were clumsy and everything seemed to tangle with him. Growling, he fisted his hand in the silky little strip of cloth high on her hips, ready to rip the panties off. She laughed and said, "Slow down there, Jones. I just bought those from Victoria's Secret—you tear them, you buy me new ones."

"Fine. I'll buy you a fucking truckload." With a vicious twist of his wrist, the fragile silk shredded. Dropping it to the ground, he turned and boosted her up onto the counter, stepping between her thighs. "We're doing something stupid again, aren't we?"

"No. We're doing something we need to do." She curled an arm around his neck and scooted closer, twining her legs around his hips. "Make love to me, Taylor."

"Gladly." He pressed his lips to hers, whispered, "I swear, one of these days, we'll do this right . . . slower, easier. Spend more time in a damn bed."

"This feels pretty damn right to me." As he pushed inside, her head fell back. A ragged moan escaped her and he dipped his head, pressed his mouth to her neck. "I love you."

"Look at me."

She lifted her lashes, staring at him. The words were there.

Trapped inside—fuck. Why had it seemed too easy for her? He started to move, staring at her, at this woman who was his everything, his world. Nothing mattered, not without her.

She lifted a hand and touched his cheek, pushed her fingers into his hair. "Jones . . ."

"My name," he muttered. He turned his head, pressed a kiss to her palm. "Say my name, damn it."

Chuckling, she pulled his head close. "Taylor." She said it against his lips. As she did that, she rolled her hips against him, squeezing down with her inner muscles so that she milked him in a teasing, taunting caress.

Oh, shit . . .

Little warning tingles were already shooting straight up his spine, but he gritted his teeth. No, damn it. He wasn't going to lose it after thirty fucking seconds. Especially since he hadn't told her yet.

But then she did it again, and again.

"I love you." It came out a broken, harsh groan against her lips, the words he could no longer keep trapped inside. The words he had to share with her, *now*.

She stiffened against him. Her hands tightened on his shoulders, her nails biting into his skin. "Taylor . . ."

"I love you," he said again, and it came so much easier. Wrapping his arm around her neck, he cuddled her against him. That burning, driving need to take, to possess, to mark . . . it didn't fade . . . it changed, morphed, settled into something different, so different. Something gentle, something he couldn't remember ever feeling before.

They stared at each other. He barely moved against her, his broken arm braced against one of the cabinets by her head. Slow, gentle movements. But it was enough. Slow, gentle movements, while they stared at each other . . . almost like it was the first time.

A shaky sigh escaped her, a delicate flush rising from the swell of her breasts, darkening the warm brown of her skin. Taylor dipped his head and pressed his mouth to her shoulder. "I love you," he murmured against her skin. "I love you . . ."

Dez laughed, a dazed, delighted sound. "I know. I love you, too."

It echoed in his mind, over and over. The release, as it came for them both, was just as slow, just as sweet and gentle. And for the first time, some of the darkness that had chased him for twenty-five years, it started to recede.

TWENTY

IN the warmth of Taylor's arms, Dez slept. It came on slowly and because she'd always felt so safe with him, it hit her unprepared. She was so tired, so drained, unconsciously, she'd let her shields slip.

And when that happened, the ghost was able to slip in and touch her.

The drop in temperature was gradual. Neither of them noticed at first. Her sleep became more fitful and she grunted absently, shifting in her sleep, one hand closing into a fist.

The girl—

Anna? Was it Anna?

She could see her.

There was a field.

Dez muttered in her sleep, the words broken, making little sense. They might not have even made sense to her. But in her mind, she could see pictures. And finally, things began to piece together.

A hand. There was a hand in hers—no. Not *hers*—Anna's.
Guiding her. *"We'll go play. It's more fun with a friend, isn't it?"*
"I thought we were going to go trick-or-treating . . ."
"Oh, but we can't. That isn't safe. I want my angel safe—"
Angel—

Images flashed. Bright and vivid. The child, she didn't understand. Jerking back, hands slick with sweat, belly clenching with
horror, she stared at her new friend. *Angel*—?

He'd called her his angel.

With a scream, Dez jerked upright.

* * *

SHE was still shaking.

Taylor sat in the bed, holding her, torn between his own grief
and the need to do *anything* to make this better. Rubbing a hand
up and down her spine, he waited for Dez. He didn't know how
long it would take, and although impatience ate at him, he said
nothing, did nothing. He couldn't rush this.

As much as he wanted to.

He'd been awake for more than an hour.

When she'd first started to stir in her sleep, it had awoken
him. He'd never slept peacefully and even though he'd given in
sometime last night and taken one of the damn pain pills, her
restlessness had pulled him straight out of his sleep.

She'd been talking, muttering to herself.

A walk—?

Trick-or-treating . . .

Anna had disappeared on Halloween. And their mother had
never allowed either of them to go trick-or-treating. It was a crass
and common thing, Elsa had insisted. Taylor wasn't going to try
to fool himself into thinking this wasn't about Anna.

In his gut, he knew it was.

But he couldn't rush this. It was about his sister, and he could do nothing but wait.

Another twenty minutes passed before Dez stopped shaking. Another ten minutes before she spoke. Her voice was hoarse as she said, "Where is Anna's grave?"

* * *

"HER flowers are missing."

The sound of his voice was startling in the early morning silence. Dez jumped and shot him a puzzled look. "What?"

That emotionless mask was firmly in place as he slid his gaze her way, but she saw that screaming, dark anguish in his pale eyes as he said quietly, "Her flowers. Every year, when I visit her grave, I bring her daisies. I just left them the other day . . . the day she disappeared. They should still be here. They aren't."

A cold shiver, one that had nothing to do with the twenty-degree wind chill, ran down Dez's spine. Shoving her hands in her pockets, she looked up at the marble angel. It was the same one she'd seen before, and now that she was focused, she could feel those whispers more acutely. Although it went against her training, she lowered her shields completely, and when she did, a blast of whispers assaulted her.

Find me . . . please find me . . . I don't want to stay lost—

She shuddered and covered her face with her hands. God, did she *know*?

Help me, please . . .

"Where are you, baby?"

The screaming, roaring chaos in her mind all but deafened and blinded her. She couldn't think, couldn't focus—

With a groan, she clamped her hands over her ears, but it did nothing to ease that chaos. *Focus, focus—*

She could do this, damn it. She could. Channeling the calm she'd always gotten from Taylor, but refusing to let his presence block everything the way it often did, she blocked out *everything* but the information she needed.

Where. Are. You.

The answer didn't come in words. Dez couldn't even be sure the answer came from Anna. It was just *there*. And it was so ridiculously simple, she knew she should have realized it before now. Swallowing, she turned and looked at Taylor.

"We need to go to the field out behind Beau's place again."

For the briefest second, there was horror in his eyes. And then gold-tipped lashes swept over his eyes, shielding them. And he nodded.

*   *   *

One hand lay over the fragile stem of a daisy.

The other held a pen.

Such lovely daisies. Did you like them? I imagine you must have or he wouldn't give them to you, I suppose. If he wasn't your brother, it would bother me that a boy was giving you such flowers. But a brother is different from a boy.

The slender fingers gripping the pen tightened.

Some boys, though, some of them . . .

A memory rose up to taunt—*My pretty angel, did you think I wouldn't hear? Little slut—*

* * *

HIS knuckles were bloodless. Dez wished she could reach over and stroke the tension away, wished she could make this better. But she couldn't. There was no easing this pain for him. Closing her eyes, she rested her head against the headrest and made herself find some level of inner calm.

It had never been more important, she realized. And it would never be harder to find. She tried to dredge up some shields that would let her find what she needed to find without leaving her totally exposed. Whether or not it would work, she didn't know.

But just in case . . .

"So." She shot him a halfhearted smile and asked, "Do you have a Taser on you by chance?"

A spasm twisted his mouth. His eyes closed for the briefest second as he slowed at a stop sign. He glanced her way. The shuttered look in his eyes spoke volumes. "Yes. I hadn't planned on needing it but I've always kept one in my briefcase. After the last episode . . ."

"Good." She blew out a sigh. "I've never had to have that particular pleasure, you know."

"Don't make me use it, please." He pressed on the gas with a little more force than necessary as he took a winding road that led out of town, toward Beau's house.

She reached over, touched his hand. "If you need it, then do it—don't think, just do it. I'd rather not be trapped in one of those visions any longer than needed."

"I know."

The rest of the trip passed in silence, a tense, unhappy silence. Dez didn't recognize the unmarked, narrow road he took, although she did glimpse what looked like Beau's house some distance ahead. They parked in a narrow little spot off the road and she braced herself as she climbed out of the car, waiting by the hood as Taylor went around. She glimpsed the Taser as he tucked it away and she grimaced, mumbling a heartfelt prayer he wouldn't need it—for both of their sakes.

As he drew even with her, their gazes connected. "Are you going to be okay?" she asked quietly.

"After you collapsed on me, you're asking me?" His gaze was unreadable.

She reached up, touching his cheek. "It's not my blood that could be out there somewhere, Taylor." She stepped closer, sliding an arm around his waist. "Are you going to be okay? If . . . I—hell." She tipped her head back and stared at him. "We just managed to find each other. I don't want to lose you already. As selfish as that seems, I'm scared it will happen. But even more, I don't want to hurt you."

"Anything you tell me is going to hurt." He hooked his hand around her neck, pulled her close. "But I've already figured out enough—you're here for this. I know that. And whatever happened to my baby sister, it's keeping her trapped here. She deserves better than that."

He pressed his brow to hers. "Help her let go. No matter what we find, it's going to hurt. But keeping her trapped here just because I can't face the truth makes me even more of a bastard than I already am. We're not doing that. And I'm not losing you, either. So let's get this done."

* * *

HE hoped he hadn't lied. Oh, he wasn't worried about the deal with losing her—he wasn't giving Desiree Lincoln up, not while he breathed. He just hoped he could face what she told him.

The frozen grass crunched under their feet as they walked along, breath foggy in the cold air.

They'd been walking for twenty minutes when he saw it starting for her. It was always a disturbing change to see. Sometimes because she'd have that little smile on her face. Today there was no smile. Today, her eyes got darker, her mouth flattened into a firm line, and there was something about the way she stared off into the distance that made him wonder if she was even *here*.

Occasionally her mouth would move, but she never said a word. Sometimes she'd cock her head, like she'd heard something, something he couldn't hear.

Then abruptly, she stopped. Her head turned. And she stared.

Taylor vaguely knew where they were—Meyer's Field. And it was pretty damn close to where they'd been the other night. Dez was staring off at some point to the north and when he moved closer, he could even see the point her gaze was fixed on.

And her lips were moving again.

In some silent, soundless conversation.

* * *

"No—stop it! Let me go!"

Anna was screaming. The lady touching her, she wasn't hurting her, but when she *did* touch her, there was pain. Pain in her head, and Anna couldn't block it off. Sometimes that happened, but usually, it wasn't like this.

It hurt, and it hurt and it was ugly, so ugly—

My angel, my pretty angel. You little slut, you let him touch you—

She tore away from the lady and tried to run, but the lady caught her. "No!" Anna screamed, swinging out, hardly able to see for the tears. Pain cramped her belly, but it wasn't really hers, it came from the lady.

"Sweetheart, it's okay," the lady babbled, trying to hug her, trying to hold her.

Earlier, those hugs had felt so nice. Mama never really hugged her like that. Taylor did, and Daddy did, but Mama never hugged her. Anna liked those hugs. But now . . . ever since the woman called her angel . . .

Whimpering, Anna tried to get away. The ugly pictures swarmed her mind. A man, she knew him—what was he doing? It was wrong, she knew that . . . so wrong. Grunting and groaning—she saw images of him looming over her, only it *wasn't* her.

Anna cried out, tried to get away, but the lady wouldn't let go. She bit her. The lady screamed, and her grip loosened. Anna ran. Blindly, she ran. She didn't care where she ran, didn't know, and it didn't matter, she just had to get away. She could see the little cabin the lady had been taking her to, but she couldn't go there, she couldn't. The roots grabbed at her feet, trying to trip her, and finally, one did. She went flying and immediately jumped back up.

Behind her, the lady called her name.

Anna shot a look behind her, didn't see—

And then she was falling.

*   *   *

THE darkness came so sudden and swift, it froze the air in Dez's lungs. Her eyes flew open and she struggled to breathe around the shock of it, struggled to separate herself from that deep connection with Anna. Too deep—she'd felt the terror, felt the pain of death.

The emptiness.

And her horror.

Finally, she managed to get in a breath. Then another. The band around her chest eased and she shoved against Taylor's chest, eyeing the Taser. "Put that thing away," she wheezed.

"If you'd made me use it, I might have spanked you." He gripped her against him with his busted arm, stroking the back of her head with his good hand. "Are you okay?"

She nodded, licking her lips. "Physically, at least." It wasn't the complete truth—her belly was in turmoil and her head ached. But that would pass in a few more minutes.

Emotionally, though . . . she wasn't sure.

Emotionally, she was a disaster.

Closing her eyes, she let her mind process what had just happened. The thoughts were jumbled, trying to settle into a weird sort of pattern. Something . . . she needed to figure out one crucial . . .

"Holy shit," she whispered. Pushing back from Taylor, she stared at him. "Taylor, your sister was gifted."

"No." He shook his head. "No, she wasn't."

Dez pulled out of his arms and stood up, slowly, not trusting her shaking legs. "Oh, yes. She was. It wasn't *her* I got those images from. *She* got them from somebody else. And she didn't understand. But the person who took her had been abused—she was the one who'd been attacked. Anna had those images in her head when she died. I . . ." She swallowed, shaking her head. "Maybe all of that is part of what kept her trapped here, I don't know. But Taylor, she was gifted."

He just stared at her, his face pale, eyes glinting. "Dez, I can recognize gifted. I've always been able to. Anna, she was special, but . . ."

His voice trailed off. His eyes closed.

* * *

SPECIAL. Yes. Anna had been special. She'd had a light about her. When their father had been having a bad day, Anna knew how to make it better. She'd been the only one who could. When their mother had been despondent or more moody than usual, some-how, even though nobody else could reach her, sometimes, Anna had been able to do just that.

And Taylor . . . no matter what, no matter how bad the day had been, she'd always been the one who could ease that, turn it around. One could easily say she'd just been a child with a way of sensing emotions.

But if he'd seen her today, what would he have thought?

Would he have wanted to talk to her longer and see if that unique way was something more . . . ?

He opened his eyes and stared at Dez, let himself think—not just about what she'd said about Anna. But the rest of it. Some-thing in his heart tried to break free, but he didn't dare let it. He got to his feet, grimacing as he had to adjust his balance, thrown off by the injury to his right arm. "Are you . . ." He closed his eyes. This was one thing he hadn't prepared himself for—that Anna might not have been hurt. One thing he couldn't have counted on. "Are you telling me that Anna hadn't been hurt?"

With a steady gaze, she stared at him. "I don't think she was." She turned her head, looking all around. "I need to find her. I think she's close." And she said nothing else as she started to walk.

*   *   *

IT was a well.

Taylor recognized the solid, sturdy covering. Many of the old wells had been filled in, but a few hadn't. Staring at it, his heart racing, he wondered. Was this the end of it, then?

Had they found her?

He looked up, saw Dez staring at him.

"She's in there," Dez said quietly. A heavy sigh shuddered out of her and he realized, although the sun was beating down on them and the frost covering the ground had started to melt, it was colder now than it had been. "I feel her."

"Is she . . ."

Dez looked down. "Just open it." Then she frowned, squatted down. She reached inside her coat and pulled out a pen.

He watched as she nudged something on the ground. A flower petal . . . What . . . ?

"She was here," Dez murmured. "The lady."

Startled, he looked at her. "Lady?"

"Yes. It was a lady who took her." She rose again, her gaze shifting off to the side. Automatically, he followed her gaze, although he knew he'd see nothing. His heart screamed—*Anna?*

But there was nothing.

Setting his jaw, he bent and grabbed the handle. Logic told him it would be hard to move. It was an old well. Never used. The cover wouldn't be easy to budge.

It came up with barely a protest.

He reached for the Maglite he'd tucked into a loop on his belt and pulled it off. "If the well's deep," he said hoarsely, "we won't see much." He looked up, focusing on Dez's face. "If it's full of water or anything . . ."

She came around and rested a hand on his shoulder. "I can look."

"No." He closed his eyes. He had to do this. He had to look. For Anna. For his father. Even for his mother. And for himself.

He looked.

It wasn't very deep, maybe thirty feet. At some point since it had been dug, it had gone dry, too. Nothing, absolutely nothing, kept him from seeing the small, forlorn skeleton lying at the bottom.

* * *

"WE'RE keeping it quiet."

Distantly, Dez was aware of the detective's voice, knew he was talking to Taylor—she knew she should be more focused on him, but for the first time, Anna was talking to *her*, and she couldn't have looked away from the girl if she'd tried.

"*You found me.*"

"Yes."

If anybody noticed her talking to thin air, Dez, at that point, didn't care. She knew she would later, but right then, she didn't care.

"*Is that . . . that's Taylor, isn't it?*"

"Yeah." She shifted her gaze away from the girl's face for a brief moment and focused on Taylor. He stood with one hand jammed in his pocket, head slightly bowed against the wind. "That's him."

"*I guess I should have expected him to look different.*" Her image shivered, wavered. "*I know a long time passed—I could feel it, even when I wasn't really able to hold on much. But I didn't expect him to look different.*" A sad sigh escaped. "*He looks so sad, so grim.*"

Dez didn't feel like she was talking to a child. She supposed, in reality, maybe she wasn't. It wasn't something that had happened before. Most often, they seemed stuck, trapped by the horror of what had happened to them, unable to progress past what they'd been.

But the horror hadn't happened to *her* so much.

Edging a little farther from those around them, she quietly asked, "He needs to know . . . if you can tell me. Do you remember what happened?"

"Not all of it, no. There was a lady. She was sad. She wanted me to go with her—I knew I shouldn't. But I hated that she was sad." Anna reached up, tugging on one of her insubstantial ponytails. The habit seemed so simple, so human. And this woman-girl was anything *but* human now. No longer part of this world. *"I told myself I'd make her feel better. I liked making people feel better. Then I'd leave. She wouldn't want me to leave, but I was good at sneaking away. I did it a lot . . . even with Mom and Dad, because they just never knew I'd know when they'd come and look in on me."*

A shiver wracked Dez's body. Perhaps not as much woman as she appeared. But she'd died before she'd had a chance to lose that naiveté.

"She wanted to keep me." Anna's eyes closed. *"She was angry at my mother. She'd heard Mama yelling at me and it made her angry. It didn't make sense, you know. But she wanted to keep me. Like I was a pet. The longer I was with her, the more I worried. But it wasn't until she called me her angel that I got scared."*

"That's when you realized something bad had happened . . . to her."

Anna opened her eyes. *"Yes."* She looked past Dez, to Taylor once more. *"He looks like them,"* she said softly.

Dez followed her gaze. "I guess in a way he is. He spends his life helping people, trying to stop people from hurting kids . . . so things that happened to you don't happen to others."

"But she didn't mean to hurt me," Anna said sadly. Her voice was tired and broken. *"And somebody hurt her worse. Can you . . ."*

Oh, God. Dez felt her heart stutter. Damn it. *Damn* it. But she let none of that show on her face as Anna asked, *"Can you find her? Find who hurt her?"*

"Hurt who, sweetheart?"

"*The lady. That poor lady . . .*"

* * *

"WE'RE keeping it quiet," Stahley said. "And we will do it for as long as we can." He scowled, then, pushing a hand through his grizzled, graying hair, staring over at the small crime unit gathered around the well. "If . . . hell. *If,* technically, it has to be if. *If* it is your sister, I . . . well, I'll take care of her. I'll do that no matter who it is, but I remember your sister. I worked her disappearance, you know. Still guts me, thinking about what happened to her."

He slid Taylor another look and sighed, shook his head. "Guess not as much as it does you, though."

Taylor didn't answer. What could be said? Instead of trying to answer, he looked away, focusing on Dez. He wasn't the only one looking at her, either. Damn near every person there had shot her a look from time to time, and more than a few weren't even being subtle with the way they stared at her.

"You got any idea how many freaking *weird* things have happened in town since that woman showed up?" Stahley asked.

Taylor smiled faintly. Oh, the man had no clue.

Dez was still staring at nothing, her face downcast, like whatever it was that held her attention was smaller than she was. Perhaps a child. And she was talking. Some of the people were looking at her like she was nuts. Stahley had more than a little suspicion in his gaze.

Taylor had an ache in his heart. But instead of going to her, he turned away. He'd already figured out that for some reason, his presence disrupted the flow around Dez if he got too close. As much as he wanted to be there—and he wanted it more than he wanted to breathe his next breath—he couldn't intrude.

Hearing the soft thud of footsteps, he looked up, watched as Blake Hensley came over. Clad in a thick jacket, his hat pulled low, he nodded at Stahley then looked at Taylor. "You turn up in the weirdest damn places, buddy."

Taylor grimaced. "Yeah."

He shot a look over at Dez, then the well. His gaze lingered there, something dark and sad in his eyes, before he looked back at Taylor. "What are we going to find out about this body?" he asked quietly.

"It's too early to know anything for sure," Stahley pointed out.

Blake ignored him, just staring at Taylor. He knew. Neither of them had to say a word. The man knew.

Somebody from the team gathered around the well called out. Stahley looked up, sighing. He reached up and scratched his head. "I'll be back in a minute." As he headed off, Taylor and Blake watched him go. Only when they were alone did Blake look back at Taylor.

"It's Anna, isn't it?"

Taylor looked away.

Dez was staring at him now. As their gazes locked, she started toward him.

Blake grunted. "You're not even going to answer me, but I know the answer. It's her. I feel it in my bones."

"You ever going to try to be something more than a small-town cop?" Taylor asked absently.

"Sure. If Stahley ever retires, I'm shooting for his position. But for now, I'm happy here. This is home." He shrugged. "Not all of us aspire to fame and glory."

Taylor slid him a look as Dez drew even. "You think I chose what I did for fame? Glory?"

"No." Blake shook his head. "You did it for Anna. And now you've found her."

Dez's brows arched up. She glanced at Taylor. He gave her a tiny shake of his head, but said nothing. Blake might take some damn good shots in the dark, but there was no way Taylor was confirming them. She slid her hand into his and looked past Blake to the other cops. "Any of them know how to process a crime scene?"

Taylor sighed. "They'll do." It wasn't like there would be much to find. And he knew what he needed to know. It *was* Anna.

He'd rather handle it himself, but he had no jurisdiction here and he was already in a gray area, just from all the shit that had gone down. Gray area—hell. He might be resigning over this. He couldn't even feel bad over any of it, either. He'd meant what he'd told Dez earlier—he might have some rough nights over what had happened to the Moore kid, but he could live with it, especially knowing Ivy was safe, and that Moore would have a hell of a lot harder time targeting other people now.

He could live with his actions. But the consequences might be walking away from his career, and it started with staying out of this now. Even if he could objectively look at any of it.

Dez squeezed his hand and he looked down at her. "Do you want to stay here?"

I'm not leaving—

He wanted to tell her that.

Blake cleared his throat. Looking up at him, Taylor lifted a brow.

"I ran into the mayor before I came out here, before I heard what was up today. He mentioned that if I saw you . . . well. I don't know if he wants to rip your ass to shreds or what, but I think he wants to see you. He's at the hospital." Then the cop grimaced. "Of course he's there. Where else are they going to be now?"

He sighed and rubbed a hand over his mouth. "You know, I never did like Brendan all that much. He wasn't a nice kid—had a mean way to him. His dad, now, the guy can be an ass, but he always did love that boy. You could tell. Joshua and Jacqueline . . . they tried. Loved him, and when it looked like he had problems, they tried to help."

Dez frowned, focusing on the cop. "Jacqueline?"

"The mayor's wife. Brendan's stepmom." Blake sighed, the sound echoing. Oddly loud. It reverberated through Dez's mind. Every last moment seemed to slow as he said, "She had a baby her senior year in high school, Taylor. You remember that? Nobody ever did hear who the father was, not that I can remember, but she was . . . what . . . six, seven years older than us? Then one day, the baby up and dies. SIDS, they said. Now this. That poor lady."

That poor lady . . .

Unconsciously, Dez tightened her grip around Taylor's hand.

TWENTY-ONE

L OST in thought, Dez barely realized they'd stopped at the hospital.

That poor lady . . .

Jacqueline—Dez had only the vaguest image of the woman. Blonde hair, sweet face, blank eyes. Doll's eyes. Sad. Grim. Death on the air—but she'd thought it was Brendan's. Brendan hadn't died. Was it death she'd sensed? Despair?

"Not making sense," she whispered. She shook her head, rubbed her temples. "Not making sense."

A blast of cold air wrapped around her. Startled, she looked up, realized they were at the hospital. Taylor was standing just outside her car door, waiting expectantly, a grim look on his face. He hadn't wanted to leave Anna's grave. She knew it, even if he hadn't said anything. Swallowing, she climbed out of the car, but he didn't move. His body kept her caged in.

"What's going on, Dez?" he asked quietly.

She looked past his shoulder toward the hospital. "I don't know."

"Bullshit." His voice, harsh and stinging, made her flinch.

Looking back at him, she said again, "I don't *know*. There's something . . . it's not coming together in my head yet—there's a piece missing and I think it's here." Then, because she couldn't leave him blind, she whispered, "But I think the woman who took Anna . . . I think she's here. And . . ."

She groaned and lifted her hands, covered her face. Anna's plea rose from the back of her mind to taunt her, haunt her. "You know how they haunt me, right? Once they get their way inside me, until I lay them to rest, I can't let them go? They can't let me go?"

"Yes." He curled a hand over the back of her neck. "Dez . . . look at me."

She lowered her hands and stared at him. Her eyes burned, her heart ached. "She won't be able to let me go now—not until I do what she asked."

A muscle jerked in his jaw. "Anna . . . you . . . you saw Anna."

"Yes." She laid a hand on his cheek. "She's held on, drifted in and out, but I don't think it was her pain that kept her here."

His hand closed around her wrist, squeezed so tightly. "Don't." He shook his head. The mask on his face started to crack.

"She needs me to help this woman, Taylor. She's held on all this time . . . for her. Whoever this woman is, somebody hurt her. Badly."

Taylor let her go and spun away so fast, it left her floundering. The car shuddered under the impact of his fist and she flinched. But that didn't keep her from reaching out and catching him. He already had blood on his knuckles—if he hit it again, he'd be lucky if he didn't end up with more broken bones. He whirled on her, fury on his face. "You're asking me to—to—what, stand by while you help the woman who killed my sister?" he snarled.

"I don't think she killed her. Anna fell." Dez shook her head. "I still have to piece more of it together from her, but I don't think this woman wanted to hurt her. And this has nothing to do with *me* or what *I* want. Nothing to do with you or what you want, either, really. I've got to do what *they* need."

She knew she was risking everything as she took a step closer. Taking that chance, she reached out, laid a hand on his chest. He froze, standing rigid. "How do you know this woman didn't kill her? To keep what she'd done silent?"

"I don't know that. Not yet." Licking her lips, she continued. "But regardless, it doesn't matter. Because your sister can't let go until this woman is helped. What's more important to you, Taylor? Justice . . . or peace for that little girl? Because I don't know that I can help you find both."

* * *

HE wouldn't let himself think.

That was the way it had to be as he followed Dez into the hospital.

He even knew where they were going. Everything had changed for Dez the minute Blake Hensley had said a name. And now he was staring at the woman who was responsible for his sister's death. Whether she'd killed her or just driven his sister into an accident, Taylor didn't know.

But Jacqueline Moore, the pretty, delicate blonde that Joshua Moore had taken as his second wife, was responsible for the death of six-year-old Anna Jones, missing for the past twenty-five years.

As they stood in the door, the Moores seemed to sense their

presence and Joshua looked up. A spasm twisted his mouth and he glanced at his wife before he stood. She caught his hand, though. "You stay here with him," she murmured. "I need to stretch my legs anyway."

* * *

DESPAIR—pain—

Dez jerked her shields up, almost knocked to her feet by the pain coming off this woman. Oh, she hid it. She hid it very well. It had spiked the second she looked at Taylor, too, something that would have made Dez's antennae quiver, if she had any, and if she hadn't already sensed something off about this woman.

There were all sorts of things off about her.

All sorts of things . . .

With that sweet smile in place, Jacqueline Moore shut the door behind her. With that sweet smile still in place, she turned around to face them. And without ever losing that smile, she said, "You two shouldn't be here. Not after what you caused."

It was almost eerie, Dez thought. Like seeing a doll speak.

"Joshua wanted to see us."

"You shouldn't be here," she said again, shaking her head. "Brendan's paralyzed. He can't move his legs, can't feel anything below the middle of his chest. It's your fault." She paused, shook her head. "You shouldn't be here."

She turned to go back inside—to barricade herself.

Dez reached up and laid a hand on her shoulder. As she did it, she lowered her shields. And all of the *wrongness*, all of that *brokenness* flooded her.

Gasping for breath, she fought the torrent, tried to break it off. Because it wasn't just one way. Dez wasn't very good at this thing and when she was receiving this much, all the channels in her mind burst open and she couldn't keep it trapped—it flooded out of her, back into Jacqueline, and she flinched as the woman whimpered, then sagged.

Angel . . . my pretty little angel. You let some dirty bastard touch you? Who was it? Who's been putting his dirty hands on my angel?

The pain blistered out of her—intense, obscene.

My pretty, precious angel. You are my angel, aren't you? No matter what—

Yes, Daddy. I'm your angel. Heartbreak. Despair. Self-loathing and hatred. Then, the memory of a face in the mirror. A child. Just a child . . . perhaps no older than Anna had been.

Another face.

A man's face. Cruel and angry. *Little slut. Who is it? Who did you let touch you?*

The girl cowered, protecting her ripe, swollen belly. *Nobody, Daddy. There's nobody but . . .* She didn't say it. She couldn't because Daddy didn't like to hear her *say* those words. Not at all.

Then there was a smile. Relief from the pain in her heart. And she held a small, precious little baby. *This* was an angel, *her* angel, and she'd treat this precious little gift the way an angel should be treated. Nobody would hurt her baby. Nobody. Even though it meant begging another for help, because she couldn't go home. Couldn't risk having her sweet little baby near Daddy. That baby who had her daddy's eyes. Even though pain and shame twisted through her, because she knew it was wrong, knew it wasn't right. Nobody had to know, nobody—

Daddy found her. More than two months after she'd left the hospital, after she'd run from him, he found her, knocking on the door of the small apartment she rented. The house belonged to the lady she cleaned for, a sweet lady who needed some company around the house, who needed a friend.

Daddy came inside like he owned the place, and he smiled when he saw her. Smiled at her like he owned *her*. Then he saw the baby, sleeping in her crib. She wanted to cry, wanted to scream. But he couldn't make her come back, couldn't force her to do anything.

She wouldn't let him. He couldn't force it on her. She would talk to him, show him that he couldn't make her do those things anymore, show him that he didn't control her.

And he didn't. But she paid the price. When the phone rang, her neighbor calling to invite her for dinner, she slipped out of the room, not wanting her father to hear that conversation—she had a *friend*, for the first time ever. A friend. Her father couldn't know . . .

Because she needed to keep that precious secret, she lost something more precious. She returned to the room only a minute or so later. And saw her father standing over the crib holding one of the pillows from the couch in his hand. He lifted his head to look at her, a smile on his face. He dropped the pillow on the floor. *Your baby isn't breathing, angel. After you deal with this, you'll come home. You belong with me. Only me . . .*

* * *

DEZ finally managed to tear herself away, sobs strangling her.

Jacqueline sank to the ground, whimpering like a caged, trapped animal. "No, Daddy . . . no . . . no . . ."

The door to the hospital room opened. As Mayor Joshua Moore stepped out and found his wife huddling on the floor, another person joined them on the hospital floor, his arrival announced by the pinging of the elevator.

Dez, her heart lurching in her chest, turned her head and looked.

His face had changed a lot—some of the images she'd gotten from Jacqueline reached back from her early childhood. But the cruelty, the possessiveness, and the malice, that was all still the same. Older, shoulders stooped, but nothing about him looked frail.

He glanced from Jacqueline to Dez, and his face twisted into an ugly, cold mask of rage. "You . . . you fucking bitch, get away from my girl." He started toward them, moving faster than he should have been able to, Dez thought.

Taylor came in between them, but he wasn't the only one. He wasn't even the one who got to the old man first. That was Joshua, his face lacking that smiling politician's glow, his eyes all but blazing with fury.

"You . . . old man, I told you, and I meant it. You won't get near her again, you hear me?" Joshua grabbed the lapels of the older man's jacket and whirled him around, slamming him into the wall.

Next to Dez, Jacqueline gasped, her eyes glazed.

* * *

EVEN a blind man would have been able to sense the fear coming off the woman huddled on the floor. The fear. And the hatred. Taylor looked down at Jacqueline, his heart torn in two. He wanted justice—but Anna needed peace.

A few feet away, Joshua snarled at his father-in-law.

"You can't fucking stop me from seeing my girl," Beard sneered. "She's my girl, my angel. I got a right to see her, and my grandson."

"*My angel* . . ." Jacqueline whispered. Her voice was ragged. Broken. She shook her head, the motion jerky, disjointed. "No.

I'm not. *Not* his angel," she muttered. Her voice was thick and when she looked up, her pupils were mere pinpricks.

Dez knelt by her side, careful not to touch her. "No, you're not. You're a grown woman, a wife. If you don't want to see him, you don't have to. He can't *make* you do anything, Jacqueline."

"Shut up, bitch!" Beard snarled. "I'll damn well see her."

"Watch your mouth." Taylor moved between them, cutting off the man's view of his daughter. From the corner of his eye, he could see how she relaxed, even if it was just a little. "You won't talk to her like that. And no. If Mrs. Moore doesn't want to see you, you can't force her."

The old man jerked his chin. "You think you can keep me away?"

Taylor smiled.

But Moore was the one who leaned in. In a low voice, he said, "I'll fucking stop you, you fucking pervert."

"And ruin your reputation, Mr. Mayor?" Beard started to laugh, a nasty, low little chuckle. "Come on. You go ahead and do it. Coward. Can't protect your wife *or* your son. Look at you—the people who did this are standing right *there*."

"You don't worry about him." Moore shook him so hard the man's head smacked into the wall. Harsh flags of color rode high on his cheeks and there was a look of livid, complete hatred in Moore's eyes. "You worry about me."

Taylor heard the familiar sound of feet on the tile floor. Cop shoes. One didn't tend to forget that sound after hearing it a few hundred times. "Moore, you're about to have company," he warned. He glanced down at Jacqueline's heartbroken, terrified face, the fear that turned her eyes black. Small shudders wracked her body every few minutes.

Worst of all, she kept whispering, "I'm not his angel. I'm not his angel. I'm not . . ."

Shit. He could try to find justice for Anna. But if Anna had glimpsed any of the hell he saw in this woman's eyes . . . *peace or justice* . . . Although how in the hell he could help this woman find peace without finding her justice, he didn't know.

He gripped Moore's shoulder and tugged. "Let him go now, before the cops decide to hassle you. He's the bastard here. Not you."

Joshua shrugged his hand off, although he did let go. Slowly he backed away, unable to tear his gaze away from his father-in-law. "You have no idea what he did."

"Yeah, I think I do." He focused his eyes on Beard. "And if this slimy fuck has a lick of sense in his brain, he'll run. Fast and far. Although he can't find a rock to hide under, not from me."

"It's too late." Joshua shook his head. "It's too fucking *late*."

Taylor continued to stare at the man. "Is it ever too late to ruin a man?"

"You can't fucking ruin *me*." Beard sneered at him. He shot a hateful glare at Moore, then looked back at Taylor. "Stupid, fucking idiots. If I want to see my daughter, I *will*, and you can't stop me."

"I can."

Her voice was a shaking, quiet sound. And when they turned to look at her, Jacqueline Moore stood on legs that were wobbling and none too steady. "I can stop you . . . *Daddy*. You fucking bastard."

As the cops drew near, she furiously dashed away tears. She wouldn't look at Taylor as she edged around him until she could lean against her husband. She took her hand in his and, in that moment, Taylor realized she was tiny. Frail, even. Almost as delicate as a child.

"I'm so sorry," she whispered, choking the words out as she stared up at him. "I'm so sorry."

Joshua brushed her hair back. "You don't apologize to me," he whispered. "Not for what he did to you, not for any of it."

She shook her head. "I can't stay quiet, though. I'm sorry."

Then she looked at the police officers who were now gathered around them, frowning like they weren't sure why they had even been called up there. "This man—my father—killed my baby when she was just three months old. He held a pillow over her face until she suffocated. The doctors said it was sudden infant death. But it wasn't." Her voice shattered and she whispered, "It was him."

As Beard lunged for her, the cops caught him and wrestled him back.

In the chaos, only three people heard what she said next.

"And it was his baby. He raped me. For years. And he got me pregnant."

Joshua stumbled back, falling into a wall as he stared at her in dumbfounded shock. "Jacqui?"

"I'm sorry," she whispered again. "I'm so, so sorry."

TWENTY-TWO

"Is she here?" Taylor lingered by the car while Dez stood halfway between him and the cemetery.

She glanced back at him, her face unsmiling, her eyes sad. "I don't know." She sighed and rubbed the heel of her hand over her heart. "For the first time, I really don't know what to tell her, either. She wanted me to help Jacqueline and I don't know that I can."

"You tell her that you did what you could," Taylor said, his voice stark. Then he looked down. "And you tell her that I love her. Can you do that?"

Tears clogged her throat. "Yeah. I can do that."

"I wish . . ." He blew out a sigh, shaking his head. "I've never really wanted to carry any of the burdens the rest of you carry, you know. I don't want any of those gifts. But right now, I wish I had something, just enough to see her once."

Unable to stand the distance between them, even though it was just physical, Dez went to him. "I think you do have a gift,

Taylor. It's quieter. It's what lets you see others. And I think you help us focus—keep us calmer. That's a gift. Maybe you can't see the ghosts or hear the voices. But you do something that lets *us* see them. That's a gift."

He turned his face to her hand, rubbed his grizzled cheek against it. "Yeah, I notice you sleep when I'm around. Is that why you think you love me?"

"Think?" She lifted a brow at him. "Jones, there's no *think* to it. I might have *thought* I loved Will Smith when I was in high school. He's cute, he's funny . . . and I didn't know him. You, however . . . you might be nice to look at, but you're not exactly funny. You're not always easy to be around."

She leaned against him and kissed him. Against his lips, she murmured, "And I still love you. That I can sleep better around you, focus better, that's just a nice benefit. But I'd love you even if there were ten thousand more screaming ghosts in my head whenever you were near. You're it for me, Jones. I like it that way."

Then she sighed and looked back at the cemetery. "I have to go in there, at least try to see if I can talk to her now."

"You don't think you will?"

"I just don't know." She stroked a hand down his uninjured arm and twined their fingers, bringing his clasped hand to her lips. "I guess I go find out."

She let go of his hand and made her way into the cemetery. The wind, cold and biting, blew through her hair. But it was a regular wind, carrying nothing but the cold of the fall. She lowered her shields and although there were whispers of the departed skittering along her senses, none of them belonged to Anna.

Dejected, she shoved her hands into her pockets and began to wander around through the silent graveyard. The sun played peekaboo with the clouds, coming out every so often to cast slivers of light on the headstones. Every once in a while, a whisper would grow louder, but never real. Never complete. Nothing got loud enough to really *call* to her. None of these ghosts needed her. They were just echoes of themselves.

She hadn't arrived in time to see them move on, and now she never would.

She'd hoped she hadn't been too late for Anna—it didn't seem that could be the case. Anna had been so real, so complete and solid, just hours earlier. But now . . .

There was nothing.

Turning, she stared back at Taylor. And she knew she wouldn't even have to tell him. He could tell, just by looking at her.

* * *

SHE sat in the car, staring up at the cottage. But Dez couldn't climb out. Their *job* here, as far as it went, was done. Ivy was safe. Mark was safe. Tristan had justice—everything that Brendan had done was likely to come out now and Tristan's family would know he hadn't killed himself. Although Dez didn't know if that knowledge would really make things any easier.

Anna—she, too, had whatever peace Dez could give her. Dez wanted to see the girl off to a real and lasting peace, but she wasn't so sure that would happen. And Jacqueline, damn it, was there anything more she could do there? Dez didn't know.

But as she sat out there in Taylor's car, she couldn't go into the warm, quiet little cottage. She just couldn't. Swallowing, she looked over at him. "Take me to your house—the manor. I need to go there."

He stiffened.

"That's . . . not a good idea." His hand tightened on the steering wheel, gripping it with a force that turned his knuckles white.

"Why not?"

"Bad memories, Dez. Too many ghosts. My mom killed herself there, my dad died there. And let's not forget Anna." He shook his head. "No. We're not doing that. It was risky enough taking you there once."

"Risky?" Dez closed her eyes and rested her head on the back of the seat. "You forget I'm comfortable talking to ghosts. I'd rather talk to ghosts than deal with what's been going on here the past few days. It's driving me nuts. I'd rather get back to what I know, what I can handle."

"You need a break."

"I can't take a break." With a heavy sigh, she looked over at him and shook her head. "You know that. At least not until I try to reach Anna. She's not all that strong, Taylor. She's not tied to her grave. She reached me where her body was left, but she wasn't completely *there*, either. Maybe that's part of the problem. She's had to waste too much strength trying to reach out and find me. Maybe I need to go to her. And my gut tells me if I find her anywhere, it will be at your house, where she was happiest."

His mouth twisted in a bitter smile. "Happy? Shows what you know about our life. We weren't ever happy." But he started the car.

* * *

HIS hands were shaking, Taylor realized.

This was something he didn't want to do. Not just because of Anna, though. Anna, his father . . . his mother. Fuck, his mother. Even after all this time, he was still pissed off at her. She'd spent plenty of her time quietly whoring around, damn near *all* of her life in the bottle. And after Anna died, instead of trying to be there for the family she had left, she fell completely into that bottle, and ended up taking her own life.

If ever he was likely to force Dez to meet a ghost, it was when he took her into his house. And he didn't want her to bear the brunt of his mother's misery, damn it.

The ten-minute drive seemed to pass in seconds. If he could have figured out a way to change her mind, he would have. But no words would come. Usually, arguing with people, talking them around into doing what he wanted, came easy—and when that didn't work, he just bullied them into it.

Of course, he'd never had that luck with Desiree Lincoln.

Why would it change now?

As he pulled in front of the graceful old manor, his gut was in knots. "I don't want you here," he bit off, still gripping the steering wheel. If he thought it would do any good, he would have just driven off.

He knew better, though. She'd just find a way to come back. Even if she didn't get inside. If she was going to make contact with anybody here, he didn't want her doing it alone.

She was quiet, sitting next to him and just waiting. He looked over at her and said again, "I don't want you here. I don't want you *in* there."

"I was in there before." She stroked a finger across his mouth. "Nothing happened. Besides, it's not like I don't deal with ghosts. It's what I do."

"But these are *my* ghosts."

"All the more reason you should want me there . . . so we can put them to rest." She rolled to her knees and leaned over, kissed him gently. "Come on, Jones. It's not like doing this is going to make things any worse."

He caught her neck when she would have pulled away. With a hard, quick kiss, he muttered, "Don't say that. Please don't say that."

"Hmm. You're probably right."

Dez stroked his cheek, a habit she'd developed that somehow managed to make his heart stutter. Then again, what about her *didn't* do that?

"Okay." He pulled away and stared through the windshield toward the manor, dread curdling through him. "Let's get this done."

* * *

THE silence of the huge house was almost suffocating. Dez could hear the soft thuds of her booted heels on the floor, the softer sound of Taylor's footsteps, their breathing . . . nothing else.

She couldn't even hear the sound of a heater kicking on, water in the pipes. Nothing.

Just silence.

And emptiness. It was a complete emptiness, too. She hadn't lowered her shields completely but they were down enough to let her get a good, solid feel of things. And there was nothing here to feel. Nothing.

After he'd led her through the house in silence, she looked at him. "Where was Anna's room?"

He didn't look at her. His right arm hung at his side, the cast a stark white. His left hand was jammed into his pocket and, judging by the way his veins were popped out on his arm, he had it clenched into a rigid fist. When he spoke, his lips barely moved. "You want to see her room."

She moved to stand in front of him. Staring at him, she wished she could just tell him, *Okay, let's go. We'll just leave . . .*

But she couldn't. Whether he wanted this or not, he deserved better. Anna deserved better. She had to try. If she didn't succeed, then she didn't succeed, but she had to try.

"Want to?" She shrugged. Did she want to spend time inside the room of a child who'd died so terribly young? No. But she knew she probably needed to. "No. I don't want to. But I think I should."

Taylor closed his eyes. His voice was gruff as he whispered, "Second floor. Anna's room was on the second floor."

* * *

IT still looked the same.

Standing in the doorway, Taylor stared into the pretty white, pink, and gold bedroom that had been his sister's. Yeah, it had been where she slept, but it had his mother's touch all over it. Anna had been very much into the girly-type stuff, he supposed, but where their mother had tried to make her into a fragile hothouse flower, Anna, at her heart, had been a daisy. Bright, colorful, and cheerful.

Dez wandered through the room, pausing every now and then to brush her fingers along the dresser, the bed. In the center of the big poster bed, there was a doll. The sight of it was like a punch, right to the heart. There was a line of pristine, perfect dolls along the shelf above the bed. None of them had ever been played with for more than a few minutes.

But the doll on the bed . . . she'd been played with. Played with. Loved.

Swallowing the knot in his throat, Taylor took a step into the room. Then another. There was a fist around his heart now, one that wouldn't let go. When he reached out to touch the worn, old little doll, his fingers trembled. Lowering himself to sit on the edge of the bed, he picked it up.

"I bought her this," he said softly. "The Christmas before she died. She'd wanted a Cabbage Patch Kid but Mother wouldn't buy her one. We didn't get toys like that, you know."

A shadow fell across him and he looked up, met Dez's eyes.

She knelt down, resting a hand on his thigh. "What in the world could have been wrong with a doll?"

"It's not the doll." He crooked a smile at her. "It's a *common* doll. We got expensive shit. Collectible things—one of a kind or designer . . . things that would hold value or look pretty. Screw having fun with it."

Emotion all but choked him as he remembered the look on Anna's face when she unwrapped the present. "So I bought it for her. Me and Dad went out shopping and I asked if it would be okay. He just laughed and said, *Just don't tell your mother you asked me.* She played with it all day long. It went with her everywhere for months after, and she slept with it every night."

Dez touched the butter yellow hair on the doll's head. "It looks like she took very good care of her." She stood up and bent over, pressed her lips to his. "You're a good brother. I would have loved to have somebody give me a doll. I never had one. Did she ever name her?"

He looked back down at the worn toy. "Yeah. Her name was Laura. Anna loved *Little House*." He smoothed down the tiny dress and then he stood up. As the blood began to crawl up his neck, he pushed the doll into Dez's hands. "Here. You take her."

Automatically, Dez clutched the doll, even as she gaped at him. "Me? You want me to take a doll?"

"I can't leave it here." He looked around the room. Shaking his head, he said quietly, "You won't find anything of Anna's here. Except that doll. Everything else in here was my mother's."

"But . . ."

Looking back at her, he said, "Take it. Please. I . . . look, I can't leave it here. I just can't. Not anymore."

Dez looked down at the doll, a soft sigh falling from her lips. Then she stroked a finger over the doll's chubby cheeks, her smiling face. "She's got freckles. And blue eyes. And blonde hair." Abruptly, she started to laugh. "I'm thirty-four years old and I've finally got a doll of my own."

Tucking her into the crook of her arm, she looked around the room and sighed. "You're right about one thing. We won't find Anna here. It's . . . empty."

* * *

TAYLOR was packing up when he heard the knock.

Not his clothes, not yet, at least. They'd be stuck in French Lick for a little while, he knew. But it was time he did something with his family's things. If there were clothes to be donated, he'd do it. He'd pay somebody to come in and go through most of his parents' stuff, but he wanted to keep a few things that had belonged to his father.

And nobody would touch Anna's stuff. Not yet, at least.

In the middle of going through old, yellowed drawings, he heard the knock and looked up.

Dez was in the depths of the house, still trying to find something, he guessed. He didn't see her as he jogged down the steps, although the doll he'd given her was sitting in the foyer. Dez's sunglasses were in the doll's lap.

The last person he thought he'd see was Joshua Moore.

He tensed, ready to shut the door fast if he had to, wishing he wasn't hampered by the broken arm. Cautiously, he said, "Yes?"

Joshua looked down and then looked back up. "Can . . . can I come in?"

"Why?"

The other man grimaced. "I've a few things to say to you. Would rather do it where it's not freezing, but . . ."

"Just give me a minute." He shut the door and went to the

front parlor where he'd kept most of his things. In his briefcase, he had his weapon. He checked the safety—awkward doing it one-handed, and left-handed at that. He tucked it into the back of his jeans. Not ideal, but he didn't have a holster he could wear and still manage to draw it with his left hand.

Not that he anticipated needing it, but too many things he hadn't anticipated had happened over the past week. With Dez in the house, he wasn't taking chances.

It took under two minutes. When he returned to the front door, Moore was pacing restlessly on the porch. "If you want to talk, come on in."

"Oh, *want* isn't the word I'd use," he said gruffly. "But things just need to be said."

Taylor remained silent, gesturing to the parlor.

Joshua walked along, hands in his trouser pockets, head bowed. In the parlor, he wandered absently while Taylor settled behind the desk. He casually palmed the weapon and slid it under the desk, ready, but out of sight.

"How's your wife?" he asked stiffly. He didn't want to ask— but Anna had cared. He had to remind himself of that, damn it.

Joshua shot him a narrow look. "How can you even ask?"

Taylor lifted a brow. "Excuse me?"

Joshua laughed bitterly. "Oh, come off it. I know what she did. I know . . ." He closed his eyes. Abruptly he jerked his hands from his pockets. Taylor tensed and then relaxed, seeing the empty hands.

His tension returned in three seconds flat, though, as he watched Joshua press the heels of his hands against his eye sockets. A harsh, ragged sound escaped him, almost like a sob. He took a breath, held it.

"I've spent most of the morning at the hospital, with Jacqui.

She's been committed for a psychiatric evaluation," Joshua said, lowering his hands. He stared at Taylor. "She asked for this. And while she spoke with the psychiatrist, she asked that I be in there, told me she was tired of carrying all of this—felt like she was sometimes two different people. My wife . . . and somebody with all these secrets. How much of that is real, how much of that isn't, I don't know."

Taylor frowned, not certain why he was being told this. He didn't *want* to hear this. He had to summon every last bit of self-control he had, every last bit of human compassion, to say, "It sounds like your wife went through a very trying time with that bastard who happened to father her. She might need a lot of help to deal with it."

"Help. Fuck. Yeah, you could say she went through a trying time." Then Joshua shook his head. "That's not what I'm talking about, either."

He reached inside his coat, and until Taylor saw the sheaf of pages in his hand, he held himself rigid, ready to do whatever he had to if Joshua Moore showed any sign of danger.

But it was just paper.

"I know what she did, Taylor."

His heart stopped as he stared at Joshua Moore. Blood roared in his ears, a cacophonic noise that drowned out everything else. He didn't ever hear Dez enter the room. Until her hand touched his shoulder, he didn't know she was there. He laid the gun in his lap and reached up, convulsively gripping her hand.

"What are you talking about?" he rasped.

"Anna." Joshua looked at the sheets of paper he held. Then he looked up at Taylor, ignoring Dez altogether. "I'm talking about Anna."

Carefully, Taylor put the gun's safety on, then, just as carefully, he slid it into a drawer. He wasn't ready to hear this—wasn't ready, wasn't ready . . . Standing up, he turned away and stared out the window. He braced one hand on it, staring outside. His gaze fell on the spot where Anna had last been seen. By the fountain. She'd loved that spot. Almost as much as she'd loved their game room—their one place.

"I don't want to hear this," Taylor said, his voice rough, ragged. It felt like he was speaking through a throat lined with broken glass. "Get the hell out."

"No." Joshua's bitter laugh rang through the silence of the house. "Look at it this way: you owe me. My son's paralyzed, in part because of your actions. You can damn well stand there and let me tell you what my wife wanted me to tell you."

Taylor spun around, fury blistering inside him. "What, how she killed my baby sister?"

"She didn't." Joshua's voice, quiet and soft, couldn't quite penetrate Taylor's fury.

But Dez could. She reached up, laid a hand on Taylor's shoulder. "We need to listen, Taylor. Come on, now."

He stared at her. "I can't do this—I . . . I can't."

"You can." She reached up and laid a hand on his cheek. "You can. And I'm right here, I'm staying right here."

"She didn't kill her," Joshua said again. "I . . ." He gave Dez a dark look before he continued. "I don't know what she is telling you, but Jacqui *didn't* kill Anna. Anna fell."

Anna fell—

"She fell . . ." Taylor, stunned, turned his head and stared at Dez.

Joshua gave her an ugly look. "You're a fucking user, Lincoln. Maybe you *do* have a gift, but—"

He didn't get anything else out of his mouth beyond that except a strangled *ugh*. Ignoring the pain shooting up his arm, Taylor pressed the cast against Moore's throat. "Shut up," he said gently. "You just shut the fuck up now and maybe I won't beat you senseless. I'm trying to remember what you've been through. I'm trying to remember you don't know Dez. But if you say anything else . . . it won't *matter* what you've been through, or what you don't know."

"Taylor." Dez curled a hand around his shoulder. "Ease up. Let him breathe."

The other man's breath whooshed out of him as Taylor eased back, staring at him.

"She's trying to tell you that my wife killed your sister and you don't want me to be pissed?" Joshua snarled, his voice ragged and hoarse.

"I don't know all of what happened, Mr. Moore. I just knew your wife was involved." Dez's voice was cool. Her gaze dropped to the pages clutched in Joshua's hand. "And she *was* involved. Wasn't she?"

The anger drained out of him. As though somebody had replaced his bones with water, he sank to the floor. "She took her. Right out of the front yard. I . . . she heard your mother yelling at her, wanted to make the pretty little angel happy. And something scared her. Anna took off running. They were out near the cabin Jacqui's mother had left her—it's on Meyer's Hill, close to . . ."

"The field. The well where she dumped my sister. Like she was garbage."

"Yes." Joshua looked up at him. "Yes. Anna ran. She fell. Her neck was broken. It . . . she kept calling her . . ."

"My angel. My pretty, precious angel." Dez spoke up when his voice trailed off.

He looked at her, his face white. "Yes."

Dez looked over at Taylor. "That's what her father always

called her. She didn't want to hurt Anna. She . . . she just wanted somebody to love. I think something inside had been broken since he killed her baby. And when she saw Anna being yelled at, she just wanted to love her. She didn't realize that Anna already had people who loved her."

She cupped his cheek in her hand. "But she didn't hurt her. I know it doesn't undo her loss. It doesn't take it away. But Anna wasn't hurt."

Taylor reached out, hauled Dez against him. Pressing his face against her neck, he struggled not to cry. He wanted to know why—why Jacqueline couldn't have told anybody. Why she'd hidden it.

But Dez had already given him that answer.

That woman had already been broken inside.

"Anna needed for that woman to find peace," Dez whispered, her voice so quiet only he could hear it. "Her father won't ever have the chance to hurt her again, and maybe she can get justice for what he did to the baby. But she didn't mean to hurt her—in her mind, she was helping her. In her mind, she loved Anna. I think she still does—at least she loves what she thinks she knew of her."

Taylor shuddered. She wouldn't say it. Fuck, he knew she wouldn't. But he also knew what he needed to do. Not so much for *her*—Jacqueline Moore. But for Anna.

Lifting his head, he stared down into Dez's face. Dark, warm eyes met his. She stroked a finger along his lip. "Are you okay?"

"No." He pressed a kiss to her finger. "But I'll manage. Just . . . just don't let me go, okay?"

She twined her fingers in his. "Don't plan to."

Gripping her hand, his palm pressed tight to hers, he looked over in time to see Joshua finally climbing to his feet. "I can't say that I can forgive her. I'd be lying. Just . . . hell. Tell her that

I loved Anna—she was a wonderful girl. Tell her that Anna wouldn't have wanted her to hurt like this."

He looked back at Dez. He couldn't do much else, not without lying.

She smiled at him.

As Joshua passed by them, Taylor made himself look at the man. "What's going to happen with your son?"

"I don't know." The other man looked ten years older—no, twenty years older—in that moment. "I just don't know. I gave the journal to the police. I had to."

Both Dez and Taylor stared.

Joshua's humorless laugh rang hollowly through the foyer. "What else could I do? He killed another boy—Tristan Haler— earlier this summer. I read it, in black and white. After I read it, I went to the bathroom and puked my guts up. I turned it in to the cops—I fucking had to, because that boy's family deserves to know the truth. Then I went back and stared at him, hating myself because part of me still loves him. He's a monster. He's my son. And I love him. But I can't ignore what he did."

He sighed and shoved a hand through his hair, shaking his head. "I just don't know what will happen. He may go to jail and I'll tell him that he needs to at least try to work out a plea agreement. But he needs rehab, he needs counseling, and he looks at me with hatred in his eyes. I don't even know if he'll let me help him."

"I'm sorry," Dez said quietly.

He shot her an unreadable look, then shifted his gaze away, not responding.

Taylor pressed his lips to her brow and then eased back. There was little indecision as he reached into his pocket and pulled out his wallet. He handed it to her and said, "I need the card for Greg Moeller."

She cocked a brow, then shrugged. As she rifled through his wallet, he kept his gaze focused on her hands. Not on Moore, not on the pages he held—for once, Taylor was perfectly happy in not knowing every last detail. Once she had the card out, she gave it to him.

He in turn gave it to Moore. "I'm calling my lawyer. He handles the financial affairs for my family estate—I'm going to set up a fund for the kid's health care costs—*only* the health care costs."

Joshua shook his head. "No."

"Yes." Taylor glanced at Dez and then back at Moore. "Your son brought this on himself. You and I both know it. People may damn well try to spin it otherwise and I'll deal with that when it happens. But . . . if I'd exercised more caution, perhaps he wouldn't have been hurt."

"*Perhaps?*" Joshua stared at him.

"Perhaps." Taylor kept his voice cool. "I don't know. He took off running, and he didn't have to. We both know that. Something else we both know—if he'd gotten out of the house that night, it's very likely he would have hurt people. He got too much pleasure from doing it. I can live with what happened to him, knowing nobody else was hurt that night. But you're going to have your hands full, just helping your wife get through what she's going through. You don't need the burden of figuring out how to care for his health needs—and they'll be many."

Joshua gripped the card. "So this is . . . what, a way to mitigate your guilt?"

"No. It is exactly what I said it is." He turned back to Dez and wished Joshua Moore were ten thousand miles away.

So he could break.

TWENTY-THREE

THEY slept in a guest bedroom.

In the morning, Dez planned on asking Taylor if they could go back to the cottage. She didn't figure it would take much to talk him into it. She also hoped they wouldn't have to stay for long. They had to see to Anna, but after that . . .

She missed home.

She missed *her* home.

She was kind of hoping she could maybe talk him into making it his home, too. His house would be too chaotic for her. There would be too many imprints from others and she couldn't handle it.

For now, though, they were together in the silent emptiness of a graceful, sad manor with a heartbreaking past and Dez lay curled against the chest of the man she loved.

With the heat of his body pressed to hers, she didn't notice the change in temperature right away.

And there wasn't that desolation, either.

But something about the currents in the air when she finally opened her eyes made her realize . . . she wasn't alone and Anna had been in there for more than a couple of minutes.

She was sitting on a chair, swinging her legs back and forth, something any child would do.

And she was smiling.

It wasn't precisely a child's smile, although there was naïve innocence to it as she stared at Dez. *"You're in bed with my brother."*

Dez winced. This was a first. She'd never had to face a ghost in her birthday suit, even though she had a sheet tucked around her. She didn't want to speak, either, for fear of waking him. Trying to communicate silently with her ghosts had never been that easy for her, for some reason.

Her brow puckered as she focused her thoughts, pushing them outward.

Yes. We . . . well, I got kind of lonely in this big old house.

Anna rolled her eyes. *"Yeah."* She stood up and wandered around, pausing to glance down at Taylor. Goose bumps broke out over his arms. Dez pulled a blanket up over him, hoping he wouldn't wake. The stress of everything had finally dropped down on him, so he might sleep through this. Might.

"I think I can go now," Anna said, shifting her gaze to Dez. *"Things feel . . . different. I feel different."* She reached out a hand, let it hover over him. Sadness turned her pretty face dark and the room's temperature plummeted. *"He can't see me, can he? Not at all?"*

Dez shook her head. *No. You . . .* She licked her lips, hesitating. *You know how you felt the lady's pain? It's a gift you have. Mine is seeing people like you. Taylor's got a gift as well. It's just different from ours.*

"*He kept me* me." She reached up and touched her chest. "*Sometimes, especially when Mother was really sick, it was awful. But all it took was for Taylor to be there, and it made it better. He kept me* me. *Does that make sense?*"

More than you know. Dez smiled. *He loves you. Misses you. But he wants you at peace, baby.*

She nodded. "*I know. I want him happy. Tell him that. And tell him I love him . . .*"

Her fading was quiet, gentle. Dez closed her eyes against the tears, but it didn't keep them from falling. And only heartbeats passed before Taylor shifted in the bed, his lean body stretching. The rough material of his cast scraped against her arm and she glanced down, saw him staring at her.

His eyes were ridiculously awake, ridiculously alert. Sighing, she reached down and brushed his tousled hair out of his face. "Nobody should look that awake without the benefit of coffee," she said, her voice husky with tears.

He said nothing, just reached up to wipe the tears away.

She caught his hand. "Anna's gone."

He closed his eyes and turned his head.

"Taylor?"

* * *

AT the soft, worried sound of her voice, Taylor looked back at her. The tear tracks on her face gutted him. "I don't even know what to say." He sat up, pulling her close, although she still wasn't close enough. Finally, he ended up hauling her onto his lap, with her legs draped on either side of him. That was better, he decided. Resting his head between her breasts, he said it again, "I don't know what to say. I . . . hell, I'm glad. I wish I could have said good-bye, but I seem to chase your ghosts away."

"She was your ghost, too." Dez combed a hand through his hair.

"My sister. Your ghost. She called you here."

"I think we were both intended to be here," Dez said. "Both of us. Because I think it was my connection to you that made everything here stronger, different. If it hadn't been for you, I think I would have helped Tristan, Ivy . . . and then I would have left. I never would have known about Anna. She just wasn't strong enough to pull at me after all this time—not without that connection to you."

He shrugged, restlessly stroking a hand up her naked back. "She's gone . . ."

"Yes." She leaned back, forced him to meet her eyes. "She saw you. Recognized you . . . and she wanted you to know she loves you."

He closed his eyes. "Fuck." His arms tightened around her and, once more, he nestled his head against her chest. *Anna . . .* she was gone. He blew out a breath, determined he wouldn't break over this. She was gone—at peace. Finally. "Do you think we're done here, then?"

"Yes." She combed a hand through his hair, wrapped an arm around his neck. "Your mother . . . hell, there's nothing of her here. It's just emptiness. I think she was too weak to leave even an echo. Your father, I don't feel him, although I don't think it's weakness on his part."

She stroked her fingers along his shoulder. "He made his own peace with it . . . maybe he had some inkling what you were doing with your life."

"He knew I was going into criminal justice." Taylor sighed. "But he died before I had any clue where I'd go from there."

"Maybe that was all he needed. But there's more than just an emptiness here now. There's peace. You can let it go, baby. You can move on."

She leaned back and cupped his face in her hands. "It's time you did just that. Whether it's back to the bureau, or whatever. You're bringing your sister home. You'll lay her to rest. And then you need to let go. Move on with *your* life."

He closed his good hand around her wrist. A strained, sad smile curled his lips. "Dez, I already did that. I did that the night I went chasing after you."

Her heart flipped over in her chest as he leaned in and pressed his lips to hers. "You did, huh?"

"Yeah." The hand on her wrist stroked downward, curving over her waist. "You're my life . . . and I moved on to you. I love you."

"Hmmm. I love you."